"Hey. I heard you were looking for me."

The men stopped dead, and Peter whipped his head around. Noa was standing right behind them.

Before they could react, she unleashed a jet of pepper spray at one of them, and jammed a Taser into the other's bicep. Peter jerked loose just in time, narrowly avoiding getting crisped by 1,200 volts.

"Come on!" Noa yelled, running back toward the computer building.

Peter bolted after her. "The parking lot is the other way!"

"The car's already been moved. Hurry!"

Noa cut a tight corner around the administration building. As Peter followed, the pack slammed against his back, the hard drive edges digging in like drill bits. As he tightened the straps, he chanced a glance back over his shoulder; the goons were in pursuit. And they didn't look happy.

DON'T LET GO

MICHELLE GAGNON

HARPER

An Imprint of HarperCollins*Publishers*

"After Persephone" by Cleopatra Mathis from *What to Tip the
Boatman?*, published by The Sheep Meadow Press, 2001,
used by permission of the poet.

Library of Congress Cataloging-in-Publication Data
Gagnon, Michelle, date
  Don't let go / Michelle Gagnon.
    pages cm
  Sequel to: Don't look now.
  Summary: "In this final installment of the Don't Turn
Around trilogy, Noa, Peter, and what is left of their army race
across the country in their search to destroy Project
Persephone before time runs out"—Provided by publisher.
  ISBN 978-0-06-210297-3 (pbk.)
  [1. Computer hackers—Fiction. 2. Experiments—Fiction.
3. Foster home care—Fiction. 4. Abandoned children—
Fiction. 5. Adventure and adventurers—Fiction.] I. Title.
II. Title: Do not let go.
PZ7.G1247Dk 2014   2014001880
[Fic]—dc23   CIP
                                                                AC

Typography by Tom Daly
15 16 17 18 19   PC/RRDH   10 9 8 7 6 5 4 3 2 1

First paperback edition, 2015

For Esmé and Taegan

Heaven got sweeter, its paperweight curve
star-crazy at its purple center.
She'd found a god, a weapon in the works.
Something I hadn't noticed in the field
fought out of the layers and took her.
I tore away the land's every color,
withered the smallest grasses. Every heartbeat
went blank, I dismantled the ticking.
They only say what I took, not what I gave:
roots and strong light, glory
in the single shoot, green currency
of the just-born. From the irredeemable,
the buried—this is how a self gets made.
Remember, that darkness contained the seed
sealed in the swollen red globe.
Hell had to pay.

—Cleopatra Mathis,
"After Persephone"

PART ONE
RUN

CHAPTER ONE

"Noa, wake up. C'mon, we've gotta go!"

Noa batted away the arm and mumbled, "Go away." She'd been having a lovely dream, sitting in the middle of a giant field of flaming red poppies. Puffy white clouds drifted past overhead as she brushed her hands across the long, waving grass. It smelled like flowers, and something else, something oddly sour. . . . And then the voice had intruded, loud and insistent.

A harder tug rocked her body from side to side. More voices, muttering urgently in the background. *What the hell?* All she wanted was a little sleep.

"Noa, they're coming in!"

The sharpness of the voice shattered the final vestiges of the dream, scattering the poppies into a blur of red. Noa frowned and forced her eyes open. Her entire body still felt unbearably heavy, leaden. As she shook her head to clear it, the person who was yanking so annoyingly on her arm swam into focus. "Peter. Leave me alone."

Peter's pinched face glowed faintly in the moonlight seeping through the window. Daisy and Teo stood behind him looking equally anxious. They were all fully dressed and had their backpacks on. Teo kept glancing over his shoulder toward the door.

Seeing that, Noa snapped upright. "Crap," she muttered, struggling to her feet. "Not again."

Peter grimly handed her pack over. "Yup."

"How do they keep finding us?" she wondered aloud. Teo and Daisy were already moving down the hall. She tried to jumpstart her foggy brain—*Where are we? Kansas? Nebraska?*

"Dumb luck?" Peter suggested. "Either that or they have really, really amazing bloodhounds."

Arkansas, Noa suddenly recalled. They were in Arkansas.

A loud crashing sound from the other end of the apartment: the front door, giving way. Noa cursed again. The gloom was nearly impenetrable, she could barely make out battered walls dank with mold and mounds of trash. They'd spent the past few months moving constantly from one ramshackle safe house to the next. Although "safe house" really wasn't the right term, since each had been raided within a few days. Somehow, no matter where they went, the mercenaries who worked for Pike & Dolan managed to track them down.

"This way!" Peter said in a harsh whisper, cupping his hand around the flashlight so that it only illuminated a hole in the wall that led to the neighboring apartment.

In Cleveland a few weeks ago, the house had been surrounded. They'd only managed to escape because a police cruiser chanced by at the right moment.

They'd learned from that. Their latest safe house was actually an apartment in a sprawling, mostly abandoned complex on the outskirts of Little Rock, Arkansas. The development huddled forlornly on the cusp of a national forest, which worked in their favor; once they got free of the buildings, they could get lost in the trees.

But first, they had to get out of the apartment. Shortly after arriving, Peter and Teo had punched holes through the sheetrock, allowing access to the apartment next door. A string of holes through the next four apartments led to the final one, overlooking the forest. An emergency exit sat right outside that apartment's front door, and a balcony provided a clear view of the trees.

It would take a small army to cover every possible exit from the complex, so with any luck, those routes would be clear. Of course, there was always a chance that Charles Pike had sent a small army.

Noa hurried ahead of Peter, ducking her head to clamber through the hole. The sound of a door closing behind her, and the dim light vanished; the windows in this apartment were all boarded up. She groped forward as quickly and quietly as possible, with Peter at her heels. Noa counted as she went: The hole to the next apartment was twenty paces ahead, then fifteen to the left. They'd mapped it out earlier, right before she fell asleep.

The pounding of boots behind them. Without breaking stride, Noa dug a Taser out of her backpack's side pouch and flicked the switch to charge it. She could hear Teo and Daisy in front of her, their shuffling feet loud in the stillness.

The four of them stumbled and tripped their way through the string of apartments, muffling curses and hissing at one another to hurry. Noa strained to hear behind them; minute by minute, they were losing their head start. Maybe this was a bad idea.

Too late now. They'd committed to the plan.

Finally, they crawled into the last apartment. Teo and Daisy raced to the balcony's sliding glass door: From there, it was a three-foot drop to the ground. They were barely visible, silhouetted by the faint light from outside.

Peter whispered, "Everyone knows where to meet up?"

They all nodded.

"Okay," Noa said in a low voice. "Let's go!"

Teo slid the balcony door open, helping Daisy through. They vaulted off the balcony one at a time. As soon as they hit the ground, they charged for the cover of the trees.

"Our turn," Peter whispered, throwing open the apartment's front door. Noa followed him into the hallway.

It was pitch-black. For a panicked moment, Noa lost her bearings. The pressure of Peter's hand on her shoulder guided her. Even though he couldn't see her, she nodded.

He murmured in her ear, "I'll break left once we get outside, okay?"

"Okay." Adrenaline sent a surge of energy through her veins. Noa mentally reconstructed the layout of the complex. The forest was on her right, but she wanted to put some distance between herself and the others. They were supposed to fan out immediately, separating into four different targets to make it less likely they'd all be caught. She'd run straight for a few hundred yards, then break toward the forest.

The emergency door suddenly flew open, and Peter's shadow darted left. Nearly tripping on the doorsill in her haste, Noa made a beeline for the next building, a hundred yards away. It was a dark night, the moon a mere sliver on the horizon. The area around the apartment buildings was barren and full of malevolent shadows. Noa kept running, pushing herself hard, fighting against the weight of her backpack.

The emergency door slammed shut behind her. She heard a yell from inside, followed by the sound of pounding boots.

Too late, you bastards, she thought grimly. There was a playground in front of her—or what remained of one. The metal slide had been hauled off for scrap metal, leaving behind a set of stairs that led nowhere. Same for the base of a seesaw, and the lilting framework of a swing set. *This would be a terrible place to raise kids*, Noa couldn't help thinking as she raced across the sand.

Another shout, closer this time. Bouncing flashlight beams captured the skeletons of the playground in stark freeze-frames.

Noa abruptly turned right, heading for the safety of the trees. Behind her, voices barked orders. She was fifty feet away from the edge of the woods, then ten. . . .

Suddenly, a shape split off from a tree to her left. She didn't have time to get out of the way as a hand reached for her. . . .

Noa lashed out with her arm, using the Taser like a club.

She had forward momentum on her side: a grunt, and the shadow dropped. Noa kept running, hoping the others were sticking to the plan. Their rendezvous point was a mile away: a culvert that emptied into a small creek. If they couldn't shake their pursuers, they were supposed to steer clear of it, though.

Plan B was to run for the car, parked a few miles away. Her energy was already sapping, her pace slowing. She was so tired of running; every time they were forced to flee it got harder and harder. The way she was feeling right now, she wasn't sure she'd even make it to the culvert.

Pull it together, she told herself sternly. *Lose them, now.*

A yell behind her. Noa tore through the trees. Branches slashed at her face and arms, whipping painfully enough to summon tears.

At least one person was still tearing after her through the undergrowth. Noa's feet pounded the dead leaves, making them crackle loudly. She might as well be lighting signal flares; any idiot would be able to track her. Her breath came in short, ragged gasps. The backpack felt like it weighed a hundred pounds. For a second, she considered ditching it—but she couldn't lose her share of the hard drives.

There was a sudden yank on the pack. Noa's feet windmilled out from under her, and she landed hard on the ground. Something sharp jabbed into her lower back, making her wince.

A dark figure loomed over her, ominous in a wasp-like mask. He gripped an automatic rifle with both hands.

"You guys really need to hire a different stylist," Noa said. "That look is so last year."

She jammed the Taser into his calf and pushed the button. His whole body shook, the sound of chattering teeth loud in the stillness. As he dropped to the ground, she added, "Idiot."

Noa staggered to her feet and spun in a quick circle: no other movement, so apparently he'd been alone. After a flicker of hesitation, she grabbed his rifle and backed away. She didn't like guns, but wasn't keen on the idea of leaving him armed.

She turned and started running again, trying to suss out which direction was north. She was a city girl, born and bred; the closest she'd ever come to camping was living on the streets. Girl Scouts hadn't exactly been part of her childhood. *But it sure would come in handy now*, she thought grimly.

A splash. Looking down, Noa saw water running over her combat boots: She'd stumbled across the creek, literally. Which meant the culvert should be close by. She slipped along the banks, trying to avoid soft muddy sections where she'd leave behind telltale boot prints.

Five minutes later, the creek widened into a small river. Noa eased around an abandoned beaver dam, jagged clumps of sticks piled nearly six feet high. That was one of the landmarks they'd noted: The culvert should be fifty feet past it. She scanned the area one last time, checking to make sure she was still alone; all clear, nothing shifted in the shadows. She hurried toward the entrance.

It was pitch-black inside the culvert. Hesitantly, she stepped forward.

"Noa?"

At the sound of Peter's voice, her knees nearly gave out from relief.

"Shh," she hissed, stepping inside. "Is everyone okay?" In the dim light she could make out Daisy and Teo, huddled together against the far wall. Peter leaned against the entrance, his face drawn and strained. "What happened?"

"Twisted my ankle," he said through gritted teeth. "I'll be fine, though. You?"

"I'm good." She glanced over her shoulder one last time, then motioned for him to make room. Peter backed up and dropped into a crouch next to Teo. Noa gratefully slid to the ground beside him. Dampness quickly penetrated her jeans, and her boots were soaked. She wrapped her arms around herself in a vain attempt to stop shivering.

"It'll be dawn soon," Peter said. "Hey, is that a gun?"

Noa looked down; she'd almost forgotten she was holding it. It was a sleek black automatic rifle, probably worth a lot of money. And they needed cash. But selling it would be tricky, and the last thing they needed was to draw attention to themselves. "I'll bury it before we head to the car."

"Maybe we should go now," Teo said anxiously. "We're still pretty close to the apartment."

"This park is a couple thousand acres," Noa said reassuringly. "No way they can search the whole place. What time is it?"

A greenish light flared in the dark as Peter checked his watch. "Four a.m."

"Nearly dawn," Noa said, relieved. "They'll pull out soon; they can't risk being seen in the daylight."

Peter fiddled with his watch. "So we hang here for a couple hours."

Daisy and Teo didn't respond. Noa could imagine what they were thinking: a few hours of sitting in a dark, gritty concrete tunnel. Damp and cold. No chance of sleeping, and they'd have to keep quiet. Good times. She sighed. Yet another glorious day in the life of Persefone's Army.

"One more minute, and they would've had us," Teo said in a low voice.

Noa tried to ignore his accusing tone. He was right: She'd held them up. Because she was such a deep sleeper, it had been a close call.

A flare of rage almost immediately replaced the guilt. It was Pike & Dolan's fault that her body was so messed up, not hers. She was doing the best she could.

And yet, if one of them had been captured . . . Noa closed her eyes and tilted her head back against the wall. She was already carrying so much guilt, the weight of all the people she'd failed to save three months ago in Santa Cruz. She didn't know if she had the strength to bear the loss of any more.

They're all I have left, Noa thought, opening her eyes. Teo and Daisy had their heads tilted together; they both looked pale and drained. Peter sat a little apart, rubbing his ankle. He met her eyes and said softly, "We shouldn't have got away."

"You're complaining?" Noa arched an eyebrow.

"No, it's just . . . these guys are highly trained, right?" Peter looked past her, toward the entrance. The first rays of dawn shimmered across his face, tinting his skin mauve.

"We had a good plan," she said firmly. "Going through the other apartments worked."

"Sure, but think it through," Peter said reasonably. "Pike could send twenty guys. Or fifty. They could surround the entire place, but they never do. It just doesn't make sense."

"Maybe they don't know *exactly* where we are," Daisy offered. "They might just be searching every dump."

"Every abandoned apartment complex and house in the country?" Peter said dubiously. "No one has that kind of manpower."

"Or maybe they're not really trying to catch us," Teo suggested. "Maybe they just want to wear us down."

"In that case, they're succeeding," Noa grumbled. She could already feel her limbs locking up. It had been months since she'd slept in a real bed. Her eyes constantly ached with fatigue, and her whole body felt like a raw, ugly bruise. She imagined this was what it was like to feel old—really old, like eighty. But she was sixteen.

"I thought we had a shot this time," Peter muttered angrily. He dug a pebble out of his shoe and tossed it against the wall of the culvert.

"Me too," Noa sighed. They'd spent most of yesterday forging a decent set of student IDs for the college on the other side of town. The plan had been to head there in the morning. In order to decode the server hard drives Peter had recovered, they needed a real computer center, with some serious processing juice.

But over the past few months, as they hopped from one campus to the next, they'd either run into laughably inadequate computer labs, or Pike's people scared them off before they could get to work.

"We need to decrypt that data," Peter pressed. "We're running out of time."

"I'm so sick of hearing about the damn drives," Teo grumbled.

"I'm sicker of carrying them," Daisy complained. "They weigh a ton."

"That data might tell us where Pike is holding the rest of your unit," Peter retorted. "And more. There might be a cure for PEMA on there."

"Yeah, yeah," Teo said wearily. "And all you have to do is find a nice, quiet place to hack into them. Except we never find that place, do we?"

"We will," Peter said obstinately. "Soon."

"Enough," Noa snapped. All the arguing was sharpening the pain in her head, honing it to a fine point. "Get some sleep."

"Right, 'cause we got a big day ahead," Teo muttered, tucking Daisy into his shoulder. "I really hope I get to spend most of it in the backseat of a crappy car. Again."

Peter and Noa exchanged a glance. For months now, their only goal had been to evade capture while trying to find a quiet place to crack those drives. And that was no plan at all.

Noa curled into a ball, resting her head against the

backpack. She tried to ignore the sharp contents jabbing out from the side as she closed her eyes and pretended to sleep.

Amanda opened her eyes and frowned, disoriented by the plain white ceiling tiles. This wasn't her dorm room. Not her bed, either, but one of those adjustable hospital beds.

She shifted her head to the side: An IV line ran into her right arm. Which, she realized with growing horror, was cuffed to the bed with soft restraints. She tugged at the strap, then tried to reach over with her left hand to free herself. But that arm was strapped down, too.

She started to scream.

Running footsteps, then the curtains surrounding her bed were ripped open by an elderly nurse in teddy bear scrubs. "There, there, Amanda," she said, rushing over. "It's all right. You're in the hospital, dear. Remember?"

Amanda squinted at her: The nurse looked familiar, but she couldn't place her. "Do I know you?"

"Yes, yes you do," the nurse said soothingly. "I'm Beth, remember?"

"Beth?" The word felt unfamiliar on her tongue. "That's a silly name."

The woman chuckled. "I suppose it is. I have good news, Amanda. You have a visitor. Isn't that nice?"

Amanda tried to sort out whether it was nice or not, but her mind was muddled and she couldn't tell. Now that she thought about it, *nice* was a strange word, too.

The nurse pulled the curtain back farther, and another old woman came in. She had a kind face and long gray hair twisted in a loose braid. She wore an enormous patchwork sweater over jeans with creases down the front. She looked vaguely familiar, too. "Who are you?"

The woman exchanged a glance with the nurse. She looked . . . *What is the word for it?* Amanda grimaced, frustrated. As she stared at her visitor—that's what the nurse had called her, a visitor—the word popped into her head and she triumphantly said, "Concerned!"

"I'm sorry?" The old woman's forehead wrinkled, and Amanda immediately felt deflated; she hadn't said the right thing after all. Frustrated, she plucked at the plain white blanket with her hand. The old woman was still talking, asking, "Why is she tied down?"

"This has been one of her bad days, I'm afraid," the nurse replied in a low voice. "They tend to wander if we don't restrain them."

They both looked down at her. Amanda felt annoyed. Deep down, she sensed that there was somewhere she should be, something important she should be doing. But when she peered into the recesses of her mind, everything was wispy, like her head had been filled with smoke.

The older woman with the braid pulled up a chair and hesitantly took her hand. Patting it, she said, "I'm Mrs. Latimar, Amanda. You used to help me at a place called the Runaway Coalition."

She paused, gazing hopefully at her. Amanda managed a slight shrug and said, "Okay."

Sadness flitted across the woman's face. Amanda felt bad for letting her down; clearly she'd been expecting more. Mrs. Latimar looked up at the nurse and asked, "Can I have a minute alone with her?"

"Of course," the nurse said. "I should be checking on the others anyway. I'll close this to give you some privacy."

After the nurse slid the curtains shut, Mrs. Latimar leaned closer to the bed and said, "Amanda, do you remember what we talked about the last time I was here?"

Amanda frowned, not entirely convinced that she'd ever seen this woman before. She shook her head. "No."

"Can you try, dear?" A note of desperation in her voice.

Amanda wanted to help, she really did. Mrs. Latimar looked nice, which maybe wasn't such a strange word, now that she thought about it. She closed her eyes and dug through the fog, trying to grab hold of something tangible. There was something just beyond her reach, a strong emotion attached to this woman. It felt like . . . anger? Betrayal?

But that couldn't be right. Mrs. Latimar was obviously kind, so she must just be confused again. "Sorry," she finally apologized. "I don't remember anything."

Mrs. Latimar closed her eyes, looking pained. A quick glance back over her shoulder, then she leaned in so close, Amanda could feel her breath on her ear. Urgently, she whispered, "Maybe this will sink in and you'll remember it later, I don't know. But those files, the fake ones?" Mrs. Latimar sounded fearful as she continued, "Mason knows, Amanda. He figured it out. He's threatening to come after Clementine, and I just don't know what—"

The curtains slid open abruptly, rattling loudly on their metal balls. The nurse peered in and said, "I'm so sorry, but we should really let Amanda get some rest. Tomorrow might be a better day for her."

"Yes, tomorrow," Mrs. Latimar said faintly. She patted Amanda's hand a final time. Her smile was tight as she said, "Rest up, dear. I'm sure you'll be right as rain soon enough."

Amanda smiled back. Mrs. Latimar had an odd way of talking. *Right as rain?* There wasn't anything right about rain. Was there? "Good-bye."

"Good-bye, dear." Mrs. Latimar gathered up an enormous

purse and slung it over her shoulder. She paused at the gap in the curtains, as if she wanted to say something else. Amanda waited patiently, but the woman simply hunched her shoulders, then left.

The nurse tapped the IV bag lightly with her forefinger, then adjusted Amanda's pillows. Straightening, she said, "Anything else I can get you, dear?"

"What's a Mason?" Amanda asked.

The nurse's reaction was interesting: She froze, donning the same fearful expression Mrs. Latimar had worn. But it vanished so quickly, Amanda was left wondering if she'd imagined it. Nurse Beth said smoothly, "I'm sure I don't know, dear. Now try to get some sleep. Your parents are coming by later. Won't that be lovely?"

Amanda stared at the curtains after they slid closed again. They swayed slightly, rocking back and forth; the motion lulled her. Another question drifted out of the recesses of her mind with surprising clarity, but there was no one around to ask. Still, out loud she murmured, "Where's Peter?"

Peter swatted futilely at the swarm of tiny black gnats that had dogged him ever since they left the culvert. Based on what he'd seen so far, mid-May in Arkansas pretty much qualified as one of Dante's rings of hell. It was hot, muggy, and filled with blood-sucking insects. Not to mention the baddies with automatic weapons. All in all, it rated a mere three out of five stars in the *Run for Your Life!* travel guide he was mentally compiling.

They'd parked their latest SUV a few miles from the apartment complex. Which was inconvenient, but they'd learned from experience that when it came time to flee, it was better to have the car stowed far away. Otherwise, they were forced to circle back to an area that was crawling with Pike's men, and that had resulted in one too many close calls.

So they were tromping through the woods, parallel to the main road. Every time a car approached, they ducked deeper into the trees. The ankle he'd twisted last night had swelled up, causing him to limp along. Plus, Peter was 99 percent certain that he'd waded through poison ivy, which meant that the real fun was just beginning for him. He smacked at something that was gnawing on his neck and swore.

Teo smirked at him. "Funny, the bugs only seem to be bothering you."

"Yeah, well. That's probably because I smell the best," Peter retorted.

"Not true. I had a shower yesterday." Teo paused midstride, then continued, "No, wait. The day before."

"Actually, the day before that," Daisy piped up. "I'm keeping track."

"So maybe I'm just sweeter than the rest of you."

"Or they only like rich kids," Daisy teased.

"I'm not exactly rich anymore," Peter muttered. Which was true. In fact, after bankrolling the group for the past few months, he was down to his last few hundred dollars. It turned out that living off the grid was more expensive than you'd think.

"What about you, Noa?" Teo called ahead. "Are the bugs chowing down?"

Noa shook her head, but didn't turn around. Peter tried to quell a surge of concern. She'd taken the lead but seemed to be struggling, stumbling more frequently than the rest of them. He considered asking if she wanted to take a break, but the last time he had, she'd practically ripped his head off.

Ever since Pike's doctors had experimented on her, Noa

had developed strange symptoms, especially when it came to sleeping and eating. She'd be awake for days, then crash hard. But last night, when he'd had such a hard time waking her up . . . for a second, he thought she might actually have slipped into a coma. He hadn't dared tell her that she'd slept for nearly thirty straight hours, losing an entire day. He figured that was a conversation they could save for the road, or maybe avoid altogether.

Even when she was awake, Noa wasn't entirely present. She'd stare off into the distance for long stretches, and she barely ate anymore. He'd initially assumed she was grieving the loss of Zeke. But as time passed, she seemed to be getting worse.

Of course, they were all in rough shape. Peter slapped at another bug on his forearm and groaned. "I gotta rest. My ankle is killing me."

"Hang on, we're almost there," Teo said. "I recognize that rock."

"Easy there, mountain man," Peter joked. "Soon you'll be starting fires with sticks."

Teo reached out and cuffed him on the arm, making him stumble. Peter jostled him back. They engaged in a silent, friendly shoving match until they rounded the boulder and spotted their SUV parked beside the entrance to a hiking trail.

Noa stared at the SUV as if it was an unfamiliar animal that had suddenly materialized before her. "This is where we left it?"

"Well, yeah," Peter said, trotting around to the back. "Don't you remember? We parked here to make it look like it belonged to hikers."

Noa didn't reply. He examined her surreptitiously as he

cracked the hatch. She appeared genuinely puzzled, which wasn't a good sign. She'd never mentioned memory issues before; was this new? Peter bit his lip. Out here, they had no choice but to rely on one another. Yet while he and Daisy and Teo became increasingly tightly knit, Noa seemed to be drifting away from them.

"You want to check this time?" Teo asked as he threw his pack into the cargo compartment.

Peter sighed. "Why not? I'm already covered in mud."

While the others waited, he crawled around the perimeter of the car, checking the tires and undercarriage for tracking devices. As usual, he didn't find anything. They'd spent hours speculating on how Charles Pike's minions seemed to find them no matter how far and fast they ran; a few states back, Peter had suggested that maybe they'd bugged the car. So they'd switched out vehicles. But two nights later, the mercenaries had shown up again.

There was another possible answer, but it was almost too awful to contemplate: that one of them was a mole.

As he got back to his feet and dusted himself off, Peter shoved the thought away. They'd been together 24-7 for over three months. Noa certainly wouldn't sell herself out, and Teo and Daisy would never risk each other. He watched as they stole a kiss in the backseat. They were good kids; a little rough around the edges, but definitely trustworthy.

So how the hell does Pike keep finding us? This last time had been too close—Teo was right, just a few more minutes and they wouldn't have gotten away. Fortunately, the perimeter alarms that he'd set up had alerted them. But those had been left behind, and there wasn't enough cash left to replace them. Which didn't bode well for wherever they landed next.

Noa had settled into the front passenger seat. "Guess I'm

driving," Peter grumbled as he rounded the front of the car. His stomach growled—they'd nibbled on trail bars while waiting for the coast to clear, but he was still starving. What he'd do for a real lumberjack breakfast: pancakes, eggs, toast, bacon. Maybe once Little Rock was just a blip in the rearview mirror, they could stop at a roadside diner. He tugged the straps of his pack tighter and shifted the seat back to make room.

"Dude," Teo grunted. "You're killing me. Take off that damn pack so I can have a little leg room."

"Sorry, man." Peter knew it was ridiculous to wear the backpack while driving, but it had become a weird sort of safety net for him. He'd nearly died for these hard drives, after all. And if he ever found a way to access the data on them, he could save a lot of people—including Amanda. So he took it off as little as possible.

Teo muttered something unintelligible as he climbed over Daisy, switching seats with her. Peter waited until they were settled, then turned the ignition.

"Which way?" he asked.

Noa shrugged.

Peter hesitated, hands on the steering wheel. "South?"

"Too hot," Daisy piped up. "I hate the heat."

"North, then? Maybe Missouri, or Kansas again?"

"I hate Kansas," Teo muttered. Noa didn't answer; she was gazing blankly out the windshield, doing her hundred-yard-stare thing.

"All right, I vote west," Peter sighed. "Nearest campus is Oklahoma State Institute of Technology."

"It's got *tech* in the title," Teo said. "That's probably a good sign."

"Maybe." They'd visited half a dozen "tech universities"

across the country, and so far none had a computer lab as sophisticated as the one back at Peter's high school. "Can't be worse than the last place."

"Oklahoma sounds nice," Teo murmured, fatigue underpinning his voice. "Bet they have lots of cows."

"Moo," Daisy lowed. They both dissolved in giggles.

Peter pulled back onto the road, adhering strictly to the speed limit.

He flicked on the radio and started humming along. Noa had her eyes closed, but he could read her well enough by now to tell she wasn't sleeping. A frown creased her features. He wondered if she was thinking about Zeke again.

Peter felt a twinge of jealousy. He'd sacrificed everything to join up with her: his family, friends, and quite possibly his entire future. He'd done it partly to save Amanda, sure. But he'd be lying if he didn't admit that a small part of him thought the time they'd spent together last October meant something.

Apparently, not so much. Because now it felt like he was constantly being compared to a ghost, and coming up short.

The edges of the hard drives dug into his back, oddly reassuring. Peter was going to get the information off them if it killed him. And that data would save Amanda's life, bring down Charles Pike, and maybe restore Noa's health.

Then, she'd see who the real hero was.

CHAPTER TWO

"Now that's what I'm talking about!" Peter exclaimed.

Noa had to agree—the computer lab at the Oklahoma State Institute of Technology was a lot more impressive than the other places they'd tried. Rows of humming terminals, all relatively new. They were so gorgeous it made her fingers feel twitchy.

"You kids need something?"

Noa jumped and spun around. A stocky older man holding a stack of manuals stood behind them. The waistband of his pants slung low under a considerable belly, and his button-down shirt strained at the seams. He had an enormous bushy mustache and small, pudgy hands.

"We've got some work to finish up," Peter said, flashing a broad smile.

"Work?" The man's brow furrowed. "School's out, kids.

Shouldn't you be at graduation? The governor goes on soon, don't want to miss that."

Noa threw Peter a desperate look; the campus *had* seemed oddly empty as they made their way here, despite the fact that the parking lot was full.

"Unfortunately," Peter explained in that overly cheery voice he always employed with adults, "I've gotta finish a term paper by the end of the day, otherwise they might not let me come back next year."

"First I've heard of that." The guy scrutinized them skeptically. "Got your student IDs?"

Noa fought to keep her face calm; all her instincts were screaming at her to bolt.

"Left them in the dorm," Peter apologized. "Sorry."

The man eyed them for a minute, then said, "Well, I gotta take these to the stockroom." He hefted the stack in his arms an inch and continued, "Can I trust you alone in here?"

"You bet!" Peter chirped. As always, Noa marveled at how convincing he was. If she'd been on her own, the guy would probably have already called campus security.

"All right, then. Don't break anything."

The door closed behind him, and Noa's shoulders slumped. "That was close."

"Nah," Peter said dismissively. "We're just a couple of nice college kids with a bad habit of procrastinating."

Noa raised an eyebrow. Their clothes were threadbare, and for the past few days they'd been washing up in gas station bathrooms. "Good thing he wasn't close enough to smell us."

Peter had already plunked down at the nearest terminal. He set his backpack on the ground, dug out a server drive, and carefully unwrapped it. "I smell like a daisy, thank you very much. Now." He cracked the knuckles of both hands, then said, "Let's hack these bad boys."

Noa sighed. Following suit, she picked a terminal and unwrapped a drive. They'd created ad hoc Faraday cages for the server hard drives, just in case they were bugged; each one was wrapped in a layer of aluminum foil, then a layer of cardboard, then more aluminum foil. Basically, that metal shield should guarantee that any signal would be blocked.

When she plugged in the drive, a command prompt appeared on-screen. That, at least, was familiar enough. The problem came when she tried to open a file: No matter which one she tried—and there were thousands of them—the only thing that came up was an indecipherable mess.

The data was protected by 256-bit AES encryption, the same level of security utilized by the NSA. To crack it, they needed to figure out which file contained the decryption key. And even if they managed to accomplish that, the archive would be password protected, too.

It was kind of like the multiple layers of security around a castle. First they had to locate the castle itself: the file that contained the key. After that, cracking the password to access that key was roughly akin to overcoming moats and dragons and all sorts of other obstacles before finally getting inside the gates.

They were both skilled hackers, but this was a brute force operation. And despite the fancy computers here, Noa didn't hold out much hope. It could take weeks just to find the key file; and they wouldn't be able to fake their way into this lab for that long.

Still, Peter insisted on trying. He muttered to himself as he tapped away, maintaining a running play by play of everything he was doing. She found it simultaneously endearing and annoying; a few times in internet cafés, she'd had to shush him. They were alone in here, though, so it was harmless enough.

Noa stared at her screen. The fluorescent lights were already making her eyes throb, and she felt a headache coming on.

"All righty," Peter murmured. "You don't like that, you little bastard? Just wait and see what Daddy's going to try now. . . ."

More annoying than endearing today, she decided. If she was going to tolerate the patter without strangling him, she needed some caffeine. Noa pushed back her chair and said, "I'm going to grab a Red Bull. Want one?"

"But we're just getting started," Peter protested.

"I slept in a ditch last night," she pointed out. "And you're talking to yourself again."

"Oh, sorry. Hey, get me one, too?"

Noa nodded and grabbed her backpack, slinging it over one shoulder. Peter had trained her well; she rarely let it out of her sight anymore, either.

In the hallway, she leaned against the wall and closed her eyes. What she would give for some real sleep. Her whole body ached, and she was covered in scrapes and bruises. For the first time in her life, she dreaded the thought of clocking hours in front of a computer.

They'd left Teo and Daisy on the grassy quad out front, ostensibly keeping watch. As Noa passed the enormous window that lined the front of the building, she spotted them lying beside each other. Daisy was tickling Teo's nose with a blade of grass. He grabbed her hand, pulling her down for a kiss.

Watching them, Noa felt a pang. She'd almost had some-one once, but she'd been too foolish to realize it. And now it was too late.

She squeezed her eyes shut, trying to blot out the image of Zeke bleeding to death in her lap. But the sound of his voice, and of that final gunshot ringing out across the water, replayed on an endless reel. She'd give anything to open her eyes and see him standing there, giving her that look that said, *I know you, better than you know yourself.*

Noa forced herself to set one foot in front of the other. She finally found a vending machine at the end of the next hallway; but of course they didn't have Red Bull. She sighed and bought two Cokes, tucking one away for Peter. Popping the top on the other, she sucked down half the can, then let it dangle from her hand while she stared blankly at the floor.

Aside from when they were running for their lives, most of their days were consumed by monotonous, unbroken hours of driving. Which provided far too much time to dwell on the mistakes she'd made, all the things she couldn't take back.

It wasn't just losing Zeke that had disheartened her so completely, although she knew that's what they all thought. It was worse than that. Right before he died, a biochemist had explained that her cells were deteriorating, overloaded by the extra thymus P&D had inserted into her chest. He'd predicted that her symptoms would worsen.

Noa didn't understand the science behind it, but he'd definitely been right. She was constantly exhausted; some days, just sitting up took enormous effort. For the first few months after the operation, she would crash hard, then be awake for long stretches; now, all she ever wanted to do was sleep. And her eating habits had changed, too. Before, she'd gorge herself, then be unable to choke down food for days. Now, she could rarely bring herself to eat anything, and half of it came back up. It was like her body was engaged in an all-out revolt.

She polished off the soda and tossed the can in a recycling bin, then shuffled back down the hall. Noa glanced outside: no sign of Daisy and Teo. Maybe they'd headed off to find a quiet corner somewhere. *So much for keeping watch*, she thought with a sigh.

Turning the corner, Noa pulled up short. Two men were walking down the hall away from her. They wore jeans and cowboy shirts, the norm in this part of the country. But the way they were carrying themselves seemed off. . . .

She checked their shoes: combat boots. Noa quickly ducked out of sight, her heart racing. They'd been found again.

Peter hummed to himself as he tapped the keys. He still couldn't understand why Noa wasn't more into this project. For a hacker to be handed a challenge like this? The old Noa would've been racing him from the car.

Her indifference was just another sign of how much she'd changed.

Frowning, Peter shoved back the lock of hair that always drove him crazy. If he had to find the archive file on his own, so be it; Noa wasn't the only hacker in town.

Maybe OSU Tech had some sort of summer school they could piggyback on, he mused. They could find a safe place to hole up; there had to be a ton of empty apartments during the summertime. Somewhere with a real kitchen, beds, and functioning showers. Catch up on their sleep. Have a shot at a few weeks of normalcy; hell, maybe even a few months.

He registered footsteps approaching; probably the older guy who ran the lab, returning to check on them. Peter hurriedly shut the open windows on-screen. Someone stepped into the room as he closed the final window.

He glanced up, then froze. Two huge men filled the doorway. Their eyes swept the lab, then came to rest on him. One of the guys broke into a broad smile. "Peter Gregory," he said. "Looks like it's our lucky day."

Daisy's waist was so tiny, Teo could touch his fingers together when he wrapped his hands around it. He never stopped marveling at that. The skin there was amazing, too, so warm and soft. . . .

They were on the side of the building, a hundred feet from the door; close enough to keep an eye on things.

Not that they'd been doing much of that. It had felt so nice, lying out on the grass, basking in the sun. For a minute, Teo had actually felt normal: He was just another kid, making out with his girl. *Nothing to see here, folks.*

Then Daisy had straddled him, bending low to brush kisses along his jawline. Followed by butterfly kisses that tickled his cheek, and tongue flicks against his earlobe. When she breathlessly murmured that Pike's men only ever showed up at night, so keeping watch was kind of silly and pointless, he was inclined to agree. After all, they could still see the door from here. And the side of the building was probably safer anyhow, since it kept them out of sight.

Of course, after shifting to the new position, they hadn't done a stellar job of keeping a lookout; Teo would be the first to admit that. But he also couldn't have cared less. He was backed against the wall, drowning in her kisses. Daisy had to stand on tiptoe to reach his mouth, and God, the things she could do with her tongue. They were both breathing hard.

Teo drew her closer until their bodies were pressed together, not an inch of space between them. . . .

"What are you doing?"

Teo jerked back so fast his head hit the wall, making him wince. Noa was standing a few feet away with her hands on her hips, looking as pissed as he'd ever seen her.

"Um, nothing. Sorry, we just figured it was better to—"

"We're making out," Daisy interrupted, a challenge in her voice. "Is that okay with you?"

"Not really," Noa snapped. "Since two of Pike's guys just grabbed Peter."

"What?" Daisy gasped. They exchanged a shocked look. Teo was immediately consumed by a wave of guilt, combined with frustration. *How the hell did they find us so fast?* They'd arrived less than a half hour ago.

"You were supposed to keep watch," Noa said angrily.

"Sorry," Daisy said in a small voice. "We weren't thinking."

"Yeah, obviously." Noa was rubbing her eyes, like she could barely stand the sight of them. She was still wearing her backpack; Teo scrambled to get his pack on, then handed Daisy hers.

"All right," Noa said, sounding resigned. "I only saw two of them, but they're probably armed. And I'm guessing there are more on the way, so we have to act fast."

"So what do we do?" Daisy asked impatiently.

A long beat while Noa examined them. Then she said, "Go back to the car."

"What?" Daisy protested. "No way. We can help."

"You can help by pulling around back. Graduation is on the other side of campus. Get the car as close to the stage as possible, but make sure we can get away fast. Okay?"

They exchanged a look. Teo wanted to argue that they could do more than shuttle a car from point A to point B, but

Noa didn't look like she was in the mood for debate.

"All right," he said. "But then what?"

"Keep the engine running," Noa said. "Because we won't have much time."

The men gripped him by the elbows as they marched him out of the building. Peter clutched the straps of his backpack as he scanned the area frantically: no sign of Daisy, Noa, or Teo. *Where the hell are they?*

He was kicking himself for letting his guard down. But then, the way these guys kept finding them was starting to seem almost magical. Peter couldn't figure it out; he'd been hacking into the server drives offline, there were no virtual tracks to follow. And the SUV was clean, he'd checked it himself.

It was getting harder to ignore the possibility that there might be a traitor in their midst. According to Noa, Pike had tried that before; in Santa Cruz, her entire unit had been lost when a girl named Taylor had betrayed them.

But after all they'd been through together, he couldn't imagine any of them doing something so terrible. There had to be another explanation.

Peter tripped and nearly fell. The guy on his right roughly jerked him back up. "Easy!" he muttered. "No need to be a douche."

"Watch your mouth," the guy said in a low voice. "You're not the one I have to bring back alive."

The other was nodding his head and saying, "Uh-huh. Uh-huh." Without breaking stride, he told his buddy, "They're ten minutes out."

"Good," the guy on the right grunted. "We'll stash him, then go back for the girl."

"Better find her this time. I want that bonus."

Peter kept quiet, listening. So they hadn't caught Noa yet—and at least for the moment, there were only two of them. His mind raced, searching for a way out. If they passed anyone, he could scream for help, maybe gain a few precious seconds to run back to the SUV. The others might already be waiting there.

Or maybe they left you, a voice needled. *You're not really one of them.*

Peter squared his jaw. The others wouldn't abandon him. He had to believe that. If only he could get to the Taser in his pack; he needed a distraction.

Unfortunately, the entire campus seemed to be at graduation, wherever the hell that was. And they were nearly at the parking lot; another hundred feet and he'd be past the point of no return.

"Hey. I heard you were looking for me."

The men stopped dead, and Peter whipped his head around. Noa was standing right behind them.

Before they could react, she unleashed a jet of pepper spray at one of them, and jammed a Taser into the other's bicep. Peter jerked loose just in time, narrowly avoiding getting crisped by 1,200 volts.

"Come on!" Noa yelled, running back toward the computer building.

Peter bolted after her. "The parking lot is the other way!"

"The car's already been moved. Hurry!"

Noa cut a tight corner around the administration building. As Peter followed, the pack slammed against his back, the hard drive edges digging in like drill bits. As he tightened the straps, he chanced a glance back over his shoulder; the goons were in pursuit. And they didn't look happy. One had tears streaming down red cheeks, the other was moving shakily.

Still, they were gaining.

He followed Noa through a narrow corridor between two buildings, emerging onto a football field. Noa broke left, barely avoiding a collision with an older couple who stared after them, startled.

The field was packed with people in folding chairs, the first few rows occupied by graduates in black caps and gowns. An older man with gray hair stood at a podium, his words amplified by speakers set throughout the field.

"I'm guessing you have a plan?" Peter managed to gasp out.

"Kind of," Noa wheezed. "Head for the stage."

"What?"

She was already shoving her way through the sea of people surrounding the stage. Ten feet from the dais, several state troopers stood shoulder to shoulder.

Peter glanced back: The thugs were less than twenty feet away.

Noa pulled up short in front of a cop. His hand leapt to his holster, an expression of utter confusion on his face.

"Those men!" Noa said, pointing at them. "They've got guns! They said they were going to kill the governor!"

Pike's men had slowed their pursuit, but it was too late. The state troopers were already reacting; one brought a radio to his lips, while others jumped onstage to usher away the governor.

Peter stood there panting, a stupid grin plastered over his face. Their pursuers hurriedly retreated, backing up directly into more cops. Protesting loudly, they were dragged away from the stage.

"Come on!" Noa said, tugging at his arm. "They might only hold them for a few minutes. We've got to get to the car!"

Obediently, he trotted after her. They wove through the crowd, which had grown restless and confused. Murmurs all around them as people tried to figure out what was going on. It was like trying to swim upstream; but they finally broke free, emerging on the other side of the field.

The SUV idled at the curb, with Daisy at the wheel.

Peter crawled in back and dropped his head against the seat, exhausted. Noa slammed the door as Daisy pulled away from the curb.

"Dude!" Teo exclaimed. "Good to see you."

"Yeah, great job keeping watch," he retorted. "Remind me to kick your ass later."

Guilt flashed across Teo's face. "Sorry, man. We were—"

"Their radios weren't working," Noa interrupted. "It wasn't their fault."

Daisy cast a startled glance back in the rearview mirror. Noticing it, Peter frowned. "Well, anyway, thanks for the save."

"We should switch out cars again," Noa said. There was a collective groan, but she insisted, "They might have seen this one."

"Great," Peter muttered. "I was starting to miss being a felon."

"Which way?" Daisy asked. Through the windshield, Peter saw the on-ramps for two freeways: One led north, the other south.

"North," Noa said decisively. "Back to Kansas. But skip the freeway. Let's stick to the back roads."

"Ugh," Daisy moaned. "I hate Kansas."

"I hate back roads," Teo added.

Peter stared out the window, ignoring the usual banter. He didn't care where they went next; he was just happy not to be stuffed in the back of a van, headed toward an operating table. Still, the thought of that gorgeous lab retreating in the distance was crushing.

Pike must have figured out that they were trying to use college computer labs. Maybe he'd narrowed down which region of the country they were in, and had men investigating every possibility within that perimeter.

In which case, they needed a new plan. One that involved a server farm, which wasn't something you'd find at a Route 66 drive-thru.

Peter had an idea, but Noa wasn't going to be keen on it. He'd have to convince her somehow. Because at this point, they were running out of options.

"Let's grab a car in Kansas, then head to Denver," he suggested.

"Denver?" Noa made a face. "What's in Denver?"

Peter shrugged, trying for nonchalance. "It's supposed to be nice there. Lots of colleges. And it's not Kansas."

"A real city would be nice for a change," Teo chimed in from the front seat.

"God, yes," Daisy said. "I seriously need some clothes that didn't come from a Wal-Mart."

"Right? Thrift stores, baby." Teo and Daisy exchanged a high five.

Peter raised his eyebrows at Noa, who threw up both hands and grumbled, "Fine. Denver it is."

"Great." Peter tilted his head back against the seat and closed his eyes. If he was right, they'd find everything they needed there.

And if he was wrong, well . . . it certainly couldn't be any worse than what Pike had in store for them, right?

CHAPTER THREE

"That's a 2011," Teo said.

"You're sure?" Peter eyed the Camry. They were sitting on a bus bench next to a public parking lot in Dodge City, Kansas. They'd spent over an hour watching cars pull in and out; none had met their requirements. Until now.

"Trust me," Teo said. "And you better hurry, she's getting out."

A heavy woman in her forties was struggling to extricate herself from the Camry, like a giant worm emerging from a tiny cocoon. Peter pushed off the bench and headed toward her. She was morbidly obese, three hundred pounds squeezed into a sundress. Her arms jiggled as she tugged a large black purse over one shoulder and waddled toward him.

Peter kept his face blank as he passed by. *I'm just another driver headed to his car,* he thought. *Don't pay me any mind.*

The woman's face went stiff, though. Her lips were bright red, tinted the same shade as her hair. In spite of himself, Peter flashed back on Terri, the chipper receptionist at Pike & Dolan's corporate headquarters who had unwittingly let him into their server room. Terri would probably steer clear of him now, too. All his clothes were the same dingy gray, the result of infrequent washes in public Laundromats. His hair was too long, and he had a three-day growth of beard. A few months ago, if he'd smiled at this woman, chances were she would have smiled back.

Instead, she scurried to the far side of the lot, giving him a wide berth.

Peter paused ten feet from her car. He held his breath as he activated the jammer in his pocket, waiting for the beep indicating that the Camry had been locked.

It never came. And the woman had been in such a hurry to get away from him, she hadn't noticed.

"Showtime," Teo announced, coming up beside him.

Peter glanced around to make sure they were alone in the lot, then followed Teo to the car. He tried the driver's-side door: unlocked. The jammer had worked, blocking the signal from her key fob. He opened the door and slid inside.

"Here." Teo handed over what looked like a small laptop. Peter switched it on and plugged the adapter into the diagnostic port under the dashboard. He hit a few keys, and the engine roared to life.

"Man," Teo said, shaking his head. "I still can't believe that works."

"Me either," Peter muttered as he slipped behind the wheel and adjusted the seat. Yet it did, at least the three times they'd tried it. A few states back—in Virginia? Or Oklahoma?—he'd stumbled across a foolproof method to hack into a car. And all it took was a hundred-dollar jamming device and the tiny laptop. The laptop had set them back nearly a grand, but it had been worth it. Originally designed for legitimate auto locksmiths, it allowed access to a car's computerized controls once you got inside.

So instead of breaking a window, or messing around with a jimmy, all they had to do was find a Japanese car manufactured between 2007 and 2011. Then he stood a short distance away and turned on the jammer. Car owners usually clicked their key fobs while walking away: He used to do the same, back when he owned a Prius. But the jammer blocked the signal, so the car remained open. And once they got inside, all Peter had to do was plug in the laptop, and away they went.

He never stopped feeling lousy about it, though. Peter could already picture the woman's reaction when she discovered her car had been stolen. Maybe she'd left something important in the trunk. Maybe there were kids waiting for her at home, or she was supposed to pick someone up later. And he'd just ruined her whole day.

Unfortunately, they didn't have a lot of other options. Public transportation was out, since Pike probably had people keeping an eye on train and bus lines. The same went for buying a car—too much contact with strangers who might ask questions.

"Pull over here," Teo said. "I'll switch out the plates."

Peter eased the car into a superstore parking lot, continuing along to the back of the building. While he waited by a Dumpster, Teo grabbed a fresh set of license plates from his pack and screwed them on. Less than five minutes later, they were pulling back out.

"They should be done by now," Teo said. "Let's go pick them up."

Peter didn't answer, suddenly exhausted. He hadn't gotten a solid night's sleep in days. He was tired of running. Tired of stealing from strangers. He was starting to fear that they were slowly but surely becoming the bad guys.

When he parked in front of the Laundromat, Teo looked over at him. "You coming in?"

Peter shook his head. "I'll hang out here."

"All right." Teo got out of the car and loped inside.

Through the plate-glass windows, Peter could see Daisy and Noa folding laundry. It was an incongruously domestic scene. Teo said something and Daisy smiled, then pulled him into a hug. Watching them, his throat tightened. They were so obviously in love.

He flashed back on the last time he'd seen Amanda. She'd looked so small and frail in her hospital bed, hooked up to all those machines. When Peter left Boston, he'd figured that within weeks, he'd be back with a cure. They'd expose Charles Pike for the monster he was, and everyone would get their happy ending. And then, he and Noa . . . well, that part had been fuzzier.

He sighed. Noa's head was ducked down, as if folding T-shirts required a tremendous amount of focus. The way she'd been acting toward him, so cold and distant . . . sometimes he wondered if she wished he'd never come.

The Laundromat door opened and the three of them spilled out, slinging on packs as they went. Noa opened the passenger's-side door and popped her head in. "You okay to keep driving?"

"Yeah," Peter said, even though it felt like if he tilted his head, sand would pour out of his eyes. "Sure."

"Good." She took the passenger seat, and Daisy and Teo crammed in the back.

"Not very roomy," Daisy complained, sliding a hand across the cracked leather.

Teo said, "Yeah. I miss the SUV."

"Then you can steal the next car," Peter retorted. "Now buckle up. I want to make Denver by tonight."

"Anything yet?" Noa asked.

"Nope." Peter sounded distracted as his fingers raced over the keys. The ever-present backpack forced him forward onto the edge of the chair. They were sitting in front of a couple of clunky, aged computers in the Denver Public Library, trying to find a local safe house. Teo and Daisy had volunteered to make a food run, since both of them were useless with computers anyway. Besides, Peter usually had a knack for finding a good place.

Tonight it seemed to be taking longer than usual, though. And they were short on time; it had taken nearly seven hours to drive here from Dodge City. Noa checked the clock on her monitor: 8:45 p.m. "This place closes soon."

"You could help look," he grumbled. "It doesn't always have to be me."

"I'm checking up on the other Persefone units," she said, lowering her voice. "Still no posts."

"Well, you told them to lie low for a while." Peter shrugged, his eyes still glued to the screen. "So they're lying low."

"Maybe." Noa had spent the past half hour trying to convince herself of that, but something still felt off.

Three units of what used to be her "army" remained, and they stayed in touch online. But there were no recent posts in their chat room on The Quad, a hidden message board for elite hackers. Nothing in any of the cloaked accounts they used to communicate, either. Complete radio silence for two full weeks.

Which worried her. Maybe the groups had disbanded, too demoralized and afraid of Pike to continue.

Or maybe Pike had captured them, too.

The thought turned her stomach. Back in Santa Cruz, his men had basically wiped out her entire unit; maybe he'd methodically gone after the others. And she was helpless to do anything about it; hell, she could barely keep three people safe. Sighing, Noa cleared her browser history and turned to Peter.

"So where are we staying tonight?" she asked impatiently.

Peter jumped, then started tapping the mouse like his life depended on it, closing windows. Noa frowned; what didn't he want her to see? She got up and peered over his shoulder: nothing there but a local news website, which seemed innocuous enough. "You're not surfing porn sites, are you?"

The computers were set in a circle, with each workstation facing in toward the others. A middle-aged woman on the computer opposite scowled at them.

"What? No!" Peter protested.

"You look guilty."

"I was checking email, okay?"

Noa eyed him; the tips of his ears had gone bright red, a clear sign that he was lying. "Bull. But hey, you don't have to be embarrassed about it," she teased. "It's totally normal for a boy your age."

The woman was doing a terrible job of pretending not to eavesdrop. In deference to her, Peter lowered his voice to a barely audible whisper and said, "I was just handling a personal thing. Okay?"

Noa wondered what kind of personal thing he'd handle on a public computer; she definitely didn't like the look in his eyes, like she'd caught him doing something wrong. But his face had shuttered. She sighed. "They're kicking us out in ten minutes."

"Well, I found a place." He gestured to the news report on-screen. "The South Lincoln Homes Housing Development. They've been demolishing it in stages, so most of the units should be cleared out. Work stalled because the money ran out, so no construction crews should be there."

"Great," Noa said, trying to muster up enthusiasm for yet another dilapidated housing project. With any luck, it would have just as many rats as the last one. "Nice work."

Peter executed a small bow. "At your service. Maybe someday I could become a real estate agent who specializes in really, really terrible properties."

Noa managed a weak smile. "Big market for that. Hopefully we can stay for at least a few days. We could use the rest."

"Sure," Peter said. "Or maybe we'll find a better place."

Noa frowned. "Like where?"

"I don't know. Somewhere."

She examined him; the flush had spread all the way down his neck, and he was avoiding her eyes. "You're being really weird tonight."

"No, I'm not."

"Yes, you are."

"Shh!" the woman hissed.

"Don't worry, ma'am. We're leaving." Peter staggered slightly against the weight of the pack as he got to his feet.

He was probably going to develop permanent indentations in his shoulders from never taking it off. As they strode toward the front door, he raised a fist. "South Lincoln awaits!"

"You're really not going to tell me what you were doing back there?" she asked, pushing open the door. The curb in front of the library was empty, no sign of Daisy and Teo. *Hopefully they made it to the store, and didn't just go somewhere to make out again,* Noa thought with a sigh. Honestly, she didn't know how they managed it. Apparently teenage hormones were more than a match for constant terror.

"Porn," Peter said resolutely. "You were right."

Noa rolled her eyes. "All right, fine. Don't tell me. But you're taking first watch tonight."

Daisy hummed along to the radio as Teo drove them back to the library to pick up Peter and Noa. She didn't mind making the food runs; it was one of the few chances they got to be alone. And besides, being trapped in a stuffy library made her twitchy.

Not that prowling the aisles of a supermarket was much better. At least in Denver, her dyed hair drew fewer horrified looks than in some of the backwaters they'd holed up in. She held out a few strands and frowned, examining the tips. She really needed to touch up the color, it had faded to the point where it looked more gray than blue. Of course, that meant finding a bathroom with actual running water, and a few hours when she wasn't being chased. She imagined running away from Pike's men in a shower cap and cheap plastic gloves, streaks of blue dye flying out behind her.

As she dissolved in giggles, Teo glanced over. "What?"

"Nothing. Just thinking that my hair looks awful," she said ruefully.

"I think it's cute." He threw her that grin that always made her stomach lurch. She'd had boyfriends before, sure, but not like this. Those guys had all wanted something from her.

But Teo actually cared what she thought about things. When she spoke, he hung on her every word. Daisy reached over and ran a hand through his hair, which looked perfect as always. It was almost long enough to put in a ponytail. "I'm going to braid your hair tonight."

"The hell you are!" he said, looking mortified.

She laughed. "I think you'd look cute with a braid."

"I look enough like a girl already," he muttered, a shadow flickering across his face.

"Hey," she protested. "Don't talk smack about my guy."

Teo blushed, which made him even more adorable. He stretched an arm across the front seat and she snuggled into it, trying to ignore the gearstick digging into her thigh. Closing her eyes, she let out a happy sigh. He had gorgeous dark skin, courtesy of his Latino parents. Dark eyes, glossy black hair. Sure, he was skinny, but she liked that. And he had the most amazing lips, so incredibly full. Her mom would have said they were wasted on a boy, but Daisy knew better. It would only have been a waste if she didn't get to kiss them.

She leaned over and did just that, pressing her lips firmly to his.

"Whoa!" he said. "Careful. You're going to make me get in an accident."

"You are a pretty terrible driver," she agreed solemnly.

"I'm not that bad."

"You're getting better, but still. Hell on wheels."

"Well, it's not like I get much practice outside of grocery runs," he muttered.

"It's easier to cuddle in the backseat."

"Yeah, but I still feel like 'the kids' sometimes. Don't you?"

Daisy ran her fingernails along his forearm the way he liked. Choosing her words carefully, she said, "It doesn't have to be like that."

"What do you mean?" His eyes flicked to her.

"I mean . . . I don't know." She sighed. "When I first joined up, I thought it would be different, you know? There was a whole group of us, and we were really doing something, saving kids. But now—"

"Now we're just running for our lives," Teo said.

"Exactly. And I just keep wondering what the point is. Remo and Janiqua and the rest of them are probably dead. If we get caught, we're dead, too. And we won't have stopped anything. Maybe we should just go off on our own."

There was a long pause. Daisy held her breath, wondering if she should have kept her mouth shut. They'd complained to each other before, late at night in the dark, but what she was proposing was practically treason.

"So you want to ditch Noa and Peter?" Teo asked.

Daisy bit her lip; his tone was impossible to read. "This guy Pike doesn't care about us, he's after Noa. If we're not with her—"

"He'll probably leave us alone," Teo said. "I know. I've thought the same thing."

The fact that he wasn't judging her, or calling her a coward, made her weak with relief. "So you don't think I'm totally awful?"

"What? No, of course not. Come here." He pulled her over and planted a kiss on her forehead. Daisy squealed as he inadvertently turned the steering wheel at the same time, almost driving them into a line of parked cars. "Let me talk to them about it, okay?"

"Sure," Daisy said. She felt light, like a burden had been lifted.

"So where do you want to go?"

"I don't know," she admitted. "I didn't really think you'd go for it."

"California," Teo said decisively, hitting the turn signal. "Los Angeles. It'll be warm there."

"Maybe we'll become movie stars," she teased.

"Maybe," he agreed with a grin.

Daisy grabbed his hand and squeezed it. "Thanks, Teddy."

He looked abashed. "I'd do anything for you. You know that, right?"

The library came into view. Noa and Peter were standing at the curb, looking impatient.

"I know," Daisy said, trying to sound cheerful. Seeing them brought the weight of reality crashing back down. Could they really just leave Noa and Peter to fend for themselves? *They don't need us*, she told herself. *Not really.* Changing the subject, she said lightly, "I hope they found a good place to stay."

"I just hope we don't spend the night running for our lives again," Teo muttered as he pulled over to the curb.

"Wow," Teo said. "This is—"

"Disgusting," Daisy interrupted, wrinkling her nose.

"Is it just me, or are the hideouts getting worse?" Teo grumbled.

"Next time you can find one," Peter muttered, scanning the room. They were right, of course: The South Lincoln Homes Housing Development was beyond grim. It was kind of amazing that it had only been scheduled for demolition a couple of years ago. The walls of the apartment were coated in mold. The windows were practically made of papier-mâché, with layers of newspaper duct-taped over the broken sections; he couldn't imagine surviving a Denver winter in a place like this. Even now, on the cusp of summer, frigid air whistled through the gaps.

Noa bent over and picked up a plastic Mickey Mouse head that must have popped off a child's toy. Holding it up, she said wryly, "And I thought *I* grew up in some nasty places."

Peter swallowed hard, abruptly overcome by a wave of homesickness; he could practically picture the walls of his room, and the bed with its crazy comfortable organic mattress. His house always smelled like furniture polish and freshly cut flowers. He didn't know what the other kids' homes had been like; it wasn't something they ever discussed. But out of all of them, it was a safe bet that he'd fallen the furthest from what passed as home. He eyed the filthy linoleum, which had cracked and peeled away to reveal a concrete subfloor. "Could be worse," he said unconvincingly.

"Ah, man, you know we're kidding." Teo clapped him on the shoulder. "This place is perfect. Hell, punching holes in the wall will actually improve it."

"Yeah," Daisy said faintly. "Really great."

Teo leaned over and planted a kiss on her forehead. "Why don't you deal with the food, Dais. Peter and me will start on the exit strategy."

"Sure."

Noa was still staring down at the doll's head as if mesmerized. Peter cleared his throat and said, "After that, we should try to get some sleep. Noa, if you want, you can lie down now—"

"I'm fine," she said, glowering at him.

He held up both hands placatingly. "I'm just saying, you've

gotten less sleep than the rest of us. We can handle this."

"I'll keep watch," she said. "When one of you is ready to take over, just let me know."

"I thought I was keeping first watch," he muttered.

Noa ignored him, moving over to one of the few windows that was still paned with glass. She swiped a finger through the lower corner, removing enough dirt to provide a view of the street.

Peter stood silently for a second, watching her. At some point they needed to talk about how she was shutting them out. *We're all barely holding it together,* he thought with a surge of anger; why did Noa think she was the only one with a right to sulk?

But there never seemed to be a good time to have that conversation. At least Teo and Daisy had each other. He was all on his own.

"I got chicken," Daisy announced, shaking him out of his reverie. "We should eat soon, before it gets cold."

She lugged two grocery bags into the kitchen.

"Don't open the fridge," Teo warned.

"Don't worry," Daisy snorted. "I'm *never* doing that again."

"Where was that?" Teo asked. "Austin?"

"Cleveland," Peter chimed in. "I still think that was a dead cat."

"Ugh, enough," Daisy said with a shudder. Wrinkling her nose, she shoved aside the moldy fast-food wrappers cluttering the countertop to make room for the grocery bags.

Like the other places they'd squatted in, the electricity and water were shut off. So they only bought prepared foods that could be eaten without reheating, and that wouldn't go bad sitting out overnight. Usually, that translated into power bars; but tonight's dinner smelled delicious. Peter's mouth watered as Daisy dug out a rotisserie chicken. He never would've thought it was possible to get sick of hamburgers, fries, and shakes; but he actually fantasized about cauliflower now.

Suddenly starving, Peter opened the package and tore a leg off the chicken. He took a big bite and practically moaned with appreciation.

Daisy smiled at him. "Good, right?"

"Yeah," he said while chewing. "Freakin' fantastic."

"We'll have to finish it tonight, it won't keep." Her brow wrinkled as she surveyed the rest of their purchases. "Maybe we should have gotten a half chicken instead."

"Trust me, we'll finish it." Peter devoured the drumstick in a few bites. Then he pulled off a chunk of breast meat, shoving it into his mouth as fast as he could chew it.

"Dude, leave some for the rest of us," Teo protested.

Peter wiped his hands on his jeans. "Go ahead."

As Daisy nibbled on a wing, she called out, "Noa? You hungry?"

No answer. They all exchanged a look; no one had to say it, they'd all noticed that she'd barely been eating.

Another conversation he needed to have with her. But that would definitely escalate into a fight, and he wasn't up for that.

His appetite suddenly gone, Peter motioned for Teo to follow him to the back of the apartment.

It took the better part of an hour to punch holes through the neighboring apartments. For the most part, he and Teo worked in silence, only exchanging a few words when trying to decide which wall to hit next. They were lucky this time; they punctured a water pipe in the third apartment, but it was empty and not a single drip leaked out.

"Remember Boise?" Teo said, letting the hammer hang by his side as he stared at the exposed pipe.

"Oh, yeah," Peter chuckled. That had been the first time they'd tried to punch through drywall, and neither of them had had a clue how buildings were constructed. Through sheer dumb luck, they'd made it through two walls. But in the third apartment, they'd hit a gas line, and the place had immediately filled with noxious fumes. They'd had to quickly relocate to another building in the complex, praying the entire time that a stray spark wouldn't cause an explosion. Noa hadn't been pleased then, either, Peter thought, his smile fading.

Teo used his hammer to knock out dangling chunks of drywall. "If we open it up down here," he noted, "we can duck through. Maybe if we're being chased, the pipe will catch them in the head."

"Maybe," Peter acknowledged. "We'll have to make sure to tell the girls about it, though."

"Right. She's different, huh?" Teo said without meeting his eyes. He carefully knocked away more drywall, widening the hole to about three feet in circumference.

"Who?" Peter said, playing dumb.

Teo swiped an arm across his cheek, smearing the dust. "Noa."

Peter shrugged. "I guess. I don't know. I mean, we only spent a few days together before this."

"Well, she's different from when I met her, but that was for just a few days, too. Then Santa Cruz happened. I'll go first." Teo edged carefully through the hole, then extended a hand back to help Peter through.

After stepping inside, Peter straightened. This apartment was marginally nicer than the one where they'd left the girls;

not as much black mold, and less trash scattered across the floor. "Maybe we should move in here."

Teo scanned the room. "It doesn't have a view of the street, though."

"Not sure that matters," Peter countered. "It's not like Pike's guys drive to the front door and knock, right?"

"Right," Teo mused, turning in a circle. "It would make Daisy happy. And actually, this might be better because it's in the center of the building. If we knock a path in both directions, there's less chance of getting cut off."

"That's smart," Peter said appreciatively. When he'd first met Teo, he'd been underwhelmed by the rangy kid who was barely fifteen. But the more time they spent together, the more he liked him. Teo only spoke when he had something important to say. He was smart and reliable. In some ways, he reminded Peter a lot of his older brother.

Especially now. Peter could sense that he was deliberately building up to something.

Teo moved through the apartment, ducking a head into each room. "Hey, there's still a mattress in here!" he said enthusiastically. "Dibs!"

"It's all yours," Peter snorted. "Probably smells like piss anyway."

"Probably," Teo agreed. "But I'll take that over sleeping on the ground."

Peter grunted in assent. They pushed open the door to the final room. The smell nearly knocked Peter back on his heels. He pulled his T-shirt up over his mouth and nose, but it barely made a difference.

"Dead rat," Teo observed, voice muffled by his own shirt. "Definitely your room."

Peter whacked him on the arm, which sent them into a

brief shoving match. This one ended after a few halfhearted blows; neither of them could afford to waste any energy, and Peter wasn't really in a joking mood. The farther they got into the building, the more somber the atmosphere grew.

"The thing is," Teo finally said as they broke through to the next apartment, "I think we might take off on our own."

Peter didn't answer for a second. It was funny—when he'd first climbed into Noa's SUV in Omaha, he'd actually been a little bummed to find Teo and Daisy staring blankly at him from the front seat. Whether he'd acknowledged it or not, part of him had been looking forward to spending time alone with Noa.

But now that it was finally a possibility, that was the last thing he wanted. "Look," he said, fighting to keep the undercurrent of desperation from his voice, "I know it's been tough, but—"

"It's been worse than tough, dude; it's been brutal." Teo's face clouded over. "I know it was hard for her, losing Zeke and the others. It was hard on all of us."

Peter swallowed, trying to come up with something that wouldn't make him sound like a total dick. He'd never met the other kids in Noa's unit, and personally, he could care less about Zeke. In fact, every time someone mentioned the kid's name, Peter felt like throwing something. Based on how they talked about him, you'd practically think Zeke had been superhuman.

Which made Peter painfully aware of how inferior he must seem in comparison. He couldn't fight. He wasn't street smart. The only skills he possessed meant nothing to Daisy and Teo; computers were barely a blip in their reality. "I know it would be better if Zeke were here," he said, unable to keep the bitterness from his voice.

"I doubt it," Teo said thoughtfully.

Surprised, Peter looked up at him. Teo ran a hand through his hair and shrugged. "I mean, I'm sure Noa misses him, but it's more than that. She barely eats, she sleeps for crazy long . . . What did Pike do to her, exactly?"

Peter hesitated before answering. Noa would be enraged if she found out they'd been discussing her; and if Teo and Daisy didn't already know about her situation, she must have kept it from them for a reason. But by sticking with her, they were risking their lives. And maybe knowing would per-suade them to stay. "They operated on her," he said. "Do you know what a thymus is?"

Teo shrugged. "I didn't pay a lot of attention in biology."

Peter laughed curtly. "Me either. Apparently your thymus regulates things; my buddy said it turns off and shrinks as you get older. It pumps out all these white cells that fight illness, which is why Pike's doctors thought it might hold the cure for PEMA." He felt a pang, remembering Cody; the premed student had practically been a brother to him. And he'd died mysteriously in a fire after helping them. No matter what the arson investigator said, it hadn't been an accident; Pike had been responsible. "Anyway, that's why Noa's sleep and eating patterns are so messed up, and why she heals super-fast."

"She heals super-fast? That's cool," Teo said. "I didn't know that. So that's why they're still chasing her, huh?"

"Yeah. We think she might be the only one the operation worked on."

"That's weird."

Peter shrugged. "I'm not exactly a doctor. I can't explain it."

"But something on those hard drives might, right?" Teo

drew back his hammer and slammed it into the drywall. "That's why we're hauling them around."

"Exactly." Peter joined him, working up a sweat as they punched through to the final apartment. They worked in silence, taking turns whacking at plaster. Finally, Peter straightened. "That should do it," he said, swiping an arm across his forehead.

"How much longer do you think it'll take?" Teo asked.

"To crack the encryption? I don't know. A while," Peter admitted. "If I had a block of computers, and a few days to sit there and try to get the key, then . . . maybe."

Teo laughed. "Yeah, hard to believe we haven't found a stack of laptops in one of these dives."

"The rats would eat it anyway." Peter wrinkled his nose at a pile of feces in the corner. The sound of rats skittering around used to keep him up nights. It probably wasn't a good sign that he'd grown accustomed to it.

Teo tapped the hammer against his thigh. "Pike probably wants those drives back, huh?"

"Maybe. But he might have backups. I honestly don't know." Peter had stolen the drives from a secret server farm that was stashed in an abandoned building. Since he'd bricked their other servers a few months before, it would be unaccountably stupid for Charles Pike not to have instituted backup measures for his precious Project Persephone. Still, the more widespread the data was, the more likely someone would stumble across it, which was a huge risk. Deep down, Peter suspected they were literally carrying everything Pike had discovered about PEMA on their backs.

He shifted the pack self-consciously. The key to saving Amanda was in there somewhere, he hoped. Not to mention the lives of hundreds of thousands of other kids. But unless he could log a solid few days at a computer terminal, ideally with a healthy and whole Noa working beside him, they might never uncover it.

Which was precisely why Peter had led them to Denver. He drew in a deep breath and said, "Listen, Teo. I know you and Daisy want to take off. But if you can just hang in there for a few more days . . ."

Teo's face clouded over. "I don't know, man. Noa's getting worse. It's like she's not even here anymore, you know?"

"I've got a plan," Peter said, fighting a mounting sense of desperation. "There's a guy here who can help us."

"What guy?" Teo asked, his brow furrowing.

"That's kind of complicated," Peter said weakly. "But trust me, he's our best bet."

Teo stared at the floor for a solid minute. A breeze skittered through, and Peter shivered as it cooled the sweat on his back.

"All right," Teo finally said. "One more day. But after that, we take off. Daisy's not handling this well. She needs a break. You won't even have to give us much cash."

Peter swallowed hard. Today's grocery run had depleted their funds even more, and they were running dangerously low on cash, but it probably wasn't the best time to share that information. He clapped Teo on the back and said, "Cool. One more day. Thanks, man."

Teo grinned back at him. "So you're going to set up a bat signal or something like that?"

"Something like that," Peter said. "C'mon. Let's see if they saved us some chicken."

Amanda blinked, and was startled to find herself staring at an enormous tree in bloom, huge white flowers bending toward the window.

She slowly turned her head. She was sitting alone in some sort of solarium, her fingers clasping the arms of a wheelchair. She was dressed in a hospital gown and a soft green robe—her robe, she realized, the fuzzy one she'd gotten for Christmas when she was fourteen years old.

She could have cried with relief. She remembered everything, with perfect clarity. She was in a PEMA ward at Boston Medical. She'd been here . . . how long? Amanda frowned. It was obviously spring outside; a window had been cracked to let in the warm breeze. Her seizure in the library at Tufts had happened in February. So unless this was an unseasonably warm day, at least a month had passed. Or longer?

Her thoughts and memories still felt jumbled. She could recall voices: her parents, Mrs. Latimar, Peter. All of them sounding concerned yet soothing, speaking like she was a child on the verge of a tantrum. An undercurrent of fear beneath their words. But what had they said?

She shook her head. It was all too vague. Her clearest memories were of the days leading up to the seizure. The confrontation with Mrs. Latimar about the medical files. Their mutual decision to feed Mason older files, of teens who'd already aged out of the test groups.

So what happened with all that? Amanda chewed her lip. She'd promised to help Mrs. Latimar come up with a way out, but then she'd ended up here. Was it too late?

Footsteps behind her. She turned to find a familiar-looking nurse standing with her hands clasped in front of her. "So happy you're feeling better, Miss Amanda," she said brightly.

"I am." Her voice sounded strange, froggy. Amanda cleared her throat and tried again. "How long have I been here?"

"A while," the nurse said vaguely, looking distinctly uncomfortable.

"Like, a month?" Amanda pressed.

The nurse bent to straighten the blanket covering Amanda's legs. "It's really best not to worry about that sort of thing."

"But I want to know."

The nurse's lips pursed. "It's been a few months," she finally acknowledged.

"Months?" Amanda's voice rose at the end. "I've been here for months?"

"I'm afraid so. It's May seventeenth, dear." The nurse straightened and looked at her. "Your parents are down the hall, we called them as soon as your condition improved. Would you like me to bring them in?"

"Wait, my condition has improved?" she said hopefully.

"Well . . ." The nurse looked evasive again. "It has, today. But I'm afraid that can happen as PEMA progresses. There are good days and bad days, just like with any other disease."

"So I'm not cured," Amanda said bluntly.

"I'm so sorry, dear. They haven't found a cure. Yet," the nurse added hurriedly. "But some of the best scientists and doctors are working on it. I'm sure that soon—"

"What stage am I in?" Amanda demanded. "When you brought me in, you said it was Stage Two. Is it still?"

"The doctor should really be the one to discuss it with you." The nurse was wringing her hands; the motion inspired a wave of déjà vu. Amanda dimly recalled a hallway, and this same nurse consoling her. . . .

"Please," Amanda said, suddenly exhausted. "Just tell me."

"Stage Three," the nurse said quietly. "But there's still time for you, Amanda."

Amanda squeezed her eyes shut, feeling a rising swell of panic. There were only four stages in PEMA. And once you hit Stage Three, best-case scenario, you had months left to live. "Send in my parents."

"You're sure you're up for it?" The nurse reached for her hand and gave it a squeeze. "If you're too tired, I can tell them to come back later."

"No, I'll see them," Amanda said grimly. "After all, this might be my last chance."

CHAPTER FOUR

Noa frowned up at the metal gate blocking the fire road. "So are you going to explain what we're doing here?"

"Hang on, I just want to make sure this is the right place." Peter shifted his backpack as he walked the length of the gate, examining it. His expression was equal parts excitement and nerves; Noa hadn't seen him this keyed up since they'd infiltrated the secret lab in Rhode Island.

Based on how that had turned out, there was a good chance she wasn't going to like whatever happened next.

Daisy and Teo stood silently beside the car. Noa sensed that something in the group had shifted in the past twenty-four hours, but she had no idea what, and no one seemed inclined to share. Last night, she'd crashed hard. The others had let her sleep through the night and a good chunk of the morning. She awoke feeling refreshed for a change, almost normal.

But she couldn't repress the sense that while she'd been asleep, they'd all decided something. There were a lot of covert glances being exchanged when they thought she wasn't looking. Growing up in foster homes and on the streets, Noa had come by her intuition the hard way. And their behavior was setting off all sorts of alarm bells in her head.

Peter had insisted on driving. As they headed northwest for more than an hour, he refused to discuss their destination, or why they were going there.

City limits vanished quickly in Colorado; all the cheery red brick buildings were abruptly replaced by a relentless march of evergreen trees. They'd ascended the foothills of the Rocky Mountains, climbing high enough for the altitude to make her light-headed. It was a glorious day outside, sunny and warm. Behind the metal gate, a large field of golden grass waved back and forth like shifting sand dunes, bookended by lumpy-looking green hills.

It looked eerily like the landscape in the dream she'd been having right before they fled Arkansas. Despite the peaceful surroundings, Noa felt a sense of foreboding.

"Okay, we're close!" Peter called out exuberantly.

"Close to what?" Noa demanded.

He squinted at a small GPS device and muttered, "Well, within a mile or so. Probably."

"A mile from what?" Noa's eyes narrowed; she was officially done with all this secrecy. "What exactly are we looking for, Peter?"

His grin faltered. Avoiding her eyes, he said, "Do you remember Loki?"

"Loki?" The name was so unexpected, it took her a second to process it. "The hacker from /ALLIANCE/?"

"Yeah." Peter looked even more discomfited as he continued, "I think he's somewhere close by."

"So?" Noa asked, stupefied.

"So I bet he can help us find the decryption key for the drives."

Noa groaned. "God, Peter. You dragged us out here because some hacker offered to help?"

"Well . . ." Peter's voice dropped as he continued, "He didn't exactly offer."

"Why do we need a GPS to find him?" Teo asked doubtfully. "Did he give you coordinates or something?"

Noa stared at the device in his hand. Slowly, she said, "You told me that Loki wouldn't have anything to do with us after bricking the server."

"That's true," Peter said, the telltale flush spreading up his neck again. "But I figure that maybe, once we explain everything—"

"Does he even know we're coming?"

A long pause, then Peter said, "No."

"So how did you find him?" Her eyes narrowed. "Did he get in touch on The Quad?"

"Not exactly," Peter hedged. "I, um . . . I built a back door into /ALLIANCE/."

"You *what*?"

"What's a back door?" Teo asked.

"Just what it sounds like," Noa said as she stared down Peter, who looked like he was hoping a hole in the ground would suddenly appear. "It's a way for a site administrator to keep tabs on who's visiting the website."

"That doesn't sound so bad." Teo shrugged.

Noa turned on him. "It is when the website administrator has promised *total* anonymity. That was the whole point of /ALLIANCE/; we couldn't be traced. Or so we thought." Anger was uncoiling inside her like a snake, and she let it;

hackers viewed what Peter had done as the ultimate betrayal. "But Peter was keeping tabs on us."

"Hey, it wasn't like that," Peter said defensively. "I had everyone's emails anyway—that's how I got in touch with you, remember?"

"Yeah, I remember," Noa snarled. "But that's different from knowing my location. What did you do? Log IP addresses?"

Peter hesitated, then said, "Yeah, basically."

"I can't believe you." Noa turned on her heel and stormed off. When she'd first stumbled across the hacktivist group, she'd joined up because she believed in what they were doing: punishing child and animal abusers, and going after bullies that the legal system was unable or unwilling to punish.

But if /ALLIANCE/ hadn't guaranteed anonymity, she never would have enlisted.

"Noa," Peter said gently, following her.

She refused to turn and face him. The sun was piercing through her tinted sunglasses, making her eyes water against the glare.

"Listen," he said. "Some of the stuff that people were doing, if it got out of hand . . . I needed a way to protect all of us."

"You mean to protect yourself," Noa said disdainfully.

"Okay, fine," Peter said more forcefully. "And I'm not sorry. What if someone got really hurt, because of a mission I didn't even sanction? A lot of people did their own thing, then claimed to be members."

"So if the cops had showed up, you would've ratted us out?" Noa asked.

Peter hesitated, then said, "Yeah, maybe. If it was for something I didn't condone."

Noa wanted to keep arguing, but the truth was, she'd experienced the same sort of thing firsthand. When she'd formed Persefone's Army, lots of kids had committed heinous acts, then claimed they were doing it on her behalf. She understood why Peter had built in the back door. But she still felt betrayed.

"Well," she said. "If I'm not happy about it, just imagine how Loki is going to feel."

"I know," Peter said gravely. "Especially since his IP was cloaked. It wasn't easy to track it."

Noa flashed back on all the hours they'd spent at public computer terminals over the past few weeks, when it seemed to be taking Peter way too long to find another safe house. "So *that's* the personal thing you were doing."

Peter impatiently brushed a lock of brown hair out of his eyes. "Loki has to have some sort of killer setup, right? Better than you and me working on crap computers, twenty minutes at a time."

Noa ran her eyes over the rugged landscape. "There's not even a house here. Are you sure you found the right IP address?"

"Not one hundred percent," Peter admitted. Off her look, he added, "But close. Ninety-seven percent, at least."

Noa considered. Teo and Daisy were still standing uncertainly beside the car. It couldn't hurt to at least take a look around, right? This road had to lead somewhere. The alternative was to stay hunkered down in that nasty safe house.

"All right," she sighed. "We'll check it out. But if we don't find anything—"

"Then we'll come up with another plan," Peter interjected, sounding relieved. "But don't worry. Loki's here somewhere, I can feel it."

* * *

The lower legs of Teo's jeans were completely soaked through, but he didn't care. It was amazing out here. He and Daisy were wading through grass that reached above his knees in places, the base of it still damp with dew. The sky was like an upended giant blue bowl; the sun warmed his bare arms. They walked in silence, holding hands.

"You okay?" he asked.

Daisy smiled up at him. "Yeah, I'm good. Really good. Better than I've felt in a while."

"Me too." There was something special about this place. In a way, it reminded him of the Forsythes' spread in Santa Cruz. He winced, remembering gunfire and waves of smoke. . . .

"Hey," Daisy said softly, pulling him back to the present. "What is it?"

"Nothing. Sorry." Teo focused on the ground. They were cresting a small hill. The plan was for them to walk a grid. He and Daisy were supposed to head a mile or so west, then turn north for another mile. Peter had pointed out the general direction, then told them to take a right after twenty minutes. He and Noa had gone off in the opposite direction to do the same thing. They'd meet back in the middle, unless one of the groups found something.

Teo patted the radio hooked to his jeans pocket. Part of him was hoping they wouldn't find anything, and Peter would be forced to admit that Loki was nowhere nearby. Then he'd have fulfilled his part of the bargain. He and Daisy could head back to Denver and catch a bus west. Los Angeles, maybe Venice Beach. Over the past few months, while keeping watch through the long, dark nights, he'd mapped out the life they'd have when this was all over. They could get jobs in a restaurant on the water. Daisy would wait tables, and he'd bus them; lots of places would probably be willing to pay under the table. Given time, they could save enough cash for false documents, then rent a place of their own. Maybe he'd even get his GED. And now, it might happen sooner than he'd hoped.

Another flash, of Janiqua being loaded kicking and screaming into a van. The memory made him squirm. After the raid, he'd been determined to do whatever he could to rescue the rest of the unit. But months had passed, and they'd never gotten any indication that those kids were still alive. Now, his only mission was to protect Daisy.

Teo stopped and turned to face her. Daisy tilted her chin up—he was a big fan of her chin, it was pert and a little knobby, in a good way—and he cupped it in one hand. Looking into her enormous blue eyes, ringed with matching eyeliner (he could never figure out how she found the time or energy for makeup with everything else going on), he felt a pressure against his ribs that had nothing to do with the altitude. Every time he looked at her, it felt like his heart was on the verge of exploding.

"I love you," he said softly.

Daisy blinked, and her mouth opened in a small surprised O. Then she smiled and swatted his arm. "Teddy, you dork. I've been waiting *months* for you to say that!"

She went up on her tiptoes and pressed her lips to his. He kissed her back, carefully wrapping his arms around her, overly aware of the delicate bones of her rib cage through her thin cotton shirt.

"How sweet," a male voice said from behind them. "Now who the hell are you?"

★ ★ ★

Noa hadn't said a word as they trudged across the hillsides. By silent accord, she and Peter were staying twenty paces away from each other, scanning the surroundings. They'd already walked at least a mile, and hadn't encountered anything except a tiny brown rabbit that startled from a bush. They both watched as it bounded away.

"I don't suppose that's Loki," Noa said wryly.

"Not unless he's a lot smaller than I imagined," Peter said, keeping his tone light. "But maybe. We don't really know who anyone is online."

"That's what I liked about it," Noa mumbled as she kept walking.

Peter opted not to reply; clearly she was still angry about the IP address tracking. And he couldn't really blame her. But his mom was a lawyer, and if she'd imparted anything to him, it was the necessity of watching your back when dealing with strangers.

He wondered what Mom would think if she saw him now, hiking through the woods in search of a shadowy internet renegade.

She'd probably think the same thing as always: that he was a loser. His parents had made their feelings for him abundantly clear, especially after his brother died. As far as they were concerned, the sun rose and set on Jeremy. After losing him, they barely bothered to say good morning to Peter.

Peter forced back the memories. He'd left home for a reason; his parents were conspiring with Charles Pike, and as far as he was concerned, they were every bit as guilty. Among other things, finding Loki represented a chance to access files proving their culpability.

He and Noa entered a spindly stand of trees at the edge of a field. The evergreens were at least fifty feet tall; underfoot, a thick carpet of pine fronds muted their footsteps. Peter stopped and stared up: above the swaying treetops, glimpses of a cerulean blue sky. The atmosphere was hushed, like a cathedral. It didn't seem like the sort of place where you'd find a world-class hacker, and he was starting to seriously question whether he'd found the right IP address after all. If Loki wasn't here, he and Noa would be forced to keep running, while Teo and Daisy went off on their own. The thought made him want to sink to the ground and stay there.

Noa was walking closer to him now. Breaking the silence, she asked, "Are you sure this is the right place?"

Peter shrugged. "Pretty sure. Loki bounced off a bunch of VPNs, but they were usually the same ones, at least when he accessed /ALLIANCE/."

"Okay." Her voice had lost that angry edge, he noted with relief. Maybe she'd forgiven him already.

The nice thing about being with Noa was that he didn't have to convert everything into layman's terms, the way he did with Amanda and pretty much everyone else. She knew exactly what he was talking about: A VPN, or virtual private network, was a good way to protect your identity and data from everyone else on the internet. It was kind of like crawling into a secret tunnel, where most people could only tell where you emerged; your starting point was hidden. But there was a way to track it back. VPNs were most easily accessed by using a gateway close to your home city; and in Loki's case, that had been Denver. Once Peter narrowed that down, he'd hacked into the VPN provider's database (no mean feat, especially on an archaic Dell in a public library); then he double-checked the time and date stamps of users until he'd landed on an IP address that matched up with when Loki logged on to /ALLIANCE/. From there, it was easy; lots of sites let you do an instant IP address search, and usually they could pinpoint a computer's location to within a mile or so.

Of course, if Loki was half as paranoid as he came across in posts, there was a good chance he'd taken extra precautions to hide his IP origins.

Peter sighed. Just once, he could really use a break.

"Look," Noa said, stopping dead. "There's something over there."

Peter followed her pointing finger. Up ahead, through a break in the trees, there was a glint of light on metal.

"That's got to be it!" Peter said excitedly. "C'mon!"

A small structure jutted out of the ground at an angle. They hurried over to it. As they got closer, Peter's heart sank and his steps slowed. "It's just a sign," he said, disappointed.

Noa's face was unreadable. "Let's see what it says." The time outside seemed to be doing her some good; she wasn't dragging the way she'd been lately, and there was some color in her cheeks.

Noa brushed away the grass covering it and read, "Warning: U.S. Air Force Installation."

Peter's eyes skimmed the rest: It was full of typical military bluster, threats about how trespassers would be handled and the right to search any visitors. Which seemed to stand at odds with the appearance of the sign itself; it was warped, rusty, and pocked with bullet holes. "Well, I don't see any sign of the Air Force."

"Still, I don't like this." Noa's green eyes looked concerned. "We haven't had great luck with government bases."

"Good point," Peter agreed. And he couldn't imagine why a hacker would voluntarily go within a hundred miles of a military base. He eyed their surroundings uneasily. Aside from the metal gate at the entrance, which had been easy enough to climb over, they hadn't seen any security. But abandoned bases were a favored location for Project Perse-phone's secret labs.

"We should find the others," Noa said, keeping her voice low. "And get back to the car."

Peter bit his lip, wanting to argue. They hadn't finished walking their grid yet. Teo and Daisy hadn't reported in, either, which meant they probably hadn't found anything. Giving up now, when he'd been so convinced they were in the right place, just felt wrong. "Just a little farther," he pleaded. "To the other side of those trees . . ."

Noa was already shaking her head. "No, Peter. It's too dangerous."

He was about to argue when they heard a loud *BANG*. They both spun around. "That sounded like a gunshot," Peter said.

Noa's jaw tensed. "It came from where we sent Teo and Daisy."

Teo's ears rang as he stumbled back, simultaneously shoving Daisy behind him. The guy had fired his gun into the air before they'd even had a chance to answer him.

"Last warning," he growled, pumping the slide of the shotgun to reload it. "So you better get moving."

"What's wrong with you?" Daisy cried out. "We weren't doing anything!"

The man was standing uphill, with the sun at his back. Teo squinted against the glare and swallowed hard: The guy was huge, at least six-five. He had a frizzy brown beard that started beneath a pair of dark sunglasses and extended all the way down his chest. Dressed in full camouflage gear and a trucker's cap, he aimed the shotgun straight at Teo's chest. "You're on my land, kid. I'd be well within my rights to shoot you right here."

"Just take it easy!" Teo protested, raising his hands. "We're not armed."

"Bullshit you're not," the guy scoffed. "That's a Taser on your belt, ain't it?"

"We were hiking, and got lost," Teo stammered. He felt Daisy quavering behind him, her hand on his back.

"And the Taser?" he asked skeptically.

Teo frantically tried to come up with an explanation. "Bears?"

"You were gonna tase a bear?" The man's eyebrows shot up over his glasses. "Son, you ever seen a black bear?"

"No, never." Teo felt a wave of relief; he seemed to be buying it.

"Tasing one'll just piss it off." The shotgun lowered a few inches, now targeting the area right below Teo's waistband. Which really didn't make him feel better.

"Wow, thanks. We didn't know." Teo nodded vigorously. "So I guess we'll just get going now, off your property. Sorry about that, we didn't realize—"

"Are you Loki?" Daisy piped up from behind him.

The guy visibly tensed. The shotgun zoomed back up as he growled, "Where did you hear that name?"

"Listen," Teo said desperately. "We don't want any trouble, really."

"Who sent you?" The guy stepped menacingly closer. "The NSA? CIA?"

"What? No." Teo almost added, *That's crazy*, but under the circumstances it seemed like a really bad idea. "We're here with friends, and they said they knew you."

"Friends?" Loki said dubiously, as if the concept was foreign to him.

"Yeah, Noa and Peter. Listen." Teo gestured to the radio hanging off his belt. "I can call them, so you can hear for yourself."

"Touch that radio and I'll blow your hand clean off."

Daisy made a small noise. Teo threw her a look that he hoped was calming and said, "Okay. Do you want to try them?"

Loki shook his head fiercely and snarled, "You think I'm nuts? You could have a whole team standing by."

"There's no team, just two other kids—"

"No!" Loki roared.

From behind him, someone called out, "Do you really think the government would have sent a couple of teenagers?"

Startled, Teo turned his head. Noa was standing twenty feet away, hands held high to show she wasn't armed. "Chill, Loki."

"How the hell do you all know my name?" he bellowed, swinging the gun from side to side like he couldn't decide where to aim it. "I want some answers, now!"

Teo swallowed hard; Loki didn't seem all that stable, his eyes were wild and his hands shook.

Noa seemed unfazed, however. Sounding more like herself than she had in months, she said firmly, "Just calm down, Loki. We came here to find you. I'm Rain, from /ALLIANCE/." Gesturing to Peter, she added, "And this is Vallas."

"Since when are you Rain and Vallas?" Teo muttered. Peter waved for him to stay quiet.

"What do you want?" Loki demanded. The gun was still raised, but at least he wasn't waving it around like a crazy person anymore.

"Can I come closer?" Noa asked. "I'm unarmed."

"That's what your friends said." Loki shook his head. "No one moves. Now who the hell are you, really?"

Daisy clung to Teo, both arms tight around his waist. He clasped her hands, cursing himself for listening to Peter. They should have left last night; he should have trusted his gut. After everything they'd been through, he and Daisy might be shot in the middle of nowhere by some freak.

"I contacted you on The Quad last October," Peter piped up. "When I was going to brick Pike & Dolan's servers."

"A lot of people know about that," Loki said. "Doesn't prove anything."

Peter and Noa exchanged an uncertain look, and Teo's heart sank. Was it possible they'd never even met this guy before? And what was up with the fake names?

"The pedophile case in Greenwich," Noa finally said. "We worked together on that."

Loki tilted his head and said, "Tell me how."

"How what?" Peter asked.

"How did we get him?" Loki snarled.

"I posed as a twelve-year-old girl and chatted with him while you sent his jpegs to the local cops," Noa said. "Anything else you want to know?"

The shotgun lowered a fraction of an inch. Loki stared at them for a beat, considering. Finally, he said, "So you are who you say you are. Doesn't matter. How the hell did you find me?"

"I, uh . . . tracked your IP address," Peter said. "Sorry."

Teo held his breath, braced for another gunshot. Based on Noa's reaction earlier, this wasn't something hackers took well.

"You *what*?" Loki sounded genuinely perplexed. "Seriously? Not cool, Vallas."

"I know, and I'm really, really sorry." Peter spoke in a rush. "We wouldn't have come, but we need your help."

Loki scowled at them. "I can't help you."

"Please, man," Peter said. "Look, I know this started off kind of weird—"

Loki grunted and waved an arm at them. "Just get off my property, before I really do shoot you."

"You have to help us," Peter said. "Please."

"I warned you, Vallas," Loki said. "Bricking that server was a bad idea."

"It's more than that!" Peter protested. "They're experimenting on kids."

"So go to the cops," Loki said dismissively. "That's not my problem."

"The cops are part of it." Peter threw up his hands. "They have people in the FBI, the NSA. . . . Hell, probably everywhere!"

Loki's eyes glimmered. Slowly, he said, "So you're saying there's some sort of massive government conspiracy?"

"Hell, yeah, that's what I'm saying!" Peter was practically shouting.

"Ho-ly crap." Loki scratched his beard with his free hand, keeping the gun tucked under his armpit. "You're Persefone's Army."

Noa looked startled, but she said, "We are. Or, well . . . we were. Just give us ten minutes to explain. After that, if you still want us to leave, we'll go."

Loki stared at the ground contemplatively; the sun was setting behind him, casting his face in shadow. For a minute he looked like a Paul Bunyan statue, with a shotgun in place of an ax. Finally, he sighed and said, "Ten minutes. But if I don't like what I hear, I'm still reserving the right to shoot you."

* * *

Peter kept his mouth shut as they followed Loki through the woods. Teo and Daisy were murmuring back and forth, probably debating whether or not to run for the car.

In spite of everything, Peter felt validated. He'd been right, Loki was here. And hopefully once they'd explained the situation, he'd agree to help.

They'd already hiked nearly a mile, deeper into the forest. A small clearing appeared through the trees. In the center was a shed, ramshackle and practically falling down. It was just ten feet by five feet, the kind of thing you'd store gardening supplies in.

"Home sweet home," Loki mumbled.

"You live here?" Peter asked incredulously. Seeing the corners of Loki's mouth turn down, he hurriedly added, "I bet it's nice inside."

Loki shook his head, then unclasped an enormous padlock and hauled open the door. It creaked slightly, carving a groove through the dirt. He ducked his head as he stepped inside. Noa glanced back at them, then followed.

"You sure this is a good idea?" Teo said in a low voice, pausing on the threshold.

"Sure," Peter said, hoping his voice conveyed more conviction than he felt. "Loki's a great guy. Me and Noa have known him for years."

"Really?" Teo said. "You use fake names with all your friends?"

"It's a handle," Peter explained. Seeing Teo's skeptical look, he said, "What, you think Loki's his real name?"

Teo still looked disgruntled, but he disappeared inside, with Daisy right behind him. Peter drew in a deep breath and stepped into the void.

It took a second for his eyes to adjust to the darkness, then his jaw dropped. A flight of rough concrete stairs led straight down. "What the hell?" he muttered.

He could hear the others' footsteps descending. The air wafting up the stairwell was cold and reeked of rot. Peter swallowed hard. He wasn't a big fan of close spaces. But then, he wasn't a big fan of letting his friends get shot, either, and he'd led them here. Tentatively, he stepped onto the first riser.

"Close the door!" Loki bellowed from below. "And lock it with the crowbar."

Through the gloom, Peter spotted a crowbar lying beside the open door. He grabbed it and wrenched the door closed, then fitted the crowbar across two iron beams. With the light cut off, he could barely make out the stairs behind him, and the sound of the others was growing fainter. Suddenly spooked, he hurried down the stairs.

They descended for a long time; after fifty steps, he lost count. The staircase abruptly ended in a plain concrete corridor lined with emergency lights in metal cages. They barely illuminated the space, and cast everything in an eerie red hue. Peter strained his ears, debating whether to turn left or right. Sounds echoed strangely down here, and his own breathing seemed abnormally loud. *Left*, he decided, and started off in that direction.

He was about to turn back, convinced he'd gone the wrong way, when the corridor branched and he spotted light up ahead. Peter scurried toward it, inordinately relieved. The door at the end of the hallway was open; through it, he heard voices.

Stepping inside, his jaw dropped again. If he'd been startled to find a staircase in an old shed, what confronted him now was mind-boggling. A large, round room, twenty feet in diameter, with an enormous gas fireplace set in the center. It was furnished like a ski lodge, with plush carpets on the floors, framed film posters on the walls, and comfortable overstuffed chairs and sofas.

"Wow," he said.

"I know, right?" Teo exclaimed. "A real underground lair! How cool is this?"

"I've still got a gun," Loki grumbled, but he sounded pleased.

"Do you have anything to drink?" Daisy asked. "I'm really thirsty."

"You're not guests," Loki snapped. "Clock's still ticking on whether or not I kick you out."

"So can I have some water while you're deciding?" Daisy said, rolling her eyes.

"You're a real piece of work, you know that?"

Daisy's face darkened. Peter quickly intervened, saying, "Some water sounds great, actually. If you don't mind."

Loki collapsed into a huge brown leather armchair, the shotgun still clasped loosely in his right hand. He waved toward the corner, looking irritated. "There's a wet bar over there. Might have to wash a glass, though, princess."

Daisy stomped toward the sink with Teo at her heels.

Noa motioned to the chair across from Loki. "You mind if I sit down?"

"Suit yourself," Loki said gruffly. "No promises, though."

Noa settled on the edge of the chair and spent the next five minutes bringing him up to date on everything that had happened over the past seven months; although as always, she skipped the part about ending up with an extra thymus. Listening to her description of the attack on the Santa Cruz compound, Peter experienced a familiar twinge of jealousy. Noa always faltered when she explained how Zeke had died on a beach while helping the rest of them escape.

When she'd finished, Loki sat there staring at her, his chin propped on one hand. "So you're Persefone now," he finally said.

"Sort of," Noa acknowledged.

"Huh." Loki grunted. "I saw your posts. Some of what you claimed sounded kind of . . . out there. But you did some good work."

"Thanks," Noa muttered.

"We can bring the whole thing down," Peter interjected. "We have hard drives from Charles Pike's private server farm. But we haven't had the processing power or the time to find the decryption key."

"And you want my help." Loki's eyes narrowed as he scrutinized Peter. "Gotta say, I'm still pretty ticked off about that stunt you pulled, tracking my IP."

"Like I said, I'm sorry about that." Loki's mood seemed to be turning again, and Peter was regretting speaking up. Maybe he should leave the talking to Noa for a change. "Listen, we wouldn't have come here, but these guys keep finding us—"

Loki sprang out of his chair. "Wait a minute. What do you mean, they keep finding you?"

"Well, yeah," Peter said, flustered. "Like, almost every night, no matter where we are—"

"And you led them here?!" Loki abruptly stormed from the room, vanishing down the corridor.

Noa shot him a withering look, then jumped from her chair to follow, muttering, "Nice going, Peter."

"Hey, he deserved to know," Peter said defensively. "You guys stay here, okay?"

Teo glanced at Daisy, then said, "Sure. Good luck with crazy mountain man."

Rushing into the corridor, Peter caught a glimpse of Noa running in the opposite direction from where they'd come in. She broke left, vanishing into the darkness.

Peter raced after her.

The corridor bent twice more before ending at an enormous metal door. When Noa caught up to him, Loki was hunched beside it, frantically punching numbers into a keypad. The keypad beeped, and he spun a wheel on the front of the door that looked like it belonged on a ship. As the door groaned open, a deep-blue glow emanated from within.

"What is this place?" Noa asked with awe as she followed him inside. It was another round room, smaller than the one they'd just been in. But this one was filled floor to ceiling with computer consoles and monitors. It looked like a government command center in an action film.

"It's an old Titan missile silo," Loki said, dropping down into a swiveling Aeron chair. "I bought it a few years ago."

"Wow," Peter said from behind her. "Now this is what I'm talking about!"

Noa knew exactly how he felt. Her eyes swept greedily across the room, taking in the array. The things she could do with all that processing power . . . it was a hacker's dream come true.

Loki ignored them. He was rapidly tapping away at a keyboard. Images shifted across the mounted monitors: Noa realized she was looking at wide, panoramic views of the landscape aboveground. Loki must have cameras hidden in nearly every corner of the compound. His eyes danced across the screen as he muttered, "Sector One, clear. Sector Two looks okay, too. . . ."

The security images flashed past in such rapid succession it was dizzying. Finally, Loki spun around in his chair. He didn't look pleased. "You said they come at night?"

"Yeah, usually," Peter said. His eyes flicked to Noa, and she shook her head slightly. Sharing the fact that just yesterday, Pike's men had showed up on a busy college campus in broad daylight might compel Loki to bring out the shotgun again.

Loki scratched his beard. "And you've checked for trackers?"

"Always," Noa chimed in. "We keep changing cars, too, and there's no way they could have bugged our clothes or packs."

Loki looked past them toward the door. Thoughtfully, he said, "Those other two. You trust them?"

"Absolutely," Noa said firmly. "If we get caught, they do, too. And terrible things will happen to them. They know that."

Loki drummed his fingers on his knee, still glaring at them.

"Listen, man. If there's any way we could plug in just one drive," Peter pleaded.

Loki snorted. "Yeah, right. That might be how they're tracking you."

"No way. We built Faraday cages for them," Peter said, slipping off his backpack. "Here, check it out." Carefully, he pulled a drive out of his pack. It was bulky, wrapped in several layers of aluminum foil and cardboard.

Loki took the drive gingerly, like it might bite. He set it down on the desk in front of him and lurched out of the chair, lumbering toward a metal cabinet in the corner. After opening it up and riffling around inside, he came back with some sort of gadget.

"Is that a bug detector?" Peter asked. "I saw something like that once, in this spy store back home."

"Does he ever shut up?" Loki muttered. He ran the scanner over the drive, then flipped it and did the same to the other side. His forehead wrinkled. "Nothing." He sounded perplexed. "Kind of hinky, but it seems to do the trick. And they're all wrapped up like this?"

"Every one of them," Peter responded, a hint of pride in his voice.

"How many?"

"Forty-two," Noa said. "We split them up, so we've each got about ten."

Loki scratched his beard again and said musingly, "So how the hell do they keep finding you?"

Noa shrugged helplessly. The same question had been dogging her for weeks. The four of them were almost never apart; they didn't even use cell phones anymore for fear of being found that way.

Loki peered up at her from under bushy eyebrows. "You said they had you, right? Back in Boston?"

Noa drew in a deep breath. She didn't really want to go into what had been done to her on that operating table. "Yeah, but if they'd implanted a device in me, they would have found us before. It's only been a problem recently."

"So what's changed?" he prodded.

"Nothing, really." Noa shrugged, her eyes unconsciously sliding to Peter. He was standing in front of the monitors with his hands jammed in his pockets, that same lock of hair dangling over his right eye. "I mean, Peter joined up with us, but . . ."

Her voice trailed off. Peter blinked, as if confused, then raised both hands as realization dawned. "Whoa, hey," he protested. "You know I wouldn't sell you out, Noa. I would never—"

"Maybe not intentionally," Loki interrupted. "But they might have put a tracker on you."

"That's nuts," Peter scoffed. "It's not like they ever even had me—" His eyes suddenly widened, and he said, "Oh, crap."

"After Rhode Island," Noa said slowly. "You woke up in a hospital, right?"

"Yeah, but it was just a regular hospital," he said weakly.

"One way to find out," Loki said gruffly, getting to his feet. He motioned for Peter to extend his arms out to the sides. After a beat, Peter complied, but he didn't look happy about it. He stood stiffly as Loki ran the scanner over the front of his body. Noa held her breath; the machine remained silent.

"This room should block any signals," Loki said, moving on to Peter's back. "The walls are lined with copper mesh, and they're built to withstand a nuclear blast."

"Kind of a more high-tech Faraday cage," Noa said.

"Exactly."

The scanner suddenly started emitting a series of high-pitched beeps. Loki's hand froze with the device an inch from the base of Peter's spine.

Peter's voice quavered as he said, "No."

Loki gingerly lifted up a corner of Peter's T-shirt and bent to examine his back. He waved Noa over, saying, "Check it out."

Reluctantly, Noa crossed the room. Peter looked absolutely terrified. The expression on his face sent her back to the moment when she first discovered the incision on her chest, and found out that strangers had been operating on her, *handling* her, without her permission. It was the worst kind of violation.

In the dim light of the room, it was hard to see what Loki was pointing at. She bent lower and squinted: There was a tiny, thin scar on Peter's lower back, just over a half-inch long.

"But if it's been inside him this whole time . . . Peter's right, they usually only come at night. And it doesn't seem like they know exactly where we are." Noa's mind was spinning—in a way, this was still her fault. She'd given Peter permission to join them. And because of that, Pike had nearly captured them time and again.

Loki hefted the backpack by the straps and peered at it. "How often are you wearing this thing?"

Peter shrugged, his arms still raised. "A lot."

"All the time," Noa said slowly, working it through. "He only takes it off—"

"When I'm sleeping." Peter met her eyes.

"That's why they only come at night." Loki nodded, looking satisfied. "Rest of the time, those little cages you built for the drives blocked the signal pretty effectively."

Noa was almost overwhelmed with relief; they'd finally figured out how Pike was tracking them, and there were no traitors in their midst. At least, not willing ones.

Destroy the bug, and they could evade him once and for all. They could find a real safe house, and stay for more than a couple of days. "We have to get it out," she said resolutely.

"Yup," Loki agreed. "I'll go get a knife."

"Wait, what?" Peter dropped his arms and backed away. "Hell no. I didn't sign up for home surgery."

"Peter," Noa said, trying to sound reassuring. "Look, I know it's scary. But this way they won't find us anymore."

"Maybe we can shut it off somehow," he said desperately. "Or I'll just stay in here. This room is safe, right?" he said, whirling toward Loki. "You said it would block any signals."

"Sure." Loki shrugged. "No bathroom, though. That's down the hall."

"So I'll wear the backpack when I use it." He sounded relieved. "No big deal."

"And what? You stay down here forever?" Noa cocked an eyebrow.

"Just until we get the data off the drives," Peter said weakly. "We'll figure something out by then."

Loki was rustling through the cabinet again. He dug out an old fishing tackle box and sifted through it. After a minute he straightened, brandishing a scalpel in a sterile plastic sheath. "Ha! Knew I had one somewhere."

Peter had retreated to the far wall. "No way, man. Keep that thing away from me!"

"All right, let's just take a minute," Noa said calmly. "I know you're freaked out, but think about it. Do you really want to walk around with some sort of P&D device lodged next to your spine? What if it's more than just a bug?"

"Jesus." Peter sank down on his haunches and clutched his head in both hands. "Like what? A bomb?"

"Well, we don't know, right?" Going over to him, she set a hand on his shoulder. "Trust me. I know how scary this is."

He tilted his head up to meet her eyes. "I know."

"But in your case, it shouldn't be hard to get out. It's probably close to the surface. Like removing a splinter."

"Gotta get through scar tissue, though," Loki chimed in. "That's gonna be a bitch."

Noa threw him a scathing look. He hunched his shoulders and grumbled, "Just want the kid to know what he's facing."

Peter had blanched even whiter. "What if it blows up when you try to take it out?"

Noa chewed her lip; that hadn't occurred to her. If there was some sort of fail-safe mechanism, that could be very, very bad.

Loki snorted. "Hell, doesn't matter if that thing is packed with C4. It needs a remote trigger, and that'll be blocked, too. Just like the signal is now."

"See?" Noa said, trying to sound reassuring. "Nothing to worry about."

Peter didn't answer. He was rubbing the small of his back with one hand.

"Listen, Peter. We're going to figure this out," Noa said soothingly. "And we won't do anything tonight. After some food and sleep, I bet this won't seem as scary. Loki, do you have anything to eat?"

His face brightened. "Yeah, of course. I've got a three-year supply of MREs. Lots of good stuff . . . except the lasagna. Not recommending that."

"All right. Put the backpack on," Noa ordered. "We should get back to Teo and Daisy anyway."

CHAPTER FIVE

Teo chewed in silence. The mac and cheese tasted oddly gummy, but the novelty of having honest-to-God hot food for a change outweighed the pastiness of it. Loki might be insane, but he'd established a pretty impressive setup. Between bites, Loki explained the layout of the place. When he talked about it, his whole face lit up, and he looked marginally less scary. He was younger than he'd first appeared, too, probably in his midthirties.

Apparently they were inside some sort of bunker where the U.S. military used to store nuclear missiles. After the base was decommissioned, they sold it to Loki, which was crazy in and of itself; Teo couldn't imagine the government just handing over a place like this. Or what would compel someone to buy it.

As Loki made his way through the biggest bottle of beer

Teo had ever seen, he went on about all the excellent reasons to live underground. Apparently there was a long list of ways the world could end. It was kind of mind-blowing for Teo; he'd never bothered worrying about that sort of thing. In his experience, the world in its current state was hard enough to deal with.

"How big is this place, exactly?" Peter had been chugging beer, too, and his cheeks were flushed.

"Forty-five thousand square feet," Loki announced, slamming the bottle down on the table; it teetered, and Noa's hand darted out to steady it. "It's got two wells dug right into the aquifer, so there's plenty of fresh water. I own the entire two hundred and ten acres of land around it, too."

"So aside from this room, how many others are there?" Noa asked, although she sounded distracted. She kept glancing over at Peter, as if checking to see if he was okay. Which was kind of funny; it was usually the other way around. This was the most alert Teo had seen her since they'd left Santa Cruz.

"Three silos total, with about a half mile of tunnels," Loki said proudly. "I've got two sleeping quarters carved out, this room, and the old control center. I'm still working on the other sections. Takes some time, since I have to do it all myself."

"Why don't you just hire a construction crew?" Daisy suggested.

Loki made a face. "This is a secret location. When it hits the fan—"

"When what hits the fan?"

"Solar flares, super volcanoes, collapse of the global economy. You name it, something's hitting the fan. And when it does, you think I want a bunch of carpenters trying to bust in with their families?" Loki snorted. "Hell, I shouldn't have let *you* in here."

"We won't tell anyone," Teo said, noting the paranoia that had crept back into Loki's eyes.

Loki muttered something under his breath, then took a slug straight from the bottle. By now, it had to be mostly gone. Teo squeezed Daisy's hand under the table. He was getting her out of here as soon as possible, before Loki decided that letting them leave was not an option.

Peter had fallen quiet. He stared down at the ring his beer bottle had left on the table. Teo noted that he'd barely touched his food.

"So what's going on?" Teo asked, unable to stay silent any longer.

"What do you mean?" Noa said, a warning in her voice.

"I mean, you guys came back and started cooking dinner, like all this is normal." He waved a hand toward Loki. "So did he agree to help us?"

Noa and Loki looked at each other. Loki cleared his throat and said, "Maybe. Haven't decided yet."

"Well, you better decide quick," Teo pressed. "Like we said earlier, those guys after us? They tend to come at night. And I don't think a crowbar will stop them. We're trapped here," he added, turning to Noa. "Only one way in and out."

"First of all," Loki slurred, raising a finger, "that's not technically true."

"There's a back door?" Daisy asked.

Loki nodded enthusiastically. "Always gotta have a bug-out plan."

"They won't come tonight, anyway," Noa said reassuringly.

"Yeah? And how do you know that?"

"I just do." Her eyes wandered to Peter and something

flitted across her face, too fast for Teo to identify.

The fact that he and Daisy were being treated like second-class citizens again steeled his resolve. They'd been through too much to keep secrets from each other. Teo turned to Peter. "Listen, man. I held up our end, and you found the guy. Now we're taking off."

"What?" Noa gasped. "You're leaving?"

Peter was still staring down at the table. He didn't react to what Teo had said, as if the words hadn't registered.

"Teddy," Daisy said hesitantly. "Maybe we should wait until tomorrow—"

"They come at night," he repeated, enunciating every word. The chagrined look on Noa's face nearly swayed him, but he forced himself to meet her gaze. "If you two want to stay, I get it. But we can't take that chance. C'mon, Daisy."

Reluctantly, Daisy followed him to the corner where they'd stowed their backpacks. He kept an eye on Loki, who thankfully appeared amused by the turn of events. The shotgun still rested by his chair, but the big man didn't make a move to retrieve it; hopefully he wouldn't try to stop them.

"Where will you go?" Noa asked in a small voice.

For a second, Teo faltered. She sounded bereft, betrayed. He swallowed hard and said, "We're not sure. Probably west."

"Okay." Noa's voice was firmer as she added, "But please, wait until morning. It's a long hike back to the car in the dark."

"Bears out there, too, remember?" Loki chuckled. "You really want to try that Taser out on 'em?"

Teo hesitated. Daisy's eyes had gone huge at the mention of bears. It would be the ultimate irony if they managed to avoid getting shot for all these months, only to be mauled by wild animals.

"We'll be careful." He unpacked the drives, setting them in a pile on the floor as Noa stood silently watching.

Daisy was following suit, though a lot more slowly. Teo finished and stood, brushing hair out of his eyes. Noa looked back at him calmly. "Good-bye, Teo," she said, extending a hand. "Thanks for everything."

"Yeah, sure," he muttered, shaking. "Take care of yourself."

They were almost to the door when Peter said, "Wait!"

Teo stopped but didn't turn around. "What?"

"It was my fault they kept tracking us down," Peter continued, his voice ragged. "It was because of me. I was bugged."

"All right," Teo said slowly. "Let me get this straight. They put a bug in your back, and that's how they kept finding us. But when you're wearing the backpack, there's no signal."

"Basically, yeah." Peter's eyes were bleary from booze, and he sounded defeated. Noa felt a pang of sympathy, although his device could be removed without too much pain and suffering. Probably.

"So you can just keep your backpack on all the time, right? And then they won't be able to find us?" Teo said reasonably.

"Or we can cut it out," Noa interjected.

Peter threw her a look; she met it, staring back at him levelly. Just one mistake and their location could be pinpointed again. Plus, she didn't totally understand his objections. If the extra thymus in her chest could be safely removed, she'd dig it out herself.

"I already offered," Loki said, swinging the beer bottle in a lazy loop. "Doctor Maoz is officially on call."

"I prefer my doctors sober." Peter glared at him.

"It's probably just below the skin, so it shouldn't be too

hard to remove," Noa said in what she hoped was a reassuring tone of voice. "Then we can destroy it."

"And what if it's not?" Peter retorted. "This . . . *thing* is right next to my spine, Noa, and I'm a big fan of walking. Last time I checked, no one here is a doctor."

"Hey," Loki protested. "I got three first-aid certifications."

"You learn any basic surgery for those?" Peter demanded.

"Well, no," Loki admitted. "But I can make a killer tourniquet." Off Peter's expression, he mumbled, "Maybe killer is the wrong word. . . ."

Noa bit her lip. Peter was right to be scared. But their options were limited.

"You need to get it out, dude," Teo said softly. "You don't want those jerks to have any sort of control over you."

Peter's face clouded over. But after a long moment, his expression shifted to resignation. "Crap. I hate this."

"I know," Noa commiserated. "It sucks."

Peter's mouth worked as if he was chewing on something. Finally, he said, "Not tonight."

"Definitely not tonight," Noa agreed, relieved. "We'll do it on a full night's sleep."

"I have an idea," Teo said hesitantly, throwing a glance her way. "Once you get it out, maybe we shouldn't destroy it."

"Why not?" Noa asked. Her energy was flagging again. She hadn't been able to choke down any food, so all she had in her system was a can of Red Bull. She'd pretty much gotten through the day on adrenaline, but that had dissipated.

"Daisy and I could take it," Teo offered.

"What?" Daisy and Peter said simultaneously.

"Just think about it," Teo said earnestly. "Right now, they probably know we're somewhere near Denver, right? We could keep the bug in the packs, wrapped up like the drives.

Every day, we'll take it out for a few minutes so they can get a signal from it. Then we'll wrap it up and take off again."

"Where would we take it?" Daisy demanded.

"California. We'd dump it before we got to LA," he said hurriedly, off her expression. "Way before, so they couldn't catch us. But that way they'd be following us, not you."

"And we stay here," Peter said slowly. "That'll give us time to try and get the decryption key."

"Oh, so you're moving in with me now?" Loki grumbled.

Peter looked abashed. "Well, I'm going to need time to recover from the surgery. . . ."

Loki glowered at him, long enough that Noa half expected him to draw the shotgun again. Then he broke into a broad grin, made an expansive gesture, and said, "Just messing with you, Vallas. What the hell. Most fun I've had in months anyway."

The beer had definitely put him in a better mood, Noa thought. Hopefully he'd remember the offer when he sobered up. Loki had seemed different during the /ALLIANCE/ missions. Saner, for sure. Listening to him prattle on about doomsday scenarios, she got the feeling he'd only let them in because a huge government conspiracy was too intriguing to resist. "So when do you guys want to take off?"

"Soon," Teo said. "Like, tomorrow."

Noa tried not to let her dismay show. Deep down, she couldn't blame them for wanting to leave. She hadn't been much of a leader lately, and there was no army left to speak of. Even though they hadn't discussed it, the rest of her team was probably long gone. Besides, Pike really only wanted her. Anyone in her vicinity could end up as collateral damage.

She drew a deep breath and looked at Peter. "So, tomorrow?"

"Yeah, sure," Peter said ruefully. With feigned nonchalance, he added, "How bad could it be?"

Peter swallowed hard. He was lying facedown on the same table they'd eaten on last night. Loki had moved it into the computer room and covered it with torn-open trash bags, although Peter got the distinct sense that was more out of concern for the table's well-being. Daisy and Teo had opted to stay in the bunkroom. He suspected they didn't want to witness a medical procedure that had the potential to go horribly awry.

He gritted his teeth. Loki had scrounged up some Advil, and he'd swallowed three; the chalky taste still lingered in the back of his throat. He didn't hold out much hope that they'd ease the pain, however.

"You're sure that's sterilized?" Peter asked, eyeing the scalpel Loki was brandishing with way too much enthusiasm.

"Yup," Loki chortled. "Man, I'm so glad I ordered these. Wasn't sure I'd ever need a full medical kit, but it just goes to show—you're never done prepping."

"Don't suppose you have any type A positive blood laying around," Peter tried to joke. Now that he was lying here, this seemed like a spectacularly bad idea. He should back out now, while there was still time. Hell, he could turn himself into a living Faraday cage, just tape a bunch of aluminum and cardboard around his torso. *Cody could have fixed this*, he thought with a pang. He would've given anything to see his friend walk through that door.

"Shouldn't bleed much. There aren't many blood vessels down there," Loki said authoritatively.

"How do you know that?" Peter demanded.

"I looked it up online." Loki grinned. "They didn't have anything specific about removing a bug, but there was a

YouTube video about cutting off a mole that came pretty close."

"All right, that's it," Peter said, pushing his chest off the table. "It can stay in my back. We'll figure out something else."

"Easy, Peter." Noa pressed down on his shoulders with both hands.

"I'm not letting him cut me," Peter insisted. "He's way too excited about it."

"I'm not excited," Loki said, but his eyes were gleaming.

"He's probably still ticked off that I tracked him here," Peter argued. "I don't want him taking that out on my spine."

Noa bent so that her face was level with his. Quietly, she said, "How about if I do it?"

Peter stared back at her. Noa's green eyes were totally calm. Looking into them, he felt inexplicably reassured. She didn't have experience with this sort of thing either, but at least she'd try not to hurt him. "Okay," he said, sinking back down. "But only you. And have something nearby to stop the bleeding."

Noa tugged on a pair of latex gloves, then silently held out a hand for the knife. Loki reluctantly handed it over. Pulling off his own gloves, he muttered, "Christ, Vallas. You didn't have to be such a baby about it."

"Okay, Peter," Noa said in a soothing voice. "I'll be as quick as I can. Just . . . try to think of something else."

Peter squeezed his eyes shut and tried to imagine that he was sitting at his desk back home. His laptop was propped open in front of him, and he was sipping some of his dad's good whiskey—

A searing sensation in his lower back made him howl.

"Try to stay still," Noa said tightly. "It might be a little deeper than we thought."

The next stab of pain almost sent him bucking off the table.

"Steady," Loki warned, bearing down hard on his shoulders.

Peter let loose with every curse he knew. The agony just kept growing. It felt like Noa was digging around, gouging his entire back with the knife. A shriek built inside him, and his whole body went rigid and tense.

"Maybe I should get hold of some morphine," Loki mused. "This would be easier if he was out cold."

Noa didn't answer. Peter felt light-headed, his view of the room tunneled and refracted. "Oh, God," he gasped.

"I need him to hold still," Noa said through gritted teeth.

"One sec." Loki's hands released; Peter saw him dig around in his pocket. "I was saving this," Loki said peevishly, drawing out a small pill. "But I guess he can have it."

"I'm not eating something that was in your pocket," Peter protested, but Loki popped it in his mouth while he was speaking. He nearly gagged on the pill; it left a chemi-cal taste in his mouth as he choked it down. "What was that?"

"The last of my oxy," Loki grumbled. "You're welcome."

Peter shook his head. "I don't do drugs."

"Well, you do now. Enjoy."

Peter's whole body felt sick and trembly. Sweat coursed from every pore. Aside from the hospital stay last fall, his only previous injury had been a twisted ankle on a ski run when he was eight years old. This was about a million times worse.

"Almost done," Noa said, still sounding strained. Peter felt something running off the sides of his back: Was that *blood*?

The thought made him even more light-headed. This had been a mistake. God, if she hit something critical, like an artery . . .

He shrieked as a spike drove into his spine.

"Got it!" Noa said triumphantly.

The pressure abruptly eased, replaced by a dull throbbing. "Let me see it," he gasped.

She lowered a pair of tweezers down in front of his eyes. Peter frowned: They were clamped around something way too tiny to have caused so much pain. "That's it?" he asked, dumbfounded.

"You'd think it would have ten fingers and ten toes, the amount of noise you made," Loki grunted. "Christ, no wonder women have the babies."

"How badly am I bleeding?" Peter asked as air slowly returned to his lungs.

"Not too badly," Noa said reassuringly. His back throbbed; it felt like gallons must be spewing out. "I'll keep the cotton on it for a few minutes, then we can bandage it."

"Too bad I'm not you," he muttered, suddenly completely drained. He sank back down on the table, his cheek sticking to the trash bag as he mumbled, "You'd probably be down to a scar by tomorrow."

"Huh?" Loki asked.

"Nothing," Noa said sharply. "Peter's a slow healer, and I'm not."

"You should see," Peter mumbled, feeling himself drift away. The oxy was definitely kicking in. He was really wishing they'd started with it, then maybe he wouldn't have felt anything at all. "She's like Wolverine, cut her and she heals instantly."

"That's not true." There was a warning in her voice, but

MICHELLE GAGNON

Peter was too far gone to notice or care.

"Seriously, they made her into a superhero, man. She barely eats or sleeps, she . . ." He tried to remember all the other changes in Noa, but at that moment something about the way his hands looked struck him as hilariously funny, and he dissolved in a fit of giggles.

Which is why he didn't notice how quiet the room had gone around him.

"What's he talking about?" Loki asked after a beat.

"Nothing," Noa said dismissively. "He's just high."

"Yeah. Guess that was a lot of oxy for a little guy like him." Loki was smiling, but his eyes looked concerned. "So you're okay?"

"I'm fine," she said curtly, silently cursing Peter.

"Great. Because from the looks of things, these kids need you."

Noa shifted uncomfortably, then mumbled, "I don't know. Lately it hasn't felt that way."

Loki's voice was unusually compassionate as he said, "I think anyone who could go up against what you have, and still come out fighting, well . . . not bad, for a kid your age. Not bad for anyone."

"Thanks." The praise made Noa uncomfortable, but at the same time, it helped. Because these past few months, she'd started doubting herself more and more. "And thanks for letting us stay, too."

"Sure." Loki grinned. "You can operate on me anytime."

"Ugh." She shuddered. "I never want to have to do anything like that, ever again." The bug had been tiny, but that was the problem; every time she tried to grab it, it had slipped through the tweezers. Peter's howls still echoed through her head.

"How'd it go?" Teo appeared in the doorway.

"Teo!" Peter called out. "You're the man, man!"

"What did you give him?" Teo's eyes widened as he took in the scene. "Oh, man, that's a lot of blood."

"I'm what we're having for dinner!" Peter chortled. "Just grab a knife!"

"He's fine," Noa said. "Grab some bandages from over there, I need to get this covered."

She eased the gauze away from Peter's lower back. The incision was about an inch long; she'd traced the line of his scar as closely as possible. The bug had been all knotted up with scar tissue, and she'd been forced to slice through that to remove it. The whole time, she'd been fighting the urge to vomit; it was probably a good thing she hadn't been able to eat for a couple of days. A career as a surgeon was definitely out.

Still, she was feeling pretty pleased with herself. The bug had been removed, and Peter wasn't bleeding that badly; it would probably only take a few butterfly Band-Aids to close the wound. He'd be sore later, but then, they were all sore. She gingerly poured saline over his lower back, then slathered it with antibiotic ointment. The oxy must be working even better than she'd hoped, because Peter's only reaction was to start singing, loudly and off-key.

"Wow," Teo said, handing her bandages and gauze. "I kind of want what he's having."

"There's none left," Loki growled.

"Kidding, dude. Chill," Teo mumbled.

Loki tugged at his beard and said, "Feels like beer o'clock to me. You in?"

"I'm fifteen," Teo said. "And I don't drink."

Loki shifted to Noa, raising an eyebrow. She just shook

her head. "All right, then. Change your minds, I'll be in the cantina."

"Beer o'clock? Isn't it, like, ten in the morning?" Teo said wryly after he left.

Noa managed a small smile. She'd slept the night before, but not nearly as long or as deeply as she would have liked. And the adrenaline of operating on Peter had left her exhausted and shaky. "I guess you lose all sense of time down here," she said, peeling off the gloves and tossing them in the trash can.

"I'll bet. That guy should really spend more time up top. Is this it?" Teo asked, bending over to examine the bug. When Noa nodded, he shook his head in wonder and said, "It's so small."

"It'll be a lot easier to carry than the drives," she pointed out.

"Yeah." Teo straightened and looked her in the eye. "Listen, I feel badly about leaving. I know we'd agreed to stick together, but I just can't do it anymore."

"No, you're right. You should go." Noa got a flash of how he'd looked when they first met: just another terrified, grubby kid in a homeless encampment. His eyes had aged eons since then. "Staying with me just puts you and Daisy in danger. And the others . . ." She bit her lip, then forced herself to say it. "They're probably dead."

"Yeah," Teo said softly. "I know." Without warning, he pulled her into a hug. Startled, Noa stiffened. After a minute, he released her and said, "Once we get to California, I can get a phone and post the number on The Quad. If you need us, just call."

"I will," Noa lied.

"Great." Teo sounded relieved. "Seriously, anything you need, we'll come running."

"It's not like you're leaving right now, though." At the look on his face, her heart sank. "You're leaving right now?"

Teo looked uncomfortable. Avoiding her eyes, he said, "We just figure the sooner we can start leading them away from here, the better. We don't know when they last got a signal off the bug, right? What if they're close?"

"Sure," she said faintly. "That's smart." The realization that her group was being sliced in half again was hard to process. Four months ago, there had been ten of them. Now it was down to just her and Peter. *Same way we started*, Noa couldn't help thinking. She wished that felt like a good thing.

Teo looked desperately uncomfortable. "We could hang out for a day, I guess."

"No," Noa said firmly. He was right, delaying their departure would only make it harder. Last night, she'd helped them map a route to Los Angeles that would hopefully throw their pursuers off track. She'd also given them most of the remaining cash, although they didn't know that. "Be careful with the bug, okay? And take care of each other."

"Of course," Teo said, drawing himself up. He was taller than her now; when had that happened? "You, too."

On the table, Peter was bobbing his head in time to music only he could hear. Teo smiled. "Tell him I said good-bye, all right?"

"Sure. Same with Daisy."

"If she comes in here it'll be the full waterworks." He threw her a grin. "Figured I'd spare you that."

"Thanks." Noa was having a hard time swallowing past the lump in her throat. They'd been through so much together. Without their help, she probably would've been recaptured in Santa Cruz, and another half dozen times after that. It was hard to repress the ominous sense that this was the last time they'd ever see one another. "Take the car, but ditch it soon," she advised. "Stick to busses."

"That's the plan."

She wiped as much blood off the bug as she could, then carefully set it in the box Loki had left for them. It was made of copper wire, a genuine Faraday cage. That was as much protection as she could offer them now. "Here."

"Thanks," Teo said, carefully taking the box from her. He paused on the threshold. "Bye, Noa," he said in a choked voice. "See you on the other side."

Noa stood staring at the empty doorway for a long time. *People are always leaving me*, she thought, fighting a familiar pang of abandonment. This time last year, she could've proudly claimed that there wasn't a single person in the world she cared about, or who cared about her.

But that no longer seemed like something to be proud of.

"Yo, can I get some water?" Peter called from the table. "Dying of thirst over here. God, you're gorgeous. Did I ever tell you that before? I mean it, you are seriously—"

"Shut up before you say something you regret," Noa warned, walking over to the sink.

"Yeah, but God. You should see yourself now, you're all glow-y. . . ."

As he rambled on, Noa found a clean mason jar and filled it with water. She caught sight of herself in the mirror above the sink: hollowed-out cheekbones and pronounced circles beneath bloodshot eyes. It was the face of someone who was gravely ill. "Glow-y, huh?" she said, handing him the glass. "I'm going to make sure you remember saying that when this wears off."

PART TWO
HIDE

CHAPTER SIX

"All right," Teo said. "You ready?"

Daisy nodded, even though her stomach was churning. This was the second time they'd unveiled the device. She couldn't stop picturing it as a literal bug, some dangerous insect that might come to life after Teo unwrapped it and sink pincers into his palm, then crawl under his skin.

They were hunched in the doorway of a slum in Albuquerque, New Mexico. As far as she was concerned, they couldn't get to Los Angeles fast enough. She'd had qualms about leaving; it felt strange, waking up in a room without Peter and Noa close by. But she hadn't been keen on staying in that creepy bunker, either. And from the sound of it, they'd be there for a while.

She'd never been to Los Angeles, even though she'd only

grown up a few hours away, right outside Las Vegas. In her mind, it was all palm trees and beaches and famous people. The Walk of Fame, Rodeo Drive, Laguna Beach. Most of her favorite TV shows were set in Los Angeles. She used to be obsessed with all those rich teenagers who dated and fought and went to exclusive nightclubs; she would have given anything to trade places with them for just a day.

Still, Daisy was fully prepared to be disappointed. In her experience, nothing was ever as nice as it appeared on-screen.

But even the worst part of LA would probably beat Albuquerque by a wide margin. "This place is disgusting," she said, wrinkling her nose as the smell of garbage wafted past on a breeze.

"We'll be out of here soon." Teo carefully unwrapped the small box Loki had given them. The box was made out of copper, and Loki had promised it would block the signal all by itself; but he'd also muttered that there were no guarantees in life. She and Teo had decided it was better not to risk it, so they'd created a shell made out of aluminum foil and cardboard. They were taking enough of a chance as it was.

"I hate this," Daisy said, staring at the box.

"I know," Teo said grimly. "I shouldn't have offered to do it."

"If you hadn't, you'd be whining about feeling guilty."

"Hey!" he protested. "I never whine."

"Oh, please." Daisy rolled her eyes. "Like I didn't hear you complaining about the bathroom last night."

"That was a bathroom?"

Daisy laughed, and Teo smiled at her. For a minute, it was almost possible to forget that they'd spent the afternoon trying to sleep next to a Dumpster in an alley. *Déjà vu all over again*, she couldn't help thinking. Maybe when they got to their next stop, she could convince him to spring for a motel room. It had been three days since they'd left Loki's weird underground shelter, and they were both starting to get ripe.

On the plus side, Teo's mood improved with every mile they put between themselves and Colorado. He no longer seemed as tense, like there was a slap waiting for him around the next corner. The dark circles under his eyes were easing. He'd fallen asleep on her shoulder during the last bus ride, so deeply she'd had a hard time waking him when they'd arrived. She'd stroked his hair, touched by how sweet his face looked when he slept, like a little kid.

"What?"

"Nothing." Daisy looped an arm around his back. "You're just so darn cute."

"The bus leaves in ten minutes," he said. "We can probably spare five for you to admire me—"

"Just get on with it," she said, swatting him. The sooner they got this done, the better. Even though they only let the signal out for a few minutes, who knew how close Pike's men were? It was like toting around a tiny bomb.

Teo drew a deep breath, then opened the box. The bug was perched on a bed of plastic wrap. He dug it out and held it gingerly on his palm.

The pose struck Daisy as funny; it looked like he was proposing with the world's ugliest engagement ring. She grinned and said, "I keep thinking it should beep, or light up, or something."

"Me too," Teo agreed. There was nothing to indicate that the bug was even working.

Daisy ticked off the seconds in her mind, holding her breath. She'd reached two hundred by the time Teo said,

"That should do it." He carefully set the bug back on the plastic and wrapped up the box. After lowering it into his pack, he said, "C'mon."

The two of them sprinted the five blocks to the bus station. Teo already had their tickets, and they climbed on board a westbound bus right before the driver closed the doors.

"That all you got?" he asked, eyeing their packs.

"Yup," Daisy said cheerily. The man was still regarding them suspiciously, so she continued. "Divorced parents. We've got clothes at Dad's place, too."

The driver grunted and punched their tickets. Daisy walked all the way to the back of the bus, finding them a seat away from the other passengers. She didn't think they'd appreciate all the cuddling she and her "brother" were about to engage in.

She settled into the window seat and immediately hunkered down, staring out the window. She couldn't stop scanning the street for men dressed in black.

"Do you think they'll come?" she asked in a low voice.

"Maybe," Teo said. "But we'll be long gone."

Daisy nestled against his shoulder and murmured, "Love you."

Teo kissed her hair. "Love you, too."

With a groaning of gears, the bus lurched clumsily forward. Daisy watched as the streets swept past. She imagined commandos storming the Albuquerque slum tonight, and their rage at not finding them. At the thought, she smiled and whispered, "Gotcha."

"Any luck yet?" Noa asked without looking up from her keyboard.

"Nope." Peter took another slug of Red Bull, wincing

when even that small movement sent a twinge of pain up his spine. The wound was healing, but it still hurt constantly.

In spite of that, he had to admit it was a relief knowing the bug was gone.

Pike had actually LoJacked him; the thought still gave Peter the willies. He wondered if his parents had known. Hopefully they drew the line at implanting a tracking device in their kid.

He couldn't stop picturing Mason sitting somewhere with a transmitter, leering at the dot pinging on-screen. No wonder he'd known that Peter was breaking into his apartment; he'd been tracking him the entire time.

Peter shuddered, then glanced over at Noa. She was leaning forward intently, her hair covering her face as she focused on the monitor in front of her. She had to be at least as tired as he was, but she'd barely taken any breaks. He was worried about her. She seemed to have lost even more weight, and it wasn't like she had any to spare in the first place.

"Want another MRE?" he offered. "I could heat a few up."

"God, no," she groaned. "I swear I preferred the road food."

"I don't know. The Salisbury steak is decent."

"Stop," she warned. "Or I'll make you eat one in front of me."

"I don't think my doctor would approve of that," Peter joked. He had no clue how soldiers subsisted on MREs for months on end; already the mere sight of them made him feel like puking.

Still, they could hardly complain. Loki had turned out to be a surprisingly good host, allowing them unfettered access to "mission control," as he called it. If necessary, you could probably oversee a lunar landing from there. The room housed twelve monitors and six computer towers with an insane amount of processing speed. It was so impressive that Peter managed to forget for long stretches that they were nearly a hundred feet underground. Almost.

Yesterday, he'd ducked outside for a few minutes. Another gorgeous day, warm and sunny. Part of him wanted to go flying down the hill with his arms winged out to the sides like a kid. Maybe he could persuade Noa to join him; she could definitely use the fresh air, and some sunlight. For a second, he allowed himself to imagine them lying in the grass beside each other, hands linked as they stared up at the clouds.

As soon as he thought it, he got a flash of Amanda, and the look she'd given him the last time they'd kissed. Peter sighed. Nothing ever seemed to be easy for him.

At least they'd managed to stay in one place for a few days, which was practically a record for them. It looked like Loki had been right: The bunker had blocked the bug's signal. So as far as Charles Pike was concerned, they'd left Denver far behind.

He didn't doubt for a minute that Teo was sticking to the plan, letting the bug ping as they traveled west. He and Daisy might already be in California. He imagined them hanging out on a beach, while he and Noa huddled in the darkness like a couple of moles.

Peter blew out a sigh and ran a hand through his hair: It felt oily. He should take a shower. It was far too easy to lose track of time down here. Three days had passed, but it could have been weeks. Last night he'd stayed up until three a.m. without realizing it. He and Noa had been working pretty much nonstop.

No luck so far, though, which was a bad sign. And of course, even if they did find the key file, they'd probably still need to crack a password.

Encryption was like a secret code, not so different from the ones Peter and his brother used when they were kids. The simplest codes replaced one letter with another a certain distance away; for example, with a two-step code, every *a* became a *c*. He'd spend hours decoding his brother's secret messages, discovering in the end that "wmsp dccr qkcjj" translated to "your feet smell." In spite of everything, Peter smiled at the memory.

Of course, this was a lot more complicated. Here, the "letters" were bytes of information, the instruction to "shift letters by some distance" was the encryption algorithm (AES 256), and the distance (2, for example) was the key. They'd need both the algorithm and the key to decode the file.

It was a long, arduous process, and so far Peter had only made it halfway through his pile of server drives. At this rate, they'd be here for weeks. He wasn't entirely certain that Loki was willing to play host for that long.

He glanced over at Noa: She looked totally consumed by what she was doing. Swallowing hard, he opened a new browser window. *Probably good to take a break*, he told himself, knowing full well it was a flimsy excuse.

After making sure that the image would only open on the screen directly in front of him, Peter hit enter.

The security camera footage was grainy, and set at an angle. But he'd gotten lucky: Today the curtains were open.

A tiny figure lay on a hospital bed. The image was black and white, and the girl was so pale, she was barely visible against the sheets. Still, he could tell it was her.

Amanda.

He'd hacked into Boston Medical's security feed months ago. On the road, it had only been possible to check every couple of days. Every time Pike's men nearly caught them he'd been wracked with guilt, convinced that despite his precautions, his online footprints had been tracked.

Still, he couldn't bring himself to stop.

The fact that a bug was responsible had actually been a huge relief, even if he'd unwittingly been the one carrying it. And here, with Loki's extensive firewalls, there was almost no chance that anyone would catch him looking.

Not that it was pervy or anything. It was just that as long as Amanda was still lying there, there was a chance to save her. And knowing that gave him hope.

As Peter watched, someone entered the room. He leaned forward with a frown: It was a man. Her dad, maybe? He sat by the bed for a minute, without touching Amanda. There was something so familiar about the way he held himself. . . .

Peter sucked in a deep breath. It was Mason. Even though he couldn't see his face clearly, he'd know him anywhere.

The fact that he was still alive, after Peter had basically left him gift-wrapped for Pike, was a shock. He should have known that somehow Mason would weasel his way back into Pike's good graces.

But what is he doing with Amanda?

It felt like all the air had suddenly been sucked out of the room. Peter's hands clenched into fists. It was bad enough that Mason had made Amanda sick in the first place; now he was hovering over her like a vulture, admiring his handiwork?

As he watched, Mason abruptly stood and left the room, closing the curtains behind him. Peter stared at them for a minute as they swayed back and forth. He had to get back to Boston to protect her.

But if he raced to her bedside, then what? Mason had to be close by with a slew of Pike's mercenaries. And Amanda needed to be in a hospital; even if he managed to get her out, he wasn't equipped to take care of her.

In all likelihood, that's exactly what Mason wanted. Maybe he suspected that Peter was keeping an eye on things from afar, and this was his way of taunting him. Drawing him in, forcing his hand.

If that was the case, it was working.

Peter stared at his shaking hands, willing his fists to unclench. He had to stay here. Once he found what they were looking for, the proof that they needed, then he could go save Amanda.

And God help Mason if anything happened to her first.

"What's wrong?"

Peter jerked reflexively and glanced over his shoulder; Noa was eyeing him with suspicion.

"Nothing," he said, quickly shutting the window. With great effort, he forced levity into his voice as he said, "This would be so much easier if someone had named a file 'decryption key.'"

"Wouldn't that be lovely." Noa sat back and stretched.

"Tired?" Peter asked, taking in her appearance. The days underground had rendered her already pale skin practically translucent, and the glow from the monitors made the shadows beneath her eyes particularly pronounced. The burst of energy she'd had when they first arrived seemed to have dissipated entirely; she was sleeping more and more.

"What, I don't look 'glow-y' anymore?" she teased.

Peter groaned. "I can't believe you're still going on about that."

"Oh, I haven't even begun." Noa crossed her arms over

her chest, an impish look in her eye. "I just wish I'd taped it."

"It was the oxy talking," he grumbled.

"Really?" She raised an eyebrow. "So you don't think I'm a gorgeous sea creature?"

"I did *not* say that," he protested. "Did I?"

Noa burst into laughter. Grinning, she turned back toward her monitor.

"Just wait," Peter warned. "Someday, you'll be saying the same thing about me."

"That you're a gorgeous sea creature? I seriously doubt it." Without looking at him, she continued in a more muted voice, "Do you think they're there yet?"

Peter shrugged. "Maybe. Depends on how many stops they made."

A long beat, then she said quietly, "I really hope they're okay."

"They're fine," he said firmly. "Hell, they're probably in better shape than we are. Riding busses and eating vending machine food. That sounds like heaven right about now."

"Wow," Noa said. "Remind me to apply to a different heaven than yours."

"Did I forget to mention the waterslides?"

She laughed again, and Peter silently cheered. It had been a long time since he'd been able to make her laugh. Despite how she looked, maybe Noa was getting better.

"So you're okay then?" he asked lightly.

A long pause, then she swiveled to face him. "Actually," Noa admitted, "I'm not feeling so hot."

"I can tell." He rolled across the floor, stopping a foot away from her. Noa flinched slightly, the way she always did when someone entered her personal space, and Peter repressed a sigh. "Listen, I know something is going on with you. Maybe I can help."

Noa was already shaking her head. "No one can help."

"But—"

"Peter," she said firmly. "You don't understand. Some of what happened, back in Santa Cruz . . ."

Peter waited for her to continue, but her gaze was fixed on the concrete floor. He asked gently, "You mean, when Zeke died?"

"Before that," she said in a small voice. "The people we were staying with were scientists, doctors. They were helping me figure out . . . well, you know."

Peter nodded. The small of his back throbbed in sympathy. He'd only known about the bug for a day before it was removed. Noa had been living with the knowledge that there was a stranger's thymus implanted in her chest for seven months. And they still weren't totally sure why it was in there, or what it was doing, aside from messing with her sleeping and eating cycles. In her place, he'd have gone nuts by now.

"Anyway, when their compound was invaded, I found out that the Forsythes used to work for Pike. They might even have had something to do with PEMA."

"What?" Peter interrupted, startled. "Why didn't you tell me this before?"

"Roy and Monica were killed that night," she said bluntly. "So I didn't think it mattered. But before he died, Roy told me that my cells were degenerating."

"That doesn't sound good."

"I know," Noa said soberly. "He wasn't sure what it meant, but that's probably why light hurts my eyes so much now, and why I'm always tired."

"Okay." Peter ran a hand through his hair again. "So is your body rejecting the thymus?"

Noa shrugged. "Maybe. All I know for sure is that I'm always tired. I'm always cold. Everything hurts, all the time. And this cut that I got in Little Rock?" She rolled up her sleeve to show him a long, ugly gash from a tree branch. "It's not healing. So I'm not exactly a superhero anymore."

Peter regarded her gravely. "I wish you'd told me sooner," he finally said.

Noa bit her lower lip. "I would have, but . . . I didn't want you guys to worry about it, not when we were basically running for our lives every night."

"So what do we do?"

She gave a short laugh. "That's what I like about you, Peter. You always think there's a way to fix things."

"That's because there usually is," he insisted. "We could find another doctor, someone we can trust—"

"After what happened to Cody?" Noa was already shaking her head. "No way. It's too dangerous."

"Well, you can't just keep getting sicker," Peter said reasonably. "I mean, what if—"

The sudden appearance of Loki looming in the doorway cut off his words. "Who's sick?"

"No one," Noa said, straightening in her chair. "Everything cool?"

"Just wanted to check the monitors again," Loki mumbled.

Peter rolled out of the way as Loki bent over the keyboard. With the press of a few buttons, views of the property started scrolling through the upper monitors. Instead of focusing on them, though, Loki seemed to be scanning what Peter had been working on. Which made Peter uncomfortable, although he couldn't pinpoint why. It wasn't like he'd gotten close to finding the decryption key.

"No luck, huh?" Loki asked, apparently reaching the same conclusion.

"Not yet," Noa said. "But we've still got more drives to go through."

"Right." Loki scratched his beard; a considerable amount of that morning's freeze-dried eggs had managed to lodge themselves in it. "So you're looking for an archive file?"

Noa and Peter exchanged a glance, and she said, "Of course."

"Well, you can rule out the duplicate files, right?" Loki rocked back on his heels. "Maybe you should be searching more than one drive at once, looking for dupes."

Peter felt like an idiot; Loki was right. They should've been scanning as many drives as possible simultaneously, composing a list of duplicate files that could be ruled out. "That's genius," he said appreciatively. "Thanks, man."

"Yeah, well. I have my moments," Loki mumbled, but he looked pleased by the compliment.

"Can we tap into a few more of these?" Noa asked, motioning to the other towers.

"Be my guest," he said expansively. "By the way, I'm making meatloaf tonight. That okay with you?"

"Absolutely." Peter fought to sound enthusiastic. The meatloaf was almost indistinguishable from the beef bourguignon and the Salisbury steak; he doubted there was real meat in any of them.

"All right, then." Loki cleared his throat, then shambled off.

Peter turned to find Noa staring after his retreating back with a frown. "What?"

"I don't know, it's just . . . something about him kind of gives me the creeps."

Peter snorted. "That's not surprising, since he's pretty much the creepiest guy I've ever met. Nice of him to take us in, though."

"I know," she grumbled, "I just don't like the way he looks at me."

"Well, he's probably never spent this much time in a small space with a gorgeous sea creature," Peter teased, adding, "or any girl. I don't get the sense he had much of a social life."

"Maybe," Noa said, sounding unconvinced.

"Can you imagine?" Peter said. "Hey, baby. Want to come check out my bomb shelter?"

"I bet there are girls who are into that sort of thing," Noa said, the corners of her mouth tweaking up.

"Sure. Chicks love paranoid dudes. That's why I'm always going on about the zombie apocalypse."

Noa laughed out loud, and Peter felt another rush of satisfaction. "All right, Torson," he said. "Enough clowning around. Back to work."

She smiled at him, shaking her head as she turned back to her terminal. "Thanks, Peter."

"For what?"

"For being here."

She gave him a real smile, and his heart flipped. "Hey," he said softly. "I'll always be here."

A shadow flitted across her face; he realized with a sinking feeling that Zeke had probably promised the same thing, then hadn't been able to deliver on it. "Noa, I mean it. Anything you need—"

"Let's get back to finding that file," she said tersely.

Peter nodded, but continued to watch as she turned to the keyboard, her pale fingers shaking slightly. Then he sighed and went back to work.

"Okay," Teo said. "This is it."

They both stared at the box. "I'm glad," Daisy said firmly. "Let's get it over with."

Teo repeated the actions that had become rote. They were unwrapping the bug in Flagstaff, Arizona. They'd cut a meandering path north for a while, then east, before heading south again. He had no idea if the signal had been received at any of the other locations; they'd unwrapped the bug every night, for a few minutes each time. Maybe that wasn't long enough for them to be tracked. But he was done risking it. Tonight, they headed west for good. If everything went as planned, they'd be in Los Angeles tomorrow.

"Ready?" he asked.

Daisy nodded, holding up the hammer. "Ready."

"Okay. Here goes." Teo held the tracker carefully in his palm and started the countdown in his head. It was earlier in the day than they usually did this; the sun had just set. They were standing beneath a highway overpass, which was clearly being used by the homeless. It looked a lot like the camp in San Francisco where he'd first run into Noa, Daisy, and the rest of them.

That felt like a lifetime ago, even though it had only been four months.

Once three minutes had ticked off in his head, Teo dropped the bug onto a chunk of concrete. Daisy angled the hammer directly above it.

"Check it out, we got roaches."

Teo spun, startled. Three boys stood ten feet away. They were all dirty and unkempt: street kids, wearing sullen expressions

"Sorry to crash your space," he said quickly. "We were just leaving."

"Yeah?" The tallest boy approached. He was wearing filthy jeans, an old pair of Converse sneakers, and a ratty green fleece even though it was still warm outside. A watch cap was pulled low over his forehead. Something in his eyes reminded Teo of Turk, which was definitely not a good thing. "We don't like people messing with our shit."

Teo shifted so that he was standing in front of Daisy; she had frozen with the hammer in her hand. "We didn't touch anything. We were just—"

"Just what?" Watch Cap interrupted, stepping forward to get in Teo's face.

"Let's go, Teddy," Daisy murmured, tugging at his arm. There was a frantic edge to her voice; they both knew situations like this could go south fast.

Watch Cap barked a laugh. "Yeah, *Teddy*. Maybe you should go."

The other two were still hanging back. Moving slowly, Teo guided Daisy toward the bushes on the far side of the highway. The opposite of how they'd gone in, but hopefully there was an exit there.

The three boys watched in silence as they walked away. Teo kept his body at an angle, still monitoring them. He saw the kid pick up the bug, holding it high to examine it.

"The hell is this thing?" he called out.

"I don't know. We found it," he lied.

"They're full of shit." A boy with a shaved head peeled off from where he'd been leaning against a support beam. "I bet they planted it."

"You're with those guys," Watch Cap spat. "The ones that took Angie."

"Wait," Teo protested, still backing away. They were nearly at the bushes. He had no idea what lay on the other side, but if they could just get there, they'd have a chance. "We're not with anyone. It's just us."

"Get 'em," Shaved Head ordered.

Teo pushed Daisy firmly on the back and yelled, "Go!"

They charged for the bushes. Branches tore at his face and bare arms as he fought through, realizing belatedly that it was some kind of cactus. Daisy yelped in pain, but he forced her forward.

A sudden yank on his backpack, and he went flying. Teo landed hard on his back, panting. All three boys stood over him. Watch Cap held the bug up and said menacingly, "Tell us where Angie is, you little shit."

"I think this is it!" Peter said excitedly.

Noa sighed. "You said that a half hour ago."

"Yeah, but this time I *really* think so," Peter replied with slightly less enthusiasm.

Noa rubbed her eyes, then wheeled her chair across the floor to him. She squinted at his monitor; the archive folder was open, and the cursor blinked beside a file that read: filename.ext.gz.

All the server drives were part of a RAID system, a redundant array of independent disks. Basically, that meant most of the drives should be redundant; the "dupes" Loki had been talking about. From the look of things, there were a total of eight file systems on the forty-two drives. So for each file structure, there were five drives that should contain exact copies of the same information.

They were counting on the fact that a bunch of researchers would hate dealing with such a high level of security. There had to be software that took the key from somewhere and applied it to the files as they were opened, so that researchers didn't have to go through the encryption/decryption process on their own every time.

Which meant that if one of them pulled a drive off the RAID to use it, they'd have to download a copy of the key file; otherwise, it would be like trying to open a locked door without a key. And if they stored that key file on the disk, rather than using the security framework, it would make the information on that drive slightly different from the others.

Unfortunately, every drive contained an insane number of files, and finding that deviation was problematic. So they were digging through the file systems, trying to unearth something that didn't match up.

And there was a chance that Peter had just found it.

"Filename," she said dubiously. "Seriously?"

"I know." Peter cracked his knuckles. "But it's definitely a deviation. What do you think?"

"Maybe." Noa puzzled it through. It was almost too whimsical for Pike & Dolan; "filename" was the default label for a computer file. Assigning it to the decryption key was roughly the equivalent of naming your kid John or Jane when your last name was Doe.

Still . . .

"I found the same deviation on another drive, too. Look." He clicked on the file to open it, and a box immediately appeared on-screen.

"You're right." She felt a rush of excitement. "So we found the key. Now we just have to crack the password."

"Right. Easy. Of course, it could be ten characters, or a hundred."

"And here we are without a supercomputer," Noa said morosely. With access to one, this could take less than a minute.

"We could break into a facility somewhere," Peter offered. "Isn't there one in Boulder?"

"Janus? Sure. But that place is a fortress. Maybe if we had more people, but . . ."

"But we don't," Peter said with a sigh. "And we still look like a couple of refugees."

"Exactly. I don't think 'naïve college kid' will play well there."

They sat in silence for a minute, mulling it over. It was ironic, Noa thought. Here they were, probably two of the best hackers on the planet; three, if they counted Loki, although so far he'd pretty much left them to their own devices. And still, even with the massive computing array in front of them, it could take months to crack this password.

They didn't have that kind of time. She could tell by Peter's downcast expression that he'd reached the same conclusion.

"Everything cool?"

They both turned. Loki was standing in the doorway holding a couple of mugs.

"Just peachy," Peter grumbled. "Don't suppose you've got a supercomputer in one of these tunnels?"

"Look at you, getting greedy." Loki raised the mugs. "Thought you might be ready for a coffee break."

"I'd love some," Noa said, gratefully taking a mug from Loki.

He passed the other one to Peter, who mumbled a thanks. Tilting his head to the side, Loki scanned the screens with a paternal air, like he was watching his kids accomplish a feat on the playground. "Anything?"

"Peter might have found the decryption key file," Noa offered.

"Yeah?" Loki bent to peer over Peter's shoulder, looking intrigued. He barked out a laugh. "Well hot damn. Filename, huh?"

"It's still password protected," Peter said, his knees tapping out a cadence against the bottom of the table. "That's why a supercomputer would come in handy."

"Maybe," Loki said. "But I'm willing to bet there's a back door built in somewhere."

Peter snorted. "No way. Otherwise, why go to the trouble of encrypting it?"

"You know how this stuff works," Loki said disdainfully. "Joe Schmoe can't remember the password, so he writes it on a Post-it note and sticks that to his monitor."

There was a lot of truth to what he was saying. Back when Noa was freelancing for an IT security firm, what they called "the human element" was the culprit behind most unauthorized accesses to computer systems. All it took was an absent-minded software developer leaving his laptop in a café, or a stranger wandering into a server room, like Peter had done at Pike & Dolan.

"You mind if I take a gander?" Loki sounded like a kid begging for a toy.

"Be my guest." Peter pushed out of the chair.

"Huh," Loki said, pursing his lips below his beard. "Whoever set this up knew their stuff."

"Told you," Peter said with resignation.

"Whoa, wait a minute." Loki ran a finger along the code, hovering an inch away from the commands. "Check out this one: .ffly."

"So?" Noa asked.

Loki straightened and stared at her, an odd glimmer in his eye. "You never heard of Firefly?"

"The hacker?" Peter frowned. "Of course. Everyone's heard of her."

"I thought Firefly was in jail," Noa said, surprised. Firefly was an Australian hacker who had masterminded a plot to bring down the prime minister. But in the process, she'd been caught. Noa was a little murky on the details, but she was pretty sure the woman had been sentenced to at least a decade in prison.

"Someone must've sprung her," Loki mused, knitting his bushy brows together. "'Cause this is definitely her framework."

"I don't see how that helps us," Peter muttered.

Loki turned the chair around and glared at him. "You think that /ALLIANCE/ was the only pot I had my finger in, kid? That's what I did before my morning coffee."

Peter visibly bridled at the implication that his hacktivist site had been small-time. Before he could retort, Noa interceded, asking, "So do you know how to get the password?"

As Loki tapped away, he said, "Firefly and I were tight. When she went down, she could have taken us all with her. But she kept her mouth shut. Gotta respect that."

"Which group was that?" Peter demanded.

"We weren't dumb enough to name it," Loki grumbled, shooting Peter a look. "But we shared things."

"What sort of things?" Noa asked.

"Things like this." Loki bent low over the keyboard. Noa watched as he hammered away, editing the source code configuration. It was impressive; until now, she'd had no idea how good he really was. Potentially even better than her, which was a little unsettling.

With a flourish, Loki hit the enter key. The monitor suddenly flooded with information.

Noa gasped. "You did it!"

Peter raced over. "Dude," he said, in a voice filled with awe. "How the hell did you figure it out?"

"I told you." Loki looked pleased with himself. Flashing a yellowed grin, he explained, "Firefly and I were tight. We shared back doors." Seeing Noa's raised eyebrows, he went bright red and mumbled, "That didn't come out right."

Peter bent over him, eagerly scrolling through the screen. "This is it! We're in!"

"You're welcome," Loki said, shoving Peter aside as he lurched back out of the chair.

Noa grabbed his arm as he passed her. Squeezing it lightly, she said, "Thank you."

Embarrassment flickered across his features, but Loki's eyes lit up. He bowed his head slightly, then lumbered out of the room.

Peter didn't even seem to notice that he'd left; he plunked back in the chair, exclaiming as file after file popped open on-screen. "Medical files!" he called out. "Emails! Noa, we've got him!"

Noa tried to match his enthusiasm. "Yay."

Peter didn't seem to notice. His fingers flew across the keyboard, sifting through the enormous stack of files. Noa thought about the original documents they'd gained access to, and the insane amount of information there. This had to comprise several times that. On just one of the file structures. And there were seven more.

Peter was so completely consumed by the information filling the screen, he didn't seem aware that she was still in the room. "All right, Pike, you bastard. You're going down," he muttered.

"You should destroy it," Teo gasped, still lying at their feet. One of the guys had grabbed Daisy; he pinned her arms to her sides as she struggled against him. "It's a bug. That's how they track us."

"Hear that? It's a bug." Shaved Head was older than the other two, maybe eighteen or nineteen. "We got ourselves James Bond here. Grab their packs."

The kid in the ragged Suns jersey wrestled Teo to his feet.

He tried to fight his way free, but the boy was stronger, his hands were iron clamps on Teo's arms.

Watch Cap had already yanked Daisy's backpack off and was digging through it. He drew out a stack of bills wrapped in a rubber band and let out a whoop. Teo winced. That was all the money Noa and Peter had given them, a few hundred dollars. Without it, they weren't going anywhere.

No way I'm letting them roll us, Teo thought, his resolve steeling at the sight of Daisy's dismayed expression.

"Looks like we got a couple of rich kids playing at being homeless," Shaved Head sneered. He snatched the money from the other kid and jammed it in his pocket. "Are Mommy and Daddy waiting up for you?"

"Bet they're worried," Watch Cap chuckled. "Especially about you, huh, princess?" He grabbed Daisy's chin and drew it up. She pulled away from him, and he laughed cruelly.

"Nope," Teo said, his insides hardening. The two of them had been through too much to be terrorized by a few punk street kids. The cash had distracted the guy holding him; his grip had eased. Hopefully, that would be enough. "I'm part of Persefone's Army."

"You're what?" Shaved Head asked, puzzled.

"Bullshit," Watch Cap said. "You remember those losers, Joe. Everyone was talking about them a few months back."

"Right, the kid army." Joe scrutinized Teo. "Thought it was a bunch of crap."

"It wasn't," Teo insisted. "Your friend Angie? She probably got taken. By the same guys who put that bug in a friend of mine."

Joe tossed the tracker in the air and palmed it one-handed. "Right," he said skeptically. "So you and your little girlfriend here are being tracked by this thing?"

"Yes," Teo said firmly.

"We're just like you," Daisy interjected. "Street kids. Only we decided to fight back."

The boys openly guffawed. "Yeah, you two seem pretty tough," Joe chortled. "Must be some army."

"It was," Teo said. "And you know what?" He grabbed his backpack. Suns Jersey was too startled to react immediately, and Teo shoved his hand through the open top. It closed automatically on the one thing he'd vowed never to leave behind. "You would've made shitty soldiers."

Teo jammed the Taser into Suns Jersey's armpit. The volts coursing through his body cut off the kid's shriek of rage.

Unfortunately, a Taser took time to recharge, and he couldn't get to the one in Daisy's pack. The other two kids were momentarily paralyzed, but that wouldn't last. Teo grabbed Daisy's arm and gave her a shove, urging, "Run!"

Noa was starting to wonder if she needed glasses; she'd been staring at the screen for hours straight, and the words kept blurring on her. *My eyes are getting worse*, she realized. *What happens if it gets so bad I can barely see?* The thought hit her like a gut punch.

She pushed back from the desk quickly. Peter glanced over. "What?"

"Nothing," she mumbled, closing her eyes to rest them. They still throbbed, matching the constant pulse in her chest. "Just tired."

"Yeah, me too." He tilted back the chair and methodically cracked the knuckles on one hand, then the other. His elation had dissipated as they pored over the files. Peter disconnected a drive, then bent to retrieve another from the backpack at his feet. Noa repressed a smile. Even though the tracking device had been removed, he still seemed loath to be more than a foot away from his pack.

Of course, hers was resting against the wall beside the door. Some habits died hard. "How's your back feeling?"

"Like it was stabbed with a scalpel," he said reproachfully, throwing her a look.

Noa smiled. "Been there."

"I know." His face grew somber. "I would have gone crazy by now."

"Gee, thanks," she muttered, feeling herself flush. "And here I was trying not to think about it."

"We could both just get hooked on oxy," he suggested. "Might make us feel better."

"Sure," she agreed. "Drugs would be a great solution."

"See, you think I'm joking, but I could use some about now." His right hand drifted toward his lower back and probed it carefully. "I really hope those antibiotics Loki shot me up with worked."

"They did," Noa said, adding with exaggerated solemnity, "Otherwise you'd already be dead."

"That's comforting. Thanks." Peter made a face. "Man, I'm starving. You want to break for dinner?"

Before Noa could respond, the air was shattered by the high-pitched wail of a siren. Peter shot out of his chair. "What the hell is that?"

Noa could only shake her head. The siren was piercing; she pressed her hands to her ears. The tide of panic that perpetually circled her depths like a prehistoric monster leapt to the surface.

Loki raced into the room, his eyes wild.

"What's going on?" Peter asked, shouting to be heard over the din.

"Alarms," Loki snapped, keying up the security feeds again. Noa barely even looked at them anymore. Aside from the occasional animal wandering through, the images never seemed to change; they were almost like a screensaver.

Not this time, though.

"Oh, shit," Peter breathed.

Noa froze. The surrounding fields and woods flitted past in a now familiar succession. But instead of a whole lot of nothing, the cameras displayed dozens of men in black, wearing familiar wasp masks and carrying rifles.

Pike's army was here.

CHAPTER SEVEN

"How did they find us?" Noa said, a familiar terror gripping her heart as she thought, *Not again*. They'd been lulled into complacency, and now they were trapped underground like a couple of rats.

On every monitor, men were moving purposefully in staggered lines. *How many did Pike send? Dozens?*

Peter spun on Loki. "You sold us out!"

"I *what*?" Loki growled. "You think I would *ever* invite a bunch of jackboots here? Hell, I didn't even want *you* here!"

"I don't think it was him," Noa said. "He could've just disabled the alarms."

"Exactly!" Loki exploded, throwing up his arms.

Peter took a step back, doubt flickering across his features. Mingled with something else . . . Was that guilt? "It couldn't have been the tracker," he said weakly. "Teo and Daisy have it."

"Maybe there are trackers in the servers?" she said.

"No way." Loki shook his head emphatically. "Told you, this room is its own goddamn Faraday cage." He jabbed a finger at Peter. "Did you take that pack off before we got the bug out? Anywhere outside this room?"

Peter looked panicked. "I don't think so. Crap, I can't remember."

"Hell, Vallas," Loki snarled. "We should have left the bug and pushed you into the river."

"It doesn't really matter how they found us." Noa gestured to the monitors. Four commandos were outside the little shed: After a series of complicated hand signals, they disappeared inside. *Okay*, she told herself. *Stay calm*. They'd gotten away before; they'd do it again. "We don't have much time. Loki, how do we get out of here? You said there was another way."

Loki pulled the greasy trucker's cap off his head and tugged anxiously at his thinning hair. His eyes darted across the room. "I'm going to have to leave it all behind." His voice was thick with shock and disbelief. "You've ruined everything."

Noa didn't have time to feel sorry for him. She grabbed his arm and said urgently, "Loki, we have to go."

"You know how many years it took to build this place?" he said forlornly.

"If we don't leave, they'll kill us. *All* of us," she emphasized. Grasping for something that might penetrate, she said, "This is exactly the sort of disaster you've been planning for all along."

Loki blinked, finally seeming to see her. Slowly, his head bobbed. "Yeah. Yeah, okay. I'll go grab my bug-out kit."

He charged out the door and vanished down the hall.

Peter was rushing around the room, cramming server drives back into his pack. Noa followed suit, her eyes skittering across everything in the room. Thank God they'd kept the packs close by, and more or less fully stocked.

Of course, with the added drives from Teo and Daisy, they'd be twice as heavy, too.

In the distance, a series of thumps: Pike's men were trying to break down the door at the base of the stairs.

Loki reappeared. He wore an enormous pack on his back, three times the size of theirs. A headlamp was strapped over his trucker's cap, and the shotgun was gripped in both hands. "This way!"

Noa followed as he moved with surprising speed down the hallway. All sorts of miscellaneous things were attached to the outside of his pack: A crowbar with a shovel attachment, a coil of rope, and other random objects jounced in time to his footsteps.

Peter was following so closely, he kept tripping over her heels. She flashed him a look the third time it happened.

"Sorry," he muttered. "But we need to go faster."

"The blast door should hold them for a while," Loki called out before darting down a side corridor. They were leaving the part of the bunker she'd become familiar with over the past week, and entering a section that hadn't been fixed up. Now she understood why he was wearing a headlamp; there were no lights in this part of the complex. Loki hadn't been kidding about the size of it, either. He guided them through a dark maze of tunnels, the concrete floors and walls caked in dirt. It looked like a world abandoned by man, pocked with dusty food wrappers and rusty machines. Her feet kicked up clouds of dust; the grit coated her throat and made her nose twitch.

They took so many turns, Noa doubted she'd be able to find her way back to the control center, never mind the surface.

Another *BOOM*, closer and louder. The entire tunnel shuddered, like a giant creature in death throes. Loki slowed the pace slightly. "Crap," he muttered. "They must have C4."

"Will that get them through the door?" Peter asked anxiously.

"Enough will, if they know what they're doing."

Noa was happy she couldn't see Loki's face; he sounded like he was considering turning the shotgun on them.

"I'm sorry, Loki," she said.

He glanced back at her; there was a fine sheen of tears on his cheeks. "S'all right, kid. Hell, this gives me a chance to test the bug-out plan."

"What is the bug-out plan?" Peter called out.

At that, Loki's face split in an impish grin, and some of the sadness faded from his eyes. "Just you wait," he said. "You're gonna love it."

As Teo and Daisy tore down the street, he was all too aware of pounding footsteps behind them. The boys were giving chase, yipping and howling like this was all some big game. He gritted his teeth and pressed on. He could go faster, but Daisy wasn't much of a runner, and he was careful to stay behind her.

He was hoping to circle back to the bus station; there were bound to be people there. The bus they were supposed to be on was probably already boarding.

Not for the first time, Teo wished he'd been graced with a better innate sense of direction. They were running straight down the middle of a desolate street. Decrepit buildings on either side, mainly storage facilities. Not a soul in sight.

The road they were on dead-ended at a cross street; the metal gate of a closed auto body shop yawed up in front of them.

"Which way?" Daisy yelled, frantic.

He hadn't a clue, but there wasn't time to mull it over. "Left!"

Daisy hooked left, and Teo pounded after her. As they turned down the next block, he glanced back over his shoulder. The boys must have split up, there was only one pursuing them. Which gave him a really bad feeling. They knew the area, and could easily try to cut them off.

Daisy skidded to a stop, and he nearly crashed into her. Teo groaned: Joe and Watch Cap blocked the road ahead. There was no way around them, and Teo didn't hold out much hope that they'd be able to plow through.

"Daisy," he said in a low voice, "grab your Taser."

"Already got it," she said, taking a step back so they were side by side.

Footsteps behind them, slowing to a walk. Daisy spun to face Suns Jersey, while Teo kept his eye on the other two. He clenched his Taser in his right hand; it should be recharged by now.

Joe and Watch Cap stopped fifteen feet away, clearly wary of the Taser. Teo swept it in an arc in front of his body. At this range, against a moving target, it wasn't a very effective weapon. Still, if they managed to take out two of them, the third might cut and run. . . .

But seeing their expressions, he reassessed. Before, the boys had been messing with them mainly out of boredom; they had nothing better to do than shake down saps who had inadvertently infiltrated their camp.

Getting tased had changed that; now they were intent on revenge.

"What kind of pussy uses a Taser?" Joe called out. Teo's heart dropped into his gut; they were no longer unarmed. Joe was holding a knife, and Watch Cap had a pipe.

"The kind who just wants to be left alone," Teo said.

"Too late for that," Joe said. "Should've stayed away from our camp."

"Idiots!" Daisy screamed in exasperation. "We were there for like five minutes, and we didn't touch anything! Get over it!"

"You scared, princess?" Joe sneered. "Don't worry, we'll take good care of you."

"Stay back!" Daisy yelled shrilly.

Teo whipped his head around; Suns Jersey had edged closer, just out of range of her Taser. He danced toward her, mockingly bobbing from side to side.

"Okay, Daisy," Teo murmured. "When I get to three, you go for him, okay? I'm going to take out Joe."

"Then what?" Daisy asked, an undercurrent of fear in her voice.

"Run like hell back the way we came," Teo said. "We need to get to that bus station. I'll be right behind you."

He brandished the Taser like a sword. Truth was, he'd probably have to hang back to give her a head start. There was a pretty good chance she'd be getting on that bus alone tonight, if at all.

But Teo wasn't going down without a fight, not this time. The way he was feeling, he could almost imagine dispatching them all by himself. They'd been pursued and shot at by professionals; scrawny street kids armed with pipes and knives weren't nearly as terrifying as they'd seemed a few short months ago.

Joe and Watch Cap seemed to sense the shift, and they put more space between them. Watch Cap was closer, but Joe was the leader. Take him out, and the other two might reassess. Teo fought to keep his face blank, trying not to broadcast his movements.

"Teddy!" Daisy suddenly shrieked, and just like that it was settled. He heard the familiar clicking sound of a Taser engaging. Reacting immediately, he lunged for Joe, hitting the button that sent the barbs airborne. Even if they just latched on to his clothing, the prongs would deliver enough of a shock to incapacitate him.

Joe's eyes widened as the barbs flew toward him. In Teo's peripheral vision, he saw Suns Jersey drop to the ground. Daisy was pounding back the way they'd come. He braced to follow, his muscles primed. . . .

But Joe dodged sideways at the last minute. The barbs clattered to the ground harmlessly, sparking off the pavement. Teo hit the button to retract them, but it was too late; the charge had been dispensed.

Joe pointed the knife at him and jeered, "That's why Tasers are for pussies." His eyes flicked to Watch Cap. "Go get that bitch."

Watch Cap raced down the street. Teo shifted like a boxer as Joe circled, keeping him ten feet away. Suns Jersey was slowly recovering, blinking his eyes.

"Cute girl," Joe said, with steel in his voice. "Bet she's a lot of fun, too."

Teo prayed that Daisy had gotten enough of a head start. "I wouldn't mess with her, she's tougher than she looks."

"Yeah?" Joe's grin widened. "Well, Rat's feeling motivated. I promised he could go first."

"Go to hell," Teo spat.

"What, you're gonna try and tase me again?" Joe snorted. "Good luck."

Teo lunged forward with the Taser, parrying with it. It was a bluff, though; the Taser was still recharging. Joe reared back, and Teo tried to get past him.

He'd only gone a yard when there was a searing pain down his left arm. He gasped and tried to keep running, but someone tackled him from behind.

Teo struggled to extricate himself, but Suns Jersey had him pinned. He barely had time to wince before the kid's fist connected with his jaw.

The punch knocked him senseless, he literally felt his brain rattle against his skull. Teo blinked in an effort to clear his vision, but before he could focus, another punch slammed into his right temple.

The whole world spun like a kaleidoscope. Teo heard Daisy's voice, frantic with fear, and tried to get up, tried to help her. But he couldn't move, he was trapped in some sort of quagmire. Distant laughter, someone trying to tell him something; but the words sounded funny, like everyone was suddenly speaking a foreign language.

A blinding light overhead. *Oh no*, he thought. *I'm dying. . . .*

Daisy needed him, he had to stay here for her; but the light kept coming closer, accompanied by a growing roar in his ears.

Shouts, and pounding feet. A yelp close by, and the pressure on his body abruptly released. Someone yanked him upright.

"Daisy?" he asked, staring blearily at his rescuer.

A pair of blank eyes gazed back through the slits in a wasp helmet.

* * *

By now, there was a good chance that Pike's people were inside, stalking them. Peter prayed that Loki really did have an escape route; it would be refreshing for the guy's paranoia to work in their favor.

"How much farther?" Noa asked, keeping her voice low. She seemed to be flagging; Peter kept fighting the urge to snap at her to move faster.

"Not far," Loki huffed.

"Then what?" Peter demanded. "How are we getting out?"

"There's a hatch at the base of the hill," Loki panted without looking back. "South side. It's my bug-out route, in case the zombies ever got in."

"Right," Peter said, thinking, *Zombies? Seriously?*

"There it is," Loki said, slowing.

The hallway ended in a huge metal blast door, exactly like the one they'd originally come through. Incongruously, a laptop lay on a rickety metal table a few feet from the door. Loki opened it up and brought the screen to life.

"Uh, not sure we have time to check email," Peter said.

Loki shot him a look. "This is connected to the security feed. Gotta check and see if they're outside."

"Oh," Peter said. "How do you keep it charged?"

"Switch it out every day."

"Of course you do," Peter muttered, picturing Loki lumbering through the halls every night with a fresh battery pack.

Noa was leaning against the wall trying to catch her breath. Looking like she was on the verge of collapsing, she gasped, "Are they out there?"

"Still checking," Loki muttered. "Give me a sec."

Peter hunkered down in front of her and dug a water bottle out of his pack. "Here," he said. "Probably a good idea to stay hydrated."

Noa managed a weak smile. She took a few gulps, then passed it back. "Same old, same old, huh?" she said wryly.

"Hell, I was kind of starting to miss these guys," Peter said. "Maybe they brought us a housewarming gift."

"Crap," Loki muttered.

Noa pushed off the wall and joined him; Peter peered over their shoulders. The base of the hill sloped into a large, overgrown field. Trees in the distance.

And six of Pike's men spread out across the monitor. Their heads moved back and forth in a way that made them appear even more like insects.

"So that's right outside this door?" Noa asked faintly. "Can they get in here?"

Loki shook his head. "They won't see the door unless they're right on top of it, it's hidden by a bramble thicket."

"How are we supposed to get through that?" Peter demanded.

"Crawl," Loki said. "Hell, it's easy. I've done a dozen test runs. You get a few scratches, but that's it."

"It doesn't matter," Noa said, gesturing to the screen. "We'll never get past them."

She was right, Peter thought with a sinking heart. They had two Tasers and a shotgun between them, against six armed commandos. The element of surprise might buy them ten feet, but after that they'd be toast.

Noa's eyes were heavy with defeat. The sound of distant boots echoed through the corridor; they were getting closer. Peter swallowed hard. This was it. The end of the line.

"Well," Loki said gruffly. "Looks like it's time for Plan B."

"There's a Plan B?" Peter said, a spark of hope igniting in his chest.

"I was really hoping it wouldn't come to this," Loki said forlornly, gazing up at the ceiling.

"Loki," Noa said. "What is it?"

"I got the whole place booby-trapped," he explained.

"Sure," Peter said, as if that made total sense. *The crazy never stops with this guy.* "But how does that help with the guys outside?"

"I got other countermeasures out there," Loki said. "Don't want to use those, though, unless we have to."

"Why didn't we do this in the first place?"

"This program brings the whole place down," Loki growled. "And everything inside it."

Peter swallowed hard. "Sorry, man."

Loki still looked like he wanted to punch him, but he said, "I'm not doing this for you. I'm doing it for Firefly."

"What?" Peter asked.

"You think something happened to her," Noa said slowly.

"I *know* something happened to her," Loki barked. "One day she's in jail, the next she's just gone. And she never came back online. Takes a hell of a lot of power to swing something like that."

"You think Pike somehow got her out, then made her construct an encryption framework for him?" Peter asked skeptically. They'd seen what Pike was capable of; he clearly had highly placed contacts in the U.S. government. But did his tentacles extend far enough to spring a notorious hacker from a foreign prison?

"That was Firefly's framework," Loki said obstinately. "I don't know what those bastards did to her, but I sure as hell am gonna make 'em pay for it."

"So how do we set off the booby traps?" Noa asked impatiently.

Loki had already turned back to the keyboard. "Just gotta put Serenity on DEFCON 1. . . ."

"Serenity?" Peter asked.

Noa shushed him, muttering, "Let him concentrate."

They waited in tense silence as Loki cycled through screens. Peter sipped more water, trying to still his racing heart. His whole body was screaming at him to run; sitting here staring at a computer felt like the exact opposite of what they should be doing.

The sound of an explosion in the distance, followed by screams. Loki looked up and said with satisfaction, "Phase one."

Peter stifled an involuntary shudder; he hated Pike's thugs, but that didn't mean he was comfortable with people getting blown up. "Bombs?"

"A little bit of everything," Loki grunted. "Gotta cover your bases."

"They're leaving!" Noa exclaimed.

Peter checked the screen: the men outside were racing up the hill like their lives depended on it. Their buddies inside the bunker must have called for help.

The last guy vanished from the corner of the screen: The field outside was wide open. Peter tightened the straps on his pack and said, "Let's get the hell out of here."

Teo tried to fight back, but his head was reeling so badly he could barely stand. "Daisy!" he shouted, but a deafening roar drowned the words out completely. He was half shoved, half carried forward. Someone pushed his head down as he stumbled into a small, metal cage.

Not a cage, Teo realized as his vision finally cleared: a

helicopter. That explained the glaring light, and the roar that seemed to swallow every other sound. He was on a helicopter.

He'd been caught.

Teo's captors yanked his hands behind his back, securing them tightly with plastic ties; the stab wound on his arm throbbed painfully. Before he could protest, they jammed a thick black bag over his head. He screamed out, but it was no use; the rotor wash swallowed it up.

The only consolation was that Daisy had gotten away. Teo wondered what had happened to Joe and his flunkies. If it hadn't been for them, he and Daisy would be on a bus headed west right now. Teo gritted his teeth; the whole life he'd planned out for them was gone, all because a few punks had showed up at the wrong time.

The floor lurched below him—the helicopter was rising. The sudden motion inspired a wave of vertigo, and Teo had to swallow hard to keep from throwing up. His legs cramped, and the zip ties dug into his wrists. Blood ran warm down his arm. The throb of the helicopter's engines was like the pain in his body made manifest. Teo slumped forward in defeat.

All that running, only to end up here.

And worse was coming. They'd try to make him betray Peter and Noa, probably torture him until he pinpointed Loki's hideout.

Honestly, Teo didn't know how long he'd be able to hold out. It had been nearly a week since he and Daisy split off and headed west. Silently, he prayed that Peter and Noa had found what they were looking for, and were already long gone.

CHAPTER EIGHT

"One more minute," Loki said, holding up a hand for them to wait. Snaky tendrils of foul-smelling gas started to crawl along the ceiling.

"Ugh!" Peter exclaimed, covering his nose and mouth with his hand. "What the hell is that stuff?"

"Phase two," Loki said, his eyes alight. "Nerve gas. Wow. I wasn't a hundred percent certain that would work."

"Nerve gas?" Peter's voice shot up an octave. "You know they've got masks, right?"

"Yeah, but no oxygen tanks," Loki said with a wicked grin. "It'll definitely slow them down."

"We have to get going," Noa prodded. Loki seemed far too interested in witnessing the effects of his booby traps firsthand. Their escape window was closing; Pike's men were nothing if not highly trained and resourceful. They were probably already fleeing the tunnels.

Plus, the gas was getting thicker; she was starting to feel light-headed.

"Best not to breathe it in," Loki advised. Out of nowhere he produced a gas mask and slipped it on with practiced ease.

Peter yanked his T-shirt up over his face. "Don't suppose you have two more of those?"

"You'll be fine. Just . . . try not to breathe too much. Almost forgot." Loki pulled a couple of handheld radios out of his pack. "Take these."

"What for?" Peter demanded.

"In case we get separated," Loki said with a frown.

"Thanks," Noa said, taking one from him. It was strikingly similar to the radios her unit had used, she thought with a pang. Peter held his like it might bite him. She motioned for him to hang it from his belt. He rolled his eyes, but complied.

Loki inhaled deeply, then shut the laptop. He cast a longing look back down the corridor and said, "So long, Serenity."

Noa awkwardly patted his shoulder, both to console him and to keep him focused on leaving. In her head, a familiar voice was urging, *Go go go. . . .*

"This place was awesome," Peter said. "I'm sorry, man."

"Me too," Loki said thickly. He eased the door open until there was a wide enough gap to squeeze through. Keeping one hand on the door to prop it open, Loki waved for her to follow. Noa drew a deep breath and slipped under his arm.

He'd been telling the truth: A thick mesh of brambles extended like a cage around the door; sunlight sifted through the branches that arced over the exit. Noa pulled on her sunglasses, wincing against the glare.

There was a narrow three-foot-wide clearing directly in front; as Peter joined them, they were forced to crowd together. Loki closed the door, then hit some buttons on a keypad beside it. A hiss, followed by the sound of a latch engaging.

For better or worse, they were out of the silo.

Noa maneuvered carefully to her knees and peered beneath the branches. A foot-high path ran under the bush, the dirt scuffed like something had been dragged across it.

"That's it," Loki said in a low voice. "I keep it clear."

"You fit through there?" Peter said dubiously.

"Watch and learn, kid." Loki dropped to his belly and started wriggling through the crawl space.

"Man," Peter muttered, tightening the straps on his pack. "This guy never stops surprising me."

"Hey!" Loki hissed from the other side of the hedge. "You coming or what?"

"Be right there," Noa muttered. Lowering herself to the ground, she commando crawled forward, inch by inch. Stray branches snarled in her hair and dragged along her spine and legs. She gritted her teeth and kept moving forward. When she got close, Loki reached out a hand and grabbed her wrist, hauling her out the rest of the way.

"Thanks," she gasped, winded.

"No problem." Loki grunted. "Vallas is on his own, though."

A minute and a lot of stifled curses later, Peter joined them. "Not a huge fan of the bug-out plan so far," he muttered.

"It's working perfectly." Loki had that crazy gleam in his eyes again.

"What next?" Noa asked. The field still looked clear: a

few hundred yards of waving brown grass, dead-ending in aspen trees.

"I got a truck five hundred yards south," Loki murmured. "Covered with a camo tarp."

"Great," she said, relieved. The run through the tunnels had sapped her energy, and she definitely wasn't up for a long hike.

"What are we waiting for?" Peter urged. "Let's go!"

"There's one rule," Loki said ominously, holding up a finger. "Put your feet exactly where I do. Got it?"

"Why—"

"We got it," Noa said, throwing Peter a look. Loki had gotten them this far. Trusting him was their best bet for survival.

Loki broke into a lope across the field. Noa kept pace, trying to stay within the tracks he left in the grass.

Peter mumbled something about crazy bastards, but when she checked he was right behind her, following the exact same path. Her legs felt leaden, so heavy she almost expected them to sink into the earth. She bit her lip, trying to tap into a hidden energy reserve, but it was no use; her body refused to respond.

"It would be better," Peter huffed practically in her ear, "if we could move a little faster."

"I'm trying!" she insisted.

A shout from behind them: Noa whipped her head around.

A mercenary loomed at the crest of the hill, aiming a rifle at them.

"Stay together!" Loki hollered. "We're almost there!"

"He's going to shoot us!" Peter protested.

Loki charged ahead, carving a path through the grass like a bull plowing through tissue paper. "Moving target! Hard to hit!"

Peter prayed he was right as they tore headlong across the field. Gunfire whizzed past his ears. Peter instinctively tucked his head into his shoulders, as if that could possibly make a difference.

Loki was moving in an odd, zigzag pattern, with Noa right behind him. Peter struggled to follow in their tracks.

Angry shouting from the top of the hill. Peter focused on Noa's back, her dark hair flying out behind her. Peter's lungs strained, every breath made ragged by the hard drives slamming into his rib cage.

A bullet whistled past his ear. Peter was nearly tripping on Noa's heels; her foot had no sooner vacated a space then he plunged into it.

The tree line was twenty feet ahead.

Ten.

Five.

More shots, closer together. There were probably more of Pike's men firing from the top of the hill, but he didn't dare check. Peter pictured himself shot full of holes, spouting blood like a leaky sieve. But somehow, the bullets kept missing.

A blast exploded straight ahead of him; Loki had stopped just inside the shelter of the trees and was firing the shotgun back up the hill. As Noa and Peter raced past, he called out, "The truck's fifty yards dead ahead!"

Another whoop as he fired at the dark figures who swooped toward them like a flock of vengeful crows.

Pike's men scattered, spreading out across the hillside.

"That's right, you bastards!" Loki taunted, fumbling to

reload the shotgun. "Come and get us!"

He unleashed another volley up the hill, then loped after them.

Peter wove through the trees. Noa was just ahead of him, more stumbling forward than running. He grabbed her elbow to help her along. She had to be in truly bad shape, because she didn't protest.

"Is this the right way?" he called out.

Loki swept past them. "It's right there!"

"I don't see anything!" Noa gasped.

"There!" Loki pointed.

Following his finger, Peter saw a dark, huddled shape. As they pulled closer, it resolved itself into a dark-green pickup truck with camo netting draped over it.

Loki was already digging keys out of the wheel well. Peter dragged off the netting and tossed the packs into the truck bed, scrambling in after them.

"Drop the gun!"

Peter spun around so fast he nearly went sprawling across the packs.

A swarm of men emerged from the trees on all sides— five total.

A shot pinged off the side of the truck inches from his hands. Peter froze, riveted by the circle it had sheared through the metal.

"Drop the gun and stay where you are!" one of the men shouted. The group was still advancing slowly, inching forward from their position twenty feet away. They looked eerily alike in their black uniforms, with their faces concealed behind masks.

Noa was already in the passenger seat. Her face was grim, filled with defeat. Loki stood at the driver's-side door, the shotgun dangling from his hands. With seeming nonchalance, he tossed the keys on the front seat.

"You're on private property," he bellowed. "Get the hell off my land!"

In spite of everything, Peter was impressed by his bravado. Not that it was any use. Peter breathed out hard, overwhelmed with frustration. They'd been so close, just one more minute and they might have made it. . . .

"I'm sorry," Noa said in a low voice. "I slowed us down."

"Not your fault," Peter said.

"Shut up!" one of the men barked.

Four of the men had stopped where they were, establishing a wide perimeter. The other stepped forward cautiously, his gun aimed straight at Peter's chest. "Under no circumstances is anyone to shoot the girl," he said loudly. "She's—"

An audible metal click, loud and discordant. Loki started to laugh deep in his chest.

"What was that?" the guy asked.

Loki whipped his head around to Peter; there was a wicked gleam in his eyes as he said, "Better take cover."

"What? Hey—"

Loki hurled himself into the driver's seat. The commandos were shouting for him to stop, but he'd vanished from sight, dragging Noa down with him. Through the window, Peter saw his lips form the word *bomb!*

Peter dropped to the truck bed and covered his head with both hands.

BOOM!

The force of the explosion slammed Peter against the truck's wheel well; the pickup rocked from the concussion. The guy who had been speaking shot straight up in the air like a rocket. Peter's jaw gaped open as his body was tossed toward the trees like a rag doll. It landed in a spray of red ten feet away.

In books and movies, everything slowed down when a bomb went off; Peter had the opposite experience. Suddenly events were occurring at warp speed. The truck started with a roar. Peter slid around helplessly as it whipped in a circle, clipping low-hanging branches. There was screaming everywhere, but it sounded oddly hollow and far away, like it was coming at him through a long tube.

Peter kept his head down as the pickup screeched forward, gunshots pinging all around him as tree branches raced past overhead.

Loki was bent so low over the steering wheel, Noa couldn't imagine how he could see anything. Not that it mattered; pierced by multiple bullets, the windshield had splintered into a dizzying array of cracks. Her ears were still ringing from the explosion—and what was up with *that*, anyway?

That's why we had to stay in his tracks, she realized. Loki must have set land mines along his escape route; it was exactly the sort of insane, paranoid thing he'd do. Sheer dumb luck must have kept Pike's men from stepping on one of his booby traps as they came down the hill.

Loki murmured to himself as he steered, zigzagging around obstacles in the road that only he could see. Although "road" was putting it generously; it was really more of a glorified hiking trail. Fortunately, the truck had four-wheel drive; what it lacked in speed, it more than made up for in sheer tenaciousness.

The forest all around them teemed with armed men; every time they rounded a bend, a barrage of gunfire rained in from the trees. How many had Pike sent?

A lot, Noa thought grimly. She just prayed there wasn't a barricade blocking the end of this road.

She straightened up to check on Peter: He was spread-eagle in the truck bed, with his hands and feet braced against the sides. Seeing her, his eyes went wide and he shouted something, but her ears were still ringing too hard to discern it. He was covered in blood, but hopefully none of it belonged to him.

A bullet struck an inch from her head, and she dropped back down, curling into the passenger footwell. So much for not shooting at her; apparently some of them hadn't gotten the memo. Although if they wanted to, they could probably turn the truck into Swiss cheese. So maybe they were just trying to disable the vehicle.

Which might be working. Smoke rose from the hood—had the engine been hit?

"Loki?" she ventured. "Where are we going?"

His eyes flitted to her. "Out."

"I got that," Noa said, trying to keep her voice calm. "But out where? Is the road close?"

"They came." He wet his lips, then repeated, "They finally came. Gotta bug out."

He seemed to be lost in his own private world. Hopefully he'd hold it together long enough to get them out of here.

A break in the trees up ahead—daylight. Noa bit her lip. This was it, the moment of truth.

A huge Humvee was parked across the road. Three armed men stood in front of it. As the truck lurched toward them, they raised their guns.

Noa hunched lower. There was a deep gully on the right side of the road. On the left, long grass that either concealed flat land, or another ditch.

She prayed for land. As they approached the Humvee, Loki swerved left. More bullets riddled the passenger side of the truck. "Hang on, Peter!" Noa screamed, even though she doubted he could hear her.

The truck dipped alarmingly, Noa's heart plummeting with it. *No*, she thought. *No, no*—

But it abruptly bounced back up; she caught a glimpse of sky through the window, then the back wheels climbed out of the rut and the truck leveled out with a hard thump. The front tires bit into pavement, and Loki wrenched the wheel right again. The rear of the truck swung wide with a squeal of tires.

They were back on a real road.

Noa breathed out hard. Her lungs ached from the strain of holding her breath. It felt like a lifetime had passed since they fled the control room, but it had probably only been twenty minutes.

"Are they gone?" Peter yelled.

"Yes!" she yelled back.

His head popped up in the splintered rear window. In a voice slightly muffled by the remaining glass, he said, "Well, that totally sucked. You guys okay?"

Noa cut her eyes to Loki. He was hunkered over the wheel, eyes darting feverishly across the road. "We're fine, I think. You?"

Peter shrugged. "I'm not bleeding. The truck's in pretty bad shape, though."

He was right: Smoke poured from the front, making it even harder to see the road ahead. "Loki," she said. When he didn't respond, Noa tapped his arm and gestured toward the smoke. "We're going to have to ditch the truck."

"Can't leave the truck," he said fiercely. "They get you if

you leave the truck. Gotta keep moving."

"We'll get a new one," Noa said. "A better one."

He shook his head vigorously. Noa bit her lip. She had to get him to snap out of this.

"He might be right," Peter called through the window. His voice was calm, but his eyes still looked frantic. "Not exactly an easy place to catch a ride. And once they find the truck, they'll send everyone they've got."

They didn't have much time to figure out a solution. Any minute now, at least one Humvee would be tearing after them. And that would be the world's shortest car chase. Nothing but trees and fields on either side of the road, and so far no other roads had intersected it. Loki's property abutted an immense national forest that occupied thousands of acres; their chances of hitting a town where they could switch out cars were slim.

The road climbed, and something glinted in her side mirror: a reflection of headlights, probably the Humvee in fast pursuit.

"This would be a great time for a plan!" Peter shouted through the glass.

"Loki," Noa said urgently. "Where are we going?"

He turned a glazed gaze on her. "My mom's place."

Noa stared at him, wondering if he was joking. But he appeared completely serious. "Where does she live?"

"Breckenridge," he muttered. "Got a trailer there."

Noa didn't hold out much hope that they'd be able to evade Pike's forces in a trailer park. "Do you have any other cars stashed close by?"

"Got an ATV," he said. "Headed for it now."

"What did he say?" Peter yelled, tapping on the glass. "They're getting closer!"

"We can't all fit on an ATV, can we?"

Loki's eyes flicked toward her. "Just me," he growled. "Gonna go save my mom."

"All right," Noa said, her mind racing. "Tell you what. Peter and I are going to jump out, okay? Get to that ATV as fast as you can."

Loki didn't seem to hear. She grabbed his arm and urged, "Loki, do you understand? You need to get far away from this truck. Don't ditch it anywhere near the ATV. And when you get to your mom's place, don't tell anyone what happened."

"They killed Firefly," he said gruffly. "I'm gonna get them."

"No," Noa argued. "Just leave it alone. They're too dangerous."

The truck was starting to cough and sputter as it slowed. Smoke seeped through cracks in the windshield, making her eyes water. In the side mirror, Noa saw the glint of the Humvee growing closer.

They needed to hold them off somehow.

Up ahead, she spotted a stand of trees—and just past them, a deep canyon. "Loki," she said. "How far to your ATV?"

"A few miles," he grumbled.

"Great. Drive the truck in there." She pointed toward the canyon.

Obediently, he steered the pickup onto the shoulder. It bumped over it, onto the grass, then started rolling toward the gorge.

"Oh no," Peter said. "No, no, no—"

"Grab the packs!" she yelled, opening her door. "And get ready to jump!"

Peter grabbed the backpacks and got to his knees, using his hands to brace himself against the side of the truck. It was slowing down, but they still had to be going at least thirty miles per hour. Noa had the passenger's-side door open. Loki was driving straight toward the lip of the canyon, showing no sign of braking.

"This is nuts," Peter muttered, frantically scanning the underbrush for a safe place to land.

"Throw the packs!" Noa yelled.

He glanced back over his shoulder; a Humvee crested the hill they'd passed minutes earlier. Peter swore under his breath and tossed the backpacks; they vanished into the tall grass.

"Now jump!" Noa yelled.

Peter drew a deep breath and got into an unsteady crouch. The truck rocked back and forth. A cloud of noxious smoke washed over the cab, thick enough to blind him. He had no idea how Loki could see anything.

"Go!" Noa screamed. She catapulted from the truck cab and started rolling down the side of a small hill.

The canyon loomed ahead, less than twenty feet away. The driver's-side door popped open, and Loki jumped out, arms wrapped around the shotgun like he was cradling a baby.

"Now or never," Peter muttered, trying to psych himself up. He counted off in his head: one . . . two . . .

On three, Peter jettisoned from the truck bed. He landed hard on his right shoulder and felt something wrench. Instantly, he realized he'd waited too long. He hurtled after the truck in a free fall, the world flipping around him: sky, ground, sky. Branches and twigs tore at him, scratching his face and bare arms. . . .

Peter was rocketing straight toward the edge of the canyon. He tried to grab hold of something to slow his descent, but clumps of grass tore away in his hands, and his body kept bounding forward. His injured arm twisted beneath him, and he cried out in pain.

The rear of the truck suddenly canted upward. It hung suspended for a long moment, gears issuing a piercing whine; then it vanished over the edge. A second later, the groan and grind of metal against rock.

Peter was about to tumble after it. He screamed as his feet scrabbled frantically for purchase; but he'd gained too much momentum. There was no stopping his plummet.

A hard yank on his shirt, slowing him. He skidded another few inches, then stopped with his heels dangling over thin air.

Another tug, and he flew backward. He collapsed against Noa. They lay there panting for a few seconds, then Peter inched forward.

The truck lay on its side a few hundred feet down, the front end smashed in and smoking. "Sometimes," he croaked, "I really hate your plans."

"Come on," Noa gasped. "We have to grab the packs and get under cover. They'll be here any minute."

They raced back to the road. There was no sign of Loki. Had he already headed for the ATV, just leaving them there?

The packs were farther back than he'd thought. The pain in his right shoulder was agonizing, and his arm hung at a strange angle. When they finally reached them, Peter grabbed the bag with his good arm and slung it over his shoulder, then limped as fast as he could toward the tree line.

The Humvee came into view. It was less than a mile away.

As he watched, it veered toward them. Peter gulped— they'd been spotted.

Noa yelled, "Run!"

They headed for the trees. Peter's entire body felt like one giant bruise; every time the pack hit his back he wanted to scream. His right arm felt strange, tingly and useless. The grass tangled around his feet, like it was intentionally trying to slow him down. Noa was pulling ahead, five feet, then ten. . . .

Peter tripped and landed hard, twisting his ankle. He tried to push back up, forgetting for a minute that his arm wasn't working properly. The blinding wave of pain was so intense it nearly blotted out everything.

Noa had stopped and was screaming for him to keep running, but his muscles refused to obey. Peter turned his head: Back at the road, the Humvee had pulled over. Four men with automatic rifles were spilling out the doors.

He closed his eyes, ready to give up. His ears were still ringing from the blast that had killed the soldier.

To his left, something bellowed loudly. Loki rose up out of the grass.

The shotgun was braced against his shoulder. A *BOOM!* as he shot off a round, followed by a loud click as he pumped the gauge. He walked toward the soldiers methodically, firing again, and again.

Noa was yelling, waving frantically at Loki. Peter gritted his teeth and staggered to his feet, bent double with pain.

"Loki!" he called out. "C'mon, man!"

Loki glanced back over his shoulder. He threw Peter a crazy grin, then nodded.

At the same time, there was a hail of gunfire from the road. Loki dropped to his knees.

"Run!" Noa screamed.

Peter stumbled toward her. Whizzing all around him, dirt and grass erupting as it was torn apart by gunfire.

They reached the trees.

Peter chanced a quick look back over his shoulder. Pike's men were racing after them.

Thank God for adrenaline, Noa thought as they ran through the forest. She didn't know how long it would hold out, but for now it was keeping her illness at bay. It was lucky she'd gotten so much rest and decent food this past week, otherwise she never would have made it this far.

Somehow, they had to lose their pursuers. She had no idea where they were, or if they'd be able to find the ATV Loki had mentioned. She got a flash of him back in the field; had he been killed? The thought made her jaw clench with rage. She was tired of leaving bodies in her wake, tired of running.

Peter was barely staying on his feet. One of his arms looked funny; it must have been dislocated. Remembering him tumbling toward that canyon, her heart clenched. If she hadn't been able to get to him, and he'd gone over the edge—

No time to think about that now. They wove through the evergreens, their pounding feet muted by the thick carpet of needles. Yelling behind them, and more gunfire.

"Can't go much farther," Peter gasped. "I have to stop."

"We can't," Noa insisted. "Let me take your pack."

He winced and shook his head, even though he was clearly barely hanging on. The pain in his shoulder had to be excruciating.

Reaching out, she tugged the pack away from him. Peter's jaw went tight, but he didn't say anything. And he started moving faster.

The trees started to thin; there was a clearing up ahead. Better yet, it was a campground parking lot. Two cars and a truck sat at the far end.

"There!" she yelled, urging him forward. Her mind raced ahead: They'd have to break into a car and pray that the locksmithing laptop was still functional. It should still be in Peter's pack, buried beneath the drives; of course, he was the only one who had ever used it, and he was doubled over with pain.

She flashed back to Loki grabbing the pickup keys from the undercarriage. Maybe hikers did that, too; it was worth a shot. Noa ran toward the nearest car and fumbled around the rear tire. She heard shouting behind them, but it sounded like Pike's men were still in the forest; they might have lost their trail, at least temporarily.

Nothing. Noa went to the next car, praying *please, please* over and over again.

"What are you looking for?" Peter asked in a strained voice.

"Keys," she said. "Check the truck."

He limped over to the truck as Noa groped along the wheel well on the driver's side. Her fingers hit something small and rectangular, tucked under the carriage. "Yes!" she crowed, pulling out a hide-a-key.

Peter shambled over as she slid open the case and dug out the key. The car was a small white Accord, covered in a thick layer of dust and pollen. She clicked a button, and the doors unlatched.

A shout from behind them. Noa spun around: One of Pike's men had emerged from the forest at the far end of the parking lot. He aimed his rifle.

"Hurry!" Peter cried, scrambling into the passenger side.

Noa tossed her pack in the back and dove into the driver's seat. She turned the key in the ignition, nearly crying out with relief when the engine caught on the first try.

As they tore out of the parking lot, she saw their pursuer talking into a radio.

"God, that was lucky," Peter groaned as he reclined his seat.

"We're not home free yet," she warned. "That Humvee will be coming for us."

"Just do me a favor," he said in a voice tight with pain. "Try to keep this car in one piece. I can't handle any more jumping."

CHAPTER NINE

Teo had lost all sense of time. The helicopter flight felt like it had taken about a half hour, although it was hard to say exactly. He tried to estimate how far they'd gone, but since he had no clue how fast a helicopter flew, that was mostly just to keep his mind occupied. The air in the sack over his head was stale, and the taste of his own breath made him gag.

Then the helicopter dropped down, landing with a jolt. Teo was frog-marched off, then led up a flight of metal stairs that clanked under his feet. Engines again, quieter and more refined sounding: definitely turbines. *A plane? For real?* Must be one of those fancy ones rich people owned; no way they'd be able to smuggle a kid onto a normal jet.

Teo considered screaming for help again, but he got the distinct sense that it wouldn't matter; if they needed him to stay quiet, they would have gagged him. Even though the air tasted foul, it was a lot easier to breathe without duct tape covering his mouth.

So he stayed silent, praying that Daisy had gotten away.

He was angled roughly into a seat. Teo's fingers brushed against something unbelievably soft and buttery—*leather?*—as the world tilted at a sharp angle. The sensation of invisible hands bearing his body down into the seat as the plane rose.

A flash of bemusement; today was the first time he'd ever flown, and he'd done it not once, but twice. It was a shame he hadn't been able to check out the view.

It was also probably the last trip he'd ever take.

"Remove that, please."

The bag was yanked up and off his head. Teo blinked against the sudden glare, trying to get his bearings. He'd been right; this was some sort of fancy plane. Creamy white leather seats arranged in groups of four, facing in to one another. Beige carpeting underfoot. Ten feet away, a curtain the same shade as the chairs was drawn across the narrow aisle.

Sitting across from him was an imperious-looking man who wore a dark suit and a disconcerted frown. He had strange eyes, so dark they were nearly black. Two goons loomed behind his seat, holding their big, meaty hands clenched. Teo craned to check over his shoulder: another curtain. The section of the plane they were in was small, about twelve feet long and eight feet wide. A sudden wave of claustrophobia hit him. Teo nearly laughed out loud; funny that under the circumstances, he was more afraid of a plane crash than the men glaring at him.

"So," he said, fighting to keep the squeak from his voice. "We headed to Maui? 'Cause I forgot my trunks."

The man's lips tweaked up at the corners. "I see you share your friend Peter's sense of humor."

"Who?" Teo said, swallowing hard. *Did they catch Peter and Noa, too?*

The man made a disapproving noise in the back of his throat. "Don't be tedious, Teodoro. This will proceed much more smoothly if we can forego the banalities."

"Was that even English?" Teo asked.

A smirk, then the man said, "I continually forget to compensate for the failings of our educational system. Put bluntly, I'd very much like to know where Noa Torson is."

So they don't have her. Teo heaved a sigh of relief. "No clue."

"But you admit to knowing her?" The man adjusted his cufflinks. His stare was unnerving, like a probe. Teo shifted his gaze to the floor and shrugged.

"Teenagers," the man sighed. "I really am so tired of dealing with them." Motioning to the flunkies behind him, he said something in a low voice.

One of the guys nodded. He was huge and bald, straining the limits of a gray suit. As he stepped toward Teo, he dug something out of his pocket and pressed a button: a switchblade.

Seeing it, everything inside Teo turned to ice. But he raised his chin and said defiantly, "You should've just killed me in Flagstaff. Getting blood out of leather is going to be a bitch."

The big guy leaned over, holding the knife right in front of Teo's nose. Teo went rigid—*What is he going to do, slice it off? Jesus, can a person live without a nose?*—then the guy lowered the blade. Suddenly, the pressure on his wrists eased; the plastic ties had been cut.

Warily, Teo rubbed some feeling back into his hands. The

cut on his arm had stopped bleeding, it must not have been as deep as he thought. Still hurt like hell, though.

"Better?" the seated man asked with a thin smile.

Teo chose not to answer. It wasn't like they'd done him some big favor; after all, he was still in a goddamn plane, flying God knew where. Unarmed, and flanked by guys who could literally rip him in half if they wanted to.

The man tapped a finger against his armrest. "So did he scream?"

"Who?" Teo asked, puzzled.

"Peter." Another creepy smile as he continued, "I'd imagine that having the tracking device removed was quite painful for him."

Teo repressed a shudder; Pike had a real thing for hiring psychos. "He didn't scream."

"I very much doubt that. I know Peter fairly well, you see. You could say we're old friends."

Teo suddenly made the connection: fancy suit, slicked back hair, shark eyes. Just like Peter had described him. "You're Mason."

Mason looked pleased. "I am indeed."

"Peter said you were probably dead."

A shadow flitted across Mason's face, but his voice maintained the same even tenor as he said drily, "Fortunately, Peter was mistaken. I'm not an easy man to kill."

"Yeah? Last I heard, you were tied to a banister. Must've been pretty humiliating."

Mason narrowed his eyes. "Not one of my finer hours, but it worked out in the end."

"Sure. You're Pike's errand boy again. Must be great." Teo felt a surge of satisfaction at seeing Mason's jaw go tight. "Bet he'll be pumped when you bring me back instead of Noa."

"Oh, but you're going to help me locate Miss Torson."

"Not a chance." Teo snorted. "You're going to kill me no matter what."

Mason contemplated him, like Teo was a nippy dog who refused to heel. "Frankly, it's been an extremely long day. I'd prefer to keep things civil if possible."

"Trust me," Teo said. "I can make it a lot longer."

As he lunged forward, Mason's eyes flew open; Teo got a nice close-up of them, right before he ducked his head and slammed it into Mason's nose. Mason's head snapped back, his jaw making a satisfying clacking sound as his teeth knocked together.

The thugs were already in motion; they had Teo pinned before Mason's head came back down. It was worth it, though, to see blood streaming from the bastard's nose.

Mason glared at Teo as he rose from his seat. He pinched the bridge of his nose with one hand while curling the other into a fist.

Bracing for a blow, Teo said, "I was kind of hoping you'd scream. Bet that's painful, huh?"

The veneer of complacency was gone; there was murder in Mason's eyes as he growled, "You're going to regret that."

"Like I said," Teo said with forced bravado. "I'm basically already dead. You can't kill me twice."

"True. But Peter should have mentioned that I like to cover my bases." Mason dabbed his nose with a spotless white handkerchief. Drawing it back to examine the blood, he snarled, "Go get the girl."

"Oh, man," Peter groaned.

Noa cast a worried glance at him. There was a fine sheen of sweat on his forehead. He'd reclined the seat back at a forty-five degree angle and was clutching his injured arm with his good hand. "It's bad, huh?"

"Really bad," he hissed through gritted teeth.

"I think I can put it back in," Noa said, although the thought made her cringe. "We just have to find somewhere to do it."

"We should get off the road anyway," Peter said. "Too dangerous."

So far there had been no more Humvees in the rearview mirror. They'd turned off onto smaller roads, cutting a serpentine path through the Rocky Mountains. "We could head back to Denver," she suggested.

"Too crowded."

"Might throw them off track, though."

"They know we stick to cities." Peter shook his head. "That's where they'll look. Besides, we can't exactly wander into an internet café looking like this."

He was right, Noa thought, taking him in. Aside from the horrible way his shoulder jutted out, his clothes were covered in mud, and his face was a mess of cuts and abrasions. She probably looked the same.

Their best bet was to stay away from urban areas. But neither of them was exactly cut out for the backcountry. And they had limited supplies: no food or water, nothing but the beat-up sleeping bags stowed in their packs.

"Did that sign say Vail?" he asked.

"I didn't see it," Noa admitted. She should be paying more attention to the road, but the fatigue was encroaching again. It was all she could do to keep the car in the right lane as they wound through the mountains.

Peter was digging through the glove box with his good hand. "I'm pretty sure it did. Hang on—"

He awkwardly unfolded a map of Colorado in his lap. "That's Loki's place," he said, pointing to a spot northwest of Denver, "and we're here now. Which means if we can get back on the Six, it'll lead us straight to Vail."

"Um, okay," Noa said. "But last I checked, we didn't have a grand to drop on a hotel room."

"Won't need it," Peter said smugly.

"Why not?" Based on what little she'd heard, Vail was an expensive playground for the absurdly wealthy.

"You keep forgetting I'm rich." Peter closed his eyes as he leaned back against the seat. "I'm going to try and go to my happy place. Let me know when we're close."

Daisy struggled as the guy dragged her up the center aisle, pushing through the curtains at the front of the plane. They'd given her some sort of shot; she still felt woozy, and none of her kicks seemed to land.

Buried under the stupor was rage: They'd been so close. If it wasn't for those dumb rednecks the bug would be gone and they'd be on a bus right now. Instead, she'd found herself running, again. The boy chasing her had caught up and knocked her to the ground. He'd punched her twice, hard, making her head spin. Then he'd started to yank up her skirt. . . .

After that, she didn't remember much. Bright lights, and a stab in her thigh. She'd awoken with her hands tied behind her back and a bag on her head.

Before she could start screaming, the bag was pulled off, and a huge brute of a guy yanked her painfully to her feet. Daisy had frantically examined her surroundings; they were on some sort of plane.

The guy shoved her through the curtain. She spotted Teo

being held down in a leather seat. He blanched at the sight of her and shouted, "Leave her alone!"

Daisy bucked against the guy holding her. "Let me go, you idiot! We're on an airplane, where the hell am I going to run?"

"Let her go."

The words came from the guy facing Teo. Daisy walked forward on shaky legs, stopping beside the two of them. The man was older and disarmingly attractive, well-dressed in a suit. He regarded her calmly, despite the fact that he was holding a bloodstained white handkerchief to his nose. Daisy felt a flash of pride; Teo must have done that.

"Teodoro and I were just having a chat," the man said blandly. "Please join us."

"Man." She shook her head. "It's like you guys all went to the same creepy bad guy charm school or something. Did you seriously just say that?"

His eyes narrowed, and Teo choked back a laugh. She threw him a look, trying to convey everything she was thinking. *Be strong. We're going to get out of this.*

Although it was kind of tricky to imagine how.

Still, Daisy thought, squaring her shoulders, *it could be worse*. At least they were together.

The man regarded her like she was a slug he'd just found in his salad. "As I was telling Teodoro here, we're trying to locate Noa Torson. I was going to talk to you separately, but, well"—he withdrew the handkerchief from his nose and frowned at it—"he's being difficult."

"Do the kids you kidnap usually cooperate?" Daisy demanded.

"Given a choice, yes, they do," he observed coolly. "And I'm going to give you both that choice now." He turned back to Teo. "Either you tell us where Miss Torson is, or I have them slit her throat."

Teo stiffened. "Don't you dare hurt her."

As one of the goons unclipped a knife from his belt, Daisy's knees shook, betraying her. She couldn't stop staring at the blade. It was long and shiny. She backed away as he stepped toward her.

"We don't know where Noa is," Teo protested, panic in his voice. "I swear!"

"Please," the man said in a bored voice. "Don't waste my time."

The guy with the knife advanced on her. Daisy took another step back, but found her path blocked by the massive man who had dragged her up here. As the blade moved toward her throat, she sucked in her breath.

"Stop!" Teo yelled. "Please, don't!"

"Tell us where she is," the man pressed.

"Don't tell him, Teddy! They're just going to kill us anyway!" Daisy fought to keep the fear from her voice. At least this way it would be quick, and she wouldn't be experimented on, right? She and Teo would die together.

The tip of the blade touched her throat, making her gasp.

"They're in Colorado!" Teo shouted.

"No!" Daisy yelled.

The man nodded, and the knife withdrew. "Where in Colorado, specifically."

The words tumbled out of Teo's mouth in a rush. "Outside Denver, in some sort of silo. I can show you on a map, but you have to promise—"

"I didn't ask where she *was*," the man interrupted scornfully. "I asked where she is *now*. They left the silo hours ago."

Teo threw her a relieved look. "That's the last place we

saw them. They didn't tell us where they were going next."

"Really?" The man cocked an eyebrow. "That seems . . . convenient."

"That was the deal," Teo insisted. "We split up, didn't tell each other where we were going."

The man examined them each in turn, then said, "I'm tempted to believe you."

"Well, you should, because it's the truth."

"Noa's too smart, you'll never catch her," Daisy added, unable to resist.

"In that you are mistaken." A fresh trickle of blood slid out of the man's nose; he stemmed it with the handkerchief. "She will be found. But more to the point, it appears that you can't help us."

"We won't help you," Daisy snapped. Teo was straining against the guy pinning him to the seat, an anguished expression on his face.

"Well then, I suppose it's settled." The man leaned back and closed his eyes. "Take them to the back of the plane. We'll deal with them after we land."

"This is a bad idea," Noa said nervously.

"Relax. We'll be fine, unless they changed the alarm code," Peter reassured her. They were in front of his buddy Rick's ski house in Vail. They'd spent ten minutes watching for any sign of movement: nothing, and the only lights inside were the ones he knew were kept on timers.

"And if they changed the code, and the alarm goes off?" Noa demanded.

"Then we run back to the car and drive away." But Peter wasn't really worried. The key had been in the usual place, tucked under a planter on the front porch. He'd known the

Shapiros since he was a kid; they were old money, which generally translated into lazy. Not the type to bother updating alarm codes on their various properties, because it was too much of a hassle to keep track of them.

There was a keypad above the deadbolt; a handy thing to have in a vacation place, since you didn't have to worry about bringing a set of keys. Peter typed in the code: 6-1-97, his buddy Rick's birthday. Which, as a hacker, he found almost criminally negligent. Really, if a couple of teenagers on the run broke into the Shapiros' house, it was their own damn fault for making it so easy.

A click: He turned the latch. The light in the foyer automatically clicked on, and the alarm pad opposite the door started beeping.

Noa stayed on the porch as Peter limped across the threshold. He flipped up the cover and punched in 4-4-94, Rick's sister's birthday.

The light stayed red: The alarm continued beeping.

"Great," Noa groaned. "How long until the cops get here?"

Peter waved for her to be quiet. This *had* been the alarm code, he was sure of it; on their ski trip last year, he'd teased Rick mercilessly about how anyone with access to Facebook could get into the house, no problem.

Rick must've told his parents, and that prompted them to change it, Peter realized with a sinking heart. The countdown on the pad said he had less than thirty seconds to enter the correct code. He tried to focus, pushing past the pain in his shoulder. What else would they use?

His eyes fell on the photos lining the walls: There was one constant in all of them. He drew a deep breath and started typing again.

"We should just go," Noa urged.

"Last try," Peter promised, typing in 4-1-06.

"Whose birthday is that?"

"Coco's," Peter said, pressing enter.

The light turned green, and the alarm fell silent. Peter dropped his forehead against the wall and said, "Damn. That was close."

"Who the hell is Coco?" Noa demanded.

"Their dog." Peter waved his good hand at the framed photo display. "Rick's mom always throws this big party for her on April first. I remembered, because it's—"

"April Fool's Day," Noa said. "I get it." Warily, she closed the door behind her and stepped into the hall, dropping the backpacks to the floor. "How can you be sure they aren't just out to dinner or something?"

"This is their winter place," Peter explained. "Summers, they go to the Cape."

"Right," Noa said drily. "And what about spring and fall? They have houses for those, too?"

"Vermont and Florida," Peter said without missing a beat.

Noa squinted at him. "You're kidding, right?"

"Yup," he said. "No one in their right mind buys in Florida anymore." He limped down the hall toward the living room. The house smelled slightly musty, like it had been months since the windows were opened. It was immaculate, though, which worried him; a housekeeper probably came in on a regular basis.

Hopefully she wouldn't show up today.

"All right," he said, wincing as he stepped into the sunken living room. "Ready to play doctor again?"

Noa had halted at the end of the hallway.

Peter turned. "You okay?"

"Yeah, just . . . wow."

He followed her eyes. The place was impressive. The living room encompassed both floors, with high-beamed rafters vaulting overhead. The furniture was top of the line, plush leather couches and chairs surrounding a huge fireplace. "Rick's dad is a hedge-fund manager," he said.

"I keep forgetting that you're actually rich." Noa turned in a slow circle. "So you used to come here?"

"Almost every year," he said, somewhat apologetically. It was funny, over the past few months, he'd kind of forgotten how polar opposite their lives used to be. This house served as a stark reminder that for all intents and purposes, they came from different worlds. Different planets, almost. "Anyway," he said, clearing his throat. "I'm kind of in a lot of pain here."

"Right." Noa stepped closer to examine his arm. Gently, she took his hand and moved it slightly; even that small motion was agonizing. He hissed through his teeth. "Sorry," she said apologetically. "I think I'm going to have to really pull on it."

"You think?" he said in a strained voice.

"They have a computer here, right?" she asked.

"Upstairs, in Rick's dad's office."

"Okay, wait here."

He perched on the edge of the sofa, trying to regulate his breathing. The operation to remove the bug had been scary, but in some ways this was worse. What if she couldn't fix it? Would he lose the use of this arm permanently?

He could hear Noa moving around upstairs, the sound of cabinets opening and closing. She came back down a few minutes later with a bottle of whiskey in one hand and a prescription pill bottle in the other.

"Found this in the desk drawer," she said, holding up the booze, "and this in the medicine cabinet."

She handed him the bottle. He read the label: "Vicodin?"

"It should help," she said. "Wash it down with the whiskey. And try to keep the mermaid comparisons to yourself this time."

He popped a pill and took a swig to wash it down. Closed his eyes; man, it had been so long since he'd tasted real, top-shelf booze. His dad used to keep a bottle in a drawer, too. In fact, drinking out of it one night when he was home alone had led to all of this . . . the discovery of Project Persephone, meeting up with Noa . . .

In spite of everything, the memory made him smile.

"What?" Noa demanded.

"Nothing." He shook his head. "Did you find anything?"

"A YouTube video."

"Great," he groaned. "That should be helpful."

"It was, actually. Lie on the couch with your arm hanging down."

He clumsily got in the right position; already, his muscles were tensing in anticipation. Noa cradled his arm in both hands, and said, "Ready?"

Before he could reply, she yanked on it. There was a loud snapping noise. The pain was excruciating, a hundred times worse than anything he'd ever experienced. He succumbed to a wave of darkness.

When he came to, Noa was sitting beside him on the sofa. She looked down at him with amusement and said, "That wasn't so bad, was it?"

"Oh, God." His arm still felt sore, but in a different way; the constant sensation of a spike driving into his shoulder was gone. "Did it work?"

"Looks like it," she said cheerfully. "Maybe I should become a doctor."

"I'd like a break from being your only patient," he groaned. "Your bedside manner sucks."

She swatted his back. "You're welcome, by the way. So are you hungry? I'm going to see if there's any food."

Peter's head was still swimming, and he could taste the whiskey in the back of his throat. He swallowed hard and said, "Go for it. I'm just going to lie here in agony for a while."

Noa threw him a grin and pushed off the couch.

Peter found the remote and turned on the massive TV mounted above the fireplace. Clicking through, he found SportsCenter. He lost himself for a while in a Rockies game recap.

He must have drifted off, because when he opened his eyes, night had fallen. His shoulder still throbbed, along with most of the rest of his body, but the pain was manageable. And something smelled amazing; his stomach grumbled, reminding him that he hadn't eaten anything since their powdered-egg breakfast in Loki's silo.

At the thought of Loki, he felt a pang. Without him, they never would have cracked that password. And he might have paid the ultimate price.

Trying to shake off the guilt, Peter eased off the couch and shuffled into the kitchen. Noa was standing over the stove, stirring something in an enormous pot with a wooden spoon. She dipped it in and took a bite, then turned and started at the sight of him.

"That bad, huh?" he said self-consciously, running a hand through his hair.

She smiled, the corners of her eyes crinkling up. "Well, you could probably use a shower."

Her hair was wet, and she was dressed in unfamiliar

clothing: a pair of jeans and a flannel shirt. Both were too small, leaving her ankles and wrists poking out. She noticed him looking and said, "I found these in a closet upstairs."

"Sure," he said. "Rick's sister's stuff. She probably won't even notice if it goes missing."

Noa flushed. "I'm only borrowing them while our clothes are getting washed. I moved the car into the garage, too."

"I wasn't being critical," he said uncomfortably. The kitchen was enormous, almost as big as the living room, but it suddenly felt small and cramped. "That was smart, moving the car."

Noa shrugged, still looking nonplussed. "They might be looking for it."

"Since when do you cook, anyway? That smells amazing." He bent over to peer into the pot. The smell of beans and tomato sauce wafted out. He was half tempted to dig out a handful and shove it in his mouth.

"I can't promise it's any good," Noa said in a muted voice. "Zeke used to say I was the only person he knew who could ruin chili."

"Well, I'm starving," Peter declared, trying to gloss over the awkwardness. She'd ducked her head, but not enough to hide the fact that her eyes had gone shiny. Even after all this time, one mention of the guy's name and Noa went to pieces. He really hated that, even though it was unbelievably petty to be jealous of a dead kid. "I'd eat a shoe right now if that's all we had."

"Hopefully it'll taste better than that." She scooped some into a bowl and handed it to him. "Here."

He blew on a spoonful to cool it, then nibbled at the chili. Through the steam, he saw Noa regarding him anxiously. "Is it okay?"

"Delicious," he lied. Truth be told, it was bland and

overcooked, but he was too ravenous to complain.

"Good." She got herself a bowl and leaned back against the counter.

"So you're hungry?" he asked.

"Yeah. It's been a few days," she replied without looking at him.

They stood in silence, polishing off the chili. Peter helped himself to another bowl, then Noa did the same. It suddenly struck him that this was the first time they'd been completely alone since Rhode Island. Peter was mildly perturbed to realize that he felt tongue-tied, like they were on a date or something.

But then, he'd never shared chili with someone in the aftermath of a crazy car chase.

"So, um . . . do you want to try going through the drives?" he suggested.

Noa shook her head firmly. "No way. I can't think straight right now."

"All right, then let's do something brainless for a change," he said, suddenly struck by inspiration. They'd spent months running and hiding. They could afford to spend a single night acting like normal teenagers.

"Brainless?" Noa raised an eyebrow.

"Sure. Let's watch a movie." Peter rinsed out the bowl before stacking it in the dishwasher. "Unless you're too tired?"

Noa hesitated, then said, "I can't even remember the last movie I saw."

"It's a plan, then." Back in the living room, he dug through the Shapiros' media cabinet. "Let's see. What are you in the mood for? Action, comedy . . ."

"No action. I get enough of that in my everyday life," she quipped.

"Yeah, me too. Oh, wait. Here's one of my all-time favorites." He dug out a copy of *The Princess Bride*. "Have you seen this?"

"When I was a kid, I think. I barely remember it."

"Well, then you're in for a treat. 'My name is Inigo Montoya. You killed my father. Prepare to die,' " he intoned.

Noa gave him a blank look. "Is that from the movie?"

Peter groaned. "Seriously? Okay, we're watching it."

Noa took the case from him, frowning as she read the back. "I thought we agreed no action."

"Trust me. This has nothing to do with our everyday lives."

Forty-five minutes later, they were side by side on the couch watching one of Peter's favorite scenes. In the middle of a swordfight with Inigo Montoya, the Dread Pirate Roberts, aka Wesley, switched his sword to the other hand, explaining, "I'm not left-handed, either." Cracking up, Peter turned to check on Noa.

She was staring at the screen, completely enthralled. Even more startling, tears coursed down her cheeks. "Hey," he said gently, hitting the pause button. "You okay?"

"Fine." Noa hurriedly swiped them away. "I'm fine."

"You're sure? Because they've got a lot of other movies. I can just—"

"I remember this," she said, cutting him off. Her voice was thick as she continued. "I watched it with my parents."

"Oh." Peter knew that Noa's parents had died in a car crash when she was a kid; she'd been the only survivor. But she'd never talked about them before. He'd kind of forgotten that she'd ever had parents; she was so self-sufficient, it was easy to imagine her emerging into the world fully grown, wearing combat boots and toting a laptop.

But in reality, the people who were supposed to protect her

had been ripped away. She'd spent her childhood shuttling from one bad situation to another, unwanted and unloved. Peter cleared his throat. "How much do you remember about them?"

"Not much," Noa said in a small voice, still staring at the screen. "I remember my mom had hair like mine. She wore it really long, though. And she used to sing me to sleep every night."

"That sounds nice," he offered.

"Yeah. And my dad was really tall. Funny. He laughed a lot; they both did. That's what I remember most—them laughing."

Peter swallowed hard. All things considered, he'd been lucky, born into a family with a lot of money. But after his brother died of PEMA, he couldn't remember ever hearing his parents laugh. "I'm sorry."

She shrugged again. "Yeah, me too."

Peter tentatively reached out and took her hand. She didn't say anything, didn't even look at him; but she didn't push him away, either. They sat in the dark for the rest of the movie, holding hands. Noa even laughed at some of the sillier lines. It was the most normal Peter had ever seen her. He kept sneaking glances at her, wondering what she would have turned out like if her parents had survived. She was stunning, tall and willowy, with thick black hair and green eyes. He couldn't picture her as the prom queen, but maybe she would've been the type to run the school paper. Or the girl who passed around petitions at lunchtime to save whales or monk seals or whatever cause she'd decided to embrace. *Like Amanda*, he realized, startled.

On an impulse, he leaned over and pressed his lips to hers. At first, Noa stiffened. But a second later, her mouth opened slightly. She tasted like chili and mint mixed together, but not in a bad way.

Peter kept his eyes closed, focused entirely on the softness of her lips, the way they parted as he moved closer. He'd thought about doing this for months, ever since they first met in person. To be honest, he'd thought about doing a lot more, too.

But oddly, it wasn't what he'd expected. The kiss wasn't passionate, or sweet. The word *comforting* leapt into his mind, and he frowned.

Noa drew back and wet her lips with her tongue. Hesitantly, she said, "That was weird, right?"

"Yeah," he agreed with relief. "Really weird."

"Not bad, though," she amended. "I mean, I'm not sorry we did it."

"Me either," Peter said, running a hand over his scalp. "It just—"

"Felt like kissing a friend?" she offered.

He nodded. "Yeah. Like that."

"I know." Noa sighed. "I'm sorry."

"Don't be." Peter shook his head. "If we hadn't, I always would've wondered."

A long beat, then she admitted, "Me too."

"So we're good?"

There was a hint of sadness in her smile as she said, "Yeah. We're good."

"Awesome." Peter inhaled deeply. He felt lighter, like a burden had been lifted. "I saw some ice cream in the fridge."

"I'm full, actually." Noa was rubbing her wrist, the way she always did when she felt anxious. "That was a great movie."

"Yeah, the best." The awkwardness had crept back in

between them. "Are you tired? I was going to take Rick's room, if you want his sister's."

Noa didn't answer. She was staring at the screen with a shocked expression.

Peter followed her eyes. The TV had switched back to live mode, and it was tuned to CNN.

Their faces filled the screen, right above the banner: TERRORIST ALERT IN COLORADO.

Teo clutched Daisy's hand. They were seated next to each other in the rear of the plane. Mason hadn't bothered tying them up again; Teo couldn't decide if that was a good sign or a really, really bad one. Daisy was curled up against him, resting her head on his shoulder. He stroked her hair, trying to silently reassure her.

As the plane started to descend, Daisy tilted her head to look up at him. "So this is it, huh?"

Tears pressed against his eyelids. Teo shook his head firmly and said, "No way. We'll be fine."

"You're such a liar," she said with a small, sad smile. The plane shuddered as the wheels touched down. It bounced once, then started to taxi. "Where do you think we are?"

The window shades were drawn, but he could tell it was still dark outside. "I'm hoping for Disneyland," he said lightly. They'd been flying for about five hours, so they could be pretty much anywhere from Mexico to Canada.

Daisy giggled. "That would be an awesome place to die. Wonder why they didn't just kill us in the air?"

"Probably didn't want to mess up the upholstery," he said grimly.

"Well, at least I finally got to ride on an airplane, right?" she said softly.

Seeing the tears in her eyes nearly killed him. Teo drew her close, wrapping both arms around her.

The hiss of a door opening, and hands suddenly pulling them apart. "Time to go," one of the guards said gruffly, digging his fingers into Teo's shoulders. "Get up."

Teo growled, "Get your hands off me. I can walk."

Holding Daisy's hand, he walked up the aisle on shaky legs, remembering the look of rage in Mason's eyes. Would they be killed right there on the tarmac?

Teo paused in the doorway. A set of stairs had been driven up to the plane, as if they were dignitaries getting off a fancy jet. Four black SUVs were parked in a half circle at the bottom of the stairs. The airfield was small, just a single runway surrounded by trees. He scanned the area, but there was nothing to indicate where they were.

"Go," a voice behind him ordered.

Slowly, Teo descended the stairs, the metal clanking beneath his boots. He could hear Daisy sniffling behind him. One of the men opened the rear passenger door of the closest SUV and motioned for them to climb in. There was already someone sitting in the front passenger seat; he leveled a handgun on them.

Mason got in a separate vehicle, Teo noted with relief. But maybe he wasn't the type to get his hands dirty, at least not directly.

Their SUV pulled away from the airplane. With a growing sense of dread, Teo watched the tarmac unfurl before them. A metal gate rolled aside to let them through. Then they were driving down a two-lane road, hemmed in by trees on either side. He kept his eyes peeled for street signs, even though that was probably pointless. Why bother finding out where he was going to die?

It felt like they drove for an eternity, although probably only forty-five minutes had passed when the SUV abruptly turned up a long, sweeping driveway. A twelve-foot-high stone wall rose up on either side of the car. The SUV stopped in front of an enormous gate. The driver rolled down his window and swiped a key card against the security box, then the gate slowly swung open.

The driveway eased left. It was lined with lights that provided just enough illumination for Teo to make out more trees surrounding them. They could be anywhere: a pricey suburb, or somewhere rural. Hell, they could be in a whole other country for all he knew.

They rounded a bend, and his jaw dropped. An enormous mansion loomed up, nearly every window lit. It looked like something out of a movie: Bruce Wayne's castle in *Batman*, maybe. Carved out of massive stone blocks, with honest-to-God turrets.

"They're going to kill us here?" Daisy said. "Fancy."

"Shut up," the driver barked.

They passed the main door, pulling around to the side of the house. The SUV stopped in front of a garage with five vehicle bays.

"Out," the driver ordered. "And stay quiet."

Teo was practically choking on the lump in his throat. *Pull it together*, he scolded himself as he climbed out. A guard motioned for them to follow him through a side door. Daisy fell in step beside him, her hand small and sweaty in his. Teo squeezed it reassuringly as he glanced back; the other guys from the car were right behind them. *So much for making a break for it.*

They entered a dark, gloomy hallway. The guy in front kept walking, and they followed him through a series of rooms. Teo's mouth gaped open: In his entire life, he'd never set foot in such a nice house. Roy and Monica's compound in Santa Cruz looked like a tenement in comparison. Huge chandeliers in every room. Rugs and furniture that even he could tell were worth a fortune. Paintings set in gilded frames on every wall. He briefly wondered if it was a museum; there was no way actual people lived like this.

"Damn," Daisy muttered. "What is this place?"

Teo shook his head. "Not Disneyland."

She stifled a nervous laugh.

Finally, the guard halted before a set of enormous wood doors. He rapped on them with his knuckles. From inside, a voice intoned, "Come in."

The guard opened the door and stepped inside. Someone prodded Teo in the back, and he followed.

They were in a living room, if you could call a place the size of a banquet hall that. Lots of plush furniture beneath a chandelier that scattered light across dark red walls.

An older man leaned against the mantle. He was dressed in khakis and a light gray sweater that matched his hair.

As he turned toward them, Teo gasped, recognizing him immediately from photos and videos. This was the man who had infiltrated all of their lives, even though they'd never met.

Charles Pike.

"Welcome," Pike said with a broad smile. "Please, have a seat."

CHAPTER TEN

"Oh, crap," Peter said, running both hands through his hair. "What the hell?"

Noa stared at the photos of them on-screen. Peter's was a school portrait; he looked younger, with that persistent lock of hair nearly covering one eye. He gazed into the camera with a cocky grin, looking self-assured and confident.

Hers was less formal. She was wearing headphones and looking down. Her hair was cropped short, and she had on her favorite scarf. She'd bought it last September, so the picture must have been taken then, before she was kidnapped.

By the people stalking me, she realized. Pike's people.

"This is not good," Peter said grimly.

Noa forced herself to focus on what the news anchor was saying: something about a murder in Colorado, and the discovery of a sleeper cell in an old missile silo. "Wait," she said. "Murder?"

Another image replaced their faces on-screen: Loki against a hazy blue background, probably from his driver's license. He stared challengingly out at them, his mouth set in a firm line, the beard consuming most of his face. His ever-present trucker cap was gone, revealing thinning brownish-gray hair.

"Loki didn't make it," Peter said flatly. "Those bastards killed him, and now they're blaming us."

The anchor's bland voice was saying, ". . . Matan Maoz was found dead by authorities who raided the compound this afternoon. The state police believe that Maoz was killed by his co-conspirators before they fled. Numerous bombs and bomb-making materials were found in this former missile silo, purchased by Maoz in 2007. While the police refuse to discuss which terrorist organization might be responsible, an anonymous source revealed that these two teenagers are persons of interest. A nationwide manhunt is currently under way for Noa Torson and Peter Gregory. They are to be considered armed and dangerous; authorities stress that if you see them, please call the tip line immediately. Do not under any circumstances attempt to make contact with them."

"Anonymous sources, my ass," Peter snorted. He pushed off the couch and started to pace. "Those bastards are framing us."

"Poor Loki." A well of emotion rose up, nearly choking Noa. He'd fought to give them a chance to get away, and now he was gone. Sometimes it seemed like everyone who tried to help her ended up dead.

Loki's photo vanished, replaced by footage of state police cruisers parked in front of the gate to his compound. The news anchor prattled on about bomb-sniffing dogs and robots being brought in to search the site.

Then the camera cut to a living room, where a well-dressed middle-aged couple sat on a couch. Peter collapsed in a chair, as if his legs had buckled beneath him.

"What?" Noa asked, alarmed.

"Those are my parents," he croaked.

Noa shifted her attention back to the screen. The resemblance was clear: Peter had his mother's brown, wavy hair, and his father's eyes and nose. His parents looked tired, and agitated. They sat in a gorgeous living room: Everything looked insanely expensive. This must be where Peter used to live, the house he'd grown up in. She swallowed hard, struck again by how different their lives had been.

His mother spoke first. "Peter was an excellent student, with a lot of friends. He's always been such a happy boy. He's not . . ." She broke down, covering her mouth with a manicured hand. Peter's dad rubbed her shoulder reassuringly.

"He fell in with some bad people," his father said gruffly. "Ran off a few months ago. We've been looking everywhere for him, even hired private detectives. And now this." He shook his head. "It's not his fault. They must have brainwashed him."

Peter made a strangled sound. "Me? I'm the one who's been brainwashed?"

"Please." Peter's mother's hands twisted in her lap. "If he is involved in all this, I'm sure it wasn't his idea. He's a very sweet boy."

"God, she's making me sound like a serial killer," Peter grumbled. "Thanks a lot, Mom."

"Peter's got a lot of anger in him," the father interjected, staring right at the camera. "I'd like to say I'm surprised to hear that he killed someone, but, well . . . we should have gotten him help sooner. That's all we have to say."

The camera abruptly cut back to the blond news anchor. As she announced a four-alarm fire in an abandoned storage complex in Flagstaff, Arizona, the picture beside her switched to a city block engulfed in flames. Peter picked up the remote and turned off the TV.

They sat in silence for a long time.

"So," Peter finally said. "Nationwide manhunt, huh? That's not exactly a change of pace for us."

"It is when *everyone* is looking," Noa said. "Not just Pike's people."

"Good point. Looks like it's time to invest in some hair dye."

Noa plucked at a hole in her jeans. This was very, very bad. The one thing they'd had going for them was relative anonymity; Pike had just stripped that away. All it would take was one phone call from a concerned citizen, and the dragnet would descend. "So. Those were your folks, huh?"

Peter's face clouded over. "Yeah."

"They look . . . nice," she offered.

Peter glowered at the blank TV screen. "Yeah, really nice. I wonder how long it took Pike to convince them to sell out their only living kid. They probably tripped over each other to volunteer."

"Maybe it wasn't like that."

"Please." He examined his hands, then started methodically cracking his knuckles. "I mean, I knew they were involved in all this. I guess I just figured that if it came down to it, they'd take my side, you know? And instead . . ." He gestured toward the TV. "My mom even did her hair and makeup, did you notice that?"

He sounded utterly bereft, like someone had just torn out a piece of him that he'd never get back. Noa bit her lip. She'd spent her entire life resenting people who had parents. But maybe she'd been better off. "I'm really sorry," she finally said.

He shrugged. "Whatever, right? Bob and Priscilla can go screw themselves."

Noa felt like she should say something, or do something, but didn't know what. *Zeke would know.* He'd always had a knack for coming up with the perfect words to make someone feel better. She brushed the thought away. "We should get some sleep."

"Right." Peter had retreated into himself; he seemed to be growing smaller by the moment.

"Do you need anything?" she offered one last time.

Peter shook his head. Noa stood there awkwardly for a minute, waiting, then left the room. At the top of the stairs, she turned back. He was still sitting there, staring at his hands. As she watched, his shoulders started shaking. Noa bit her lip: She wanted to go back down, to comfort him in some way. But she got the feeling that more than anything, Peter wanted to be alone.

Suddenly exhausted, she shuffled down the hall to her room and quietly shut the door.

Daisy perched on the edge of the sofa, surreptitiously checking out their surroundings. Teo was sitting next to her, still holding her hand. The windows were all the way across the room, and closed: No way she could get to them without a guard tackling her. And for all she knew, there were dozens more surrounding the place. This was more like a prison than a house.

Charles Pike held a drink in his hand as he stared down at them. He swirled it, making the ice clatter, then took a sip. "I'd offer you some," he finally said. "But you're underage. And I wouldn't want to get in trouble for that."

Humor played in his voice, like this was all a big joke. He was attractive for his age, tan and athletic looking. Salt-and-pepper hair, piercing blue eyes, and a cleft chin. Daisy imagined leaping off the couch and clawing her nails down his cheek; that would wipe the smug grin off his face.

"What do you want?" Teo demanded.

Daisy felt another flare of pride for him; in spite of every-thing, he didn't sound afraid. He'd come a long way from the scared kid they'd rescued in San Francisco just a few months ago.

She was terrified, though. Because despite the opulent surroundings, if Pike gave the word, their throats would be slit right then and there.

Mason appeared in the doorway, and Pike waved him in. He walked over and murmured something to Pike; she strained to hear, but couldn't make out what he was saying. His nose had swollen to twice the normal size: probably bro-ken. *Good*, Daisy thought. She hoped it hurt like hell.

Pike shifted to face them. "Mr. Mason claims you weren't very helpful on the plane."

"We don't know where Noa is," Teo said.

"That's unfortunate." Pike set his glass down on a side table. "She's very important to me, you know."

"Yeah, we've heard," Daisy said. "You can hardly wait to start cutting her up again."

Pike actually looked wounded. "I'm afraid you don't have all the information about her . . . condition."

"We've lived with her for months," Daisy said disdainfully.

"We know more about it than you, for sure."

Teo gave her hand a hard squeeze, and she realized belatedly that she should've kept her mouth shut. Too late—Pike's eyebrows had shot up. "So she's not well?"

"She's fine," Teo snapped, but his tone wasn't convincing.

"Interesting." Pike took another sip. "The doctors thought something like that might happen."

"Something like what?" Daisy demanded. Teo squeezed her hand again, but she ignored him. Pike didn't know where Noa was, and they were probably going to be killed as soon as they left this room. She might as well find out what the hell was going on.

"Well, I suppose she told you about the extra thymus?" Seeing their blank looks, he continued, "Perhaps she doesn't even know herself. But I'd imagine that she's been getting weaker, and that her eating habits are . . . odd."

Daisy swallowed hard. She and Teo had spent hours discussing Noa, and what exactly might be wrong with her. Sometimes she seemed to go days without eating, then she'd scarf down everything in sight. Back when Daisy first joined up, Noa hardly ever seemed to sleep, but recently that was practically all she did.

Still, to share all that with this monster seemed like the ultimate betrayal.

Charles Pike was still regarding them with interest, as if they were a puzzle he was trying to solve. Abruptly he said, "I have something to show you."

"Thanks, but we're not into old dudes," Teo retorted. Daisy could tell he was trying to be brave, but there was an unmistakable tremor in his voice.

"You won't be harmed," Pike said with a sigh. "Please. It's this way."

And with that, he walked out of the room.

Daisy hesitated, then started to get off the couch. Teo clutched at her hand, restraining her. In a low voice he said, "This could be a trick."

"They're going to make us go no matter what." She indicated the goon squad with a tilt of her head. Two of their escorts had already stepped forward, looking eager to mete out punishment.

Teo hesitated, then got to his feet, muttering, "I really hope he's not going to show us a bunch of chopped-up kids."

Pike was waiting for them in the hallway. His expression was unreadable as he waved for them to follow. Daisy exchanged a look with Teo, then fell in step behind him. Two men followed as they walked through several more rooms. Pike finally stopped in front of an innocuous-looking door and said, "She's in here."

He actually sounded choked up. Daisy frowned. *What the hell is going on?*

The door opened into a room that was a huge departure from the rest of the house. The walls and floor were bare, the lighting dimmed. In the center of the room, a teenage girl lay on a hospital bed.

"You're doing experiments here, in your house?" Daisy exclaimed. Even given all the awful things she'd heard about Pike, that seemed beyond the pale.

"Experiments?" He appeared genuinely puzzled. "No, of course not. This is my daughter, Elinor. I've always called her Ella, though."

Daisy stepped closer to the bed, with Teo at her heels. Ella was around her age, fifteen or sixteen. Tiny, maybe five-two. Even paler than Noa, like she hadn't seen the sun in months. Her eyes were closed, and she was lying so still that she looked dead.

Even more disturbingly, she was strapped down like some sort of criminal.

"You tied up your own daughter?" Teo said indignantly. "That's sick."

"It's for her own good." Pike bent to kiss her forehead. Ella didn't react. His voice sounded distant as he continued, "Although it's purely precautionary. She hasn't moved in weeks."

Daisy vaguely remembered Noa explaining that Pike's daughter was dying of PEMA, which was why he was doing those horrible experiments; he wanted to find a cure in time to save her. Honestly, at the time she hadn't cared what his reasons were; she'd seen his victims, and nothing justified his crimes against them.

Seeing him standing there holding Ella's hand with tears in his eyes, though . . . in spite of herself, she felt a twinge of sympathy.

Without looking at them, Pike said, "Ella's mother died when she was six years old. She's all I have left."

Daisy stared at the girl on the bed. Ella's dad loved her enough to do anything to keep her alive. She might not have had a long life, but it had probably been a pretty decent one. A hell of a lot better than hers, at least. "My mom died, too," Daisy said. "And my dad took off. I spent my last birthday eating out of a Dumpster."

"I'm so sorry," Pike said, with what sounded like genuine warmth in his voice. "That must have been terrible."

"Yeah, it really sucked." Daisy felt the rage rekindling inside her. "And it got a lot worse when your people tried to kidnap me so I could be sliced open. Spare me the fake pity."

Pike stroked his daughter's hand, then gently set it back on the bed and smoothed out the sheet. Turning to face them, he said earnestly, "Please understand, I wasn't involved in the day-to-day operations of Project Persephone. I had no idea what was being done on my behalf. I only found out later how my employees were securing . . . volunteers."

Teo snorted. "Volunteers? Seriously?"

"I'm truly sorry," Pike said. "Once I found out what was going on, I put a stop to it immediately."

Daisy watched his eyes, trying to gauge whether or not he was telling the truth. She was having a hard time reconciling this grieving father with the monster Noa and Peter had described.

"So you've stopped kidnapping kids?" Teo snapped. "Because guess what? Here we are."

"Yes, but have you been harmed?" Pike held out his hands, palms up. "Has anyone hurt you? If they have, please let me know. My orders were very strict."

"Mason threatened to cut Daisy's throat," Teo snapped.

"He did?" Pike looked startled. His gaze shifted to the door, and he frowned. "Well, rest assured, I'll have a word with him about that."

Daisy exchanged a glance with Teo. This was all too weird. "Why are we here?"

"You're here because I really hoped you'd be able to help us find your friend Noa," Pike said. "I'd like to try and make amends to her, if that's even possible anymore."

"By cutting her open again?" Teo asked. "Yeah, I think she's going to pass on that."

"You really don't understand," Pike said wearily. "Noa is very ill, possibly even dying. And if we don't get to her soon, I'm afraid it will be too late."

* * *

Peter leaned into the mirror, examining the results. A stranger stared back at him; the clippers had only left a quarter inch of hair all around. "I look like I'm ready for boot camp," he muttered to his reflection. He picked a lock of brown hair out of the sink and stared at it for a minute, feeling oddly melancholy.

"Stop being such a girl," he said aloud. It was just hair, it would grow back. He rinsed the sink until it was clean again.

Other than the new hairdo, there wasn't much he could do; growing a beard or mustache would take a few days anyway. He'd just have to hope this was enough. Peter dug some Bengay out of the medicine cabinet and rubbed it on his shoulder. It still throbbed in unison with the incision in his back, but not nearly as badly as yesterday. Despite his popping four Advil, the rest of his body ached; but all in all he felt okay.

Certainly better than Loki, he thought grimly. Peter felt a twinge of guilt; if he hadn't traced that IP address, Loki would still be living happily underground.

It's not our fault, he reminded himself. *It's Pike's.* And this was yet another death Peter was going to make him pay for.

As he closed the cabinet, Peter got an unexpected flash of his last visit to this house. Spring break, a little over a year ago. Playing beer pong in the rumpus room with Rick and a couple of girls they'd met on the slopes. He'd passed out drunk in the middle of the night, and woke up with the worst hangover of his life.

Sighing, he shoved the memory away. It was hard to believe that life had ever been so normal.

Coming out of the bathroom, he heard the sound of typing down the hall. Peter shuffled toward it, wiping his newly shaved head with a hand towel. He found Noa in the office, tapping away at an older PC.

"Anything new?" he asked.

"Nope. The news feeds are all saying the same thing. Nationwide manhunt, call the hotline, blah blah blah." She turned to face him, then did a double take. "Wow."

"Yeah, I know. I'm calling it my Seal Team Six look," he said wryly.

"It's not so bad." Noa got to her feet and turned a slow circle around him. "You definitely look different."

"Better?" he joked.

Noa gave him a small smile. "Different. Older, actually."

"Perfect. First chance I get, I'm buying some beer." He let the towel drop by his side. "I gotta say, you're pulling off the red nicely."

"Really?" She sounded uncertain, but pleased by the compliment. Since the photo showed her with short hair, Noa had left it long and dyed it auburn with some henna they'd found in the master bathroom's medicine cabinet; apparently Rick's mom wasn't au naturel. She was wearing a blue tank top and jeans.

"Sure. Your eyes look greener. You look hot." The words slipped out before he could stop them. Noa's eyes widened in surprise, and he hurriedly added, "I mean, not that you weren't, you know, pretty before. But now—" Her smile widened, and Peter blew out an exasperated breath of air. "You know what? I'm just going to shut up."

Noa cocked an eyebrow. "First I'm glow-y, and now I'm hot. Maybe I should have gone red a long time ago."

"Maybe," Peter agreed. "Honestly, you don't look that different, though. You're kind of . . . distinctive."

"Distinctive? How am I distinctive?"

"I don't know." He felt himself flush a deeper shade of red. "You're tall, and thin, and you kind of walk different."

She glowered at him. "You're making me sound like a freak."

"But a good freak." Her smile faltered, and Peter said, "Man, I'm sorry. I just mean, you don't look like a regular teenager. People are going to notice you."

"Why would they notice me?" she asked, sounding genuinely puzzled.

"Well, hell," he said. "You look like a supermodel, for one."

"You're so full of it," she groaned. Suddenly, she bent double, clutching her chest.

"Noa?" Peter said, alarmed. "Hey, I was kidding. There's nothing wrong with how you look."

"I . . . just . . ." She staggered across the room and fell into the desk chair. "God, it hurts."

He crossed the room quickly and dropped into a crouch before her. "What can I do?"

Noa winced in pain, rocking back and forth. "Nothing. I . . . I'll be fine. Just . . . give me a minute."

She was breathing hard through a clenched jaw. Peter watched helplessly, feeling utterly useless. Finally, Noa exhaled, closed her eyes, and sat up straight. "All right. I'm good now."

"What the hell was *that*?" Peter demanded.

Noa shook her head. "I don't know. It's been happening for a while."

She was avoiding his eyes. Peter ran a hand over his head, startled for a second to encounter nothing but a thin layer of peach fuzz. "Why didn't you tell me?"

"I thought I had it under control," she said in a low voice. "But . . . it keeps getting worse."

The fear in her eyes scared the hell out of him. "Do you want . . . I don't know, some Advil or water or something?"

She was already shaking her head. "It won't help. I've tried that."

"Okay." Peter sat back on his haunches, thinking. "So this is because of the extra thymus, right? I mean, that guy Roy said it might be making you sick."

"He said my cells were degenerating," she said tonelessly.

"Crap." Peter blew out hard. They were hiding out in a house in the middle of nowhere, with the entire country convinced they were murderous terrorists. There was no one left to turn to for help.

"I'll be fine, Peter," Noa said with effort. "Don't worry about me."

"Well, that didn't look fine. I mean, first there was all the extra sleeping, and now this . . ." He stood up resolutely. "We need to see what's in the rest of those files. There might be something that explains it."

"Yeah, right. The files." Noa waved at the computer on the desk. "It'll take forever on this thing. I've been trying for an hour and still haven't found any mention of Pike." She held up a drive that had a bullet hole straight through it. "Hopefully there wasn't anything on this one."

Peter took the drive from her and turned it over in his hand—it must've gotten hit yesterday, while they were running through that field. He shivered involuntarily. What if the drives hadn't stopped the bullets? Would he or Noa be dead right now? "How many were ruined?"

"I'm not sure yet." Noa rubbed her temple with her thumbs. "Aside from the bullet holes, they got banged around pretty badly. Some of the data must've gotten corrupted."

Peter tossed the drive in the trash. "Well, it's not like we can go anywhere anyway, right? Nothing but time on our hands."

"What if someone shows up here?" Noa asked weakly. "You said there might be a maid."

"Yeah, there might be. So we stay quiet, and try to keep everything looking the way it did when we came in. If she shows up, we hide."

"Hide?" Noa cocked an eyebrow.

"Sure," he said, trying to sound convincing. "As far as she knows, no one has been here for months. I bet she doesn't even come upstairs anymore."

"That sounds risky," Noa said dubiously.

"No riskier than strolling into an internet café when our faces are front-page news," Peter argued. He put his hands on the arms of her chair. "Look. You're not doing so hot, and I feel like I just got hit by a truck. We need to rest up, and while we're doing that, we can try to get something off these drives that we can use. Something to end this."

"But what if there's nothing there?" Noa said weakly.

"If that's true, we'll deal with it. But I think there is," he argued. Noa had a look in her eyes that he'd never seen before—like she was giving up. That was almost scarier than what had just happened. "There's something in those files that Pike doesn't want anyone to see. And we're going to find it."

Noa leaned back in the chair. Her skin was pale, and a fine sheen of sweat covered her forehead. Swiping it away with a shaky hand, she said, "So what do we do if we find something?"

"We use it to make Pike release a cure."

"What, we blackmail him?" She laughed weakly. "And you're always down on *my* ideas. That's a terrible plan."

"He'll do it," Peter said firmly, wishing he felt as certain as he sounded. "He'll save you both. Or I'll ruin him."

"And then what?" Noa demanded. "We just let him get away with everything?"

"To save all those kids out there who are dying of PEMA? Yeah, definitely. I mean, it sucks," he added, seeing the expression on her face. "But we'll probably have to let him off."

"I hate that," Noa said bluntly. "I mean, we don't even know how many people he's killed. What about Cody, and Roy, and Monica? And Zeke?"

Peter shook his head, suddenly exhausted. Everything they'd seen, everything they'd been through flashed through his mind. The photos of kids laid out on tables like dead butterflies. The coolers filled with body parts. Could he really just let Pike walk away after all that?

He had to. It was Amanda's only chance, and Noa's, too. "I hate it, too," he said. "But it's the only choice we have."

"And if he needs me for the cure?" she said, so softly he almost didn't hear it.

"We'll make sure it's in his best interest that you survive. Otherwise, we'll expose him."

"You mean, you will," Noa said with a crooked smile. "Because I'll be gone."

"It won't come to that," Peter said fiercely. "I won't let it."

They sat there for a long time. Noa's breathing was still labored as she said, "You really think this will work?"

"Sure," he said weakly, suddenly completely drained. "What could go wrong?"

Noa choked out a laugh in response. She reached out, and he took her hand. They sat in silence for a minute, lost in their own thoughts. Finally, Noa said, "I guess I'll keep looking through the files. Gotta make sure whatever we have on him is airtight, right?"

"Right." Peter ran a hand over his head again, the spiky hairs tickling his palm. "I'm going to see if there's a laptop around here somewhere."

Noa turned back to the stack of drives. Without meeting his eyes, she said, "Oh, and Peter?"

"Yeah?" He turned back at the threshold.

"I like your hair this way." She threw him a wicked grin. "Makes you look tougher."

He held up a finger warningly and said, "Careful. I might try to kiss you again."

Noa rolled her eyes. "Give it your best shot, navy boy."

Teo lay on the bed, curled around Daisy. Weak daylight streamed through the windows, but she was still fast asleep. He, on the other hand, had lain awake since they were brought to this room. Pike had acted like they were guests; there were even minisoaps in the bathroom, for God's sake. And bandages and antiseptic, thankfully, which he'd used to clean and patch up the knife wound on his arm. It still throbbed, but he could handle that. He kept waiting for the door to pop open, and guys with guns to come streaming in. Mason, maybe, ready to finish the job.

But they'd been left alone.

Daisy lay on top of the comforter, still fully dressed. Her eyes were closed, lips slightly parted. He was tempted to kiss her, but didn't want to risk waking her. Not after the night they'd had.

He rolled over on his back and stared at the ceiling, hands crossed behind his head. Things had taken a turn for the surreal, that was for certain. After showing them his dying daughter, Pike had offered them some food. When they'd turned that down, he told his men to make sure they were comfortable for the night.

He and Daisy had spent ten minutes casing the room: The windows opened, but they were on the top floor of the house, easily a fifty-foot drop to the ground. Every few minutes, a guy walked past on patrol down below. There was no other way out that they could find.

So after conferring in low voices about their options, they'd decided to try and sleep, and see what happened in the morning.

Easier said than done, Teo thought grimly. He was completely wiped out. They'd spent the past few days crashing on busses and in squalid alleys. Living on candy bars, chips, and sodas. And then they'd fought those street punks, had the showdown with Mason, and met with Pike. Busy week. He should have dropped off immediately.

But these might be the final hours he ever got to spend with Daisy, and he didn't want to waste them. When she was dreaming, she did this thing that he found absolutely adorable, where her mouth tweaked up in a faint smile. He definitely didn't want to miss seeing that one last time.

Daisy's eyes moved back and forth beneath the lids, then it happened: Her lips curved up, ever so slightly. Teo was glad that even in the middle of all this, she was able to escape into a good dream. He leaned in and lightly brushed his lips across her forehead. Her mouth tweaked again, and she made a small noise in the back of her throat. Carefully, he eased an arm around her. In her sleep, she nuzzled into him, settling against his shoulder. Teo tucked his cheek against her hair, inhaling her scent. He finally drifted off to the sound of rain pattering against the rooftop.

CHAPTER ELEVEN

Noa blinked her eyes, trying to get them to focus. Her head was throbbing, and her throat was dry. At least the chest pain had dissipated, although there was an uncomfortable tightness in her rib cage, like the extra thymus inside her was straining to break free.

She took another sip of water and attached the tenth server drive to the computer. The decryption key was working perfectly. But every single drive contained an insane amount of information, and none of it was organized. It reminded her of when she first hacked into the Project Persephone files; only those had contained a mere fraction of what she faced now.

Most of the files were both familiar and discomfiting. On the surface, it was all bland post-op reports, emails, and other forms and abstracts written in incomprehensible jargon. She hated the way the researchers used science-speak to gloss over the atrocities they were committing against kids. Last time, at least, she'd had a medical student to help her wade through them. Peter had recommended that they search the files by keywords: "Charles Pike," "cure," and "Noa Torson."

Typing her own name into a search engine was really unsettling. Noa wasn't sure whether or not to be happy about the fact that so far, it hadn't yielded any results.

Unfortunately, neither had any of the other terms; and searching for "cure" returned too many to count. In dozens of reports, the researchers had written stuff like, "With any luck, we're fast approaching a cure." None of them actually claimed to have discovered it, and their tone struck her as defeat thinly cloaked in false optimism. These doctors didn't seem to be on the brink of solving anything; most just sounded like they were desperately trying to keep their jobs.

Bastards, she reminded herself as she swapped in another server drive. They were more concerned about saving themselves than helping kids.

Peter was holed up in his friend Rick's bedroom; he'd found an ancient HP laptop in a closet, and carted half the salvageable drives in there. Hopefully he was having better luck.

"Anything?" she called out.

He grunted in reply, which she took as a no.

Even though she'd slept nearly twelve hours last night, Noa was wiped out. The thought of lying down for a nap was unbelievably tempting. She tried to rationalize it; all they could do right now was sift through the drives and rest up. She'd logged four hours so far; why not take a break?

But if she lay down again, she might not wake up for another twelve hours, or longer. It was a strange sensation, like her body was slipping away from her. She'd always been healthy, almost abnormally so; even when a particular nasty virus tore through one of her foster homes, she rarely caught it. And since the surgery, she hadn't gotten so much as a head cold. Maybe that was a by-product of whatever made her heal so quickly.

But now . . . she lifted her arm and examined it. The cuts she'd gotten while running through the woods in Arkansas were still there. A normal person would have healed by now; and she should barely have been able to see them by the next day. Yet they looked as raw and angry as they had a week ago.

Which probably wasn't a good sign. Noa rubbed her eyes: Even though she had drawn the blinds to block out the daylight, the bright monitor was making them ache. She keyed it down a few more notches and typed in the search parameters again.

Skimming the list of results, her heart leapt into her throat: For the first time, the word "Pike" had returned an item. Quickly, she clicked on the file and started to skim it. It was an email exchange, between Pike and a Dr. Johnson:

> Mr. Pike—
>
> As promised, here are the results of our latest tests on the blood samples from Subject #050207. As I mentioned before, with renewed access to the subject, we should be able to isolate specific markers and hopefully synthesize a vaccine. I don't want to get your hopes up, but given the results so far, I believe it's entirely possible that we'll be able to slow down the progression of the disease, or even eradicate it entirely.
>
> Of course, all of this is contingent on whether or not we are given direct access to the subject. Do you have a clearer sense of when that will be possible?

The email was dated April 18; a little over a month ago. Dread blossomed in the pit of Noa's stomach. With trembling fingers, she initiated a search for subject #050207.

Nothing.

She tried the next drive, then another. On the fourth, a result finally came up. Noa drew a deep breath and clicked on the file.

It was a jpg. Opening it, she immediately recognized the photo. It was taken in one of Charles Pike's ad hoc operating rooms, shot from above. A girl lay on top of a metal table in a hospital gown, with a sheet pulled up to her waist. Her eyes were closed, dark hair reflecting the overhead surgical light.

It was her.

Noa sat back and closed her eyes. Even though Peter still had the original Project Persephone files stored on backup servers somewhere, she'd never looked at them again. Once she'd discovered the broad strokes of what had been done to her, all she'd wanted was to exact revenge.

Seeing herself laid out like this, unconscious and vulnerable, hurt just as much as it had the first time. And in spite of everything she'd done to try and spare other kids from the same fate, Pike had continued the experiments anyway.

The absolute worst part was that it seemed to have worked; he was close to a cure for PEMA. Even if they found incontrovertible evidence of his involvement, they'd have to keep their mouths shut. Pike would end up hailed as a hero.

The thought made her stomach curdle. Her chest began throbbing more persistently. Noa gripped the edge of the desk, battling against the pain. She was sitting there, drawing deep breaths, when there was sudden whoop from the other room.

"I got it!" Peter cried out. "Yes!"

"Got what?" Noa managed to say.

The sound of feet padding down the hall, then Peter appeared in the doorway. His brow immediately furrowed with concern. "Is it bad again?"

"Not as bad," she gasped, although that was a lie. It was agony, a hundred times worse than anything she'd felt so far. Her chest seized up, and she fell to the floor. Noa tried to move, but discovered to her alarm that she couldn't; her entire body was shaking uncontrollably.

"Oh, crap," Peter said, rushing to her side. "Noa!"

He placed his hands on her shoulders, but the shaking continued. From far away, Noa heard her teeth chattering. She lost all sense of time and place, retreating to somewhere else, somewhere dark and quiet.

When she opened her eyes, Peter was looking down at her, panic contorting his features.

"It's okay," she said, alarmed to hear the words slur. "I'm fine."

She tried to sit up, but his hands tightened on her shoulders. "Just chill for a sec, all right? Christ, you nearly gave me a heart attack."

She tried to respond, but her mouth was incredibly dry. "Water," she croaked.

"Yeah, okay." Peter scrambled to his feet.

A foot from the door, he stopped short and cocked his head to the side.

Noa was about to ask what was wrong when she heard it, too: the sound of a car turning up the gravel driveway.

Teo wouldn't stop pacing, and it was driving her nuts. "Just sit for a minute," Daisy said. "Please."

"I can't," he muttered, his hands opening and closing in fists at his sides. "We need to come up with a way out."

"There isn't one." Daisy tried to sound patient, even though she felt like she was crawling out of her skin, too. "We can't go out the window, we're too high up. The door is locked and guarded. Unless you've got some sort of teleporting trick you haven't told me about, we're stuck."

"Teleporting trick?" he said with a small smile, raising an eyebrow.

Daisy shrugged. "I watched *Star Trek*."

"You're a Trekkie?" He came back over to the bed and plunked down beside her. "Man, that makes me love you even more."

She punched him lightly in the arm. "I'm not a Trekkie. I just liked the movies."

"The new ones?" He groaned. "Those don't count."

"Please. Chris Pine is a total hottie."

"I guess. If you're into that sort of thing," he mumbled. "He's no Shatner, though."

"Oh my God." Daisy rolled her eyes. "You're such a dork sometimes, Teddy."

"I love it when you call me Teddy," he said with a small smile. "Did I ever tell you that?"

"Only, like, a million times," Daisy said, but she flushed with pleasure. He rocked into her, bumping her shoulder. She bumped him back.

"I can't believe I'm complaining about being locked in a bedroom with you," he joked.

"Yeah, this is really romantic," Daisy said wryly. "Nothing like an armed guard outside to really set the mood."

"I know," he said, suddenly serious. "But we haven't really been alone, since . . . well, you know."

He stared down at her hand as he stroked it with his thumb. The truth was, they hadn't really been alone together since the night they'd shared a bunk in Santa Cruz. After that, they'd been with Noa and Peter 24-7. Followed by a week of sleeping on busses, and in skanky alleys and homeless camps. Their entire relationship had consisted of stolen kisses and cuddling, in between running for their lives.

Now, for the first time, they were alone. *Kind of*, she amended.

Teo cleared his throat. "Listen, I don't mean . . . what you think I mean. We don't have to do that."

"Sure you did," she said with a small smile.

Teo blushed deep red. Daisy eased her hand under his shirt and lightly skimmed her fingers across his back. He had the most amazing skin, incredibly soft. He shuddered and closed his eyes.

"It's okay," she said softly.

"It's not." He shook his head. "It's really not. I just wanted you to know . . . I mean, just in case this is it . . . you're the only person I've ever really loved. And I wish—"

A click, and the door to the room sprang open. Daisy yanked her hand back.

Pike was standing there in jeans and a polo shirt. He looked like one of those old guys in an ad for men's cologne. He smiled and said, "I hope you both slept well."

"We're hungry," Teo said, getting to his feet. "Are you ever planning on feeding us?"

Pike looked genuinely distressed. "I'm so sorry, I just assumed they'd bring you breakfast."

"Well, they didn't." Daisy crossed her arms over her chest.

"My apologies." Pike's tone remained even as he said, "Good news, then. I came to invite you to join me for lunch."

Teo scoffed. "Yeah, that sounds awesome."

"It will give us another chance to talk." He stood aside,

gesturing for them to join him.

Looking at Teo, Daisy saw her own confusion mirrored on his face. *What is this guy playing at?* Whatever she'd expected, it hadn't been a lunch invitation.

But at least they'd be on a lower floor; maybe they could try to run. As Teo took her hand, he leaned in and whispered, "Whatever he wants, don't give it to him. Because the minute we do, he'll kill us."

She managed a small nod, although her throat had gone dry. He was right, of course. But that didn't mean Pike wouldn't kill them anyway, once he got tired of being stonewalled.

As they walked down the hall together, their guard fell in step behind them. Pike clapped his hands together and said, "I hope you like grilled salmon."

"Who is it?" Noa asked breathlessly. Her chest was still heaving from the seizure. There was a blue tinge around her lips, and her pupils were seriously dilated.

"Probably the maid. Shh." He'd pretty much carried Noa down the hallway, dragging her into the walk-in closet in the master bedroom. He'd cased it earlier; the room was immaculate, not a dust bunny in sight. He silently prayed that the Shapiros' housekeeper was lazy by nature.

Because if she came up the stairs . . . the computers were still open, the drives scattered everywhere. He'd been extra careful with the downstairs, cleaning up their dishes and restacking them, smoothing out the couch cushions. But if the housekeeper decided to take a look around, she'd know instantly that there were intruders in the house.

A stair creaked. He drew in a deep breath. In spite of himself, he flashed back to when Mason's maid had nearly caught him. *What is it with me and cleaning ladies?* And what would they do if she discovered them?

If that happened, he and Noa would have to grab what they could and run.

Another creak: She was coming upstairs. Hanging dresses kept brushing his face; Peter swatted them away.

Creak.

Noa leaned against him, breathing shallowly. She let out a small moan, and Peter winced. It sounded incredibly loud in the stillness.

"Who's there?" a frightened female voice called out.

Okay, Peter thought with resignation. *We're done for.* She was probably already dialing 911.

He started going over the next steps in his head. Get Noa to the car, then come back for the drives and packs. Grab the laptop: The Shapiros would already know someone had broken in, they might as well take what they needed. Food for the road. Cash.

Where the hell are we going to get cash?

He flashed back to last spring break. They'd wanted to make a beer run, but were both tapped out. Rick went upstairs, and came back with a hundred-dollar bill, boasting about his dad's secret stash. . . .

Peter carefully eased Noa over so that she was leaning against the closet wall. He got up on the balls of his feet and started pawing through clothing; mostly women's dresses. He crab walked to the other side of the closet, moving as silently as possible.

Please still be here, he prayed. *Please.* Peter's fingers fumbled along a line of hanging suits. He groped through them, feeling the lapels. Finally found one that felt satiny: a tuxedo jacket.

He dug into the right front pocket: nothing. Reached around to the left, and was relieved when his fingers closed around a wad of bills secured by a money clip. *Thank you, Mr. Shapiro*, he thought. *I promise to pay you back.*

Noa groaned again, and he winced. The sound practically echoed through the still house. He heard running footsteps downstairs, followed by the door slamming shut. Peter bit his lip. *Dammit.*

He went back to Noa and slung her arm across his shoulders, then hauled her to her feet.

"Where . . . what . . .?" she mumbled.

"I'm getting you to the car. We're going."

"I can walk," she slurred.

"Great. Any help would be appreciated." He was already huffing, and the pressure of her body weight on his sore shoulder was excruciating. He manhandled her down the stairs and into the garage. Awkwardly, he opened the Camry's passenger door and shoved her inside. Then Peter raced back into the house, an invisible clock ticking off seconds in his mind. How long until the cops showed up? Three minutes? Four?

He threw the drives and laptop into the packs and dragged them downstairs. Grabbed another duffel from the top of Rick's closet and tore through the pantry, shoving anything he could grab into it.

By the time he got back to the car, three minutes had passed. He threw everything in the backseat, then climbed in. The engine started on the first try: Thank God for small favors. He realized that the garage door was still down, and stumbled out of the car, frantically slapping the button to raise it.

Sirens sounded in the distance. The door opened painfully

slowly while his fingers drummed the steering wheel. When the door finally cleared the rear of the car, Peter gunned the engine and threw it into reverse.

A Subaru wagon blocked the driveway; an older, heavyset woman with frizzy blond hair stood beside it. Her mouth gaped open as he tore past her, bumping onto the grass to avoid ramming her car. The accelerator climbed to thirty, then forty as he raced down the driveway. When he hit the road, he yanked the wheel right. The back of the car swerved out, nearly going into a spin before he righted it.

Peter forced himself to slow to the speed limit, blinking sweat out of his eyes. A half mile down the road, two patrol cars screamed past with lights and sirens blazing.

He glanced over at Noa. In that weird, slurred voice she asked, "Where are we going?"

"Away from here," he muttered, checking their rearview mirror.

"Boston," she murmured.

Peter wasn't sure he'd heard her correctly. Dumbfounded, he asked, "Did you just say Boston?"

Noa nodded. "We can't keep running. It's time to finish all this."

The only sound was the clink of silverware against china. Teo and Daisy sat across from each other, with Pike between them at the head of an enormous dining table. Teo had never eaten a meal like this in his life: There were cloth napkins and fancy plates. One of their guards brought out each course: bowls of soup, then salads, followed by slabs of orange fish surrounded by vegetables.

The dining room was on the ground floor, but the guards posted at each door eyed them menacingly the entire time.

Which wasn't exactly helping his digestion.

Teo had been chewing the same bite for five minutes; the acid in his throat overwhelmed his taste buds. He had no appetite and had barely touched most of the food on his plate.

When he tried to swallow, he started choking on the fish. Teo gulped water from a crystal goblet to clear it.

Looking up, he found Pike regarding him with concern. "I apologize for my chef. The salmon is a bit dry."

Teo issued a sharp laugh. "I can't stop thinking about Hansel and Gretel. You know, how the witch was fattening them up to eat them."

Pike set his fork down and said with bemusement, "You can't seriously think you're going to be eaten?"

Across the table, Daisy snorted and muttered, "Chopping us into bits isn't much better."

"As I explained last night," Pike said with a frown, "you won't be harmed here."

"Why keep us, then?" Teo demanded. "Why not just let us go?"

Pike looked at him levelly. "You'll be free to go as soon as I've gotten what I need from you."

"What's that?" Daisy asked. "Our hearts? Kidneys?"

"Noa Torson," Pike said sternly.

"So you can chop her up." Teo tossed his fork down. It landed on his plate with a satisfying clatter. "Sure, why not. I mean, she only saved us from you."

Pike abruptly pushed back his chair and stood. "I have something else to share with you."

"I'm not done with my salmon," Teo said obstinately, scooping up a piece with his fingers. He shoved it in his mouth and stared challengingly at Pike, chewing with his mouth open. "Besides, isn't dessert coming?"

Daisy stifled a laugh. Pike glowered at him, then sat back in the chair. Teo cherished the small victory. If Pike wanted to play at being the good guy, let him. Soon enough, he'd show his true colors.

And until then, Daisy might as well get a good meal. Unlike Teo, she'd devoured everything set in front of her, even scraping the plate to get the last few bits. Teo derived great pleasure from seeing how that sound made Pike wince.

"So where are we headed after this?" Teo said conversationally. "You got a dungeon or something?"

"Torture chamber?" Daisy chimed in. "Or ooh, I know. A shark tank."

Pike cleared his throat. "It's about your friend, Noa. I can prove she's sick. Dying, in fact. And my people are the only ones who can save her."

"I bet you say that to all the street kids," Daisy commented as she sat back in her chair and delicately wiped her mouth with the cloth napkin. Teo felt a flash of pride: That was his girl. He could tell how terrified she was by the little twitch in her right eye, and the way she kept twisting her hair. But she was putting up a good front for Pike.

Pike gave her a grim smile. "I understand the lack of trust, given the circumstances. But you'll see that I'm telling the truth."

"All right, then." Teo tossed his napkin on the table and pushed back his chair. "I'm not in the mood for dessert anyway. Let's get it over with."

Noa turned over on her side and groaned: Her chest was pulsing again, it felt like the pressure was crushing her lungs. She tried to sit up, but immediately fell back against the pillows. She frowned as a mottled, dingy ceiling swam into view. "Where are we?"

Peter suddenly appeared by her side. "Hey! You're awake!"

He sounded relieved, like he'd been afraid she wouldn't wake up again. "How did we get here?" she whispered.

"Let's just say it wasn't easy," Peter muttered. "Here. Drink."

He lifted her head and held a glass of water to her lips. Noa wanted to protest that she wasn't an invalid; but when she tried to lift her hands, they felt impossibly heavy. She opened her mouth and gulped down most of the glass.

"Better?"

"Yeah," she said. "Thanks." Looking around, she saw that they were in a seedy motel room, the carpet and rug matching shades of puke green. The dingy drapes were drawn, so the only light came from the laptop that sat open on a crooked desk.

"Nice place," she commented.

"They take cash," Peter said defensively. "And didn't ask for IDs. So yeah, it's pretty much perfect."

It all came back to her in a rush: doubling over, Peter dragging her down the hall after the maid came in. The long car ride. Peter leaving her alone, then showing up with another car and transferring her into it. "Where are we?"

"Outside Omaha," Peter said.

She laughed. "Omaha, again? Seriously?"

"Yeah," Peter said wryly. "And guess what? It looks even worse in the daytime."

Noa flashed back to a bus station in the middle of the night. Peter sitting on a bench waiting for them, looking small and scared in the glow of the headlights. Teo and Daisy in the front seat, while she sat in the back, digging her fingernails into her palms. Her overwhelming relief at seeing him again, knowing that she wouldn't have to do this alone. Mingled with grief over having just lost Zeke. "Are we still going to Boston?"

"According to you, we are," Peter said. "But feel free to let me know if you've changed your mind. After all, it is Pike & Dolan ground zero."

Noa's throat went the kind of dry no amount of water could fix. Still, she said firmly, "No more running. We have to confront him." She didn't add that unless they hurried, she might not make it, judging by how fast she was deteriorating. And she didn't want to die without looking Pike in the eye.

"Well, I've got some good news." Despite the circumstances, there was enthusiasm in his voice. "Back at the house, right before maidzilla came in, I found proof in one of the files. Enough to put Pike away for life. Definitely enough to blackmail him."

"What proof?" Noa asked wearily. Keeping her eyes open took too much effort, so she closed them.

"Everything." Sounding downright gleeful, he continued, "Forms he signed off on, approving the experiments. Emails where he and Mason discussed targeting more 'test subjects.' Even messages between him and some senators where they talk about huge campaign contributions. Crazy stuff. Man, if we could put this out there, we'd bury him and about half of Congress!"

"So that's how he keeps getting the cops to cover for him," she said, hating how weak her voice sounded.

Peter nodded. "Someone high up in the FBI must be in his pocket; bet we find out who, if we keep looking. Plus it sounds like a lot of his buddies in Washington have sick kids."

"And he promised them a PEMA cure," Noa said slowly.

"Not just PEMA," Peter said. "He's claiming to be able to fix pretty much everything, maybe even cancer."

"And all he needs is me," Noa concluded. She was so tired. She knew that what they were talking about was important, but she was having a hard time focusing. Her mind kept wanting to drift off.

"Yeah, but don't you see?" Peter said urgently. "We've finally got him. I've already spread copies of the most damaging stuff across a bunch of different servers, and put in fail-safes so that if I don't check in regularly, it posts everywhere. Pike will never risk this getting released to the public."

"Maybe," she acknowledged. "Or he could just torture you for the codes. Then he'll kill you."

"There's a happy thought," Peter said, sounding nonplussed. "I thought you'd be pumped. This is exactly what we've been looking for."

Noa sighed. She locked eyes with him and said, "Peter, listen to me. I know you're trying to do the right thing. But honestly, I'm beyond helping at this point."

"No, you're not," he said forcefully.

"I am," she insisted. "Blackmailing him is too risky. Just release the files."

Peter shook his head. "No way. This plan will work."

"I'm not letting him kill you, too." It was frustrating that he didn't seem to grasp how sick she was. He was still convinced there was a way out that didn't involve her dying. *But that's Peter all over*, she thought. *Mr. Glass Half-Full.*

If it hadn't been for him, she probably would have given up a long time ago. After the others were taken, and Zeke died, she hadn't really seen the point in going on. But she'd felt responsible for Daisy and Teo. Peter joined them, and he wanted so badly to make everything better . . . and she was persuaded to let him try.

He couldn't wrap his mind around a world without happy endings. But that's all she'd grown up with.

"I don't want you to risk your life anymore." It was taking an enormous amount of energy just to form the words. "I'm pretty sure I'm dying anyway. I might not survive long enough to get to Boston."

Peter's jaw was set obstinately; she could tell he didn't want to acknowledge the truth in what she was saying. He glared past her, as if Pike himself was standing there. Finally, in a low, fierce voice he said, "This bastard ruined my life. He turned my parents against me. He infected Amanda, killed Cody, and hurt you. Yeah, it would be great to see him go down for all of that. But not if it means you and Amanda die. Those files are going to make him fix you."

Noa closed her eyes. She was too weak to keep arguing. "I'm so damn tired."

"You just need to hold on." Peter gripped her hand. "I'm going to get us through this. I promise."

Pike led the way from the room. Teo was developing a rough sense of the house's layout, which was the main reason he was going along with this weird charade. The more they knew, the better their chances of escaping. Noa had taught him that.

They hadn't passed any outside doors yet, which was a bummer. And all of the downstairs windows were shut. Not that that would stop him. If there was a chance to flee, he had no problem hurling a priceless heirloom through the glass.

But only if they had a real opportunity.

As Pike glanced back, Teo pasted a look of studied nonchalance on his face. They approached the study. Instead of entering, though, Pike kept walking. Teo and Daisy followed in silence, clutching each other's hands.

Pike stopped at the end of the hallway and opened a door. Stepping inside, Teo found himself in a giant media room. A flat-screen TV took up one entire wall.

Pike gestured toward the plush couch facing the screen and said, "Please, have a seat."

He and Daisy settled on the couch. "What, no popcorn?"

Daisy giggled again, and Pike frowned. He picked up a remote and pointed it toward the screen. "This is the recording of a Skype conversation I had last August," Pike said. "Dr. Johnson is the head of Project Persephone."

That explained the grainy quality, Teo thought as the video started to play; clearly this wasn't meant to be blown up to more than life-size. A dumpy middle-aged man in a white lab coat stared back at them. Wisps of reddish hair barely covered his scalp, and the overhead light gleamed off his pate. Occasionally, he blotted sweat from his forehead with a handkerchief.

"Gross," Daisy commented. "He's like my old gym teacher. I wonder if he likes to keep girls after school for 'extra credit.'"

Pike glared at her, but didn't say anything. Suddenly, his voice blared out from the speakers. "I understand your enthusiasm, Ron, but we've been here before."

"It's different this time, sir." The scientist leaned in close enough for Teo to discern individual pores on his nose. "I believe we're ready to move on to phase two."

"Phase two," Teo snorted. "Let me guess. That's the part where you start kidnapping kids and operating on them?"

Pike looked uncomfortable, but he hit the pause button and said, "I received reports like these regularly; mainly, my researchers only told me that the experiments had failed. I assumed they were doing animal testing; I wasn't involved in the day-to-day process. And when I found out what had been going on, entirely by accident, I shut it down immediately."

"So you never visited one of your own labs?" Teo demanded.

Pike squared his jaw. "Of course I did. But the lab I visited—this one, in fact—only used mice and rats as test subjects. I assumed that phase two meant they would be moving up to larger animals."

"They did that all right," Daisy muttered.

"So when did you find out, exactly?" Teo asked. "And how?"

"A few months ago, I was frustrated by the lack of progress." Pike started to pace. "So I decided to review all of the files associated with Persephone, not just the ones passed along to me. When I discovered what had been done, in all those labs I was funding . . . I was horrified." The remorse in his voice sounded genuine as he continued, "I'm a parent myself. I never would have agreed to experimenting on children."

"Not even if it might save your daughter?" Daisy demanded.

"Not even then," Pike said firmly. "Unfortunately, I had established a bonus program; the first researcher to hit certain benchmarks would receive an enormous amount of money. Because as you saw last night"—he gestured toward the door—"Ella doesn't have much time left. The thought that we might discover a cure, but too late to save her, haunted me. In retrospect, that might have been a mistake. In order to receive the bonuses, Dr. Johnson flagrantly violated dozens of international laws. So yes, to some degree, I suppose I am to blame. But he was not following my orders."

Teo stared at Pike, trying to figure out if he was for real. He'd spent so long despising this guy; the way Noa and Peter had described him, he'd pictured some sort of arch-villain, complete with a cat and an evil laugh.

Instead, it sounded like Pike hadn't meant for anyone to get hurt. *Is that possible?* Noa and Peter had never met Pike. In fact, they had no hard proof of his involvement; that's why they'd been so desperate to get the information off those hard drives.

What if they'd been wrong about him all along?

"We've been chased for months," Daisy interrupted. "By guys with guns. Are you going to lie and say you didn't know about that, either?"

"Those were my men," Pike said earnestly. "But my orders were clear; none of you were to be harmed, under any circumstances. And you weren't, were you?"

Teo looked at Daisy. There was uncertainty in her eyes, and he could tell she was thinking the same thing he was. Everything Pike was saying made a kind of crazy sense.

"So you're the good guy," Daisy snorted. "But everyone who works for you is an asshole."

"I know it's difficult to believe. But if we'd gotten to you sooner, you would have been brought here completely unscathed." Pike opened his arms wide. "I would have showed you this video, and explained everything, just the way I'm doing now."

"So no operating tables?" Teo asked dubiously.

"Of course not."

"Friends of ours were taken," Daisy interjected. "By your men in Santa Cruz. What happened to them?"

"That was . . . regrettable." Pike appeared genuinely

downcast. "But all of those teenagers have been released, and given enough cash for a fresh start."

Teo frowned. Pike sounded sincere; but Remo, Janiqua, or any of the others would have tried to get in touch with them. There was no way they would have just taken the cash and left.

Unless they thought that Noa had been killed at the compound in Santa Cruz. And maybe after what happened there, they decided to steer clear of the other units. Given the circumstances, he might have done the same thing.

"Please, can we continue?" Pike said pleadingly. "There's not much more."

"I don't understand a word coming out of this guy's mouth," Teo complained. The way he'd learned to view the world was being turned upside down, and listening to a bunch of science jabber was only making it worse. "What's the point?"

"You'll see," Pike said. "Just watch."

The image of the researcher abruptly vanished, replaced by a close-up of three mice in a cage. One was tearing around like he'd been given uppers. Another sucked at the water bottle like its life depended on it, and the third was chowing down on a bowl of food in the far corner. The scientist droned on about senescent cells and spontaneous healing. Daisy rolled her eyes and said, "Seriously? You know I dropped out of school in eighth grade, right?"

Pike dialed down the volume. "Maybe I should explain it. These mice"—he pointed at the screen—"were part of an experiment to use thymuses to boost t-cells."

"Yeah, that's not any clearer," Teo said sardonically.

Pike cleared his throat, then said, "Basically, they were given a section of a human organ—a thymus. The thymus produces cells that keep you from getting sick. Does that make sense?"

"Sure," Teo said.

"We're not idiots," Daisy grumbled, glaring at him.

"All right then." Pike ran a hand over his jaw, then continued, "The thymus stops working when you're a teenager. Basically, after that, you have a limited number of cells to fight infections. That's why people get sicker as they get older. When you're young, your body is even strong enough to fight off cancer cells."

"So you gave these mice a new thymus," Teo said, suddenly understanding, "because you thought it might make more of those good cells. And that would stop people from dying from something like PEMA."

"More or less." Pike nodded. "At least, that was Dr. Johnson's theory. Initially, he was simply trying to slow the progression of the illness. But these results got him very excited. The mice were infected with a variety of different diseases, any of which should have killed them. And yet they remained extraordinarily healthy. Even their cuts healed at several times the normal rate."

Teo stared at the screen, focusing on a mouse that was frantically stuffing its mouth with food. He swallowed hard. He'd seen Noa eat like that, when she thought no one was looking.

"But here's what I really wanted you to see." Pike pressed another button, and the image whirred forward at several times the normal speed. The screen went black, then snapped back to the mouse cage. "This was taken three months after the initial surgery."

Teo stared at the screen. One of the mice was lying on its side, struggling to breathe. "Where are the other two?" he asked, dreading the answer.

"Dead," Pike said curtly. "The healing process reversed itself. Their bodies started to attack the thymus, and their systems shut down. And this," he said, fixing them both with a grave expression, "is exactly what's going to happen to your friend Noa if you don't help me find her. Unless we remove that thymus, it will kill her."

"Man," the motel desk clerk said, holding the bill up to the light and squinting at it. "Is this thing real?"

"Nope, made it in my basement," Peter replied with a nervous laugh, silently cursing Mr. Shapiro. The emergency cash fund had been a roll of hundred-dollar bills, which unfortunately attracted a lot of attention in a small town like this one. "Figured I'd better not put it in the vending machine."

The guy laughed. "Hell, it probably wouldn't work anyway. Damn thing barely takes a single."

"I'll bet," Peter said with a grin. He was sweating bullets; hopefully the guy would chalk it up to the humidity. "Can you break it for me?"

"Sure." The guy wasn't much older than Peter, pimply faced and dressed in a Metallica T-shirt and jeans. "I'll try to find some crisp ones for you, so you don't have to iron them out first."

Peter laughed again, then wondered if he was overdoing it. The guy didn't seem to notice, though. He slid the hundred under the cash drawer, then started sorting through bills. "All right, I got a couple nice, crisp fives, that should do you. Okay if I give the rest in twenties?"

"Sure!" Peter said with enthusiasm. That got a raised eyebrow, but hell, at this point he was already going to be remembered.

A TV sat behind the counter, turned toward the clerk's stool. The volume was off, but as he watched, the scene from Loki's compound flashed on-screen. A second later, those same photos of him and Noa, with the headline: NO LEADS ON HOMEGROWN TERRORISTS.

He swallowed hard, praying the kid wouldn't choose that moment to turn around.

"Here you go," the guy said, handing him a thick stack of bills. "Let me know when you're making some more of those hundos, I sure could use a few."

"Thanks," Peter said brightly. "See ya."

"Hey." The guy leaned across the counter on his forearms. "You famous or something?"

Everything inside Peter turned to jelly. "Who, me?"

"Yeah, I gotta say . . ." The kid pointed at him. "I'd swear I know you from somewhere."

"Oh," Peter said, slowly backing toward the door. "I get that a lot. People think I look like Matt Damon."

The kid's brow furrowed. "Nope, that's not it." He cracked his gum, then shook his head. "Man, it's killing me. It'll come to me, though."

"Great," Peter said, his heart hammering. "Let me know when you remember."

"Sure thing," the kid said, already turning back to the TV.

Peter had to force himself not to run back to the motel room. When he got there, Noa was still lying on the bed. "What's up?" she asked blearily.

He raced around, packing up their things. "We gotta get out of here. I think the desk clerk recognized me."

"Crap," Noa groaned.

"I know."

"Um, Peter?" she said.

"Yeah?"

She'd pushed herself up on her elbows. "We've got another problem."

"Fantastic," he muttered, winding up the power cable for the laptop and stuffing it in his pack. "What now?"

"I can't see."

"What?" He stopped dead and turned to face her.

Noa's eyes looked normal, but her pupils were fixed on a spot to his right. "I closed my eyes while you were gone. And when I opened them again, they just . . . I don't know. I think I've gone blind."

PART THREE

FIGHT

CHAPTER TWELVE

Daisy flipped through another magazine, then tossed it aside. Who knew that being held prisoner by an evil mastermind would be so damn boring. Moodily, she plopped back down in the window seat.

After showing them the video three days earlier, Pike had announced that considering their ages, he was uncomfortable with them sharing a bedroom. So he'd separated them. They'd protested; Teo actually took a swing at one of the guards, and had to be pretty much dragged from the room.

She'd tried to run, but they'd grabbed her, too. Since then, she'd been locked up in the original bedroom they'd shared. Three times a day, her guard escorted her down to the dining room. It was so freaking surreal: She and Teo were seated across from each other at the fancy table, being served amazing food on real china. But they couldn't talk, not really; not with Charles Pike hovering over them like an anxious hen. Sometimes, it felt like she'd stumbled into one of those fairy tales where the princess was held captive in a tower.

At every meal, Pike asked if they'd reconsidered his offer: Hand over Noa, and he'd let them leave.

And each time, they told him to go to hell.

He was persistent, though. Asked all sorts of questions about how the units had coordinated with one another, how Peter and Noa communicated. She knew all about the online message boards, but there was no way she was sharing that information.

Daisy lay awake at night fantasizing about a classic Noa rescue attempt. The door to her room would suddenly burst open. Pike would shake uncontrollably as Noa or Peter tased him. She and Teo would laugh as they ran across the lawn hand in hand, alive and free. . . .

But that would only have worked months ago, when Persefone's Army was still up and running. Noa and Peter alone . . . they could barely save themselves. And if she did contact them, they'd feel obligated to try, which would play right into Pike's hands. The only conceivable reason he was keeping them alive was to act as bait.

She had to believe that Noa and Peter would find something on those damn hard drives. And that any day now, a slew of cop cars would come tearing up that driveway. Because if they failed, she and Teo were as good as dead.

So Daisy spent her days waiting. She slept, skimmed old magazines for the umpteenth time (God, what she'd do for a TV), and plotted out exactly what she'd do to Pike if she ever got the chance. Last night they'd been served steak, and she'd actually been given a sharp knife. She'd spent the entire dinner toying with it, trying to get up the nerve to plunge it in his chest. Teo frowned and shook his head slightly, casting his eyes to the guard a few feet away. And he was right; she probably wouldn't be quick enough to do any real damage.

Still, it was so tempting to try. Daisy was going to lose her mind if she stayed cooped up like this much longer. It was funny; she'd spent her life cycling through all sorts of terrible, filthy living situations. If someone had told her it would be worse to be stuck in the nicest bedroom she'd ever seen, with nothing to do but hang out, she never would have believed them.

A tentative rap at the door.

She sat up straight in the window seat and called out, "Yeah? What now?"

The door cracked, and Pike stuck his head in. "I had a thought."

"Awesome," Daisy scoffed. "Those always work out great for me."

"This one, I think you'll like." He smiled tentatively at her, but Daisy wasn't buying it. The other day, she'd almost fallen for his sad dad routine. But three days of house arrest had proved he wasn't a good guy; they'd been kidnapped, even if he wasn't operating on them. Yet. And she didn't doubt that in the end, he'd have them killed.

Pike gestured for her to join him. Daisy hesitated, then flounced off the bed. Leaving the room represented a chance to get away, although separating her from Teo had been smart. Together, they would have busted free by now. But she wasn't willing to leave without him, and she knew he felt the same way. Daisy didn't even know where he was being held; but this little expedition might help her suss it out.

They'd brought her clean clothes: jeans and a polo shirt. Probably the kind of thing a girl like Ella wore every day;

Daisy hated them on principle. But her own clothes were filthy and threadbare, so she'd begrudgingly changed into them. They'd left her combat boots, though, which meant she got to stomp across the room toward him. "Field trip, huh? Yay."

Pike looked perfect as always, dressed in the male equivalent of what she was wearing. As he strode down the hall, she pictured him twirling a tennis racket over his shoulder. The thought made her choke back a laugh.

"Something funny?" he asked, raising an eyebrow.

"I was just thinking you could use a makeover," she said. "Your outfit is pretty lame."

He grimaced, then said lightly, "That's exactly what Ella used to say."

He led Daisy down the narrow flight of stairs that had become all too familiar. She was gradually developing a blueprint of the house in her mind: A right at the bottom of the staircase led to the study, dining room, and media room; left, to the room where he kept his daughter tied up.

He went left. Daisy's footsteps slowed as they approached the door. "We're going in there?" she demanded, stopping in her tracks.

Pike paused with his hand on the doorknob. "Ella's awake today. I thought it might be nice for her to talk to someone her age for a change."

"What, she doesn't have any friends?"

"They stopped coming," Pike said shortly. "There are so many misconceptions about PEMA. Some people still think it's contagious."

Tough to have guests when you're holding teenagers hostage in your house, too, Daisy thought. She really didn't want to go in there. She wasn't a big fan of sick people in general. Her aunt had died young, of cancer; she and her mom spent a lot of time visiting her toward the end. Daisy had hated everything about it: the nasty cafeteria food, that hospital reek, and the way her aunt was more sunken and withered every time they saw her. Until finally, one day, she was gone.

Daisy swallowed hard. Could that really be happening to Noa right now? She hadn't been well since Santa Cruz, that was obvious. But was she dying?

No, she told herself. Pike was just trying to trick them into giving her up.

Pike stepped into the room and motioned for her to join him. Daisy hesitated, but a sharp prod from one of the guards forced her inside. Slowly, she approached the bed.

It was tilted up at an angle. The same girl was lying there, in a different nightgown. Her eyes were open, and she looked less like a doll; she wasn't tied up anymore, either, although there were marks on her wrists from the restraints.

"Who's this?" the girl asked in a tired voice.

"A friend," Pike said brightly.

Daisy snorted, and he threw her a stern look. He pulled a chair up alongside the bed and took one of his daughter's hands. "You look so much better today, sweetheart."

"Well, I feel like crap," Ella muttered.

Daisy laughed out loud. Maybe Ella wasn't so bad.

"This is Daisy," Pike continued gently, like he was speaking to a small child. "She'll sit with you for a bit."

"Whatever." Ella pulled her hand away and closed her eyes.

Pike held the chair for Daisy. She sat down cautiously and folded her hands in her lap. Glanced back over her shoulder: Pike had left a guard posted at the door.

Daisy sighed; she should have known he wouldn't trust

her alone with his precious daughter. She examined the room: A huge hedge rose halfway up the window, blocking the bottom. Even if she managed to distract the guard, she'd have to get past that . . .

"Plotting your escape?"

Daisy snapped her head back around; Ella was regarding her curiously. She debated how to respond. The guard was staring straight ahead, pretending he wasn't listening.

What the hell, she thought. *Worst-case scenario, they take me back to that damn room.* "Yeah," she said. "You got any ideas?"

"Please. I've been trying to get out of here for months," Ella said moodily. "I won't leave until they carry me out."

Daisy was tempted to reply that it would probably be the same for her, but the goon glowered at her warningly. She swallowed hard and said, "So how long have you been here?"

"You mean how long have I been dying?" Ella said wryly. "I don't know. What month is it?"

"May," Daisy said, startled that she didn't know.

Ella put a hand to her forehead. "A year and a half," she finally said. "I got sick around Christmas."

"That sucks," Daisy said sympathetically.

"Tell me about it," Ella groaned. "It wasn't so bad at first, but the last few months . . ." Her voice sounded smaller as she continued, "I haven't been out of this room. Or this bed. And it's like, I close my eyes, and when I wake up, a whole week has gone by."

"Wow. That's awful."

"Plus I'm always afraid it'll be the last time I wake up." A tear rolled down Ella's face. She swiped it away angrily. "I know, I'm a serious bummer."

"You really are," Daisy agreed.

Ella laughed; it was a nice laugh, high and full. Daisy

smiled back at her. "So how'd he talk you into hanging out with me?"

"He didn't give me much of a choice," Daisy said truthfully.

"Yeah, that sounds like my dad. He can be pretty convincing when he wants something." A shadow flitted across Ella's face, then she said, "So do you know Z?"

"Z?" Daisy asked, frowning. "Who's that?"

"The other 'friend' my dad has visit me. He's in a wheelchair."

"Nope," Daisy said, her mind spinning. "Never met him." *Is another kid being held captive here? And if so, why haven't we seen him yet?* The wheelchair didn't sound good, though. Maybe Z was a Project Persephone victim?

"Too bad. I thought you might've, since you're from the same community service program. He's pretty cool." A small smile spread across Ella's face as she added, "And hot, too."

"Yeah?" Daisy said lightly, thinking, *Community service? Yeah, right.* "Then I definitely haven't seen him. I have a boyfriend, though, so it wouldn't matter."

"You have a boyfriend?" Ella's whole face lit up. "Tell me about him."

"Oh, I reall—"

"Please?" Ella wheedled. "I'm so jealous. My boyfriend dumped me as soon as I got sick."

"That's terrible." Daisy looked back toward the window; the top of a guard's head passed by as he made his rounds. She sighed, then said, "His name is Teo, but I call him Teddy."

"That is *so* cute," Ella exclaimed.

"I know, right?" Her enthusiasm was contagious.

"So what's he like?"

Daisy brightened, thinking of him. "He's kind of shy,

but really sweet. He gets really red when he's embarrassed, which is, like, all the time. He'd do anything for me."

Ella sighed. "That must be nice."

"It is." Daisy felt a pang. If she'd known they'd only have that one night together, she would have done things differently.

"Is he a good kisser?"

"The best," Daisy said, feeling herself flush. "Like, he could give lessons."

They both laughed. Daisy felt lighter than she had in months. This seemed almost normal, trading gossip about boys with a girlfriend.

Although this girl had a death sentence hanging over her head. The thought sobered her.

"Oh, crap. You got that look on your face," Ella groaned.

"What look?"

"The 'poor you' look. Trust me, I see it all the time." Ella picked at the blanket covering her legs. "Listen, I know we're not really friends. But can you do me a favor?"

"I guess."

"It's just . . . I know I don't have a lot of time left, no matter what my dad keeps saying. But I don't want to spend it with someone who feels sorry for me. So if you're going to be that way, maybe we shouldn't hang out."

She said it so frankly and sincerely that Daisy was taken aback. Ella gazed openly at her with pale gray eyes, waiting for a response. Daisy cleared her throat and said, "I get it. And to be honest, I don't feel sorry for you."

At that, Ella's eyebrows shot up. "You don't?"

"Are you kidding? I would kill for your hair."

Ella laughed again, and Daisy joined in.

"Hey, you want to see something?" Ella offered.

"Sure." If nothing else, this beat sitting alone in her room, reading an article on smoothies for the umpteenth time.

"It's in the drawer." Ella nodded toward the bedside table.

Obediently, Daisy opened it—and caught her breath. Inside was a hairbrush, a headband, a bracelet, and a few other odds and ends.

Including an iPhone.

Daisy hesitated, her eyes shifting to the guard at the door. He was checking his watch with a bored expression. She quickly grabbed the phone and handed it to Ella.

The sick girl didn't seem to notice her reaction. She was already skimming through the photo albums. "There it is."

She held up the phone. There was a photo of her in a stunning gown, clinging to a tall blond kid in a tuxedo. He looked like the bully in every high school movie ever, but Daisy said politely, "Was that your boyfriend? He's cute."

"Yeah," Ella sighed. She stared at the screen for a minute, then brushed a fingertip along her own image. After handing the phone back, she said moodily, "You can put it away. It's not like anyone calls anymore. I don't even know why I bother keeping it."

"That's too bad," Daisy said, but her breathing had gone shallow. *A phone.* Obviously, there wasn't one in her room; not even a TV, so she had no idea what was happening in the outside world. But with a phone, she could potentially get in touch with Peter and Noa. . . .

Unless that's exactly what they want me to do, she thought with a frown. Was this all some sort of elaborate trap?

Either way, the phone should have GPS; at least she'd be able to figure out where they were. Deciding, she palmed it, then slid the drawer closed. The guard glanced up at the noise and frowned. Daisy gave him her best innocent look and said, "So. Do you watch Real Housewives?"

They spent the next few hours talking about bad TV shows. Before Daisy knew it, Pike had returned. He stood there, beaming at them. "I knew this was a fantastic idea."

"Ugh, Dad," Ella groaned. "Enough."

"I'm going to see Daisy out," he said, bending to kiss her forehead. "If you're well enough tomorrow, should I see if she can come back?"

Like I have a choice, Daisy thought. A shadow crossed Ella's face, but she nodded and said, "Yeah, that would be cool."

"Wonderful."

Daisy gave Ella a small wave. The girl returned it, but her face had already shut down. She turned her head toward the darkening windows.

Outside the door, Pike clapped his hands together. He still looked ecstatic. "So you enjoyed yourself?"

She shrugged, keeping her features composed. "It was fine."

"My daughter is a very special girl," he said seriously. "And she doesn't take to just anyone."

Daisy wanted to retort that Ella didn't have much of a choice, since no one else was stopping by. But that felt unfair. Ella seemed pretty cool. In a different world, maybe they would have ended up as friends, even without the house arrest. Daisy lowered her eyes and asked, "So what's for dinner?"

"Fettuccine Alfredo." Throwing her a look over his shoulder, Pike added, "My men think it's a bad idea to trust you with any more knives."

CHAPTER THIRTEEN

Peter basically carried Noa from the car to their motel room on the ground floor. She'd slipped into one of her deep sleeps, and as he dragged her across the parking lot she mumbled something about a fire monster.

They were at yet another crappy motel, right outside Springfield, Massachusetts. He shifted her weight, struggling to get the key in the lock. Even though she weighed a buck and change, the pressure on his still-aching shoulder brought tears to his eyes.

It was early afternoon; not his favorite time to check into a place like this, when people were still wandering around. But he'd driven seven straight hours, all the way from Buffalo, New York, with nothing but brief refueling stops. And each of those had been stressful as hell. Since he was paying cash, he'd had to go inside and deal with a cashier every time. He'd rushed through the transactions, keeping his hat brim low, avoiding eye contact, terrified of being recognized again. He'd switched out cars twice since leaving Colorado a few days earlier; they were now driving a beat-up Accord acquired at a mall on the outskirts of Utica. Still, he kept expecting to see flashing lights in the rearview mirror.

They'd been lucky; aside from that close call at the motel in Omaha, they'd made it nearly all the way across the country without incident.

For the first couple of days, it seemed like every television he passed had their faces flickering across it. But thanks to a massive chemical plant explosion in Texas, they'd finally been shunted to the media back burner.

Which didn't mean they were safe.

Peter had been tempted to keep driving; they were less than two hours away from Boston. But he wanted to make sure the plan was airtight before walking into the lion's den. And he'd rather face Pike on a full night's sleep.

The key turned, and he forced the door open with his shoulder. Noa's head lolled forward as he awkwardly dragged her across the threshold.

"What's wrong with her?"

Peter twisted his head: A guy filled the open doorway of the neighboring room. Midthirties and burly, he was dressed in jeans and a sleeveless T-shirt that declared, "CHOKE: The Official Drink of the Yankees." He clutched a can of beer in one hand, and a lit cigarette in the other.

"Nothing," Peter said, trying for nonchalance. "Just tired."

"She looks sick," the guy said skeptically.

Noa chose that moment to let out an anguished moan. Fighting to keep the desperation from his voice, Peter said, "We had a late night, and she's got a wicked hangover."

It sounded thin, even to his own ears. Noa's skin looked waxy, and she was panting like a dog left in a car. Definitely not the symptoms of a typical hangover.

The guy took a gulp of beer and said, "Uh-huh."

Turning his back on the guy, Peter maneuvered Noa into the room and dropped her on the bed. She landed lifelessly, like a giant doll. As he went back to close the door, the guy appeared on the threshold.

"What do you want?" Peter demanded, hating that he sounded like a scared kid. But the guy outweighed him by at least fifty pounds, he was covered in tattoos, and the bends in his nose testified to the fact that he was no stranger to fighting.

"I sure do like redheads," the guy said as his eyes roved over Noa. "You mind sharing?"

"That's my girlfriend!" Peter snapped, clenching his fists.

The guy smirked at him. "Yeah? 'Cause she looks roofied."

"Get out," Peter ordered.

The guy sized him up. Peter stood his ground, although inside he was quailing. This guy could toss him aside with one hand, get inside the room . . . and then what? It wasn't like Peter could call the cops on him.

Throwing one last leer at Noa, the guy flicked his cigarette toward Peter, who batted it away, feeling the sear on his palm. "Whatever, dude," the guy said. "I don't get off on that creepy shit anyway."

Sure you don't, Peter thought, relieved when the man stepped back. The guy sucked away at his can, peering at him over the top as he shut the door. Suddenly, his eyes narrowed and he asked, "I know you?"

Peter's heart clenched, but he tried to sound dismissive. "No, you don't."

He slammed the door, locked it, and fell back against it. Noa stirred. Groggily, she opened her eyes and croaked, "What's up?"

"Nothing," he said, going over to her. "Just some jerk. You want something?"

She nodded and closed her eyes again. "Water."

Peter got some from the bathroom, where he found cups wrapped in plastic; a pleasant surprise in a dive like this. Some of the abandoned buildings they'd camped out in were nicer than the motel rooms. He'd considered going back to those, but at least here the door locked, and there was a bed. He didn't like the thought of dragging a semiconscious Noa into an abandoned slum; if they were attacked, there would be nothing he could do.

He brought the water to her. Noa gulped it down quickly, then fell back against the comforter. "Ugh," she said. "This place smells even worse than the last one."

"Well, we're almost there," Peter said. "No more motels after this."

"World's worst road trip, huh?" Noa commented.

Peter pulled off the ball cap and swiped a hand over his head: His hair was already longer, he should have remembered to take the shears from the Shapiros' house. "Yeah, that's pretty much become our specialty."

The corners of Noa's mouth tweaked up and her body started shaking; he tensed, thinking she was having another seizure. It took a beat to realize she was laughing silently.

"Glad you're enjoying yourself," he said moodily. "Meanwhile, I get to do all the driving and deal with potential rapists. Man, that never gets old."

"Sorry, Peter," Noa said soberly.

Peter waved a hand, feeling guilty. She was clearly in

enormous pain, and her vision still hadn't returned. She had to be scared as hell. But she hadn't complained once. "Don't be. None of this is your fault."

"I'm a little hungry," Noa confessed after a minute.

"Yeah? That's probably a good sign." Peter's eyes felt sore and gritty; all he wanted was to plop down on the bed and drift off for the next day or so. Instead, he dug a power bar out of his pack and placed it in her hand. "Here."

Noa ate it lying down. Between bites, she said, "Stop staring at me."

Peter started; how could she tell? "Sorry. I'm just zoning out. I'm pretty wiped."

"So get some sleep. I'm guessing we're sharing a bed?"

"'Fraid so. The presidential suite was booked."

"Then come here." Noa shifted sideways to make room for him. Peter pulled off his sneakers and eased onto the bed. They lay there in silence while she finished eating. When she was done, she tossed the wrapper to the floor.

"That'll probably be there until sometime next year," Peter commented, "based on what I've seen of the maid service."

"Not exactly four star, huh?" Noa teased.

"Not even one star." Peter closed his eyes.

He was surprised a minute later when she took his hand. Noa gave it a squeeze and said, "Thanks. For everything."

"Stop that," he grumbled.

"Stop what?"

"Acting like every conversation we have is going to be the last one. It's getting old."

A long pause, then Noa said, "I know I've been . . . difficult the past few months."

"You've always been difficult," he remarked. "I'm used to it."

The old Noa would have punched him in the arm for

that. She settled for digging her nails into his palm. "Ow!"

"You deserved it."

"Are you really not going to let me sleep?" he groaned.

"You have to let me go, Peter," she said softly. "Just call Pike and post the files. I've changed my mind. I don't want him to get away with all this."

"Well, that's too damn bad," he said, drawing his hand away. "Because we're following my plan now. We're going to rest up here, get our strength back. Then I'll call Pike and have him meet me at Back Bay station during rush hour. It'll be crowded, and there are lots of ways in and out; he won't be able to cover all of them. I'll show him what we've got, and explain that if anything happens to me, it'll all be released online. We won't give him a choice: He'll be forced to help you and Amanda."

A long beat, then Noa said, "Wow. You came up with a plan."

"Well, I kept waiting for you to do it, but you decided to sleep instead," Peter said. "And we want this to be over, right?"

"Yeah," Noa said. "Definitely."

Peter watched her eyes move sightlessly back and forth. Her brow was creased. "What?"

"It's just . . . risky."

"I didn't say it was perfect," Peter grumbled. "If you have a better suggestion—"

Noa sighed. "I wish I did. It feels wrong, sending you in there."

"Because you don't think I can handle it?" Peter asked, bristling.

"Of course you can," Noa said, sounding surprised. "It's just . . . all this started because of me. I hate that you have to confront him alone."

The fact that she trusted him to handle this meant more than she knew. His parents always acted like he was a liability. Before she got sick, Amanda sometimes treated him like he was a difficult child. Even Cody had acted like he was an occasionally pesky younger brother.

Of course, back then, they might have been right. But things were different now. *He* was different now.

Noa pressed balled fists to her eyes and whispered, "Dammit. Why couldn't my eyes have held out for just a little longer?"

Tentatively, Peter reached for her. She shifted closer and tucked her head against his shoulder. For a second, he flashed back on their kiss. It seemed silly now, that he'd thought they could ever be more than this. Because this was enough. He'd trust her with his life. But not his heart; both of their hearts belonged to other people, and it was too late to change that.

"If I could take you with me, I would," he murmured.

"I know." Noa shook her head. "This is so frustrating. So what do I do, just wait here?"

"In this dump? Hell, no." Peter had already thought that through, too; the main benefit of all the dreary hours spent driving was that he'd had plenty of time to pick apart every facet of this plan.

There were still a dozen ways it could go wrong, but he was trying not to dwell on those. "I got in touch with Luke, from the Northeast division. They have some sort of safe house in South Boston. I'll drop you there first."

"So I can be babysat," she said darkly.

"It shouldn't take long. Couple hours, and I'll be back for you." Watching her, Peter bit his lip. He just hoped it wasn't already too late. In a way, it was good she couldn't see herself. Noa looked so much sicker than she had in Colorado; her skin was practically translucent, and he could see the blue lines of her veins through it. There were deep, dark pouches under her eyes, and there was an ashy quality to her, as if she was slowly turning to sand and drifting away.

"What?" she demanded.

"Nothing."

"Why don't I believe you?"

"Because you have some serious trust issues." Peter held up his hands to fend her off as she halfheartedly batted away at him. "Easy! My arm is still sore."

"If I can see when I wake up, you're in big trouble."

"Great," Peter said, turning over on his side. "Do your worst. Just wait until I've slept for about a day and a half, 'kay?"

Teo took a deep breath and checked the ground below for guards; he'd been timing their sweeps, and had a pretty good sense of their patterns. Still, the last guy had been off by a minute, which was worrisome.

If one of them happened to look up . . .

He checked the clock above the mantel: 2:15 p.m. Which hopefully allowed him some time. The first few days of captivity, his guard would pop open the door randomly. But when he always discovered Teo sitting there with an innocent expression on his face, he'd frown, then shut it again.

The past two days, his guard only came in to escort him to meals; so if luck held, he'd be left alone until 6:15, when it was time for dinner.

The next patrol would be coming by any minute now. So he'd better get moving.

Gathering himself, Teo hauled his body up and out the narrow bathroom window. He fought the urge to look down; a fall would definitely kill him. He inched along the narrow ledge, finding the footholds he'd identified on two previous attempts.

This time, he planned to make it all the way to the other side of the house. He'd already checked the bedrooms over here: No sign of Daisy. Hopefully they hadn't moved her to another floor.

Using his fingertips, Teo found gaps in the roof tiles and hauled himself up. Swinging a hammer to bust through drywall was finally paying off; no way he would have been strong enough for this a few months ago. But now, he hauled his body weight onto the roof with relative ease. The healing cut on his arm throbbed painfully, but he'd bound it tightly with surgical tape. Hopefully it wouldn't open again.

As soon as his feet found a purchase, he scrambled up and flipped over on his back, gasping. Teo allowed himself a minute to catch his breath. Then, trying to block out the knowledge that one careless step would result in a death plummet, he eased up the steep slope.

From the top of the roof, he could see past the dense forest that entombed the property. There was water on three sides; Pike's mansion was on some sort of peninsula, which wasn't great news. The shore looked rocky, and there were whitecaps far out on the waves. The sun was descending on the opposite side of the house, which made this the East Coast. But they could be anywhere from Maine to Florida, and he wouldn't be able to tell the difference.

Probably not Florida, he amended; it wasn't that warm out. Seventy degrees in the daytime, cooler at night. This was May, so that would be normal in the Northeast somewhere.

Way to narrow it down, he thought disconsolately.

A guard passed by on the lawn below; Teo ducked his head. He counted out a full minute before checking again;

the guy was rounding the corner of the house.

Teo felt shaky: He shook his hands to loosen them up. This was insane. Even if he figured out which room Daisy was in, he had to pray that her guard was also stationed outside, and that her window would be open. And after that, they had to get through the house, past all these guards . . . and then what?

Don't give up, a little voice in his head insisted. *Find Daisy. You'll figure out the rest later.*

Teo inched down the opposite side of the roof, lowering himself along the shingles. His toes finally hit the gutter, and he paused, bracing himself. This next part was where it got truly dangerous. He had to trust that the gutter would bear his weight, and that there would be a ledge below for his feet.

He eased onto his belly and peered over the other side. At the sight of the fifty-foot drop, his insides clenched. With effort, Teo forced his gaze higher. There it was: a ledge, identical to the one outside his bathroom window. If he was careful, he should be able to make his way along the second story without too much trouble.

Teo drew a deep breath and lowered himself down. A panicked moment when his right foot slipped off the ledge, followed immediately by the left. He dangled by his arms, legs scrambling frantically. He could feel his fingers slipping, his grip starting to give. The gutter groaned, the sound unbearably loud. . . .

His right foot found the ledge. Panting, he got his left foot braced and clung there, too terrified to move. Sweat coursed down his face, fogging his vision. He blinked it away.

"Teddy?"

Startled, he nearly lost his grip. Daisy was staring at him through the window, her mouth slack with shock.

"Oh my God!" she said in a loud whisper, throwing the window open.

"Hey," he said weakly as she grabbed him and dragged him inside. He winced as his shins butted the windowsill. "Easy."

"What the hell are you doing? You could've fallen!"

"I was looking for you," he said. Taking in their surroundings, he realized this was their original room. He should have thought to check here first. Lucky thing he stumbled upon it, almost literally.

Daisy had her arms crossed over her chest. Her blue eyes blazed with fury as she hissed, "What were you thinking?"

"It's a rescue attempt," he said defensively. "We're getting out of here."

Daisy's face softened, and she threw herself into his arms. Teo buried his nose in her hair and inhaled deeply.

After a minute, Teo forced himself to pull back. The clock on the bedside table read 2:45. "We don't have much time. How many guards do you have?"

"Just one," she whispered. "But he's pretty big. And he's always got a gun."

"My guy, too." Teo dropped onto the bed for a minute, his mind racing. *Maybe if we could overpower him, and get the gun. . . .*

"I have something to show you," Daisy said excitedly. She dropped to a crouch and felt around under the mattress. Then she dug out an iPhone and handed it to him, a victorious expression on her face.

"Where did you get this?" he asked, dumbfounded.

"Long story. It works, but the battery only has a few hours left." The words came out in a rush. "I was going to call Noa, but I was worried they might be tracking it."

Teo turned the phone on. The screensaver was a young girl; it took a second to recognize Pike's daughter, back when she was healthy. He frowned. "This is hers?"

"They haven't missed it yet, but they probably will soon. What should we do?"

Daisy sounded so hopeful, like she had every faith in him. Teo swallowed hard. He opened up the map app; in seconds, it zeroed in on their location. "Kennebunk, Maine," he said softly. He enlarged the map, getting a clearer view of the property. There was one road on and off the peninsula. But if they cut through the woods to the right, there was a state highway two miles down. And past that, a town. If they could only get there . . .

"We can't call Noa," he said decisively. "You're right, this might be a trap. And I don't want to risk it."

Daisy visibly deflated, her shoulders drooping. "Yeah, okay. But then what do we do?"

"I have another idea," Teo said slowly. Peter had established protocols in case they ever got separated. He'd repeatedly made Teo memorize them, a fact he was overwhelmingly grateful for now. "Keep an eye on the door, this should only take a minute."

It took time to access the website since the wireless signal kept dropping out. Cursing, Teo navigated as quickly as he could, entering the password for The Quad. He wasn't nearly as adept at this as Peter or Noa; hell, he'd never held a smartphone before in his life.

"Hurry!" Daisy hissed. "I think he's coming!"

Teo quickly tucked the iPhone back under the mattress. He'd sent the message; now they just had to pray that the right people saw it, and decided to respond. Long odds, but it was the best chance they had of getting out of here.

The knob turned. Daisy squeaked as Teo threw himself under the bed.

Peering out, he could see the guard's combat boots step

inside. "Everything okay?" he rumbled.

"Fine." Daisy's voice was a little shaky, but hopefully the guy wouldn't register it. "Why?"

"Thought I heard something."

"Oh, that was just me singing. I do that when I'm bored."

A long beat. Teo held his breath, praying that the guard wouldn't decide to investigate further.

"Pike wants you," the guard finally intoned.

"Great," Daisy said brightly. "Right now?"

"Yeah, now," the guy said with irritation. "Let's go."

The door closed behind them. Teo mentally counted out five minutes. His whole body felt sore and shaky, both from the exertion of climbing over the roof, and from nearly getting caught.

But he had to get back before his guard realized he was missing.

He crawled out from under the bed and went to the window, raising the sash to check below. He didn't know how often guards patrolled this side of the house; he'd just have to chance it.

He was about to climb out when he caught movement in his peripheral vision. Ducking back down, he watched three guards round the corner.

Two guards, he amended a moment later. They were flanking someone smaller and leaner. Based on the formation, it looked like they were escorting him somewhere: Another prisoner? The smaller man limped slightly, and paused frequently as if he were in pain. The guards seemed impatient, yanking on his arm if he stopped for long.

Teo frowned. Even though he couldn't see the prisoner's face, there was something familiar about him. Maybe someone from one of the homeless camps he lived in? But what would he be doing here?

He couldn't worry about it. If anyone answered their SOS, his sole priority was to get Daisy out safely. The other prisoner, whoever he was, was on his own.

Peter awoke to find Noa standing up facing the window.

"Hey!" he said, scrambling up. "What's wrong?"

"What's that bright light?" she asked, pointing at the flimsy curtains. A rectangle of light was diffused through them. Peter walked over and opened the curtains slightly to peek out. Storm clouds had rolled in, darkening the sky. Steel columns were sunk into the edge of the motel's parking lot, supporting an enormous screen that faced their room. "There's a billboard over the highway, one of those electronic ones. Can you see it?"

"Kind of," she said. "I can see the glow."

"Your vision must be coming back!"

"A little. But you're still just a big blur."

"Well, that's a relief." Peter cleared his throat. Noa should have been turning cartwheels, but she looked despondent. "This is good though, right?"

"I guess," she said. "It's weird. I feel totally fine, my chest stopped hurting. But I still can't really see." Noa turned in a slow circle, then shook her head. "Just shapes, mostly. That's the bed over there, right?" She pointed.

"Yeah."

"Okay." She breathed out hard. "God, I really hope it's coming back."

"Me too." Peter watched as she edged back toward the bed, groping with her hands before carefully sitting down. "So you want to get more sleep?"

Noa shook her head. "I'm not tired anymore. I feel really awake, actually."

"Great." Peter tried to sound enthusiastic, but he was still utterly wiped out. It was a little after 5:30 p.m.; he'd only slept for a few hours.

"Can you show me some of the stuff you found on Pike?"

"Sure," he said. "Just let me eat something first."

"I'm hungry, too," she said tentatively.

"Yeah? So maybe you are getting better!"

"Maybe," she said doubtfully.

Judging by her tone, she wasn't in the mood to discuss it. Peter shambled across the room and grabbed the laptop out of the pack, along with a couple of power bars.

"Ugh." Noa wrinkled her nose after taking a bite. "So sick of these things."

"Yeah, I know." Peter choked down the bite he was chewing. The bar was stale, and had a chemical aftertaste. He'd mostly grabbed cans of food from the Shapiros', but no can opener. And they had no way to cook beans anyway. Shortsighted; he should have gone for the cereal. "I can try and find something else, if you want. Maybe there's a vending machine."

"That's okay." She polished hers off. "Tell me what you found."

Peter powered up the laptop. He'd saved the files that looked most promising to the desktop. Clicking open a jpg, he explained, "This has the earliest date stamp. It's a picture of Pike with a bunch of researchers. I think they probably took it close to when Project Persephone first started."

"Are any of them named?" she asked.

Peter looked at her: She was sitting bolt upright, an eager expression on her face. "Yeah. Dr. Jeremy Holmes, Dr. Ronald McCall, Dr. Ray Forbes—"

Noa inhaled sharply and said, "Is there a Monica Forbes, too?"

There was only one woman in the photo. Peter read the name: "There's a Monique Forbes. According to this, she and Ray were project heads."

"Ray and Monique," she said resignedly. "They changed their names to Roy and Monica. I was kind of hoping that Cole had lied about them, but it turns out he was right. They sold us out."

Peter put a hand on her shoulder and squeezed it. "Maybe not totally. I saw some other files with their names. Want me to pull them up?"

She nodded. He leaned over and tapped some keys, instituting a search for "Forbes." He had to click through a few files before finding what he was looking for. "Here it is." He drew a deep breath; this was the file that had been churning through his mind for days, the one he'd mulled over endlessly as the miles slipped past.

"What does it say?" Noa asked impatiently.

He hesitated; based on what little she'd said about the couple, they'd served as sort of stand-in parents for her. And what he was about to say would probably destroy that image entirely. "It explains how they caused PEMA."

"What?" Noa's eyes widened. "They did it intentionally?"

"I don't think so." Peter shook his head, forgetting that she couldn't see the gesture. "This talks about developing brand loyalty, marketing shampoo and makeup to teens. Nothing about any disease. I think it was an accident."

He'd spent every spare moment poring over documents from the decrypted files while Noa slept. He'd made copies of copies, and scattered them across servers on nearly every continent. Outside Buffalo, he'd left the actual server drives in a bus station locker, then mailed that key to a PO box that belonged to the one person left who he trusted: Luke, the head of the Northeast chapter of Persefone's Army. Luke had rescued him the night he'd stolen the hard drives; they'd only spent a few days together after that, but Peter knew in his gut that he could rely on the kid. He'd enclosed a note detailing what was going on, and explaining what Luke should do if he didn't hear from Peter by the end of the week.

The information in these files had weighed heavily on him. After all this time, he'd finally gotten the answer to how PEMA came into existence, and why they thought Noa could cure it.

The thing was, now he understood what they meant about ignorance being bliss. Because after everything he'd discovered, the thought of allowing Pike to skate on this was even more galling.

"So what did they do?" Noa pressed.

Peter hesitated, not sure he wanted to burden her with it. This was the first time in days that she was wide-awake and coherent. Would the truth really do her any good at this point?

"Peter," Noa said warningly, "don't you dare try to protect me."

"All right." He blew out a breath of air, debating where to begin. "Well, I don't exactly understand all of it. But basically, your friends were in charge of the research and development team that was trying to get people hooked on Pike & Dolan products. They called it 'the lifetime initiative,' like it was a good thing."

"But they were scientists," Noa said, puzzled. "Doctors. It wasn't their job to sell stuff."

"They were researchers, Noa, working for a big corporation," Peter explained. "They weren't trying to cure cancer, they were trying to figure out a way to make sure that people only bought Pike & Dolan's shampoos. So they came up with some sort of transmission system—prions, which are like a protein combined with a germ."

Noa's brow furrowed. "They intentionally tried to make people sick?"

"Nope, it wasn't like that at all." Peter ran a hand over his head. "From what I can tell, they thought this prion thing would be harmless. It was only supposed to affect the brain's pleasure center, and not even that much. So when people were exposed to it, they'd start associating P&D products with being, like, abnormally happy."

"That's so creepy," Noa said slowly. "They actually put this in the stuff they were selling? Like, toothpaste and everything?"

"Not all of their stuff," Peter clarified. "Mainly in what they marketed to teens. They wanted to start with that group, and get them hooked for life. If it was successful, they planned to go after even younger kids. I found a few files that talked about introducing it into baby products."

Noa shuddered. "That's sick."

"And totally illegal," Peter agreed. "The thing is, all these teen products had already been on the market for years, and the additive was hush hush. So they didn't think anyone would find out. But then, PEMA started." He tilted his head toward the screen. "Your buddies Ray and Monique—or Roy and Monica, whatever the hell their names were—figured out right away that the prion might be responsible. They sent a whole bunch of angry emails to Pike, demanding that he put a stop to the project."

"But he didn't?"

"Not right away. And by the time he did, the Forbes also had proof that the prion didn't do what it was supposed to anyway."

"So everyone who used the wrong shampoo or toothpaste got it?" Noa asked. Her face had gone pale.

"Not everyone. Some people only got a little sick; that's why the government couldn't figure out what was causing it. I found one really twisted memo to Pike from his lawyer.

The guy goes on about how, since the additive was in so many products, the CDC was unlikely to trace it back to a single source."

Noa stared at him. "So PEMA was Pike's fault, all along."

"Yup. And I get the feeling that your friends tried to stop it," he said. "I did a search for them, and supposedly they died in a car crash a few years ago. Pike was at the funeral and everything."

"They faked their own deaths," Noa said slowly.

"Or Pike tried to kill them, but they survived and ran." Peter cleared his throat. "Hell, I can't say I blame them."

"But they had proof, right?" Noa said. "So why didn't they go to the cops?"

"I don't know." Peter shook his head. "Maybe they didn't think they had enough, or they were too scared."

They sat in silence for a few minutes. Noa finally said, "If Roy and Monica knew all this and didn't use it, they must have had a good reason. We could threaten Pike with these files, and he might just laugh in our faces."

"I don't think so," Peter said firmly. "We've got too much proof, more than they had for sure, and we know how to get it out everywhere. Trust me, these files are going to be popping up in Uzbekistan. There's no way he'll be able to quash them all."

"It's a big risk," Noa finally said.

"So is sleeping on this comforter," Peter said, nodding toward it. "But I already did that today."

Noa cracked a grin, and he smiled back at her. There was concern in her eyes, though. "So are you really ready for this?"

"Sure," he said, trying to inject confidence into his voice. "What could go wrong?"

CHAPTER FOURTEEN

"So you really haven't done it yet?" Ella whispered.

"No!" Daisy swatted Ella's arm gently. "What do you think I am, some kind of ho?"

"But you've been together for months." Two bright red dots stood out on Ella's cheeks, and her forehead was flushed. Her eyes sparkled as she said, "I mean, don't tell me you haven't thought about it."

"We haven't exactly been alone," she hedged. This was the third straight day she'd spent with Ella, and she was finding it increasingly difficult to lie to her. But Daisy wasn't a fool. If she spilled what was really going on, Pike might hurt Teo.

God, she hoped he'd gotten back to his room safely. She could throttle him for taking such a risk.

Still, he'd known what to do with the phone. Daisy's eyes shifted to the bedside table. It was hard to believe Ella hadn't realized it was missing yet; every time she was with her, she kept waiting for the girl to ask for it. And when they discovered it was gone . . . at the thought, Daisy went prickly with nerves. She drew a deep breath and forced herself to focus back on what Ella was saying.

"Well, I'd find a way," Ella declared.

Daisy shifted uncomfortably. "How are you feeling?"

Ella laughed shortly and said, "Same as always."

"Well, you look amazing."

"You're such a liar." Ella rolled her eyes. "I know how I look." She plucked at the blanket, the way she always did when the conversation turned toward her illness.

"I thought kids with PEMA were in worse shape," Daisy confessed. "Like, their brains got all mushy and stuff."

"Mine was. Man, you should have seen me last year, I swear my three-year-old cousin knew more words than I did. A few weeks ago, I was even blind for a few days."

"But you seem normal now," Daisy pointed out.

"The doctors said that might happen." Ella shrugged. "You get a good week or two before the very end. Sort of a last gasp."

"Oh," Daisy said, instantly uncomfortable. So Ella would be dead in a week? That totally sucked. She wondered how she'd feel, knowing that her life was almost over.

Of course, it was probably her last week, too. The thought was sobering. The past few days, she'd been lulled into believing that maybe they'd make it out of this place. But unless by some miracle Teo's plan worked, she'd die as soon as Ella did.

They sat there in silence. In spite of everything, Daisy felt sorry for this girl. It wasn't Ella's fault that her dad was such a crazy bastard.

"Hey, can I show you something cool?" Ella said in a low voice.

"Uh, sure," Daisy said, praying it wouldn't be another picture from her iPhone.

"You can't tell anyone," Ella hissed. "It's seriously secret. Like, if-you-told-I'd-have-to-kill-you secret."

"I'd like to see you try," Daisy said with a smile.

"Oh, I can still do some damage. You should have seen me with a field hockey stick," she said wistfully. "Anyway, come here."

Daisy leaned in. Ella pushed herself off the pillows, grunting from the effort.

"You want help?"

Ella waved her off, an expression of intense concentration on her face. She pulled herself up until she was sitting. Ella glanced over at the guard, then shifted slightly to block his view. She tugged down the top of her hospital gown. Daisy's eyes widened: There was a scar there, identical to the one she'd seen on Noa's chest.

"That's why I'm still here," Ella said in a low voice. "At least for now."

"You had an operation?" Daisy asked, trying to sound surprised.

Ella nodded. "They put an extra thymus in me. It's supposed to help my body attack the disease. My dad says that without it, I wouldn't have lasted this long."

Daisy swallowed hard, picturing Noa. "So if it's working, then why are you still . . . you know."

Ella's face clouded over. "I guess there's some sort of problem with it. But my dad says there's a way they could still save me. He's working on it."

Daisy kept her hands clenched in her lap, knowing full

well what Pike was counting on: finding Noa, so he could use her to cure Ella once and for all. She swallowed hard, then said, "Sounds risky."

Ella smiled wanly. "What's it going to do, kill me?"

Daisy tried to smile back, but she'd suddenly gone cold. She glanced at the guard, then said, "So where did the extra thymus thingy come from?"

Ella shrugged. "Some kid who died in a car crash. We were a match."

"That was lucky," Daisy noted, thinking, *Yeah, right.* The perfect match just happened to show up.

"Not for the kid who died," Ella said soberly as she tugged the hospital gown back up. "Poor kid."

She sounded genuinely sympathetic. Daisy flashed back to the faces of all the kids she'd known who'd been sacrificed to save this girl. A rising tide of rage built inside her; she had to fight to quell it.

"Anyway," Ella said obliviously. "I gotta ask you something."

"What?"

Ella looked embarrassed. "It's just . . . I can't find my phone. I haven't seen it since I showed it to you a few days ago."

Daisy's heart stopped. She tried to keep her face blank as she said, "You think I stole your phone?"

"Well, stole is a strong word," Ella said, fingering her blanket. She looked uncomfortable. Her eyes darted to Daisy's blue hair, and she said, "Look, it's cool if you wanted to borrow it. It's just . . . . I need it back. I haven't told anyone it's gone yet."

"What's gone?"

Daisy nearly fell out of her chair. Turning, she discovered

Charles Pike glowering down at her.

"Hi, Dad," Ella said brightly.

"Is something missing?" His voice was calm, but there was an ugly undercurrent to it.

Ella's eyes flicked quickly to Daisy, then back to her father. "No, it's cool. It'll turn up."

Pike leaned forward, his knuckles pressing against the bedding. In a low, threatening voice, he asked, "What's missing?"

Ella shrank back against the pillows, a frightened look on her face. In a small voice, she said, "My phone. But I'm sure—"

"Daisy needs to come with me," Pike said abruptly, straightening.

"But we weren't done—" Ella protested.

"Now."

Daisy slowly got to her feet. Her heart was hammering against her rib cage. She braced to run, but Pike's hand clamped down on her arm. "You should say good-bye," he said sternly. "Ella, I'm afraid this is Daisy's last visit."

Daisy threw Ella a panicked look. Ella's eyes shifted to her, then back to her father. Slowly, she nodded her head. "Okay, Daisy. It was great hanging with you."

Pike started to drag her from the room. "Wait! No!" Daisy cried.

"Do not make a scene," Pike hissed.

When they were nearly to the door, Daisy yanked her arm free and raced back to the bed. In a rush, she said, "Ella. I don't go home after I leave you."

"What?" Ella asked, looking perplexed.

"Your dad locks me in a room upstairs. My boyfriend is here, too. He's holding us prisoner. Why do you think a guard always brings me in and out?"

Pike grabbed her arm again; the guard was rushing to join him.

"That's crazy," Ella said dismissively, but her eyes darted to the guard. "My dad just keeps these guys around for protection."

Daisy had to get the full story out; even if Ella didn't believe her, she should know what was really going on.

"That thymus your dad is trying to get? It's inside a friend of mine. Her name is Noa, and he's going to kill her to give it to you. He's kidnapped other friends of mine and killed them," Daisy said, speaking as fast as she could. "Your dad has been kidnapping runaways for a long time now—probably since you got sick. And his doctors have been doing horrible experiments on them. I've seen it with my own eyes."

Ella stared at her incredulously. "What's wrong with you? Are you crazy?"

"They're going to drag me out of here now," Daisy said, turning to glare at Pike. His expression was unreadable, but the rage in his eyes was clear. "And they're going to kill me. That's why you're never going to see me again."

"Dad?" Ella was regarding her father like he was a stranger.

"I'm so sorry, dear," Pike said soothingly. His face was beet red, and his blue eyes were hard as ice chips. "I had no idea this poor girl was so disturbed. Trust me, I'm going to have a word with the community service people about who they send to us."

"I'm not crazy!" Daisy yelled. The guard grabbed both of her arms and started dragging her away from the bed. "Open your eyes, Ella!"

The door slammed shut behind them. Daisy screamed and kicked and struggled, but the guard was too strong. Pike drew back his hand and slapped her across the face.

The blow snapped her head sideways, and she saw stars. Daisy choked out a sob as Pike leaned in and hissed, "You will pay for that, you little bitch."

He nodded at the guard, then stalked toward his office. The guard dragged Daisy behind him; she fought hard, but he didn't even acknowledge the blows.

Pike held the door for them. Dread blossomed in her stomach as she was hauled inside: That awful man from the plane was standing by the desk. Pike snapped, "Your turn to deal with her, Mason."

Teo had a bad feeling. A few minutes earlier, he'd heard Daisy screaming and yelling, swearing a blue streak. It had definitely been coming from downstairs. He'd had to resist the urge to charge out the door and rush to her aid.

Then, silence. He'd stood with his ear pressed to the door, his whole body tense with fear. If they hurt her . . .

He couldn't stand it anymore. Whether or not help was coming, they had to get out of this house, now. He just prayed it wasn't too late.

It was nearly dinnertime; his guard would be unlocking the door and coming to collect him soon. Tonight, he'd be ready for him.

Teo clenched the clock from the mantelpiece in both hands. It was heavy, made of solid brass. His shoulders ached from holding it—if this took much longer, he might not have enough strength left to swing it.

A click as the door unlatched. It slowly opened.

Teo held his breath. He was standing in the shadows behind the door. It was the usual guy, Baldy. He stood at least six-five, with huge meaty arms that strained the sleeves of his black shirt. Baldy peered around the room, muttering, "Where the he—"

Teo swung the clock forward with everything he had. Baldy's eyes went wide a second before it connected with his forehead. The guard staggered a few steps, then dropped to the ground.

Teo let the clock fall to the floor, gasping from the effort. Baldy's gun was tucked in a holster—hurriedly, he grabbed it. Teo had never held a handgun before, it was heavier than he'd imagined. And he wasn't confident that he'd be able to hit anything with it. But if he was going to get Daisy out, he needed a weapon.

Teo peeked into the hall: empty. Moving silently, he made his way down the corridor, toward the room where they'd been holding Daisy.

But the bedroom was unlocked and empty, and there wasn't a guard in sight. His apprehension built; they hadn't escorted Daisy back to her room. He tried not to imagine all the horrible things that could have happened to her in the past five minutes, all the ways they could have killed her. He needed to get downstairs.

At the end of the hall, he encountered a second staircase. This one was unfamiliar: plushly carpeted, with a polished mahogany banister. The enormous stained-glass windows above it gathered the dying light and fractured it into hundreds of tiny colored fragments. This must be the main staircase: He'd been hauled down a much less impressive one for meals. Teo quickly padded down it, wincing every time a stair creaked. He checked the second floor hall: also empty. *Where the hell is everyone?*

He was starting to despair; Baldy would be coming around any minute now, and he'd sound the alarm. And if all the guards stationed outside rushed into the house, well . . . he didn't like his chances. There were at least a dozen of them, based on the patrols he'd been monitoring. And he didn't even know how many bullets this gun held.

Teo fought to quiet his breathing. He was gripping the gun so hard, his hands shook. In the front hall, he heard voices: more guards, coming this way from the sound of it.

"Christ, I hate these kids," one was grumbling.

"Yeah, me too. I hear they'll be gone soon, though."

"Not soon enough. This little punk gives me any trouble, I'll snap his neck."

A low laugh from the other guard. Teo scrambled back up the stairs, taking them two at a time. They were heading to his room. He'd let them pass; hopefully that would leave the downstairs hall clear, and he'd have a narrow window to grab Daisy and go.

He reached the landing as the first guy came into view over the banister. Teo hustled back down the hall, checking doorknobs: Every room was locked. He got a flash of kids huddled inside each room—but that would be ridiculous, right? Still, why the hell did Pike keep his entire house locked up so tightly? It didn't make any sense.

He had to find a place to hide quickly; they were almost at the top of the stairs.

Teo pressed himself into the shadows and started praying.

Suddenly, the door behind him opened, and he fell backward. Someone grabbed him under the armpits and dragged him into the room. Teo struggled for a second, until a familiar voice hissed, "Quiet!" in his ear.

All the hair on the back of his neck stood up. Teo scrambled to his feet as his savior eased the door shut.

"Zeke?" Teo said disbelievingly. "But . . . you're dead!"

* * *

"I wish I could read these myself," Noa complained.

"Me too," Peter said. "My throat is killing me." He'd been serving as her eyes, reading files aloud for over forty-five minutes. He understood her need to finally know everything, but honestly, he was sick of staring at them. Aside from driving, it was all he'd done the past few days.

Plus, he couldn't stop going over every element of the plan in his mind. Unable to shake the sense that no matter what, it was going to go horribly awry. By this time tomorrow, they might both be dead.

"Sorry," she mumbled, looking crestfallen. "I know it's a drag."

"It's fine," he said, feeling guilty. It wasn't her fault she couldn't see. "Really, I get it. I just need a break."

"Okay." She squinted at the screen, then shook her head with frustration. "I feel so useless. This is torture."

"It'll get better," Peter said encouragingly. "Maybe when you wake up tomorrow, you'll be able to see what a shithole this place is."

"Maybe." She sighed.

Peter rolled his head from side to side to loosen his neck. "I'm still starving. I think I'll go check out that vending machine."

"Get me a Red Bull, if they have them."

"You got it." Peter grabbed his wallet and went to the door. The clouds had thickened, causing night to fall prematurely. A smattering of raindrops were spiking the pavement. He paused, suddenly uneasy; aside from the hum of traffic on the overpass, it was eerily quiet, especially for this time of day. All the other motel doors were shut, the interiors dark. Even the neon sign that proclaimed KNIGHT'S INN: VACANCY had been extinguished.

And the parking lot was filled with dark sedans.

Quickly, he stepped back into the room and locked the door.

"What is it?" Noa asked with concern.

"Time to go," he said, rushing past her. Peter scooped up the laptop and shoved it in his pack. There was a single window in the bathroom. Small, but they could squeeze through. *And then what? How am I supposed to get a blind girl out of here?* He'd figure something out. Peter threw open the window and hissed over his shoulder, "This way! We've got to go, now!"

He was suddenly blinded by the glare of a spotlight. Holding up a hand to shield his eyes, Peter staggered back.

An amplified voice called out, "FBI! Drop your weapons and come out slowly with your hands up!"

CHAPTER FIFTEEN

"Sit," Mason ordered. Daisy tried to bolt backward, but another guard had joined the first, and the two of them formed a human wall. Mason rolled his eyes and said, "Please, Miss Stoia. No need to be impolite."

Daisy's shoulders slumped with defeat; she was trapped in this room. And after what she'd just done, they'd never let her leave alive. She'd just have to pray that Teo's plan worked, and that he was rescued. It was already too late for her. *I'm so sorry*, she thought, tears spiking as she pictured his reaction. Wordlessly, she crossed the room on rubbery legs and perched on the couch farthest from Mason.

He smirked, then came over and sat down next to her, too close. His nose was still swollen, and there were fading bruises around his eyes. Mason examined her with those awful black irises. "Has anyone ever told you," he finally said, gesturing to her hair, "that the blue looks tacky? Shame, because you could be a very pretty girl."

"How's the nose?" she asked defiantly.

"Painful," Mason replied smoothly. "I'm looking forward to having another chat with your boyfriend. Now, then. I understand you took a phone from Ms. Pike's room?"

Daisy kept her mouth shut, lips pressed in a firm line.

"Who did you call?" Pike growled.

"No one," Daisy snapped. "We thought it might be a trap."

"We?" Mason's eyebrows shot up, and Daisy's heart sank. Crap. She'd basically just told them that Teo knew about the phone, too. Still fixing her with his cold, beady stare, he said, "Could someone please escort our other young friend down here?"

One of the guards started talking into a radio as he left the room. Daisy chewed on her lower lip, stealing a glance at the clock. They'd figured it would take at least a day for someone to respond to their SOS, and it had only gone out a few hours ago. By the time anyone showed up to save them, it would be too late. If anyone even came.

"So you didn't call anyone." Mason's eyes narrowed. "But of course, there are other ways to contact people."

Daisy glared at him, refusing to respond.

Pike snorted. "Haven't you learned by now that the police can't help you? It doesn't matter who you contacted. No one is coming."

"Really, Charles," Mason said with a sigh. "If you'd allowed me to supervise your guests, we wouldn't be dealing with this situation in the first place."

Pike glowered at her. "You're right. I should have."

"Well, water under the bridge and all that," Mason said,

waving a languorous hand. "I don't suppose they've been helpful with the Torson situation?"

"We don't know where Noa is," Daisy said obstinately.

"Perhaps not," Mason said, crossing his legs. "But I'm willing to bet you know how to get in touch with her. And Charles has finally agreed to let me use my considerable powers of persuasion."

Daisy shot Pike a murderous look. "You're a monster."

Pike snarled, "I gave you a chance. If you'd just done what I asked, I would have released you."

Daisy snorted. "Yeah, right." Mason had her fixed with a predatory gaze; it felt like he was stripping off layers, carving her up. She repressed a shudder. "You were always going to kill us."

"Not necessarily. I don't like the idea of killing children. Not even when they're a waste of the world's resources." Pike gave her a thin smile.

"Which leads us back to the issue at hand," Mason said. "Either you tell us how to find Noa Torson, or you become expendable. I'm assuming there's some sort of message board?"

Daisy squared her jaw and shrugged. "I don't know. I'm not very good with computers."

"Really? A girl your age? I find that surprising," Mason said.

"We didn't exactly have a computer center in my trailer park," Daisy retorted. "If you know so much about me, you should already know that."

She met his gaze, forcing herself to glare back into the dark pits he called eyes. Was she mistaken, or did he throw her a small smile?

"I believe her," Mason finally said. "She doesn't know."

Daisy released her breath, relieved. "Great. So can I go now?"

"It hardly matters," Pike said dismissively. "The manhunt will pay off soon enough."

"What manhunt?" Daisy asked.

Pike came over and bent low, until his face was inches from hers. Daisy shrank back. Pike's demeanor had completely changed: The kind, caring dad had been replaced by something much uglier. She'd been right, it had all been an act. "Do you think I brought you here, to my home, out of the kindness of my heart? I could have had you killed at any moment." He snapped his fingers.

"So why didn't you?" she demanded, trying to keep the quake from her voice.

"Because once your friend Noa arrives . . . and she will, I can assure you of that . . . she might need some persuading. She's threatened to harm herself before, and I need her alive and breathing. Healthy. So you, my dear, are an insurance policy."

"She won't come," Daisy said.

"She won't have a choice," Pike barked.

"Really, Charles. No need to frighten her." Mason was watching the exchange with what appeared to be amusement.

Pike straightened and stared down at her. His nostrils still flaring, he said coldly, "I only need one of you. Remember that."

Daisy caught her breath. She was done being threatened, done being scared. Tired of pissy old men bullying her. Before she even realized what she was doing, she was on her feet. She lashed out, slapping Pike with everything she had, leaving an angry imprint of her hand on his cheek.

"My, my." Mason shook his head. "I must say, I like this one. Feisty."

Pike's lips twisted with rage. He shoved hard, hurling her back onto the couch. Daisy slammed against the cushions. "You will regret that," he said, emphasizing each word. "And so will your boyfriend."

"They told me you were dead, too," Zeke said with a wan smile. "Hey, where'd you get the gun?"

Teo blinked, still disoriented. Zeke looked almost the same as the last time he'd seen him, three months ago. Except his hair was shorter, and he was pale, as if he hadn't been outside much. "I can't . . . what . . ."

"We can talk about it later," Zeke said authoritatively. "I heard someone scream. Is Noa here?"

Teo shook his head. "No. That was Daisy."

"Daisy's alive, too?" Zeke's face lit up. "Awesome. What about the others?"

"Just us." Teo's mind was still playing catch-up. Zeke was alive, and being held here by Pike, too? How was that possible? He'd seen him on that beach, bleeding out from a gunshot wound. "I thought you died, man. We heard the shots."

Zeke's face went grim. "I thought I had, too. Then I woke up here."

"Why wasn't your door locked?"

"It was." Zeke grinned. "But hell, I was picking harder locks than that when I was a kid. I was just waiting for the chance. When I heard the yelling, I figured this was it."

Teo hesitated. He had so many questions; Zeke showing up like this was beyond strange. In his experience, when something looked too good to be true, it usually was. But

Daisy was still downstairs, and any minute now the guards would discover what had happened to their buddy. "I have to go."

"So let's go." Zeke was scrambling around the room, grabbing things from hiding places: a pack of matches from behind the oil painting over the fireplace, a small wad of cash from the bed frame. "I was going to take off tonight anyway. The guards are on ten-minute shifts, we can get past them if we time it right."

"I still can't believe it," Teo said. This whole thing was too weird; it was like Pike was running some sort of ad-hoc foster home. "I mean, why is he keeping any of us alive?"

"Because he wants to use us. If he gets Noa, he'll torture us in front of her, and force her to do what he wants. We can't let that happen," Zeke said firmly. "We need to get gone, now."

"Three months is a long time," Teo said skeptically. "Why'd you wait until now to try and escape?"

"Dude. You don't trust me?" Zeke stopped dead in the middle of what he was doing and fixed Teo with a wounded look. "Seriously?"

"I don't know, man." Teo shifted uncomfortably. "It just seems kind of . . . convenient."

Zeke stalked forward and drew up his shirt. Teo winced: Zeke's side was a mass of ugly scar tissue. In a low, angry voice, he said, "Up until last week I was still in a wheelchair. So yeah, I figured I'd wait until I could walk before busting out of here."

"Okay." Teo held up both hands placatingly; Zeke looked like he was ready to punch him. "So Pike saved your life and brought you here? That—"

"Doesn't make any sense, I know," Zeke interrupted. "He

spent a couple months asking about Noa, then pretty much just gave up. Did he give you his whole nice guy routine?"

"Yeah," Teo said. "Fed me salmon and everything."

"Well, don't believe him," Zeke growled. "He's an evil bastard."

"No kidding," Teo agreed. "And he's got Daisy."

"All right, then." Zeke crossed to the fireplace and reached up the flue, drawing out a knife.

"Where'd you get that?" Teo asked with awe.

"Steak dinner," Zeke explained. "I've been waiting to use it for a month. Between that and the gun, we've got a shot. Now let's go."

Noa heard a window slam shut, then the sound of Peter scrambling back into the room. He was breathing hard, clearly agitated.

The voice from the bullhorn echoed through her mind. The FBI had found them. They were totally screwed. In a flat voice, she said, "I'm guessing they're in the parking lot, too?"

"You win the teddy bear," he muttered. "Crap. That creepy guy must have recognized us."

Everything felt strange, dreamlike. This was it, she realized. There would be no going to Boston. They'd be arrested, then handed over to Pike. Noa squeezed her eyes closed, then opened them again. The details of the room were still fuzzy; no matter how hard she tried to focus, there were only dark, looming shapes. Like the shadows were slowly slouching toward her. "I really wish I could see."

"Actually, right now I'd trade with you," Peter muttered. A glow appeared to her right: the laptop. She heard him feverishly tapping away at keys. "All right," he said with determination. "I'm reconfiguring the fail-safe passcode. If it doesn't get entered every . . . what do you think, three hours?"

"Sure," Noa said, although it felt like she was far away, staring down at the scene from above. "That works."

The sound of his fingers flying across the keyboard. Noa stared toward the window. It looked like full daylight had blossomed outside the curtains; they were backlit and glowing. "How many cars are out there?"

"A lot," he said curtly.

"So we're surrounded."

"Yup."

As he tapped away, the bullhorn blared, "Leave all weapons behind and come out one at a time."

"They're going to come in if we don't go out," Noa said. For some reason she pictured Star Wars storm troopers, in blank white masks.

"Just one more sec," Peter muttered. "All right, this is good to go. What do you think? Should we go out there?"

"They'll just hand us over to Pike," she said slowly. "And we still don't know if he'll care about the files. He might think he can stifle them."

"Well, we don't really have any other options."

Noa could still barely make out his form, but his agitation was clear. "We have one," she said. "It's risky, though."

"Anything that doesn't involve getting shot by the feds sounds pretty good right about now."

"At the very least, it should give us some leverage." She laid it out for him.

A long beat, then Peter said, "I can tear a lot of holes in that without even trying."

"I know." Noa managed a weak smile. "But I think it's our

only shot. And there's less chance of Pike doing something crazy if everyone's watching, right?"

"I guess. So you're sure about this?" he asked.

"No."

Peter laughed sharply. "All right, then. Hell, you've had crazier plans before."

"And they worked, right?" Noa struggled to sound confident, even though she felt anything but.

"There's always a first time," he mumbled. "You better get down on the floor behind the bed, just in case. Here, I'll help you."

She felt his hand in hers: It was hot, and a little sweaty. Peter carefully led her around the bed. Noa settled down, feeling the press of the frame against her back.

"Ready?" he asked.

"Ready."

Peter gave her hand a squeeze, then called out, "I've got a hostage! If you come in, I'll kill her!"

CHAPTER SIXTEEN

All the anger Daisy had been storing up exploded out of her. She shrieked and lashed out with pure, primal rage, slamming both feet into Pike's gut.

Pike grunted and doubled over. A firm grip on her shoulder; she jerked around. Mason was gazing down at her with an inscrutable look. "I must say, you're only making things worse for yourself."

She shook him off, keeping her eyes on Pike. Like her, his chest heaved from exertion. His eyes were wild, enraged. The mask he'd been wearing for the past week had vanished, leaving behind sheer contempt and fury.

"I'll kill you both myself," he spat, still bent double.

A low chuckle. They both turned their heads. Mason was regarding them with a sardonic smile. "My, my, Charles," he said, sounding bemused. "Undone by a couple of teenagers?"

Pike snarled, "If you'd delivered what you promised, I never would have had to take matters into my own hands."

"Yes, and what a fine job you've done." Mason didn't seem at all perturbed by Pike's crazed demeanor. He shook his head, then added, "A full week, and they haven't told you anything? I'm surprised you waited so long to call me back in."

Pike's jaw was set. "She's yours now."

Mason inclined his head. "Of course."

Daisy went cold. Based on what she'd seen of Mason, she'd honestly prefer to deal with Pike; at least then it would be over quickly. "I told you, I don't know how to get in touch with Noa."

"Oh, my dear girl," Mason sighed. "We've gone so far past that now."

Pike's cell phone rang, the trill incongruously cheerful. He dug it out of his pocket and glared at the screen. Confusion flitted through his eyes. He put it to his ear and snapped, "Yes?"

As he listened, his eyes roved back to Daisy. A slow smile crept across his face.

"Thank you," he said crisply, sounding once again like the guy who'd offered her more salmon. "I'll be there shortly."

"Good news?" Mason asked after he hung up.

"Yes." Pike's eyes were as cold and deep as a frozen sea. "We won't be needing her anymore. I believe the boy will suffice."

"Really?" Mason sounded mildly surprised. "So they've located Ms. Torson?"

"She's in a motel outside Springfield. I'm going there now." Pike checked the enormous Rolex on his wrist. "We should be back soon."

"Well, that is a nice turn of events," Mason said.

Pike was already striding toward the door. At the threshold, he paused and threw a final glare at her. "Clean up this mess before I get back."

The door shut behind him. Daisy gulped in air, then turned to Mason. He was still sitting on the couch, gazing at the door contemplatively. After a moment, his black eyes turned on her. "Well, well," he said. "It looks like I have my marching orders."

Teo crept down the hall after Zeke, who held the gun out in front of him like it was lighting their way. He was the better shot, so Teo had gladly handed it over. In the past, they'd always used Tasers. His fingers were itching for one; it was the perfect way to disable a guy who had at least fifty pounds on you and a hell of a lot more training.

He drew a deep, shuddery breath as they approached the staircase.

"I think she's on the ground floor," Teo whispered. "Probably in Pike's office."

Zeke nodded, keeping his eyes on the stairs. Teo was forced to admit that it felt good, letting someone else take the lead again. Zeke and Noa were made for this sort of thing; he definitely wasn't.

He wondered how Noa would react to the news that Zeke was alive—if she ever even found out. First they had to get Daisy, and slip past a slew of guards. Then, they had to pray that Zeke's escape plan worked.

He wasn't feeling very hopeful.

Suddenly, agitated voices from above; they must have found the guard he'd knocked out. The squelch of radios, and feet pounding down the stairs.

"C'mon!" Zeke said urgently. "Move!"

They raced down the staircase and into the main hall. Without hesitating, Zeke turned left, headed toward Pike's office. Teo followed so closely he nearly tripped on Zeke's heels. God, he hoped he was right. If she wasn't in there . . .

There was a shout behind them. Teo checked back over his shoulder: two guards, less than twenty feet away. Their guns were drawn, and they looked pissed.

"Zeke!" he cried out.

Zeke spun and fired a wild shot toward them; it hit a vase, sending it crashing to the floor. Teo yelped, covering his ears; the gunshot had been loud enough to pierce his eardrums.

The guards started to return fire. They raced through a series of rooms, while bullets ricocheted and sent chunks of wood and other shrapnel flying at them from all sides. Teo kept waiting to feel the hot fire of a bullet piercing his body. Pike's office was down the next hall. They were so close. . . .

A guard stepped out of the adjoining hallway. It was Baldy, and he had an automatic rifle leveled at them. Seeing Teo, his eyes narrowed beneath the ugly bruise on his forehead.

"Drop it," he snarled.

For a second, Zeke wavered; Teo saw the gun shake in his hands. Then slowly, he lowered it to the floor. Straightening back up, Zeke raised his arms in surrender.

"Damn," Baldy said, sounding disappointed. "I was really hoping you'd give me an excuse to kill you."

The battered phone on the bedside table started ringing. Peter looked at Noa: She nodded for him to pick up. The handle was greasy; he'd never held a phone before that actually smelled bad. Wrinkling his nose, Peter placed it an inch from his ear and asked, "Who's this?"

"Peter Gregory?" A man's voice, as smooth and polished as a river stone.

"I asked first," Peter said petulantly. Noa was settled on the floor beside the bed with her knees drawn to her chest, her hair pulled back into a loose ponytail. He still couldn't get used to the red.

"This is Agent Smith."

Peter snorted and said, "Smith, huh? That sounds fake. You're with the FBI?"

"Yes, I am." The man cleared his throat, then said in the same even tone, "I've got some concerned folks out here, Peter. They'd like to know who's in the room with you."

He drew a deep breath, then said, "Tell them I've got Noa Torson."

A long pause, then the man said, "Are you claiming that Noa Torson is there with you against her will?"

"Oh, yeah," Peter said. "I had to keep her drugged the whole time." Which should jibe with what the creep in the next room had told them. He glanced at Noa, who was staring at a spot a foot to his right. Everything depended on whether or not he could sell this guy on their story.

"We don't want anyone to get hurt, Peter."

"I've got some demands," Peter blurted, talking over him.

A long beat, then the man said, "What kind of demands?"

His voice sounded weary, and for a second Peter felt for him. It must be a pretty sucky job, trying to reason with lunatics who took people hostage, then asked for planes and cash. *This should come as a pleasant surprise for him*, he thought with a smirk.

"I want to talk to Charles Pike," Peter said decisively. "In person."

A longer pause. Incredulity in Smith's tone as he asked, "The businessman? Why?"

"Just get him," Peter ordered. He checked the clock; it was just before seven. If Pike was in Boston, it would take about two hours to get here. "Tell Pike that if he's not here by nine p.m., I'll start releasing files."

Let him chew on that, Peter thought smugly. Noa was grinning at him. In spite of everything, he felt a little giddy.

"Peter," Smith said calmly, "you've got to understand, I don't even know if I'll be able to get in touch with Mr. Pike, never mind get him to come here. If you would just—"

"Oh, he'll come," Peter said with certainty. "Trust me, you're not going to believe how fast he gets here."

He hung up the phone, cutting off Smith's sputtered protests.

"Good job," Noa said approvingly. "They definitely won't come in now."

Peter sank down on the floor beside her, picturing Smith and his FBI buddies scratching their heads as they tried to figure out what the hell was going on. He was struck by a flash of inspiration. "I've got an idea," he said, pulling the laptop onto his crossed knees.

Noa cocked her head. "What are you doing?"

"You'll see." It only took a minute to find what he was looking for: A local search quickly produced the name of the company that owned the billboard. Their home page proudly declared, "Reach over 20,000 Mass Pike drivers/day!"

Peter let out a low whistle. "Wow, that's a lot of people."

"Care to fill in the blind person?" she said, an edge to her voice.

"The billboard," he explained. The website's firewalls were pitiful, so weak that just a small nudge tipped them over; after all, who would bother hacking into a billboard company? As he sifted through code, trying to find the database where they stored images, he explained, "It faces the parking lot. I'm thinking Pike might need a little incentive to get here."

"That's brilliant!" Noa said with enthusiasm.

"Of course it is. It was my idea."

Noa swatted his arm, but she was still grinning. "So what should we show our friends?"

Peter sifted through the icons on the desktop, although he already knew which one he wanted to feature. "We start with the one from Senator Braun."

"Good choice," she said approvingly. "Hey, can I press enter?"

"Be my guest." He finished setting the upload, then handed her the laptop.

Her hand hovered over the keyboard for a minute, then she tapped the right key. Noa sat back, looking pleased with herself.

"Got it on the first try. Not bad," he said.

"It's getting better," Noa said, sounding relieved. She leaned in until her face was inches from the screen. "The letters are fuzzy, but I can make them out. Black on white must be easier."

"So you want to check it out?"

Her smile broadened. "Hell yeah."

Together, they crept over to the window on their hands and knees. Peter lifted up a corner of the curtain, and they peeped out, careful to keep the tops of their heads below the ledge.

Peter had to restrain himself from crowing. The email he'd chosen blared across the billboard in enormous letters:

From: Sen. Greg Braun
Sent: Thursday, November 1, 12:10 PM

To: Charles Pike
Subject: no more screwups

Chuck—

My guy in the FBI handled it, but it wasn't easy. That was a massive screwup—how the hell did a couple of kids stumble across one of your labs? People are starting to ask questions, and I can't take another risk like that. So get your house in order—next time, you're on your own.

Greg

Peter could see heads turning toward it, a few people pointing up. He dropped back down and pounded the floor with glee. "Yes!"

"He's not going to like that," Noa observed. Smiling at him, she said, "That's just the kind of thing /ALLIANCE/ would do."

"I know," Peter said ruefully. "I was just thinking how much I miss it." They were hackers, after all, and kids. They were supposed to be pulling pranks like this, not running around trying to avoid being chopped into pieces.

"Me too," Noa said softly. "Life was a lot simpler then, huh?"

"Much," he agreed. "But you know what? I wouldn't trade it. If we hadn't figured out what was happening, kids would still be dying."

"They might still," she said soberly. "If this doesn't work."

"Trust me," he said, trying to inject certainty into his voice. "It's all going to be fine." He reached out and took her hand, giving it a reassuring squeeze. "You want to upload another file? We can set them to post every half hour until he shows."

"Definitely."

They crawled back to the laptop on the other side of the bed. Setting it back in his lap, Peter asked, "What do you think? A jpeg, maybe? Or a video? The billboard can show those, too."

"We can't push too hard," she warned. "Otherwise Pike won't have a reason to keep us alive."

"Right. How about this one, from my dad? It's only a little slimy."

"Up to you."

Peter cracked his knuckles, thinking it over. "Screw it," he finally said. "Let's see how Bob likes being famous."

They sat shoulder to shoulder, sifting through files, trying to ignore the barked commands outside the window.

"My, it sounds exciting out there," Mason said with bemusement. "I hope they don't hit the Manet. That would be tragic."

"What?" Daisy asked, stupefied. It sounded like World War III was happening right outside the office; she'd jumped to her feet as soon as the shooting started. The gunfire was loud, and men were yelling. She prayed that Teo was okay.

"Do you drink?" Mason asked.

"Do I what?" Even though she'd spent the past week— hell, the past few months—waiting for the hammer to drop, now that it had, she was in shock. She wondered if the end would be quick, or if Mason was the type to draw things out for his own enjoyment.

She had a bad feeling that he preferred option two.

"I asked if you'd care for a drink." Mason had sauntered over to the bar in the corner.

Daisy stared at the crystal decanters filled with dark liquids. She swallowed hard and said, "What, no last meal?"

"I've always wondered about that," Mason said conversationally. He poured whiskey into two glasses, then added a single ice cube to each with a set of silver tongs. He crossed the room and offered one to her.

It was disconcerting. After a second, Daisy took it. Her hand shook, making the ice cube jangle.

"Careful," he warned as he settled back on the couch. "This Scotch is older than you, it would be a shame to waste it. Anyway, as I was saying. I've always wondered if the condemned are actually able to eat. I suspect the answer is no."

In spite of everything, at the mention of food, her traitorous stomach emitted a loud grumble. Mason smirked and took a sip from his drink. "But you might be the exception."

Daisy clasped the glass hard, trying to still her quivering. "I bet you've never missed a meal."

"Oh, you'd be surprised." A shadow crossed his features, and his mouth pinched at the corners. "I suspect we have more in common than you think."

Daisy scoffed. "Yeah, right."

Mason lifted an eyebrow. "You're from Harrison, Nevada. Just outside Las Vegas."

"So?" she said defiantly.

"I know the area." Mason gazed around the room with a disapproving frown. "People like Charles Pike have the world handed to them, literally on a silver platter. They could never grasp how difficult it is to wrest away just a small piece of it. How tenuous it always feels, even if you succeed."

Daisy had no idea what he was going on about, but as long as he was talking, he wasn't hurting her. And she might as well be a little drunk for whatever terrible thing was coming.

Carefully clasping the glass with both hands, she raised it to her lips. The whiskey slid down her throat, warm and harsh. "What are you going to do to me?" she demanded, trying to keep her voice steady.

Mason regarded her over the rim of his glass, and her heart recoiled even deeper into her chest. "I don't suppose you know much about Waterloo."

"Water what?" Daisy asked. The liquor was helping; she felt less shaky. The guard at the door had left with Pike. She surreptitiously eyed the exit. She could strike Mason with the glass, try to knock him unconscious. Then run like hell and take her chances.

Mason was regarding her with bemusement. "Plotting an escape?"

"What? No," Daisy protested.

"Good." Mason straightened his tie. "Because that would be inordinately foolish of you."

"Peter beat you," she said. "He told me all about it."

"Did he now?" Mason flashed a sharklike grin. "Well, you have me there. I must say, he surprised me on that particular occasion. But we were discussing Waterloo." He draped his arm across the back of the couch. "Why don't you take a seat?"

Daisy hesitated, then carefully eased onto the couch, sitting as far away from him as possible. If he made a move, she'd fight him off.

But he kept talking, sounding for all the world like he was lecturing a class. "Waterloo was the battle where Napoleon was defeated. You have heard of Napoleon? Or are the public schools even more deplorable now?"

"Everyone knows who Napoleon is," Daisy muttered, although in truth she only knew that he was short and

French and died a long time ago. *What the hell does this have to do with me?*

"Napoleon was, without question, a military mastermind." Mason swirled his drink as he stared into it. "He really should have won that battle, but he made a few critical oversights."

Daisy decided to humor him. Half her drink was gone, and her skin was starting to feel tingly. Maybe if she played nice, he'd give her more. "Like what?"

"Hubris," Mason said. "Napoleon started to believe that he was a god, and could not be defeated. He stopped listening to his most astute generals. He claimed that no army of man could beat him, he was destined to win." Finishing off his drink in a single gulp, he said, "It's a common enough failing."

"Whatever," Daisy muttered. The alcohol was coursing through her system. It hit her empty stomach hard, and her eyelids started to droop. She was so damn tired. She morbidly wondered if Mason would let her take a nap before he killed her.

The door was suddenly thrown open, startling her to her feet. Mason remained where he was, as if such intrusions were the norm.

Daisy gasped as Teo was shoved into the room. She was so fixated on him that it took a second to register the other boy's face.

"Zeke!" she exclaimed. "Oh my God!"

"Got 'em," one of the goons grunted. He was huge and bald and had a lump the size of a robin's egg on his forehead.

"So I see," Mason said complacently. "Well done. Although to be honest, the fact that you needed weapons to apprehend them is not a credit to your training."

"Hi, Daisy," Zeke said, as if they'd just run into each other on the street, and everything was totally normal. His eyes were already scanning the room, looking for a way out.

"You want us to take them to the shed?" The guy with the lump was staring at Teo with open malevolence.

Teo was bent double. "What happened?" Daisy demanded, rushing over to him.

"That jerk hit me," he said through gritted teeth. "I think he broke some ribs. Are you okay?"

"I'm fine," she said, running her hands over his arms. "Oh my God, I was so scared for you!"

His nose wrinkled. "You smell like whiskey."

"Shut up," the bald guy snarled, slamming his gun's muzzle into Teo's head. Teo dropped to his knees.

Daisy lunged for the bastard, but arms around her waist jerked her to a halt. She thrashed against them, but they were too strong. A voice in her ear muttered, "Calm, please. I will handle this."

Something in Mason's voice stopped her. She relaxed, and he lowered her to the ground. The guard was leering at her. "I'll take this one, too," he growled. "No problem."

"I'll handle it from here," Mason said coolly. "Please close the door behind you."

The guard's jaw dropped. He looked to his buddy for help, but the other guy was already walking out. "Hey," he protested. "I got knocked out by this little asshole. I'm expecting more than a slap on the wrist."

"Mr. Pike and I have already decided on a course of action," Mason said. When the goon still didn't move, he fixed his dead black stare on him and added, with a note of menace, "I would hate to tell Charles that you didn't follow orders."

The bald guy hesitated a moment longer. Finally, he cast

one last, ugly look at Teo and said, "I hope they take their time with you."

Then he slammed the door.

Daisy helped Teo to the couch. He collapsed on it with a groan. "Man, everything hurts."

"You're lucky you didn't get shot," she said, brushing the hair out of his eyes.

Teo shook his head and said wryly, "It's all part of our big escape plan."

"Nice job," Daisy said.

"Well, I never said it was perfect." He winced and put his hand to his chest. "I think half my ribs are broken."

Zeke was standing between the couch and the door, hands held loosely at his waist. Daisy recognized the stance: His body was coiled, prepared to strike.

Apparently Mason did, too. He said, "I'd offer you a drink, but frankly I don't trust you with glass at the moment."

"Where's Pike?" Zeke snapped.

"Gone. Apparently we'll be seeing your friend Noa soon." Mason set his glass on the end table and continued, "Perfect timing, really, since it gives us a chance to chat."

Teo groaned. "They found her?"

He was giving her a funny look, as if she'd done something wrong. "I didn't say anything!" she protested hotly. "He got a phone call."

"Chat about what?" Zeke asked. "And who the hell are you, anyway?"

The door was suddenly thrown open. The nurse who was always hovering around Ella stood there wild-eyed. Her eyes flicked across them in turn, then she frowned. "Where is Mr. Pike?"

"The question of the hour," Mason answered. "Do you require assistance?"

The nurse's eyes settled on Daisy, and she motioned with her hand. "Come quickly. Miss Ella is asking for you."

Zeke had gone pale. "Is she—"

"Quickly!" the nurse said, before taking off down the hall.

Daisy turned to Mason. He raised an eyebrow at her, then said, "Interesting development, don't you think?"

"Ella wants me." Daisy jutted up her chin. "Pike will be pissed if he finds out you didn't let me go."

"Perhaps," Mason acknowledged. "Although as far as he knows, you're already dead. I could certainly tell him that, if he asks."

Teo tensed. Mason was eyeing them all contemplatively, as if mulling over his options.

"She's probably dying," Daisy said in a hard voice. "You'd really let a kid go through that alone?"

A long moment passed. Mason's eyes revealed nothing, but one long, tapered finger tapped his thigh. Finally, he said, "I don't suppose it can do any harm. As long as we all go, of course."

"Big of you," Zeke muttered. He still looked braced to run. Teo wondered if he'd bolt at the first opportunity, leaving them behind. He still wasn't sure whether or not to trust him.

Mason sighed heavily. "Well, then. I suspect we'd better hurry. But please, no more escape attempts. I find them truly tedious."

Nearly an hour passed before the phone rang again. Peter glanced at Noa. She gave him a small nod, and he picked up.

"This better be Charles Pike," he said immediately.

"Peter?" It was a woman's voice, fearful and uncertain. And utterly familiar.

"Mom?" He dropped down hard on the bed.

"What are you doing, Peter? They're saying you're a terrorist."

Peter flashed back to the news broadcast, the way his parents had pretended this was all his fault. Flinging the words at her like they were arrows, he snapped, "You're still pretending you don't have a clue, Mom? That's cold, even for you. Want to talk about your investment in Project Persephone? Because I do."

A long pause on the other end of the line; Peter could picture her weighing what to say, knowing that others were listening in. Finally, she said querulously, "If you give yourself up, they promise not to hurt you. All you have to do is walk outside and leave the girl in the room."

"Right, and no one will have an itchy trigger finger." Peter shook his head with disgust. Noa was watching him with a look of concern. She mouthed, "You okay?"

He nodded, even though he really wasn't. He hated himself for it, but in spite of everything, hearing his mother's voice pierced him to the core. Sure, she'd sold him out for the promise of future cash, but still. It was his mother.

"Please, Peter." His mom's voice cracked as she said, "I don't want to lose you, too."

"You lost me a long time ago," he spat. "As soon as you got in bed with Pike."

He slammed the phone down on the receiver and stood there, breathing heavily.

"You better get back down and stay close to me," Noa advised. "They might have had her call just to get you in their sights."

Knowing she was right, he plunked back down beside her and wrapped his arms around his knees. His breathing was still ragged, and there was a hot ball of pain in his gut. More than anything, he really wanted to cry.

But he was done crying over them, he reminded himself. If his parents had managed to stop caring, the least he could do was return the favor. "Almost done?"

"Almost." Noa glanced over at him and said, "You want to take a turn?"

He shook his head, then tilted it back and stared at the ceiling. "So you're really sure about this?"

"I'm sure." Noa looked up from the monitor. "Are you okay with it?"

"Yes," he said decisively. "You're right. It's the only way."

"All right, then. What time is it?"

He checked the clock in the corner of the laptop screen. "Almost eight."

They sat in silence. Peter wondered if his parents would call back, maybe say the right things this time. Admit they'd made a mistake.

That was about as likely as Pike showing up in a bunny costume.

"You still haven't cooked me dinner," Noa said awkwardly. "I mean, all that talk about what a great chef you are, and for months now it's been nothing but food out of a box."

"Hang on. Are you actually trying to make a joke?" he asked, raising an eyebrow.

She shrugged. "What? I'm funny."

At that, he actually laughed. The phone rang. They exchanged a glance, then he slid over to the table and reached up to answer it. Dragging the phone back with him, he said, "Yeah?"

"We've got Charles Pike here." Peter caught a harried undertone in the negotiator's voice.

"Put him on." Peter gave Noa a look, and her eyes went wide.

A second later, a different male voice said, "Am I speaking to Peter Gregory?"

"The one and only."

"What can I do for you?" Pike asked.

He had an oddly cavalier tone. *The bastard thinks he's already won.* "I want to talk, face-to-face."

"I'm not sure that will be possible," Pike said, clearly choosing his words carefully. "The agent in charge here won't allow me to risk my life."

"Well, you better figure out a way," Peter said. "Because I don't think you want to be holding this conversation over the phone. You've got five minutes. Any longer, I kill the girl."

He hung up.

"I love how easy it's gotten for you to talk about killing me," Noa commented. "It's heartwarming, really."

"Maybe I should get into acting when all this is over." Peter's heart was hammering in his chest. Charles Pike was somewhere close by. He felt like he'd just invited the bogeyman in for tea and a chat.

"You really think he'll find a way to get inside?" Noa asked hesitantly.

"Yeah," Peter said slowly. "I do. He's coming."

CHAPTER

SEVENTEEN

Daisy rushed to the bed as soon as they got in the room. Ella was lying against the pillows, looking even worse than before.

Daisy took the girl's hand gently and bent low to whisper something to her. Teo suddenly felt awkward and unsure, like he was intruding.

Zeke stared at Ella with a look of regret. "Shit," he breathed.

"You know her, too?" Teo asked, puzzled.

"Yeah. Pike had me keep her company for a while, until he decided I was a bad influence."

Teo watched Daisy brush sweaty strands of hair back from the girl's forehead.

"She's not so bad," Zeke said in a low voice. "For a rich kid."

Teo took a few hesitant steps closer to the bed, until he

was standing just behind Daisy. Ella was awake. Her chest was working hard, moving up and down as she wheezed. Her face was flushed, her pupils enormous. She looked past Daisy toward Teo. Faintly, she said, "Is that him?"

"Yeah," Daisy said in a choked voice.

Ella smiled slightly, then said, "He is hot."

Daisy issued a surprised laugh, her eyes shiny with tears. She swiped at them with her free hand, then said, "Your dad will be back soon. He went to get something to make you better."

At that, the girl frowned. "You mean someone."

Daisy didn't reply. Teo gaped openly at the girl, wondering how much she knew.

The nurse came over to fiddle with the IV drip, but Ella waved her away. "Just stop," she said in a low voice. "It's too late for that."

"You're going to be fine," Daisy said fiercely.

"No way. I don't want anyone else dying for me." Ella raised her head slightly, her eyes blazing as she croaked, "Tell my dad I want him to stop. You hear me?" She shifted back to the nurse. "You too. Tell him I said so."

The nurse gave her a funny look, but didn't say anything. Teo wondered if she'd spent some of her shifts carving up his friends. All those kids had died, in a futile effort to save one teenage girl.

Still, looking at her now, so weak and riddled with pain . . . he wanted to hate her, but couldn't. It wasn't her fault, not really. Ella was as much a victim as the rest of them.

A small smile tweaked her lips. She turned back to Daisy and asked, "Do you think you would have been my friend anyway, if you'd had a choice?"

Daisy nodded. "Of course."

"Liar." Ella's smile widened, and her eyes closed. Her chest shuddered a few more times, then fell still.

"Ella?" Daisy whispered.

"She's gone." The nurse looked composed, but as she reached out to smooth the blankets one last time, Teo could see that her hands were shaking.

Daisy turned and buried her face against Teo's chest. He winced at the renewed pain in his ribs as he rubbed her back, trying to console her.

Behind him, Mason said, "Well. That's unfortunate. I suppose I should let Charles know immediately."

Teo had briefly forgotten that he was still in the room. While he watched, Mason started tapping away at his cell phone. Jesus, was he going to send that information in a text?

"Unfortunate?" Zeke said, his voice thick with emotion. "A girl just died right in front of you, and that's what you call it?"

"I didn't mean to sound callous," Mason said dispassionately. "It's just—"

"Shut up!" Daisy sputtered. "All of you, just shut up!"

The nurse was drawing the sheet up. Ella had gone still as a statue, the color already fading from her cheeks. Teo suddenly realized that this was their chance to run. Force their way past Mason and hope for the best.

Because now that Ella was gone, Pike had no reason to keep them alive anymore.

He squeezed Daisy's shoulder, hoping she'd get the message. Caught Zeke's eye; he gave a slight nod, and Teo knew that the same thought had occurred to him.

A cell phone ring pierced the stillness. Teo watched Mason check the screen. He sighed, then answered it. "Yes?"

Teo tensed. They should try to get past Mason now, while

he was distracted. Bending low, he whispered in Daisy's ear, "We've got to go!"

Suddenly, there was shouting outside the house. Mason looked up and frowned, muttering, "Now what?"

More gunfire, close by.

Zeke threw Teo a puzzled look. "What the hell? Are the guards shooting at each other?"

"No," Teo said slowly, realization dawning. "The cavalry is here."

A double knock at the door. Noa opened her eyes: Her vision was improving, she could actually make out individual pieces of furniture. Peter was right, this was definitely one of the ugliest motel rooms she'd ever seen.

"I think that's him."

She turned to face Peter: His face was pale, his eyes too shadowed for her to read. The fear in his voice was plain, though. "Okay," she said. "We're all set?"

"Ready as we'll ever be." He squeezed her hand. "Hey, is this the dumbest thing we've ever done or what?"

"Definitely the dumbest." Noa's throat had gone dry, and her chest throbbed painfully. Still, she was possessed by an overarching sense of calm. She'd waited a long time for this. She was ready for it to end, one way or another. "Peter?"

"Yeah?"

"Thanks for everything. Just in case."

"Great," he groaned. "Can we at least pretend this might work?"

Grinning, Noa climbed up on the bed and leaned back against the pillows. She tried to keep the pain from show-ing—her sight was returning, but it felt like the rest of her body was one big pulsing wound. She swiped away the fine sheen of sweat from her forehead and croaked, "Ready."

"Showtime," Peter muttered. He perched on the edge of the bed, just out of the window's sight line, and called out, "It's open!"

Charles Pike stepped into the room and closed the door.

He was smaller than Noa had expected, probably no more than five-eleven. Lean and tan, and dressed like he'd just strolled off a golf course, save for the bulletproof vest. As he surveyed the room, his lips curled up with distaste.

"I know it's not much to look at," Peter said. "But it's home. You got here faster than we thought."

"Yes, well. I figured time was of the essence, so I took the company helicopter."

"Must be nice," Peter said. "How long does it take to get here from Boston, anyway?"

"I didn't come from Boston," Pike said curtly. His eyes had settled on her. Noa had to resist the urge to shrink back: It was a predatory, hungry gaze, like he was considering vaulting across the room to consume her. "Noa Torson," he said in a deep baritone. "I've been waiting a long time to meet you."

"We've been trying really hard not to meet you," Peter offered. "But it hasn't been easy."

"So I've heard." Pike eyed the desk chair they'd set in front of the bed, facing them. He gestured to it and said, "May I?"

Noa nodded, and he settled into it, crossing his legs as if he was completely at home. "So," he said. "I understand you want to have a private conversation."

"We have a proposition for you," Peter said. "A kind of trade."

Pike's eyebrows shot up. "A trade?"

"Yes," Peter said firmly. "You probably caught the show

we're putting up on the billboard out there."

A flicker of rage flitted across Pike's face, but his voice remained level as he said, "Yes, I had noticed. Mind you, all of that is easy enough to explain away."

"Well, we started with the small stuff," Peter said. "I'm happy to go bigger, really give the folks something to go with their popcorn."

The way Pike was staring at her made Noa feel naked, exposed. She had to fight the urge to wrap her arms around her chest. The thymus was throbbing again, probably reacting to the adrenaline coursing through her bloodstream. Her breathing got ragged, and her vision started to blur again. *No*, she thought. *Not now. Don't have another seizure, not in front of him.*

"You don't look well, Noa," Pike noted. "I have doctors who can fix that."

"It's like you're psychic," Peter said with a whistle. "That's the deal. You fix Noa and Amanda."

"Amanda?" Pike's brow furrowed. "I'm afraid I don't know who that is."

"Amanda Berns, the girl Mason injected with PEMA," Peter spat. Noa saw his fists clench, and she mentally willed him to stay calm. This would only work if Pike agreed to their terms, and he was less likely to do that if Peter broke his nose.

"Right, your parents have spoken of her. I'm assuming you want her to be cured?"

"Yeah, that would be nice," Peter said. "If it's not too much trouble."

"Then I need Noa." Pike leaned forward and said urgently, "You can save so many people. Don't you want that?"

Noa hesitated. It was like he'd read her mind; this was

exactly what she'd been grappling with for months. She finally said, "So the only way to cure them is for me to die?"

"Not necessarily," Pike said. "If the thymus is removed, you might be fine. The PEMA has probably already been negated."

"You injected her with PEMA, too?" Peter exclaimed.

Pike continued as if he hadn't spoken. "You're already dying, Noa. If there's even a chance that we can save you, and help others, don't you want to try?"

Helicopter rotors reverberated overhead; probably a news crew. Speaking loudly to be heard over them, Peter said, "Here's the deal. If Noa survives the operation, I won't release any more of the files. But they're set on a timer. If I don't enter a password every few hours, they'll be leaked. And trust me, there's no way you're figuring out that password."

Pike smirked. "That's your plan?" he said incredulously. "Blackmailing me?"

Peter shrugged. "Best we could come up with on short notice."

Pike vaulted from the chair. Towering over Peter, he said icily, "You little ingrate. No one threatens me. No one. Do you have any idea what I'm capable of?"

"I've got an idea." Noa wished she could get to her feet to confront him, but her legs felt too weak to stand. "You had street kids kidnapped so they could be used as lab rats." Her voice gained strength as she continued, "You've killed how many people, dozens? Hundreds?"

Pike spun on her. "More," he spat. "And you know what? Few even noticed, or cared. Those kids were nothing: grubby little bastards who begged for money and drowned themselves in drugs." He jabbed a finger into his chest, saying, "*I* found a way to make them useful, to have them contribute to the greater good."

"And when you were done experimenting on them," Peter said, "they were chopped up and dumped where no one would find them. That about right?"

Pike raised his hands, palms up. "Why do you even care? You're not one of them. Hell, your parents were in this from the beginning. You think that house you live in comes without a price?"

"I didn't ask for any of that," Peter retorted.

"Those grubby little bastards were *people*," Noa said. "They were our friends. Alex Herbruck. Cody Ellis. Zeke Balewa." Her voice faltered on the last name. She bit her lip, then continued, "You murdered all of them."

"And you created PEMA in the first place," Peter added. "The lifetime initiative, right? How does it feel, knowing you made your own kid sick?"

Pike drew himself up to his full height. His eyes spat fire as he said, "Listen, you pathetic brat. I'm taking the girl, and there's nothing you can do about it. Do you know how many people I have in my pocket? Senators, CDC officers, the goddamn vice president of the United States! Out of deference to your parents, I've saved you before. Now, you're about to find out exactly what I'm capable of."

"Whoa, dude," Peter said, rearing back. "Easy on the bad guy routine."

"You need me," Noa pointed out. "I'm the only one who survived, right? I'm the cure."

"Ha!" Pike threw back his head and barked a short, cruel laugh. "You think you're special? There's nothing special about you, you're just another piece of garbage."

In spite of herself, Noa flinched at the words.

Pike continued, "It's not you that I need. It's what's inside of you. That damned thymus. That's why the operation never succeeded on the others. It wasn't the procedure that worked; that thymus was special. And we wasted it on you."

Peter threw her a look of surprise. "Hey! That actually makes a crazy kind of sense."

Noa sat there in shock, processing what he said. She could feel the thymus pulsing inside her, could picture it large and swollen and angry. All this time, she'd been thinking there was something unique about her.

It turned out there was, but only because she'd been given a piece of some nameless kid. She wondered if Pike even knew who it had come from.

"So," Peter said. "About that trade . . ."

Pike leaned in and hissed, "You're dead. Your parents are dead. Your little girlfriend, too. And they'll die screaming, just like your friends from Santa Cruz. Plus, I have more of them at my compound in Maine. One phone call, and my men put a bullet in their heads. You dare threaten me?" A vein throbbed in his temple, and his face had gone purple. He roared, "I will destroy you!"

Peter looked at her. Cocking an eyebrow, he said, "I think that should do it. What do you think?"

Noa nodded, trying to sound steady even though her heart was racing. "That's everything."

Pike looked back and forth between them, a puzzled expression on his face. Clearly, he wasn't used to having his threats dismissed. He straightened his shirt collar, drew a deep breath, and said, "I'm going to have them pull up an ambulance for Noa."

"I don't think so." Peter shook his head. "See, you're missing something."

Pike's face darkened again. He opened his mouth, obviously preparing to spew another tirade. Noa motioned toward the window and said, "You might want to take a look outside."

He glared at her for a few seconds, then stalked to the window. Ripping aside the curtains, he blinked into the floodlights.

"The billboard," Peter said smugly. "Check it out."

Pike raised his head. From where she sat, Noa had a clear vantage point. It was still fuzzy around the edges, but the image was clear enough:

The billboard displayed the chair Pike had been sitting in less than a minute ago, blown up to several times normal size.

He turned back to them, his features twisted with consternation.

"Here's the thing," Peter said. "We realized that you're right, we didn't have any concrete proof. I mean, sure, lots of files with your name all over them, probably enough for some sort of investigation."

"But you're good at making those go away," Noa said. "We learned that back in Rhode Island."

"Exactly," Peter said. "Friends in high places and all of that. I mean, the vice president. Wow."

"Impressive," Noa agreed.

"Definitely. What we didn't have was an actual confession. Until now."

Pike stared at them, the vein in his temple still pulsing. His eyes darted back and forth. In a harsh whisper, he demanded, "What did you do?"

Peter shrugged. "We did what we do. We're hackers. That's the thing; we didn't have much of a shot out there, when we were just a bunch of kids going after guys with guns. That wasn't a level playing field. But this"—he nodded toward the laptop that was humming away on the desk—"is what we're good at."

"Hacktivism." Noa exchanged a smile with Peter and added, "Just like with /ALLIANCE/."

Pike turned toward the laptop. In a single motion, he swept it off the table and sent it crashing to the floor.

"Dude." Peter winced. "I was just growing attached to that one."

"There was no sound," Pike spat. "It's just a billboard."

"True." Peter nodded. "Noa pointed that out."

Pike seemed to regain some of his composure. Exhaling hard, he said, "This changes nothing, then."

"Oh, I think it does," Peter said. "You see, we realized something else while we were sitting here waiting for you. Well, Noa did." He turned toward her and said, "That was brilliant, by the way."

"Thanks." Noa inhaled deeply, fighting back the pain. Her whole body was in sheer agony, but she only had to hold on for another few minutes. And the look on Pike's face made it worth it.

"What?" Pike demanded.

"The thing is, you need me; or, rather, you need the thymus." Noa looked at Peter, who was staring back with an expression of frank pride. "But what I realized is that now, *we* don't need *you*."

"Of course you do," Pike said dismissively. "All the research—"

"Is in the files," Noa said, cutting him off. "Which we now have. Sure, we aren't doctors or experts or anything. But if we hand this research over to the right people, they'll get to the cure. It might take days, or weeks. Maybe longer. But honestly, I trust them a lot more than your creepy doctors."

"You don't have a choice," Pike sneered. Waving toward the billboard, he said, "I have dozens of people on payroll who are already making this go away."

"I'll bet," Peter said. "I mean, hell, you are a bad guy, right? I'd be kind of disappointed if you didn't have minions. But you see, the thing is . . ."

He glanced at Noa, waiting. She drew a deep breath and said, "It's not just the billboard. It's everywhere."

"Where did we post it again?" Peter asked, screwing up his forehead like he was trying to remember.

"CNN, Fox News, all the major networks," Noa said.

"Right. In prime time, no less; thanks for getting here so fast, that really helped. Oh, and YouTube, of course," Peter said. "Plus, I threw it up on the Jumbotron at Fenway. No sound there, either, but I thought it was a nice touch."

"You're lying," Pike said, his voice thick with disbelief.

"Nope. Check it out yourself." Nodding toward the computer, Peter added, "I'd show you, but you just sent this guy to laptop heaven."

Pike tore a smartphone out of his pocket and jabbed at the screen. A second later, his face blanched. His voice radiated out from the tinny speakers.

"That's my favorite part, where you talk about killing kids for the greater good. The sound came out loud and clear," Peter noted. "Thank God. I was worried about that."

Pike looked at Peter, then at Noa, his face oddly blank.

"It's over, Pike," Noa said. "And you lost."

Pike's mouth set in a tight line. He shook his head like he was trying to clear it, then stared out the window again. The billboard screen had gone blank.

His cell phone trilled. Looking dazed, Pike squinted at the screen, as if the text were written in a foreign language. When he looked back up, his eyes were empty and eerily still. "It's too late," he said in a hollow voice. "She's gone."

"Who's gone?" Peter asked, sounding perplexed.

Abruptly, Pike bent over, fumbling at his ankle. Noa frowned, wondering what the hell was going on.

When Pike straightened back up, he was holding a gun in his right hand. Pointing it at her, he said, "I brought this for Peter. But now, you're both going to die."

"What cavalry?" Zeke asked, puzzled.

Teo raced to the window. Over the top of the hedge, he could see guards swarming the lawn, shooting into the woods. A couple of scruffy-looking kids darted from tree to tree, firing back at them.

"The Northeast chapter!" Teo practically shouted. He could hardly believe it—despite his doubts, they'd responded to the SOS. Luke and his people had come to rescue them.

His eyes flicked to Mason, who was still on the phone. He was acting oddly oblivious. His eyes were far away, focused on whatever the person on the other end of the line was saying. *Is it Pike, on his way back with Noa?*

Daisy had gotten to her feet. Her cheeks were still damp with tears, but there was clear resolve in her eyes. Zeke had edged closer to Mason and the door, taking advantage of the distraction.

Abruptly, Mason tucked the phone away. His gaze shifted to Zeke, and he frowned. In one swift motion, he drew a handgun, leveling it at Zeke's chest. Teo sucked in a deep breath and shifted protectively to block Daisy. "Easy, Mr.

Balewa. This could still end well for you."

"Doubtful," Zeke scoffed, but there was a tremor in his voice.

"I'm afraid you aren't privy to the latest information," Mason said, eyeing them speculatively. "It appears that my employer just encountered his Waterloo. Earlier than expected, I have to admit."

"What?" Teo asked, puzzled.

"Was it Noa?" Daisy asked eagerly. "She beat him, didn't she!"

"Clever girl," Mason said, although it wasn't clear if he was referring to Daisy or Noa. "I warned against underestimating his opponent."

"So he's been arrested?" Teo's head spun. *Did Noa and Peter really do it?*

"Hubris," Mason said disdainfully. "Of course, as a general policy, I do prefer to honor existing contracts. Which means that I should, by all rights, carry out my final orders."

Teo was finding it hard to breathe. They were so close. If only Luke's team had arrived a few minutes earlier, they might have breached the house by now.

As it was, they'd burst in just in time to discover their corpses.

"You won't do it," Daisy said confidently.

Mason cocked an eyebrow. "And why do you say that, Miss Stoia?"

She stepped out from behind Teo, shrugging off his restraining arm. "Because," she said defiantly. "You hate Pike. And we have more in common, right? You said so."

A few beats passed. The gunfire outside was intermittent, but clearly getting closer to the house. Mason hardly seemed to notice; he was regarding Daisy with bemusement. "True,"

he finally said. "And the only thing I hate more than breaking a contract is wastefulness. Despite your many failings, I
do believe that killing you would be a terrible waste."

"So let us go."

She reached out for Teo's hand and clasped it in her own.
Her spine was rigid, her gaze fixed on Mason. She looked
like a warrior. Teo felt a swell of pride that combated with the
instinct to get her out of harm's way.

Zeke was staring at the gun as if weighing his chances.
Mason noticed, and narrowed his eyes. "Really, Mr. Balewa.
There's no need for any more bloodshed. Wasn't getting shot
once enough for you?"

"You're just dragging it out, toying with us," Zeke spat.
"That's what you do."

"Or perhaps," Mason said blandly, "I've decided that it's
time to cut my losses."

In the distance, the wail of sirens.

Mason cocked his head to the side and said, "That's a
much faster response time than I would have anticipated."

Teo groaned. Traditionally, cops had not been their allies,
and Pike's local department had to be deep in his pocket.

"At Waterloo," Daisy said. "Did any of the generals survive?"

Teo threw her a look; *what is all this nonsense about Waterloo?*
But Mason broke into a wide smile that only served to make
him look more sharklike. "They did, in fact. Tremendous
losses on both sides, but that's a regrettable by-product of any
war. Including this one."

An explosion close to the house made Teo flinch, and
Daisy reflexively squeezed his hand. It did sound like a
war out there, making the relative calm inside all the more
jarring.

"Well, then," Mason said decisively. "It's been an unexpected pleasure, Miss Stoia. Do consider a return to your natural hair color."

Daisy snorted. "No way."

Mason smirked. "Shame, but I admire your desire to flaunt convention. That should serve you well in the future." He was backing toward the door as he spoke, keeping a wary eye on Zeke.

"You're just going to let us go?" Teo blurted, astonished.

"You're already free. You just don't know it yet." As Mason abruptly turned on his heel, he tossed back over his shoulder, "Give my best to Peter when you see him."

And he was gone.

They stared at each other, dumbfounded. From far away came shouting, and the sound of heavy feet running.

"What the hell just happened?" Zeke asked, sounding as mystified as Teo felt.

"No idea," Teo said.

"Come on." Daisy was already marching for the door, tugging him along by the hand. "Let's go."

The nurse was staring blankly at the lump on the bed. It was almost as if she'd turned into a statue; she didn't move or say a word as they bolted from the room.

Mason was nowhere in sight, as if he'd simply vanished.

More gunfire as they hustled along the empty hallway. "How do we get out?" Teo asked.

"The back," Zeke said. "This way!"

They hurried through a series of rooms, headed away from the ones Teo was familiar with. Zeke pushed open a double door, and they found themselves in the kitchen.

Across the room was a door to the outside. It almost seemed too easy.

Right before they reached it, the door exploded inward. They drew up short. A big kid, probably nineteen years old, raced in. Teo had never seen him before, but he had to be one of Luke's guys. "Run!" he screamed as he tore past them. "They're coming!"

Zeke didn't hesitate, he bolted back into the depths of the house. Cursing, Teo followed, clinging tightly to Daisy's hand. He could hear her panting in time to his racing heart. It would really suck to be killed by guards who were about to discover that they were unemployed.

Zeke overtook the first kid, yelling, "This way!"

They darted through room after room, retracing their steps until they reached the front door. Zeke flung it open, then stopped short.

Teo's heart sank: A guy in a uniform blocked their path. He was brandishing a gun.

"State police!" the officer said, holding the gun steady. "Hands in the air!"

Slowly, they all raised their hands. Daisy threw Teo a questioning look, her eyes darting back the way they'd come. He shook his head slightly: no more running. They wouldn't make it ten feet.

"Do you have any weapons?" the cop asked.

"None," Teo said.

The cop's eyes flicked over them, then he frowned. "Are you the kids Pike kidnapped?"

Daisy gasped. Zeke threw Teo a puzzled look, then said, "You know about that?"

"Anyone else with you?" the cop continued, peering past them. "How many guards?"

"We're not sure, exactly," Teo said. "A lot."

Another cop appeared behind them, huffing slightly as he asked, "Is this them?"

"Ayup," the cop said. "Safe and sound."

"Sorry," Zeke said. "But what the hell is going on?"

The cops exchanged a look, then the first one said, "You're being rescued, son. What does it look like?"

"Hey," Peter protested, backing away. "You don't want to do that."

"Why not?" Pike said in a hard voice. "Thanks to you, they'll already hold me responsible for killing dozens of teens. What's two more?"

"But, your daughter," Noa said weakly. "Kill me, and she dies."

Pike's face darkened, and he swung the barrel of the gun toward her. "She's already dead."

Peter felt the nascent hope inside him wither. If Pike's daughter was gone, they'd just lost their ace in the hole. Now Pike had nothing left to lose.

"You don't want to do this," Noa said weakly. "There's no point anymore."

"How do you know what I want?" The words exploded out of Pike. He stepped forward menacingly, his gun arm stiff and straight. "How could you possibly have any idea?"

Peter backed up toward the headboard, trying to keep himself between the gun and Noa. He held his hands in front of his chest, as if they would somehow stop a bullet. It was hard to breathe, staring down the barrel of a gun; it felt like the air had turned to syrup, too thick for his lungs to handle.

Pike's mouth was set in a furious sneer, and the crazy look in his eyes had only gotten worse. Past reasoning with, probably, but Peter had to try. "There's a parking lot full of FBI agents looking in," he pleaded. "Probably camera crews, too. You're Charles Pike, the head of Pike & Dolan. You don't want the world to see you mowing down two kids in a motel room."

Pike blinked, and for a minute, Peter thought he'd actually gotten through to him. The gun lowered slightly, pointed at an angle; if he pulled the trigger, he'd take off one of Peter's feet.

Noa's breathing was shallow; she must be just as scared. He wanted to throw her a reassuring glance, but it didn't seem like a good time for sudden movements.

"It's too late." Pike sounded resigned, which was even more frightening, like he didn't have a choice anymore.

"So do it." Noa's voice was threaded with steel. Peter jerked his head around, shocked. She was propped up on the pillows. Her skin was pale and waxy, but her eyes shone with a fierce fire. "You've been trying to kill me for months, you sick bastard. At least you finally got the courage to do it face-to-face."

She was focusing on Pike's torso. Following her gaze, Peter saw a series of small red dots running up and down Pike's side like angry ants.

Peter forced his eyes back to Pike's face. Slowly, he inched farther up the bed until he hit the headboard. He reached out and took Noa's hand. It felt cool. She clasped his palm tightly in hers.

Pike's chest was heaving, making the bulletproof vest flex. "You've ruined everything," he said, raising the gun back up.

Peter dove, trying to cover Noa with his body as the window shattered into a million pieces. The sound of gunfire, impossibly loud, like bombs were blowing up right beside them. Followed by the smell, acrid and thick.

Then, silence.

"Ouch," Noa said. "You're crushing me."

He rolled off her and whipped around. Pike had been hurled halfway across the room. He lay facedown on the carpet. The vest was riddled with bullet holes, and a thick stream of blood poured from what was left of his head.

"Don't look," Peter advised.

"Don't worry," she said. "I can barely see again."

"What?" he asked, turning back to her.

Noa had a glassy look in her eyes, like she was staring past him at something he couldn't see. A dark bloom was spreading across her torso.

"Shit, he shot you!" Frantically, Peter cupped both hands to the wound. Blood pulsed out, fast and warm and thick.

"It's okay, Peter," she said softly. "Just let me go."

"No!" Peter heard shouting behind him, sensed other people entering the room. But it sounded far away, distant; tears streamed down his face, blurring his vision. The blood seemed to be coming faster; her entire shirt was soaked with it. "Please, stay with me."

Noa's lips curved up slightly. In a tight voice, she said, "We got him. Did you see the look on his face? That was perfect."

Someone was trying to drag him away from her; he fought against them. "You're going to be fine," he insisted. "They're going to make you better."

A tear slid down her cheek. "Thanks, Vallas," she said faintly. "For everything."

Peter clenched her hand fiercely. "Don't you dare give up. Not now."

But her eyes had closed. As he watched, her chest rose, then fell.

It didn't rise again.

"Noa!" he screamed, shaking her. Her body was limp, and

her eyes stayed closed. "Noa, wake up!"

Paramedics were already bending over her. Someone at his shoulder was shouting questions, but he couldn't make out what they were saying, couldn't tear his eyes from Noa. She was so pale against the dark comforter. Her features had gone still, like she'd been cast in marble.

One of the paramedics started CPR; another clamped a plastic mask over her face. Her chest moved reflexively, sending more blood pooling out. But she didn't open her eyes.

Peter hardly noticed the tears running down his cheeks as they finally led him away.

Teo kept his arms wrapped tightly around Daisy's shoulders; the space blanket the cops had provided enveloped them in a warm, crinkly cocoon.

"I can't believe it's really over," she said, staring back at the mansion.

"I can't believe we finally got out of that damn house," Teo muttered.

She laughed. After a second, he joined in. It was high-pitched, hysterical, the giddiness of two people who couldn't quite accept that they'd survived.

Zeke stood off to the side conferring with a tall, broad-shouldered guy: Luke, the head of the Northeast chapter. He'd gotten their SOS, and managed to convince what remained of his cell to attempt a rescue mission. Fully armed, no less; apparently once the Santa Cruz group fell, Luke had given up on less lethal weapons. Two kids hadn't survived the battle with Pike's men.

Teo wondered how Noa would feel about that.

News was trickling in slowly. The cops didn't seem to know much, except that they'd been ordered here based on some sort of televised confession by Pike. Rumor had it he was dead, too, but they were unwilling or unable to provide any details. Apparently the FBI was en route, along with a half dozen other organizations that went by acronyms. The state troopers had told them to hang tight, since there would be a lot of people who wanted to talk to them.

All Teo wanted was to curl up somewhere with Daisy and get some sleep. But not until they knew Peter and Noa were okay. Every time he asked, the cops gave terse, evasive answers.

A slew of state troopers were searching the peninsula for Mason, but so far he hadn't turned up. Which wasn't really surprising. Teo suspected they'd never see him again.

A cop approached Luke and Zeke and said something to them. Zeke's voice rose angrily in response; the cop laid a hand on his shoulder, his voice set at a low murmur.

"What do you think's going on?" Daisy asked, her voice filled with dread.

Zeke's legs suddenly gave out, as if a string had been cut. On his knees, he threw back his head and wailed up at the rising moon.

"Oh, no," Teo breathed. "No, no, no . . ."

Daisy started shaking, crying into his shoulder. Teo clasped her tightly in his arms, resting his head against hers as his own tears started to fall.

CHAPTER EIGHTEEN

Noa opened her eyes and frowned. She was lying on a hospital bed in a windowless room. Looking down, she saw that she was wearing a cotton gown; no markings on it, though. An IV line jutted into her right arm.

Anxiously, she reached down: There was an enormous bandage on her chest. "Oh, no," she groaned. "Not again."

"Hey."

She turned toward the voice. Zeke was sitting in a chair a few feet away, smiling at her. He looked different: His dark hair was shorter, his eyes deeper set. He smiled tentatively at her. Noa frowned. "Is this heaven? Because I was really expecting the clothes to be better."

His eyes crinkled up at the corners. "Nope. Not unless Boston Medical counts."

"But..." Noa shook her head, trying to clear the cobwebs;

they must have drugged her, everything was cast in a watery haze. "You're dead."

He pulled the chair closer to the bed. "I made it. Pike got his doctors to fix me up."

"You're alive?" It didn't seem possible; she must be in some weird dream state. Or she really was dead. She could still feel the weight of him in her lap, the sticky warmth of his blood flowing over her legs. There had been so much of it. . . . "You're really alive?"

"Yup." Zeke grinned at her. "And so are you."

Noa took a minute to process that. The last thing she remembered was that awful motel room. Pike dropping to the floor. Peter screaming at her to hold on. "But Pike's dead."

"He sure is." Zeke looked downright gleeful. "And everyone knows what he did."

"So the plan worked." She closed her eyes, relieved. "Peter's fine?"

"Worried about you, but yeah. Other than that, he's fine."

Frowning, she asked, "So where the hell have you been?"

Zeke burst out laughing, his teeth flashing white. "Pike was keeping me at his place in Maine. Trust me, if I could have gotten out sooner, I would've. I escaped with Daisy and Teo."

"Wait, what? They're in California."

"They never made it." Seeing her puzzled look, he added, "It's kind of a long story."

"Are they okay?"

"We're fine," Teo chimed in from the doorway.

Daisy rushed past him and hurled herself at the bed. "Oh my God, Noa, you had us so scared. I seriously thought you were dead when I first saw you."

"How long have I been here?" Noa asked as Daisy threw both arms around her.

"Careful, Daisy," Zeke warned. "The doctors said to watch her chest."

Daisy pulled back so fast she nearly tumbled into Zeke's lap. "Oh my God, I'm sorry, Noa. I keep forgetting—"

Noa touched the bandage again. "The thymus?"

"They took it out," Zeke explained. "Said it was killing you. Then they put you in a coma for a week to make sure your body adjusted."

Noa ran her hand across the bandage. For so long, she'd thought she had the ability to sense the thymus, keeping time with her heartbeat. Now, she felt nothing but a void.

Daisy was gripping her hand like she was trying to haul her onto a life raft. "That kind of hurts, Daisy," Noa said, wincing.

Daisy quickly released it. "Sorry. I'm just so happy you're okay!"

"We all are," Teo added.

"Where's Peter?" Noa tried to peer past them, but the corridor outside her room was empty.

"He's been here the whole time, pretty much," Daisy said. "I mean, the FBI has been questioning him a lot—like, every day. But he made them do it here, in case something changed with you."

"So where is he now?" Noa demanded.

Zeke was staring at her silently, a question in his eyes. The frankness of it was discomfiting.

"They operated on Amanda yesterday," Teo offered. "Peter's been going back and forth between your recovery rooms." Glancing at Zeke, he seemed to catch on. "Uh, Daisy and I could go get him. Right, Daisy?"

"What?" Daisy's head moved back and forth between them, then she exclaimed, "Oh! Sure. We'll be right back."

She grabbed Teo's hand and dragged him from the room. Noa was left alone with Zeke. He hadn't taken his eyes off her. Self-consciously, she ran a hand through her hair: It was knotted and oily. She probably looked awful.

"So you went red, huh?" Zeke said. "Gotta say, I kind of like it."

"Ugh. I can't wait to dye it back." Suddenly struck by the absurdity of worrying about her hair when she'd almost died, she laughed.

Zeke wrinkled his forehead. "What?"

"Nothing, just . . . I guess I'm kind of surprised to be alive."

"I know how you feel." Zeke examined his hands. "It takes some getting used to."

"I'll bet."

The silence between them quickly grew awkward. It was weird: They'd been best friends for months, and much more than that at the end. The things he'd said to her, on the beach when he thought he was dying; Noa's cheeks flamed as she remembered. And now they were supposed to do what? Make small talk?

Zeke cleared his throat and said, "You probably have a lot of questions."

"Lots," Noa said, although at the moment she couldn't come up with any.

"They didn't cure PEMA, not yet," he said. "But they took the thymus out of you and put part of it in Amanda, and part in another kid who wasn't going to make it otherwise. The rest they held back for research. They've got teams of people working on all the files you and Peter found."

"That's good," Noa said. It was weird, knowing that something that had been inside her was in another girl now;

weirder still that it was Peter's ex-girlfriend.

Zeke was clasping and unclasping his hands nervously. She was reminded of the first time she saw him, how self-assured he'd been, rushing into danger. But now, sitting beside her in a hospital room, he looked terrified.

"What's wrong?" she asked.

"This past week, I've just sat here waiting for you to wake up. I was so scared that you wouldn't." Zeke shook his head, avoiding her eyes as he continued, "And now you have, and I don't know what the hell to say to you. I mean, our last talk was kind of intense."

"You think?" Noa managed a laugh. Tentatively, she extended a hand across the bed. Zeke clasped her fingers and shifted closer. "I still can't believe you're actually okay. The past few months, I kept going over and over what happened." She dropped her eyes, studying their interwoven hands. "I never should have left you there."

"If you hadn't, you'd be dead, too," Zeke said firmly. "So would Teo and Daisy. And I would've been angry as hell at you for not listening to me."

"Sure you would've." Noa rolled her eyes. "Like you said, we'd all be dead."

"Trust me. I would have made your afterlife total hell." Zeke grinned.

Noa swallowed hard. The longer she waited, the harder it was going to be to say the things she needed to say. And she didn't want to just gloss over all this, and go back to the way they'd been. So she forced herself to meet his gaze. "I was an idiot. I felt all these things for you, and I didn't know what to do about them. And I was scared. Everyone I ever loved ended up dying," she said in a small voice. "And then, when I heard that shot, and thought you were dead, too . . . it nearly killed me."

"Noa," he said softly. "I'm so sorry."

"No." She blinked back tears. "*I'm* sorry. I should have done something about it. Then all of a sudden, it was too late, and I—"

Zeke leaned forward and pressed his lips to hers, cutting her off. His lips were soft, and tasted slightly of cinnamon. He released her hands, and Noa slipped them into his hair, feeling the silkiness of it against her skin.

The last time they'd kissed, it had set her on fire. This felt different. Deeper, gentler. Like a raft floating her out across a warm lake under the moon, or a soft blanket she could wrap up in.

Zeke drew back and looked at her. "Was that okay?"

"Yes," she gasped. "That was definitely okay."

"Good." He ran a hand down her cheek and grinned. "By the way, I think that was pretty much the most I've ever heard you say."

She punched his arm and Zeke drew back, raising both arms in protest. "Hey! I'm serious. You were never exactly known for big speeches."

"Um, hi? Is this a bad time?"

Noa turned her head. Peter was standing just inside the door, looking wildly uncomfortable. She flashed back to that awkward kiss in Colorado and flushed.

"Come in, dude," Zeke said. "She was just asking about you."

Noa noticed that he sounded completely normal; whatever issue the two boys had had with each other, apparently they'd resolved it. Peter shuffled in with his hands jammed in his pockets. His hair had grown out enough that his scalp wasn't peeking through anymore. "How's Amanda?" she asked.

Peter's face brightened. "Really good, actually. She's awake and everything. The doctors think the thymus should hold her until the cure is ready."

Zeke was stroking her hand lightly with his thumb, which felt amazing but was incredibly distracting. "That's great."

"Yeah, it is." Peter cleared his throat. "I'm glad they fixed you up, too. Because frankly, I was getting tired of carrying you around."

Noa snorted. "You and me both."

A slow smile crept across his face. "We did it, huh?"

Noa nodded. "Yeah." It seemed impossible, considering all the terrible things they'd been through. She flashed back on their first meeting in Back Bay station, when neither of them had a clue what was happening. It was hard to believe that was less than a year ago.

And now, Charles Pike was dead. And they'd survived.

"Oh, I almost forgot." Peter dug something out of his pocket and held it up. Seeing it, Noa gasped involuntarily. Her hand automatically went to her wrist.

"Is that my bracelet?" she asked, stupefied. "Where did you find it?"

Peter came closer to the bed and handed it to her. Noa held the thin green band up to the light; it was smaller than she remembered. She slipped it over her right hand, and it slid into place. The weight of it brought tears to her eyes.

"That's the weird thing," Peter said carefully. "Someone left it for me at the nurse's station."

"So how did you know it was mine?"

"There was a note inside," he said, pulling a folded piece of paper out of his pocket. "Here."

Noa took it. The message was handwritten in a tight, elegant cursive on a standard piece of office paper:

Dear Peter,

I sincerely hope there are no hard feelings. That being said, it would be best if our paths didn't cross again, for both of our sakes. I wish Miss Berns a speedy recovery. Please return this bracelet to its rightful owner.

—MM

"Who's MM?" she asked, puzzled. "And how did he get my bracelet?"

"Mason, I think," Peter said. "Maybe he was there when they kidnapped you."

"Ugh," she said. "Glad I never met him."

"You really are," Peter agreed. "Honestly, it's weird to think of him having a first name. Trying to figure out what it is has been driving me crazy."

"Manson?" Zeke suggested.

Peter laughed. "That was my first guess, too. But I'm kind of hoping it's something really freaky, like Marjory. Anyway, I should let you rest." He held out a hand, and Zeke shook it. "Take care of her, man."

"I will," Zeke promised.

"See ya, Rain." Peter winked, then walked out of the room.

Noa stayed silent for a moment after he left, her fingers working the jade bracelet like it was a string of prayer beads. "That sounded an awful lot like good-bye," she finally said.

"Nah, he'll be back," Zeke said. "He's just got some stuff to handle."

Noa cocked an eyebrow. "Since when are you two such great friends?"

Zeke shrugged. "We hung out while you were in the coma. He's not so bad."

"He's actually pretty great."

"For a rich kid." Zeke flashed a wicked smile, then continued, "It helped that he swears you two never hooked up."

"He told you that?" Noa exclaimed, pulling herself up on her elbows.

"Oh, Peter told me a lot of things," he said smugly. "I hear you're a whiz with a scalpel."

"I missed you," Noa blurted, surprising herself. "So much."

"Me too." Zeke leaned forward, resting his forehead gently against hers. "You're stuck with me now."

"Good," Noa said weakly.

Hesitantly, she lifted her chin. Their lips met again, and this time there was nothing comforting in the kiss, it was fire and lightning and devouring intensity. It tapped into a hidden reserve, buried deep inside her: all the feelings she'd repressed for so long. Noa couldn't see again, couldn't breathe, but that was okay. The whole world condensed into a single moment: his mouth on hers, their shared breath. She'd never felt anything like it, and she never wanted it to end.

Zeke abruptly drew back, and she made a small noise of protest.

Cupping her chin in his hand, he said, "I love you, Noa Torson."

"I love you, too." In his eyes, Noa could see everything he felt, all his emotions laid bare. And for once, she wasn't afraid. She swallowed hard, then said, "So why aren't we still kissing?"

"Doctor's orders," Zeke said gravely. "No serious making out until you're on your feet."

"That's a terrible rule," Noa grumbled.

"Don't worry," he said softly. "We've got all the time in the world."

Peter stood in the foyer of his house—his *parents'* house, he corrected himself. The smell of wood polish and fresh gardenias was cloying. Even though he'd only been gone a few months, it felt surreal, like this was a place he'd only visited in a dream.

The alarm had chimed when he entered, announcing his arrival. While he waited, his mind reflexively wandered through the mansion. Upstairs and to the right: his bedroom. Straight ahead through a set of double doors: the kitchen. And if he walked ten feet and turned left, he'd be in the living room.

His mom unexpectedly appeared in that doorway, as if he'd summoned her by visualizing the room. Priscilla put a hand to her chest and said, "Peter?"

"Hi, Mom." The urge to run into her arms was almost overwhelming. Peter had to force himself to remember how horribly she'd betrayed him. That steeled him, and he continued, "Where's Dad?"

"He's right—"

"Who is it?" His father appeared beside her. Bob looked smaller than Peter remembered; his slacks hung off him, like he'd lost weight, and there were new flaps of skin around his jawline. Bob's eyes narrowed. "You."

"Yup." Peter stood there awkwardly, feeling like a stranger in his own home.

His parents exchanged a glance, and Peter stiffened. He'd almost forgotten about the silent threads of communication that passed between them. It was one of the many ways they'd always shut him out.

"Come in and have a seat, dear," Priscilla said, gesturing toward the living room. "We should have a chat to clear the air."

Peter almost laughed; she made it sound like he'd broken curfew or something, and this would be a standard family meeting. "I'm good right here, actually," he said. "I can only stay for a minute."

Priscilla's forehead wrinkled. Hesitantly, she said, "I assumed you'd want to move back in."

"Live here?" he scoffed. "Seriously?"

"Don't use that tone with your mother," Bob snapped.

"Honey." His mom laid a restraining hand on his father's arm. Bob had already gone beet red, gearing up for one of his classic rages. "Please. Let's all just stay calm."

"Yeah," Peter retorted. "After all, you don't want to piss off the terrorist."

At that, Priscilla had the good grace to look uncomfortable. But Bob squared his jaw and retorted, "What were we supposed to think? You took off to live with those . . . whatever they were. And next thing we hear, you killed someone."

"I've never killed anyone," Peter retorted. "Unlike you."

His shoulders were heaving, his fists clenched. Peter chastised himself. He hadn't come here for a fight. He'd spent twenty minutes outside gearing up for this, lecturing himself about staying cool. But less than a minute into the conversation, they were already at one another's throats.

"Peter, I understand you've heard a lot of things about Charles Pike," Priscilla said carefully, the lawyer in her automatically coming to the fore. "We all have."

Bob muttered, "Stupid son of a bitch."

Peter wondered whether Bob thought Pike was dumb for what he'd done, or because he'd gotten caught.

Knowing his dad, probably the latter.

"However," Priscilla said, raising her voice slightly to underscore the point. "Your father and I had no idea what was happening. Our investment in Project Persephone was strictly that—an investment. We were not privy to how they conducted their research."

"Bullshit," Peter snorted.

Bob's eyes flashed. He was opening his mouth to yell again when Priscilla interjected, "If you've seen the files, you know we're telling the truth."

Peter shook his head; he'd known it was a long shot. Deep down, he'd really hoped that once everything came to light, his parents would express some sort of regret. Instead, they were being utterly predictable, covering their asses. Again. He drew a piece of paper out of his pocket and handed it to his mother.

Without looking at it, Priscilla asked, "What's this?"

The dread in her voice was palpable. "Just read it," he said quietly.

The grandfather clock marked off the seconds as she scanned the page. Priscilla's face blanched. Wordlessly, she handed it to his father.

Bob skimmed it quickly, then swore under his breath. "Chuck said he'd gotten rid of this."

There was panic in his mother's eyes, and Bob seemed to have shrunk another inch. Peter wished he could relish their reaction; but this was a hollow victory. The evidence of their complicity, how much they'd actually known, had shaken him to the core when he found it. It made him realize that he'd never really known them at all. "That's the thing about data, Dad. It never really disappears. And I'm pretty handy with file recovery software. Didn't take much to find it."

"So the FBI doesn't have this?" Priscilla asked quickly.

Peter cracked his knuckles one at a time, making his mother wince. "You know, I wanted to believe that you got involved in all this because you didn't want anyone else losing their kid, the way we lost Jeremy. But the thing is, knowing you, it was probably just about the money."

Bob's hands were shaking, making the page tremble. Gruffly, he said, "You can make this go away permanently, right? Isn't that the sort of thing you do?"

Peter almost laughed; this was the first time his parents had ever demonstrated any interest in his hacking skills. It was beyond ironic. He nodded. "Yeah, I could. You probably never realized it, but that's what I'm best at."

"Thank God," his mother murmured.

"But the thing is," Peter said, "I'm not going to."

While they watched gape-mouthed, he went back to the door and opened it. An FBI agent stood there, flanked by five cops.

"All set?" she asked.

"Yeah, thanks." Peter turned back to his parents. They seemed to be diminishing by the minute; he almost felt sorry for them. Almost. "This is Agent Rodriguez. She's going to be arresting you now."

As the cops swarmed in, he stepped out onto the stoop. He could hear his parents protesting: Priscilla's voice high-pitched and panicked, Bob swearing loudly.

"You okay?" Agent Rodriguez asked.

She was a good-looking woman in her late thirties, wearing a black blazer and no-nonsense shoes. Peter managed a weak smile. "Yeah, I'm good."

"You have a place to go?"

Peter thought about that for a minute. He'd been crashing

with Luke and the other kids who used to comprise the Northeast division of Persefone's Army. They were living in an abandoned warehouse on the outskirts of the city. It wasn't as bad as some of the places he'd shared with Noa, Teo, and Daisy; but it wasn't much better, either. He could probably call some old friends from high school, or even Amanda's parents, but somehow that didn't feel right. "I'll be okay," he finally said. "I'm going to take off soon, anyway."

At that, Rodriguez raised an eyebrow. "Headed where?"

"Anywhere, I guess." Peter shrugged. "I figured I might start with Costa Rica, maybe learn how to surf."

Agent Rodriguez looked bemused. "Surfing, huh? Well, I don't know if I can beat that. But I promised my boss I'd try."

"Try how?"

"By offering you a job." Seeing his look of confusion, she said, "Our tech division could use some help going through all this information, and you're already familiar with it. Plus, we have an entire unit devoted to cybercrime."

"I'm only eighteen," Peter said, puzzled. "I haven't even graduated high school yet."

Rodriguez shrugged. "Age doesn't really matter, I don't think we have a single techie over thirty. Here's my card. Think about it."

"Sure." Peter tucked the card away in his back pocket. A slow grin spread across his face. "So you could make me a G-man?"

"Technically, you'd be a consultant," Rodriguez clarified with a smile. "But down the road, maybe."

"Cool."

She laughed and held out her hand. "Take care of yourself, Peter Gregory."

"I will."

Peter shook her hand, then headed down the stairs, walking away from his house for what would probably be the last time. He expected to be overwhelmed with nostalgia, or grief. Instead, he felt about a thousand pounds lighter; like he'd been carrying around an invisible weight, and it had finally dispersed.

Noa rocked slightly back and forth as the T rattled through tunnels, balancing an Apple store bag on her lap. She'd finally decided to invest in a fifteen-inch MacBook Pro. She and Zeke were swamped with freelance work now, and she needed the extra screen space. Still, when they'd handed her the bag, she'd flinched at the extra weight. Even though months had passed, she had a hard time shaking the thought that this would be much harder to take on the run.

No more running, she reminded herself. In fact, this laptop would rarely leave the confines of their house. She still had difficulty wrapping her head around that, too; thanks to a huge settlement from Pike & Dolan, they had a real home now, a sprawling four bedroom in Brookline. They'd moved in right before school started. Not that she and Zeke went; they'd both gotten their GEDs, and since Zeke was eighteen, he was officially the adult in charge of their chaotic household. Teo and Daisy had been less than thrilled when Children's Services mandated that they attend the local high school, especially when they found out they'd both be sophomores. But that was part of the deal they'd struck: The kids could stay with Noa and Zeke, as long as they went to class.

So far, it had been going surprisingly well. Teo was rapidly becoming Brookline High's track star, and Daisy was heavily involved in the school's radio station. They spent most of their free time volunteering at the Runaway Coalition, which Amanda had taken over when Mrs. Latimar died of a sudden heart attack.

Noa and the others had donated a serious chunk of their settlement money to the Coalition. She'd originally wanted to give it all away, but Zeke insisted on keeping a cushion for themselves, and setting some aside for Teo and Daisy in case they wanted to go to college.

Daisy, in college. Noa smiled at the thought.

Peter should be calling tonight from Thailand. He was on his tenth country in five months. They received postcards regularly, and he Skyped with them at least once a week. Still, after living on top of each other for months, it was strange not having him around. Sometimes when she was working on a particularly tricky hack, Noa would catch herself talking back to the monitor, the same way he used to.

Peter always sounded cheerful, relaying anecdotes about his crazy backpacking experiences. But even through a webcam, she could see the shadow behind his eyes. After all they'd been through, neither of them would ever be whole again, not completely. She'd lay awake nights, wondering which of them was following the right path. Could the past be outrun? Or had she made the right choice, staying here to try and put it behind her?

There was a map of the Green line overhead; her eyes zeroed in on the Newton Centre stop. That's where all this had started; somewhere between her apartment and the T station, they'd taken her. And that's why she never felt completely safe on the subway.

The train shuddered to a stop. Noa slung the bag's straps over her shoulder and climbed off, shuffling along with the rush-hour commuters. Daisy and Teo should be home from school by now. Zeke was probably in the home office, working on their latest IT contract. Amanda might be at the house, too, stirring some sort of disgusting vegetarian mush on the stove.

Not that she minded. Anything hot still tasted good, and not having to cook was an added bonus. There were times that acting as den mother to a bunch of foster kids was even more exhausting than running for her life.

As she passed the ticket agent's booth, Noa caught the reflection of a beefy bald man directly behind her. The back of her neck suddenly prickled, and her pulse kicked up. Noa walked faster, murmuring apologies as she pushed past other passengers.

She was slightly out of breath as she emerged from the station, and the scar on her chest throbbed uncomfortably. Glancing back, her heart sank; the bald man was still close on her heels, wearing an intent look on his face.

Their house was five blocks away. She could make it in three minutes if she ran.

But then he'd know where they lived. Maybe that's exactly what he wanted.

Adrenaline surged through her veins as the familiar flight response kicked in. She'd almost forgotten how it felt to be hunted.

But she was done being prey.

Noa let the bag drop to her side as she turned to face him. She clenched the box in both hands; the laptop was heavy, and solid. If she swung hard enough, it might knock him out.

The bald man was dressed in black jeans and a heavy over-coat that was perfect for concealing a weapon. She checked his feet . . . dress shoes. Noa frowned. That was unusual. Maybe they'd gotten better at concealing themselves. She braced, discreetly drawing back the box, preparing to use it as a club. . . .

A smile broke across the guy's face, and he threw his arms wide. As Noa hesitated, confused, something large and red flitted past her—a young girl, maybe eight years old. She hurtled into the bald man's arms. He swept her up, whipping her in a circle and laughing.

As he kissed the girl's forehead and tugged playfully at her ponytail, Noa slowly lowered the bag. She was still breathing hard, her whole body taut with tension. The man set the girl on the ground. Hand in hand they walked by her, the girl chattering while her father nodded indulgently.

Noa choked out a relieved laugh. Still feeling shaky, she slipped the straps back over her shoulder and adjusted her knit cap. Turning, she headed for home.

It was late October, and most of the leaves had already fallen. They crunched under her feet as she walked up the path to their house.

A year ago, she'd been perfectly content living alone in a studio apartment, shying away from human interaction; she never would have expected to enjoy sharing a house with a bunch of other kids. *My family*, Noa reminded herself. The word still felt foreign at times, but that's what they'd become, for better or worse. A family.

The front door popped open. Light spilled from the hallway, framing Zeke in silhouette. His hair was slick from the shower, and he was wearing low-slung jeans and a black T-shirt. "Hey! I was getting worried." Taking her in, his brow furrowed. "Everything okay?"

"Everything's great," Noa said, mounting the final step. She wrapped her arms around him. "I love you."

"I love you, too," he said, sounding surprised.

Noa nuzzled his neck, inhaling deeply. She still couldn't get enough of him: the way he smelled, how his skin felt, the softness of his mouth.

"I've got dinner on the stove," he murmured, brushing his lips against her ear. "It'll burn."

"I don't care," she said, going up on her toes to kiss him. "Let it."

This will be my final post. By now, the whole world knows about what happened to me . . . what happened to all of us. Most of the people responsible have been brought to justice. So if you joined our fight, thank you.

We lost a lot of people along the way. Some of their names we know: Janiqua. Remo. Alex. Loki.

But so many others were reduced to a file number. Kids who suffered terribly at the hands of Charles Pike and his "scientists." Kids who screamed and suffered and died alone.

These are the kids we need to remember. Because in spite of everything that's been written, all the horror and shock and outrage, the truth is, it could happen again.

So stay vigilant. Look out for each other. And remember that we're all stronger than we think. Someone once said that the only way to fight monsters is to become the bigger monster. I used to think so, too, but it's not true.

The truth is, the only way to fight monsters is to become something they cannot defeat. Like Persephone, the only way back from hell is to walk toward the light.

Posted by PERSEF0NE on October 25th
/ALLIANCE/ /NEKRO/ /#PERSEF_ARMY/

<<<<>>>>

Acknowledgments

Three years ago, I sat down and wrote, "When Noa Torson woke up, the first thing she noticed was that her feet were cold." And from there, this incredible journey with Peter, Noa, and so many other characters who stole my heart began. I'm terribly sad to be saying good-bye to them, and I hope I did them justice.

My good friend Lisa Brown was instrumental in helping get this trilogy off the ground; I owe her and Dan Ehrenhaft a debt that truly cannot be repaid.

The PERSEF0NE trilogy found the perfect home at Harper Teen; I couldn't have asked for better champions for these books. Publicist Olivia deLeon went above and beyond the call of duty; if it weren't for her, I'd probably still be wandering the bowels of the Javits Center, hopelessly lost. The Tea Time ladies, Margot Wood and Aubry Parks-Fried, were the best book shimmy buddies ever; along with Alana Whitman and Alison Lisnow, they made the Pitch Dark Days fall tour an incredible experience.

Speaking of which . . . my fellow "Beautiful Weirdoes," Rae Carson, Sherry Thomas, Mindy McGinnis, and Madeleine Roux, were tourmates extraordinaire. Sending five women on a four-day, four-city road trip sounds like a recipe for disaster; instead, it was hands down some of the most fun I've ever had in my life. Maddie and Mindy even went above and beyond, offering line edits for *DLG*; so any and all mistakes are clearly their fault ☺. Seriously, I love these ladies and their books, and everyone should rush out and buy multiple copies.

Dudley, Ryan, Amara, Wendy, and all the other amazing teachers and fellow dancers at ODC helped keep me sane during some truly challenging life events over the past few years.

My team of white hat hackers/tech experts, Keith Nordstrom and Bruce Davis, exhibited tremendous patience while wading through versions of these manuscripts, doing their best to explain encryption technology to a Luddite. They both deserve free cold beer for life (the good stuff); I couldn't have done it without them.

Kate Stoia generously donated money to Live Oak School by buying character naming rights: Matan and Ella Maoz, I hope that you're not too angry about me killing off your namesakes; at least they both died honorable deaths.

My editor, Karen Chaplin, has gallantly shepherded these books through every draft; her keen eye for detail and gentle insistence on which darlings to kill has been a true gift. She's a real pro, and I was lucky to have her on my team.

Copy editors are the unsung heroes of manuscripts. Aaron Murray and Bethany Reis pointed out inconsistencies and errors that would have proven hugely embarrassing had they made it to print—so thanks for making me look good.

Two poets generously allowed me to use their work as epigraphs: the esteemed Rita Dove ("Persephone, Falling") and Cleopatra Mathis ("After Persephone"). If you love these poems as much as I do, you can find more of their work in *Mother Love* and *What to Tip the Boatman?*, respectively.

Stephanie Kip Rostan has been so much more than my agent, she's also a friend with an unerring knack for talking me down from the proverbial ledge and putting out fires with aplomb. We're all lucky that she chooses to use her powers for good.

With this trilogy, I tried to shine a light on some of the failures of the U.S. foster care system. There are organizations devoted to improving the lives of these kids. The Jim Casey Youth Opportunities Initiative is a group that helps ensure that young people make a successful transition from foster care to adulthood. They help improve policies, promote youth engagement, and create community partnerships, among other things (http://www.jimcaseyyouth.org/). One Simple Wish (onesimplewish.org) matches donors with kids, helping grant wishes that range from new shoes to music lessons. Any amount helps; it's almost heartbreaking to see what an enormous difference a small gift can make for a foster kid. So please consider donating today.

Booksellers, librarians, readers, and bloggers: What can I say? You've done so much for this trilogy. Thanks, from the bottom of my heart. I hope you enjoyed the ride as much as I did.

Finally, in some ways it feels like I was undergoing a trial by fire at the same time as Noa: and we both emerged stronger than before. I owe a lot of people for that, especially my family, both old and new. My parents, for fostering a love of reading and writing. My sisters, for always listening. Taegan and Esmé, for making me laugh when I really needed to.

And Kirk, for showing me the way back to the light. I love you, sweetheart.

Turn the page for a peek
at the book that started it all.

CHAPTER ONE

When Noa Torson woke up, the first thing she noticed was that her feet were cold. Odd, since she always wore socks to bed. She opened her eyes and immediately winced against the glare. She hated sleeping in a bright room, had even installed blackout curtains over her apartment's sole window so that morning light never penetrated the gloom. Noa tried to make sense of her surroundings as her eyes adjusted. Her head felt like it had been inflated a few sizes and stuffed with felt. She had no idea how she'd ended up here, wherever here was.

Was she back in juvie? Probably not; it was too quiet. Juvie always sounded like a carnival midway: the constant din of guards' boots pounding against metal staircases, high-pitched posturing chatter, the squeak of cots and clanking of metal doors. Noa had spent enough time there to identify it with her eyes closed. She could usually even tell which cell-block she'd been dumped in by echoes alone.

Voices intruded on the perimeter of her consciousness—two people from the sound of it, speaking quietly. She tried to sit up, and that was when the pain hit. Noa winced and fell back on the bed. It felt like her chest had been split in half. Her hand ached, too. Slowly, she turned her head.

An IV drip was taped to her right wrist. The line led to a bag hanging from a metal stand. And the bed she was lying on was cold metal—an operating table, a spotlight suspended above it. So was she in a hospital? There wasn't that hospital smell, though—blood and sweat and vomit battling against the stench of ammonia.

Noa lifted her left hand: Her jade bracelet, the one she never took off, was gone. That realization snatched the final cobwebs from her mind.

Cautiously, Noa raised up on her elbows, then frowned. This wasn't like any hospital she'd ever seen. She was in the center of a glass chamber, a twelve-by-twelve-foot box, the windows frosted so she couldn't see out. The floor was bare concrete. Aside from the operating table and the IV stand, rolling trays of medical implements and machines were scattered about. In the corner stood a red trash bin, MEDICAL WASTE blaring from the lid.

Looking down, Noa discovered that she was wearing a cloth gown, but there was no hospital name stamped on it. She tried to get her bearings. Not juvie, and not an official hospital. She got the feeling that whatever this place was, bad things happened here.

The voices grew louder; someone was coming. Noa had spent the past ten years fending for herself. She'd learned better than to trust authority figures, whether they were cops, doctors, or social workers. And she wasn't about to start trusting anyone now, not in a situation like this. Slowly, she eased her feet off the table and slid to the floor. She wrapped her arms around herself, repressing a shiver. The cement was freezing, like stepping barefoot onto a glacier.

The voices stopped just outside the chamber. Noa strained her ears to listen, catching a few fragments: *"Success . . . call him . . . what do we . . . can't believe we finally . . ."*

The last bit came through crystal clear. A man's voice, sounding resigned as he said, "They'll handle it. She's not our problem now."

Fighting to keep her teeth from chattering, Noa desperately scanned the room. A few feet away, a metal tray held a variety of medical instruments. She'd nearly reached it when the door at the far end of the room opened.

Two men dressed in scrubs crossed the threshold. The first was a thin white guy, a few strands of blond hair pasted across his forehead beneath a surgical cap. The other doctor was Latino, younger and stockier with a straggly mustache marring his upper lip. Seeing her, they froze. Noa seized the opportunity to edge closer to the tray.

"Where am I?" she asked. Her voice came out weaker than usual, like she hadn't spoken in a while.

The doctors recovered from their surprise and exchanged a look. The blond one jerked his head, and the Latino rushed from the room.

"Where's he going?" Noa asked. She was two feet from the tray now, and he was three feet past it.

The doctor held up his hands placatingly. "You were in a terrible accident, Noa," he said soothingly. "You're in the hospital."

"Oh, yeah?" Her eyes narrowed. "Which hospital?"

"You're going to be fine. Some disorientation is to be expected." The doctor glanced back over his shoulder.

"What kind of accident?"

The doctor paused, his eyes shifting as he searched for a response, and Noa knew he was lying. The last thing she remembered was leaving her apartment and walking toward Newton Centre station to catch the train into Boston. She'd been heading downtown to pick up a new video card for her MacBook Pro. Noa had turned right on Oxford Road, passing Weeks Field on her way to the T stop. The last heat of an Indian summer day was soft on her skin, daylight sifting through trees already shedding their leaves in a riot of fiery oranges and reds. She'd been happy, she remembered. Happier than she'd been in a long time, maybe ever.

And then, nothing. It was all a big blank.

"A car accident," he explained, a small note of triumph in his voice.

"I don't own a car. I don't even take taxis," Noa said warily.

"A car hit you, I mean." The doctor looked back again, increasingly impatient. Clearly the other guy had gone for help. Which meant she was running out of time.

Noa suddenly fell forward, as if the wooziness had overwhelmed her. The doctor lunged to catch her. In one smooth motion, Noa scooped a scalpel off the tray and pressed it against the side of his neck.

His mouth opened wide in a surprised O.

"You're going to get me out of here," she said firmly, "or I'll slit your throat. Don't make a sound."

"Please." The doctor's voice was hoarse. "You don't understand. You can't leave, it's for your own—"

A rush of footsteps pounding toward them.

"Shut up!" Noa shoved him in front of her, keeping the blade pressed against his neck as they went through the door. She paused outside: not a hospital at all, but a giant warehouse the size of an airplane hangar. Makeshift aisles composed of cardboard boxes and long lines of metal filing cabinets surrounded the glass chamber.

"Which way out?" she hissed, keeping her mouth close to his ear. They were nearly the same height, five-ten, which made it easier.

The doctor hesitated, then pointed right. "There's an exit, but it's alarmed."

Following his finger, Noa spotted the narrow hallway leading off to the right. She propelled him toward it. Someone was shouting orders. As they entered the hallway, she heard the chamber door being flung open behind her. More yelling as they realized she was gone. It sounded like at least half a dozen people were after her.

The hallway was long and narrow and lined with more boxes stacked to shoulder height on both sides. One of the fluorescent tubes overhead flickered, casting them in a pulsing strobe. Noa fought to ignore the stabbing pain in her chest, and the ball of panic right alongside it.

Ten feet farther and the hallway turned right. They rounded the bend and came face-to-face with a large metal door. It was chained shut.

"That's not an alarm," Noa said flatly.

"There's no point hurting me," he pleaded. "You can't leave. He'd never let you go."

Beside her, the top box on the stack gaped open. Noa dug her free hand inside, then risked a glance: metal bedpans, nothing she could use to break a padlock. She was trapped. Noa fought the urge to scream in frustration. Out in the expanse of the warehouse floor, she'd stood a chance of escaping. Now, she was a rat at the end of a maze. At most, she had a few minutes before they found her.

"Take off your clothes," she ordered.

"What? But—" he sputtered.

"Now!" She pressed the scalpel deeper into his neck.

A minute later, the doctor shuddered in his underwear as she stepped into his crocs and pulled the mask up over her face. Good thing he'd decided to stay—the Latino's scrubs would never have fit her.

"It won't work," he said.

Noa frowned and responded with a double-fisted upper-cut: a trick she'd learned the hard way, by being on the receiving end once. It connected with the doctor's jaw and his head jerked back. He dropped hard, knocking over boxes on the way down. He didn't get back up. "I hate negativity," she muttered.

The Latino doctor suddenly darted out of the hallway, skidding to a stop in front of them. Noa reached into the box beside her.

"Jim?" he said, eyes widening as Noa raced toward him. As she ran she drew her arm back, then swung the metal bedpan as hard as she could. He shied away, drawing his arms up to protect his face. The bedpan made a loud, hollow sound when it connected with his temple. His eyes rolled back in his head, and he dropped to the floor beside the other doctor.

Noa dashed back down the hallway, pausing at the end. She was still clutching the scalpel in her left hand, but chances were the people she was up against had knives, maybe even guns. The warehouse was dimly lit, which worked in her favor. It was enormous, too, so the people searching for her would have to split up. The scrubs might fool them at a distance, but that trick wouldn't work for long; they were sure to find the doctors any minute now. She had to find a way out.

Noa edged along, keeping to the shadows. Ten feet down the adjoining wall she spotted a gap: another hallway, about thirty feet away. It was a risk—she might get to the end only to discover that the door was bolted like the other one. But spending too much time on the warehouse floor was suicide.

She moved as quickly as possible toward the opening, hoping that at a distance she'd be mistaken for the blond doctor. The crocs weren't exactly ideal: They squeaked against the raw concrete, and there was no way she'd be able to run in them. Better than being barefoot, though. At least her feet were finally warming up.

She'd nearly reached the corridor when someone shouted, "Hey!"

Noa slowly pivoted.

The guy facing her was large and lumpy; he looked like a kid had stuffed clay into an oversized security uniform, dabbing on a stubby nose and ears as an afterthought. There was a gun in his right hand.

"I already checked down there," the security guard said, indicating the space behind her with the gun barrel. "Don't waste your time."

Noa nodded her thanks, hoping he wouldn't find it strange that she wasn't answering. He sauntered off toward the next hallway, the one where the doctors were stashed.

She was about to slip down the corridor when someone across the room hollered, "Stop her!"

Turning, Noa spotted the blond doctor standing at the

edge of the opposite hallway. In the darkness, his bare skin practically glowed. His arm was extended, finger pointing at her accusingly.

The security guard swiveled back toward her with a frown. Their eyes met, then Noa spun and broke into a run.

Peter Gregory was bored. He spent most weekends at Tufts University with his girlfriend. But Amanda was swamped with a huge paper, and she'd told him in no uncertain terms to not even consider showing up to distract her. His parents were away in Vermont celebrating their thirtieth wedding anniversary at the type of pseudo-bed-and-breakfast they loved, an alarming amount of chintz the only thing that differentiated it from a regular hotel.

At first, Peter had been kind of psyched—a whole weekend to himself, no one to put up a front for. He could spend it online, monitoring the projects birthed by his brainchild, /ALLIANCE/. Yesterday, a Croatian member announced he was on the verge of tracking down the kid who posted a video of setting a cat on fire. That had been a particularly gruesome attempt to garner fifteen minutes of fame, but sadly not an unusual one. Peter had been checking all day, though, and there were no new posts. Hardly anyone on /ALLIANCE/ at all. Maybe everyone was busy logging rest bubbles on World of Warcraft, he thought with a grin.

Peter liked to think of these vigilante hackers as his minions. Since he'd founded the underground website a year earlier, it had snowballed. It turned out he wasn't the only one ticked off by all the hypocrisy out there. They'd become a loosely knit community of hackers with a mission: to target Internet bullies, animal abusers, sexual predators, and everyone else who took advantage of the weak. Peter's only rule was no violence. He saw /ALLIANCE/ as a way to wreak justice by pranking the bad guys, and so far, that hadn't been an issue: After all, the people who counted themselves as /ALLIANCE/ questers could wipe out someone's credit history or destroy their privacy with a few keystrokes. In the end, that was a lot more effective than beating someone up.

Peter had already made the circuit of the house a few times, absently flicking lights on and off. It was big, a four-thousand-square-foot McMansion, so that consumed some time. He ended up in his dad's office. He plopped down in the Aeron chair and spun a few times, then propped his feet on the desk as he tilted back. Through the picture window beside him their lawn stretched away from the house like a rolling black tide, stopping at the street where it lapped at towering elm trees.

Saturday night, and he was home alone. There was a party at his buddy Blake's house, but he wasn't really in the mood. After going to college parties with Amanda, the high-school equivalent struck him as a lame waste of time. Still, there was nothing to stop him from having some fun. His dad kept a bottle of twenty-year-old bourbon in his lower right-hand desk drawer. He wouldn't miss a few pulls.

Peter punched in a code and the bottom drawer popped open. Ridiculous of his father to think that a three-digit lock would keep anyone out. Peter shook his head as he uncorked the bottle. It was insulting, really.

He took a swig and leaned back. Someone had inscribed a note on the label: *For Bob Gregory, with sincere appreciation.* The signature was illegible; probably another jerk his dad had thrown money at to achieve some awful end.

His father was the reason Peter had initially started

/ALLIANCE/. A self-described "do-gooder investment banker," his dad was the kind of guy who insisted on driving a Prius with all the bells and whistles, but couldn't be bothered to drop his Pellegrino bottle in the recycling bin. He'd make a show of tucking a five-dollar bill in a homeless guy's cup if people were around, then go home and donate the maximum amount allowed to a campaign geared toward keeping that guy on the streets. And Peter's mother was no better. As a high-priced defense attorney, she spent her time ensuring that Boston's most lethal lowlifes never saw the inside of a prison cell. The two of them were perfect for each other, Peter thought with a snort. No wonder they'd made it thirty years.

It had been a while since he'd checked out what Bob was up to, Peter mused, scratching his chin with the mouth of the bottle. Couldn't hurt to take a look.

A stack of papers and files filled the rest of the drawer. Peter dug them out and splayed them across the desk, then started flipping through. Mostly dull stuff: stock reports, investor statements, prospectuses from a variety of hedge funds. One file was thicker than the others. He recognized his father's careful writing along the tab, *AMRF* in block letters. Peter frowned. He went through the drawer fairly regularly. This was a new addition.

He perused the papers inside the file: more quarterly reports, meeting minutes in some incomprehensible short-hand. His father was listed on the letterhead as both a board member and financial adviser. No surprise there—Bob always jumped at the chance to join a board roster, and "financial advisers" surely got some sort of kickback.

Peter took another tug from the bottle of bourbon, then eyed it. If he drank much more, Bob would be able to tell. Reluctantly, he replaced the cork.

He was about to tuck the various papers and files back in the drawer, rearranging the bottle on top of them, when his eyes alit on the line item "Project Persephone."

That was pretty exotic for a financial company; they tended to have a penchant for testosterone-driven names like "Maximus" and "Primidius." Peter scanned the page, but all he could tell was that whatever Project Persephone was, it consumed a hefty chunk of AMRF's significant annual budget. As in, almost all of it.

Something about the name, though, struck him as familiar. Peter keyed up Bob's laptop, typing in the password when the box appeared on-screen: his mother's birthday, of course. He did a quick web search for *Persephone*, and realized where he'd seen the name before: When they studied Greek myths back in middle school. Persephone was the girl who got kidnapped and dragged down to Hades, but her mom cut some deal where half the year, she returned to live back on Earth.

Peter sat back in the chair, puzzled. His eyes fell on the clock across the room: nearly seven thirty, *SportsCenter* would be on soon. The Bruins had played a game earlier, and he wanted to see the highlights. He debated closing the drawer and going on with his evening, but something nagged at him. Peter sighed and ran his fingers back over the keyboard, instituting a basic search on AMRF.

A long list of organizations went by that acronym, including the Algalita Marine Research Foundation and Americans Mad for Rad Foosball. Skimming the list, none of them jumped out as the kind of company Bob would invest in. Peter hesitated, then decided to dig further. He shut down Bob's computer and went to retrieve his laptop.

Twenty minutes later, he was pretty sure he'd found the

right site. From the look of things, it was some sort of medical research company, although whatever they were researching was buried under a string of code names. He dug around some more, but the majority of the company's files were locked behind firewalls that resisted his first attempts to throw a ladder over. Peter knew that given enough time, he could surmount them—in the past, just for fun he'd hacked unnoticed into the Pentagon, FBI, and Scotland Yard databases. The question was, could anything Bob was involved with possibly be worth the time commitment?

Probably not, Peter decided. With a yawn, he powered down the laptop.

A minute later, his front door was kicked in.

JOIN THE

Epic Reads

COMMUNITY

THE ULTIMATE YA DESTINATION

◀ DISCOVER ▶
your next favorite read

◀ MEET ▶
new authors to love

◀ WIN ▶
free books

◀ SHARE ▶
infographics, playlists, quizzes, and more

◀ WATCH ▶
the latest videos

◀ TUNE IN ▶
to Tea Time with Team Epic Reads

   Find us at **www.epicreads.com**
and @epicreads